Horse Country

Christine Meunier

Horse Country
A World of Horses

by Christine Meunier

National Library of Australia Cataloguing-in-Publication Data

Meunier, Christine

Horse Country

1st ed. 2013

ISBN 978-0-9875332-0-3 (pbk.)

Cover design by Graphic Design City
Cover photo by Christine Meunier

FOREWORD

Horses are an incredible animal that offer a multitude of employment opportunities. I am blessed to have been able to work on a number of properties and travel overseas because of horses.

The horse industry offers many opportunities for those willing to seek them and work hard. Careers can be formed by curious minds, willing hands and an enthusiastic attitude.

Horse Country was written in the hope that it will open peoples' eyes to the wonderful world of working with horses. If horses are your passion, I hope this book will encourage you to learn as much as you can about them, pursue a career and take advantage of opportunities to travel.

A special thank you to Nev and the crew at Larneuk for helping me to learn so many skills and gain contacts in the industry. It was the encouragement from working here that helped me to shape this book, travel overseas and I feel so blessed through being able to do a job that I love.

A big thank you to my husband for supporting me and just being you.

Christine

Horse Country

A World of Horses

Year 1

February

Lise Hemmingway smiled to herself, studiously reading the available jobs listed on the sheet in front of her.

She silently thanked whichever genius had decided to start a company that focused solely on advertising jobs in the equine industry and lining up capable people to take on these jobs anywhere across the globe.

At nineteen years of age, the slim brunette already boasted a strong love of horses and had proven herself capable of handling and caring for excitable thoroughbreds many a time.

Just recently, she had finished up a six-month stint at a large stud in the Hunter Valley, working with weanlings and previously foaling down mares. Now in February and barely scraping the surface of what the year had to offer her, she had traveled to South Australia with a friend, helping out with a few yearlings for the Magic Millions Adelaide Yearling Sale to earn a bit of extra money before moving on to Victoria.

Having given up on school at the age of sixteen Lise had quickly learnt what hard work was involved in working in the thoroughbred field.

This was now especially true, with the equine industry quickly adopting the idea of employing those who had taken the time to learn the theory and gain the piece of paper.

Eager to improve herself though, she had delighted her past employers by asking lots of questions, often volunteering for tasks others shied away from and consistently turning up early or staying behind late. It was obvious to others that she was aware that working with horses wasn't at all a nine to five job, but rather, a lifestyle.

Now, two and a half years later, she had an attractive resume behind her and was ready to take on a more challenging role in Victoria. All she had to do was find the job, she reminded herself, moving out of the way of a colt that was prancing excitedly on the end of his lead.

"Your horse is about to slip that shoe," she observed an older man telling the handler as they led the yearling up to the ring.

The handler paused, looked at the horse's foot, then shrugged and continued on their way.

"But hey, that's fine when the nail punctures his sole and an infection builds up and suddenly you don't have a viable racehorse. Moron," the man muttered, shaking his head in disgust before following the animal up to the pre-sale ring.

Curious, Lise followed the older male, placing herself casually beside him. Her gaze also followed the horse and handler around the ring.

The same colt, discovering a filly in front of him increased his pace, the handler oblivious of the horse in front of them. Squealing, the colt lunged forward, nearly gaining a kick from the filly.

He then jumped back in surprise, pulling the confused handler with him.

This exertion on the loose shoe half pulled it from the colt's foot, leaving the shoe dangling and nails sticking up. The excited animal pranced on a tight lead, the handler now in control but in danger of the young animal piercing its foot.

The older male observing this at the ring sighed.

"I told him," he muttered to himself, flicking a cigarette to the ground before stamping it out with his foot.

"People don't always recognise a knowledgeable piece of information," Lise responded, gaining his attention.

The male nodded.

"You're telling me!"

"Farrier? ... or just particularly aware of how true the saying *no foot, no horse* is?" she queried, realising that the clinking noise that resounded every time the colt put weight on the foot with the loose shoe should clue in anyone who had been around shod horses awhile.

He nodded, pulled out his wallet and extracted a card, handing it to her.

"Guess it's not worth giving advice to people who don't ask. Stuart Hunter," he introduced himself.

"Lise Hemmingway," she smiled, shaking the hand he offered.

"When I land myself a job, I'll keep you in mind," she smiled.

"Looking for anything in particular?" he queried, lounging against the rail, his gaze drifting to the colt as its handler led it through to the inside sale ring.

"Find out who that guy works for... I'm sure his boss will be looking for another worker soon," he grinned.

Lise laughed.

"Wrong time of season, but I want to focus on foal care."

He cast his eye over her, taking in her small frame.

"Had much experience?" he questioned dubiously.

She smiled.

"I'm competent enough... don't let the young age fool you. I was up Hunter Valley way but actually want to be situated in Victoria."

"So why the Adelaide sales?"

"Just helping out a mate with a couple of horses."

He nodded, kicking the ground.

"Nirvana Park... I heard through the grapevine they're taking on a couple more stallions for the next breeding season and they usually have a lot of weaners. Probably could do with an extra pair of hands at this time... Barn C. The guy's name is Kingsley... David Kingsley."

"I'll keep that in mind, thanks," she shook his hand again and strolled back to the barn where her friend's yearlings were stabled.

The young brunette smiled. The name rang a bell and although she knew little about the stud, she was aware of their reputation for turning out yearlings to a high standard and receiving good sales prices.

Topping up some water buckets, she glanced down the aisle at a television that was set up, showing each lot as it was taken through the ring.

Noting that her friend's first horse to go through, a chestnut filly by Rory's Jester, wasn't due to be in the ring for another hour or so, she finished filling the buckets, checked each horse had food and strolled out of the barn, heading toward where Nirvana Park was stabled.

***

Glancing out of the school window across the green oval the bored sixteen-year-old sighed, admitting to herself that it would be a lot more exhilarating racing her palomino gelding around the emerald surface, rather than sitting in a stuffy room while their teacher marked the roll.

Calling her name he gained her attention, marking her off before addressing the class.

"Morning everyone. Over the next fifteen minutes or so, I want you to have a think about what you're going to do after year twelve.

"Because you're in year eleven, I know most of you have already picked subjects that coincide with what you plan on studying in University. But, today I'd like you to have a think about what you want as a job after your studies and list five different possibilities for me. This year you're going to do two bouts of work experience, so we will try and line these up with your preferences," a balding fifty something pedagogue informed the general consensus of bored teens before him.

She smiled to herself, mentally correcting the teacher as she stared at the blank piece of paper in front of her. She didn't want a job – she wanted a *career*.

And she wouldn't spend fifteen minutes deciding on one either, she'd spent just short of fifteen years deciding on horses. Flicking through the University/TAFE guide before her she stopped on the letter *E*, her eyes scanning the page until she came across the word she was looking for.

Finding a list of seven or so careers, she mentally crossed out those that didn't appeal to her, writing down the few that did before her attention returned to the green surface outside the classroom.

Replaying in her mind the conversation with her "Careers Teacher", she smiled ruefully, more than aware of how she should have handled the conversation.

"Horses aren't a career, dear. Every girl goes through a stage where she wants a pony; you'll grow out of it. Aside from that, it's too dangerous working with these unpredictable animals."

It'll be even more dangerous me working with them if I'm not initially trained to do so.

"*Girls* that want *ponies* do quickly grow out of it, generally by the time they've discovered the male population. I own a *horse*, have had this infatuation for the past ten or so years and don't believe I'll be growing out of it anytime soon. Though, if I am going to do so, surely I'd tire of the animals more quickly if I was put to work with them?"

Aware that this response from her could have turned the conversation either way, she was curious to know if it would have worked to her advantage.

Thankful she had a mother whom was insistent on her following her heart, there'd been no need for *her* to have a follow up conversation with the older male however, and it was all thanks to her *mother's* "little conversation" with the man. She'd managed to convince the teacher to agree to let her daughter work with horses, at least for the first lot of work experience and that's all that mattered to the teen.

Grinning, she scanned the list of horse properties in the phone book before her, highlighting those that were close enough for her to consider working at and therefore send a letter to.

***

Smiling excitedly, Lise exited Barn C, concluding she was up for a rather long drive if she was to start working at Nirvana Park come April. Hearing racing hooves meeting hard ground she glanced around, expecting to see a loose horse. Spying the culprit - a young colt racing backwards on the end of its lead while its handler tried to keep up - she watched curiously, waiting for the inevitable.

Surprisingly the handler managed to hold on and she watched, impressed as he quietly talked to the colt, gaining some ground - and lead - as he came to stand beside the horse's shoulder, encouraging the young equine forward. The colt took a couple of prancing steps forward before dancing on his hind legs, his handler responding by lifting the lead high into the air so his charge wouldn't get his legs caught up in it.

Once the colt had calmed down, Lise cast an experienced eye over the bay animal, taking in his well-conformed body.

Curious, she made a note of the number on the handler's hip tag and looked the animal up in her catalog, glancing over the colt's pedigree. She grinned as she took in the name of the mare, recognising it to be one she had dealt with a few years earlier at the racetrack.

Small world. She always was a wranger of a horse... this boy must have inherited it.

Overhearing lot number 130 being called to the outdoor parade ring, she quickened her step with the realisation that her friend's filly would be going through in twenty lots. *Time to get her ready.*

March

"Now turn left here, dear," her mother directed her father, the car turning the corner before coming to a stop as the vehicle full of people took in the view of painted white fences, green grass and grazing horses before them.

The youth smiled, turning her focus to her mother as the older woman started to speak.

"So! I guess this is where you'll be doing work experience... you should see the look on your face!" she smiled at her daughter who had turned her gaze back to the impressive looking property.

"Ready to go horse riding now?"

"Stupid question," she replied, grinning as her father turned the vehicle around heading for the property a few minutes away where her gelding was agisted.

***

"Michael?"

"That would be me. I take it you're Stuart?" the young man inquired, offering his hand.

"Definitely am. New to the property?" Stuart inquired after shaking the taller man's hand.

"New to horses in general," he smiled, gesturing to the tall gelding that was badly in need of having its feet trimmed.

Taking in the sight of the underweight animal under an experienced eye, Stuart grimly patted the horse before lifting up a front foot to inspect the damage. *At least someone has told him the feet need doing... People should need a license to own horses... not that it was this man who left this horse in its current condition...* He shook his head, clearing his thoughts before addressing Michael.

"You own this horse then?" he queried as he stepped away from the animal, putting his chaps on before grabbing his tools and once again picking up the equine's leg.

"Not yet. I'm leasing him for six months with the option to buy... it was suggested to get his feet in better shape before taking him for any rides though and I'm eager to get started. I've had a few lessons at a nearby riding school and then found this guy advertised in the paper."

Stuart nodded as he cleaned out the foot with his hoof knife before moving on to clipping the unneeded growth with a pair of pincers.

"Well his feet aren't too bad... it just looks like they haven't been trimmed in awhile."

Michael nodded, looking on curiously before turning his attention back to the young girl whom he had been watching have a jumping lesson in the arena opposite.

"Eye's up, Jacinta. Make sure you're focusing on the centre of the jump and beyond. Good," her instructor informed her, watching intently.

The young woman frowned, focusing all of her being on the jump in front of her, approached the centre, lifted, rose over the jump, landed and directed herself toward the next jump, just as determined as before. She stayed focused; telling herself the time to relax would be once she'd finished the course.

The sixteen-year-old completed the course, making it a relatively easy clear round before trotting her mount toward the end of the arena where her instructor was standing.

"That was great. I just want you to remember where your focus should be and make sure Geira's strides are even. She still wants to rush just before the spreads where you need to keep her collected. You don't want her coming up short before a jump she's really going to need to stretch over," he reminded the determined young woman, speaking of her Arab mare.

Jacinta nodded, taking in the information and reminding herself to put it to good use each time she was riding.

"Other than that," her instructor spoke up, grinning, "I'd say you're ready for the show on Saturday. You'd better bring us home another blue!" he smiled, wandering out of the arena before the young woman dismounted, rolled up her stirrups, loosened the girth and walked her mare around to cool her down.

Jacinta finished cooling down her mare and headed to a spare stall, tying up Geira before removing her tack and giving the Arabian a good curry followed by a light brush over.

As she worked the familiar routine, she went over in her mind the dressage test she was to execute the next weekend. Satisfied that she had it memorised her thoughts traveled to how she would plait up Geira to best show off her not too lengthy neck and strong quarters.

***

Relaxing in her seat, the sixteen-year-old reminded herself she would communicate a lot better with her horse if she were at ease. Grinning, she lined up the prancing gelding alongside her friends' horses, waiting for a signal.

"One, two... three! Go!"

Touching her legs to her mount's side she spurred the animal forward, racing the children surrounding her.

As she crossed the paddock she laughed at her horse's nature. Set in the middle of the pack he was eager to overtake those in front of him but so focused on those drawing in close from behind and too eager to send a kick in their general direction that he didn't catch the leaders.

Content with his antics but still eager to give her friends a run for their money, she lined up her gelding as the group reached the end of the paddock, ready to do it all again. She keenly waited for the chance to jump out ahead of them.

Halfway across the paddock she glanced to her right, taking in the sight of another palomino - a pony mare - keeping in line with her and consequently pushed her frame further forward, lifting her weight off her gelding's back in an attempt to encourage him to increase his pace.

A few strides later she came to realise her mistake as the cantankerous equine let fly with a couple of bucks, sending her flying over his shoulder before landing with a thud, banging her head on the ground.

She groaned and stood slowly, shaking her head to disperse of the stars that were interrupting her view of the paddock. As things cleared she grinned at the sight of her plump gelding - a few metres in front of her, grazing earnestly.

"Reign!"

He lifted his head, stared at her for a second, snorted and took a step toward her before lowering his head to the grass once again.

"I'd be tempted to tell you off... but it was my fault for being too forward out of the saddle," she muttered half to her horse, half to herself as she came to stand alongside him and gather up the reins before returning herself to sitting astride the animal.

"Shall we try that again?" she asked, grinning as he snorted and tried to lower his head for some more food.

"Didn't anyone ever tell you that you're not supposed to eat with a bit in your mouth?" she chastised, keeping a firm grip on the reins so as to stop him from grazing.

Shaking her head, she pushed the horse into a walk, grinning as a friend cantered up to her, shortly followed by the rest of the racers.

"You ok?"

She nodded, patting the gelding's neck.

"Think I can only blame myself for that one."

"Ten out of ten for the fall," a youth cut in, grinning.

She laughed in response.

"Thanks, I think... Ninety four to go!"

"And are you planning on having all one hundred of your falls on this overweight pony?" he questioned, smirking.

"Jake, he's not a pony - he sits on 15 hands, thank you very much. And he's festively plump, *not* overweight!" she replied, barely managing to hide her grin, "but if I keep going at this rate... yeah, I should be able to manage becoming a rider, thanks to this horse alone."

He chuckled, pushing his mount into a trot to keep up with her as they exited the paddock and headed toward another.

"Up for some jumps?"

"Are you that eager to see me reach my hundred falls?" she questioned in mock alarm, earning another laugh from him.

"Jumping's not that bad, you know."

"Works better for me when I'm on a horse that enjoys going over obstacles more than sending his rider over them without him," she muttered but still followed as he led the way to the jumping paddock.

"Man, I wish we could go back to doing this every day of the week," she sighed as she sat comfortably while her gelding jogged after the chestnut in front of him.

"Speaking of which, how has your first couple of weeks of school been?" Jake questioned, turning back in time to see her screw up her face in disgust.

"That good, huh?" he grinned.

"I shouldn't complain with it only having been such a short time. Plus, I have a heap of frees on Wednesdays... but I can't wait until next Wednesday when I start my VET course," she grinned.

"I can understand why! Do you get to spend the whole of Wednesday studying horses?"

"Yup," she smiled, bringing her horse to a halt as Jake paused beside her, the jumps momentarily forgotten.

"You can't complain about school at all... at least you've only got two years left... unlike my four," he muttered, frowning as she nodded, grinning.

"Thanks for that reminder. Just what I needed!" she called out as she spurred Reign forward and trotted him over the first cross rail before pushing him into a canter and taking the two three tyre spread.

Shaking his head, the younger male pushed his horse into motion, following the path of the entertaining pair that was now headed toward their fourth jump.

April

Lise looked around her new home, wiping the dust off her hands and transferring them to her faded jeans. Her gaze was rewarded with the tiring sight of boxes - many boxes that still needed unpacking.

"They can totally wait," she commented to no one in particular, ignoring the voice that was telling her it'd be smarter to at least have her bedroom and breakfast for the morning organised before she went wandering.

Closing the door on her logical thoughts, she stepped away from the house and headed over to the nearest building - a stable. She paused at the entryway, a risen voice thickly accented causing her to just stop and listen.

"I wish they wouldn't interfere sometimes! Those girls think they can do everything. Women!" the young Irishman muttered, holding a yearling while an older male cleaned a cut on its near hind cannon.

The young horse had escaped the day before and hurt itself. All, Declan concluded, because two of his coworkers were trying to prove a point about females handling high-strung colts.

"Well, taking that outburst into consideration, I guess you're going to have a problem with me," Lise commented suddenly, leaning casually against the nearest box as she gazed down the breezeway at the two men treating the young horse.

"And who are ye?" the broad Irish fellow asked in a bored tone, not bothering to hide his disinterest.

"Your new work mate," she grinned, stepping forward and offering her hand.

"I'm Trevor," the older male with slightly greying hair stepped forward, taking her hand in a firm shake while the younger stayed where he was, holding the horse.

"Lise Hemmingway," she responded, smiling at the man before her gaze traveled to meet the eyes of the other male.

"...and this is Declan. Generally we both deal with the stallions."

"Mmm... I guess you won't have to deal with me that often then. I'm possibly taking on the assistant neo-natal position when the breeding season comes back around," she told them, referring to the numerous young foals that were born and raised on the property.

Declan raised a brow, taking in the young woman properly this time. She stared back, not impressed with his sudden appraisal but willing to sum up the two figures. She noticed a considerable contrast between the older man's kind brown eyes, well worn clothes and rough hands, and the younger male's taller frame, neater clothes and challenging blue eyes fitting well with his ebony hair.

"How old are ye?" Declan blurted out suddenly, his gaze returning to her face.

"How old do I look?" she challenged.

"Sixteen, seventeen," he shrugged.

"That's an awfully young age to be working in such a specialised field, don't you think?" she commented, turning from the pair and heading down the breezeway.

"It was nice meeting you, Trevor."

The older man chuckled as he looked up at Declan; quickly discerning the younger man wasn't impressed.

"I like her already."

Declan grunted, turned the horse around and lead it back into its box, removing the bit and head collar before exiting the box and sliding the door shut.

"Another one to put up with who probably thinks she knows everything. *Just* what we need."

"I bet you twenty bucks you'll have changed your mind by the end of the month," the older male smiled at him, his look telling Declan he knew something the younger male didn't.

Not likely!

"I'll take that bet."

***

Madison grinned as she watched Jacinta manage yet another clear round while under the tuition of Jack. *Talented, indeed. I hope he doesn't push her too hard.* She was all too aware of how seriously Jacinta took her competing and riding. *But you're supposed to enjoy it, too.* Glancing at her watch she strolled over to the tie up area, aware that her four o'clock lesson would be here shortly. The two young girls that were to be riding were new clients, meaning she'd need to go through the run down of approaching the horse, moving around the horse, untying and leading over to the arena for a lesson.

Many that turned up for lessons were well aware of being around horses and had done so for years but because she never knew how much they knew and how much they *thought* they knew, it was always safer to explain how things were done at the East Riding School.

She cast her eye over the two ponies that were waiting patiently, half dozing in the shade, taking advantage of the rest before two new bodies were placed on them. Bodies that often represented beginners, legs flapping, insistently asking the loyal creatures to move forward, reins being yanked on, asking them to slow - sometimes the legs and arms at the same time; just to make things a little more confusing. Tucking a strand of auburn hair that had escaped back behind her ear, Madison looked up slowly as she heard excited laughter followed by the constant sound of running feet.

"Well, glad they know how to behave around horses," she muttered sarcastically, stepping away from the horses and towards the two children; a friendly smile making its way onto her face.

"Geordie and Hannah?" she queried, stopping in front of them, her gaze flicking up to the two mothers behind the pair before refocusing on her students.

The pair nodded, both smiling widely.

"Great! We might as well get started. You can call me Emmy and over here," she gestured, turning her attention to the two steeds in the tie up area, "are Sheila and Dundee. Geordie, you're on the chestnut mare Sheila, and Hannah you'll be riding Dundee today."

Both girls rushed towards their mounts for the lesson, causing Madison to half smile at her mistake.

"Before you both rush in there," she called out loudly, strolling after them, "I'd like to show you how we prefer people to move around the horses while at the East."

"Oh, we already know all that," Geordie spoke up, stroking the face of Sheila.

"Wonderful! Then you'll know that I'd much rather you walk up to the side of the horse and pat her from there as a way of hello, rather than directly in front of her," she commented easily, still smiling.

Frowning, the pair of girls both turned to face her.

"Ok. So let me go over how we approach and handle the horses here," she stated again, this time having both girls' attention.

Madison did some math in her head, well aware that she'd easily have two horses untacked, brushed and put away within twenty minutes, but with two horse crazy girls who didn't appear to be interested in leaving any time soon, she questioned if half an hour was even going to be doable.

She smiled at the two parents as they wandered over to the tie up area while the young girls headed the ponies into their stalls. The open toed shoes of the parents didn't go unnoticed as she commented on how well suited to each of the mounts their daughters had been. *Or rather, how well each pony put up with the two who constantly wanted to canter, tried to talk her into letting them jump higher than would be safe and who spent a reasonable amount of time pulling on the ponies' mouths. Boy am I glad that Mel is taking these two next time.*

Madison frowned as it became further evident that the parent's weren't overly horsey as they stood directly in front of the ponies with plastic bags full of apples and carrots, distracting the animals, making it hard for either girl to be able to tie up their ponies.

"Can you help me, please?" Geordie queried, relief evident when Madison ducked under the rail and pushed Sheila back far enough to be able to get the head collar on.

"Me too!" Hannah whined, pulling on her reins with all her might in an attempt to get Dundee to back off the rail so she could reach her head collar.

Madison questioned not for the first time why parents couldn't stay away until the kids had tied up and untacked their horses. *I doubt insisting on that would go down very well with anyone... except me, of course. Oh well, deal with them for the next half hour and then Mel can worry about it. But how do I convince her to take them on again without her being suspicious of me not wanting to teach them?*

She grinned, questioning whether telling her twin that she'd *enjoy their energy* when teaching them would be giving too much away. A frown marred her features as one of the mothers questioned her about whether or not the riding school ran day programs over the holidays. *Dear God, no!* Plastering on a smile she prayed with all her might that the last couple of places had already been taken.

"Indeed we do. Remind me to give you some flyers before you leave and if you ring the office tomorrow between eight and four, you should get a hold of my mother who runs bookings."

I may just be lucky enough considering school holidays start next week. We should already be all booked up for the day programs... I think I need a new job.

Realising both girls had brushed most of the sweat out of their ponies' coats, she picked up a rug, flinging it over the back of Dundee, quickly explaining the order in which the buckles and straps should be done up. *The sooner we get these on, the sooner these poor ponies can go out and you two energetic girls can be on your merry way.*

***

"Watch this here filly. I think she's just slightly over having had IV needles for the past three days," Declan warned, holding the young animal as Lise pulled the cap off the needle.

"Well, you'll just have to save me if anything goes wrong," she commented dryly, expertly putting her thumb to the equine's jugular groove, inserting the needle smoothly into the vein and pulling back with the syringe, noting with satisfaction the red liquid that coloured the small tube before administering the previously clear liquid.

Declan was slowly becoming impressed with Lise. He'd seen a lot of her over the past week as any work that had required two; Trevor had made some poor excuse to not help but not so surprisingly, always seemed to know what Lise was up to and where she could be found to help. Declan grinned as he realised the older man's plan was working. A figure came to stand in front of the box the pair were working in, his body blocking out the light as he peered in curiously. Declan rolled his eyes at the sight of the older male's sudden interest as his gaze fell upon Lise.

"Well hello gorgeous! Why doesn't anyone tell me when we get a new worker? I don't believe we've met. I'm Tony. And you are?" he questioned as she brushed past him out of the box.

"Uninterested," Lise commented dryly, never taking her gaze off the treatment chart she had picked up to fill in.

Still in the box with the sick yearling, Declan chuckled softly, amused at her bluntness.

"What have the others already told you about me? It's all a pack of lies, I promise you," Tony commented, winking at her.

"So you being found hung over in Declan's bed *wasn't* really a mistake? The girls swore it was," she stated sincerely.

"I... what?" he asked, suddenly confused.

Declan thrust his hand over his mouth, barely managing to contain the laughter that was now coming out in bursts. This girl knew exactly how to treat males like Tony... and pick them it appeared, as he was sure she hadn't yet been warned about the sleazy stud hand. The female staff hadn't exactly taken a liking to Lise, something he found surprisingly appealing.

"Give it up Tony, she knows about us. I guess everyone does," he commented as he exited the box, sighing dramatically to add emphasis to his statement.

Lise grinned as the young Irishman winked at her before strolling down the breezeway whistling YMCA. Observing the whole display from the other end of the stables, Trevor shook his head, grinning wryly.

"I should have made that bet fifty bucks," he muttered, entering the next box with a full hay net.

***

The young woman sat down at the end of the day, her back resting against a stall door. The second week in April marked the start of the school holidays which for her meant two weeks of work experience at an impressive looking racing property. Her mother had dropped her off early that morning and now at the end of her first day, she was going back over things she'd seen and learnt while waiting for the same parent to come and pick her up.

She chewed on her pen thoughtfully as she opened up the small notebook she'd been carrying in her back pocket on her mother's suggestion. This way she could make notes while the day was fresh in her mind, making her diary report for school that much easier.

Day one...

The horses are kept on straw in boxes which is around 20 centimetres deep (not to be exact, or anything) and it's even higher around the edges. Supposedly, the higher walls are to stop the horses from getting cast. That is, stuck in their box and unable to get up. Making them sound pretty stupid animals, isn't it? But, I've been told that when a horse rolls it's possible for them to get stuck, especially in the corner of a box and this extra height around the walls either keeps them away from the corners, or perhaps it gives them something to scramble up on? I haven't worked out which, yet.

Routine for the day – visit the horse boxes, search for horse poo (can you say "yay"?); remove the wet straw (read: empty the whole box); replace with new straw and in the afternoon do another poo hunt, removing this.

In between is the constant emptying of water buckets, cleaning out and refilling each one before replacing. I believe this resulted in me having at least five impromptu showers and that was just in the morning. Must fill buckets less...

After the poo and water madness, feeds are made up consisting of chaff and many other feedstuffs I don't yet recognise... oh, and a good amount of hay that is supposed to go into hay racks well out of my reach. Many a wash due to water buckets and then getting covered in bits of hay! Think I got those two round the wrong way...

Currently occupying the stalls are thirteen horses, seven bays, four chestnuts and one gorgeous roan. I wonder if they'd notice if I put her in the car and took her home? Oh, and the coolest thing so far? One of the chestnut horses is worth $250,000. A quarter of a million dollars! And they let me brush him and pick horse poo out of his feet. The best, huh?

She paused from her writing with a smile, looking back down the breezeway of the stables. Her grin widened as she heard the crunch of gravel under tyres. *Mum's here! Wait till I tell her about my day!* Calling out a goodbye to her boss she ran toward the car, flinging the door open with a grin, not even giving her mum a chance to ask about her day before she started relaying every little event. Her mother listened with a smile, driving them both home.

"You know what I've decided mum? From now on, I'll have them all call me Wes."

"Wez?" her mother clarified.

"W. E. S – work experience slave. None of them could remember my name and I fear it'll be the same for each of my placements," she stated cheerfully.

"Wes it is," her mother agreed with a laugh, heading home.

The rest of the week consisted of many firsts for Wes and lots of learning, nothing deterring her interest. She continued to keep a record, realising things would need to be changed a lot if her teacher was going to mark the diary well, but preferring to interject with her random thoughts as each day passed.

Day five...

Groomed horses; put on one's blanket. Heavy! When horses are led out, the halter is left on when they are being walked. Makes sense, really... we wouldn't want a loose quarter of a million dollars now, would we? Also put on an anti-rearing bridle. Main strap of leather that goes over the horse's head and down the nose. There's a metal piece like the bit on a bridle except this one's rounded, but odd shaped where it goes in the horse's mouth. Looks rather like a... very uncomfortable giant metal peanut. You heard me.

Attached to it is a long lead. This bridle is so you have better control of the horses when walking them and the bit helps to stop rearing, apparently. Perhaps it has something to do with the almost half moon shape, or that of one of those jellyfish you often find at the beach. You know the ones that you can squish and let leak through your hands? You don't? Oh...

When putting a horse back, you take the halter off as they could get their feet caught in it. Racehorses really don't sound too smart, do they? Stuck in a box... feet caught in a head collar...

When picking out the feet, all this is done from the near side (left of horse). When doing the offside foot (right side, just in case you were unsure what the opposite of left is), put it in front of the horse's other foot so that if they kick out, they get themselves and not the person grooming them. As if they'd be that *stupid... oh.*

The stall doors have numbers on them and a bolt up the top and catch down the bottom. There are twenty in all, the floors being cement and the walls being wooden. I'd like to have twenty boxes filled with horses... or perhaps, just one horse in each box. Yeah, that sounds better... and safer.

Day seven...

Don't mix up the feeds! If you do, panic and leave the property at a fast pace! Or... just take the feed bucket out from the wall and switch it into the other stall it was supposed to be in. Easier, isn't it? I really don't like running that much, anyway.

The total property's 150 acres with a racetrack located on a large part of it, paddocks situated in the middle. I got to see two of their weanlings today, one being worth $600,000. It's by Danehill, funny how that can explain things!

"I paid a million dollars for a horse today."

"Are you crazy?"

"No, it's a Danehill."

"Oh, fair enough."

Can anyone say designer horses?

There's a separate feed shed; the mares get two scoops of... something, and one full of oats. Other horses get one scoop of... something, and half of oats. Think I should have asked what the something was...

Mares that have just had foals and the weanlings get the same as previous, plus some other stuff. Insightful, huh?

Each horse has a separate paddock, just under an acre. Our house is on quarter of an acre... maybe we could keep a Quarter Horse at home... There are five broodmares to the five acre paddocks, all of which are located in the middle of the racetrack, which is used for morning workouts. The racetrack obviously, not the five acre paddock.

One of the guys was telling me that when you purchase a horse, you should look for package deals. For example, rather than invest in one horse, you can pick up a mare with a foal at foot that is also in foal and get her for a decent price.

Over the top example – they got a mare in foal to Danehill with a foal at foot for $60,000. Can you say bargain? Cheap designer baby!

I guess it's a gamble to buy a pregnant mare and expect everything to work out, but work out it did. They sold the foal she had as a yearling and kept the mare and other foal she had at foot. The yearling sold for $240,000. Not a bad twelve months work, if I do say so myself... and I do.

Now if I had a lazy $60,000, I'd be set! Must bug parents for higher rate of pocket money...

We got around the paddocks inside the racetrack by a little buggy that moves along the gravel road between the track and paddocks. Much fun! All the fences in the paddock are apparently electric (I admired them from a distance). Oh, and they're solar powered. Perhaps I'll closer inspect them on a cloudy day...

Near the stables is a large area round in shape and full of sand. A sand roll apparently... sounds like a rather gritty type of food...

All feed, brooms and pitchforks are in a spare stall in the stables. And when the horses are fed they are given about an eighth of the two green bales and a sixteenth of the yellow. I know these are types of hay and really should work on finding out a more descriptive way of noting the horses' feeds rather than just by the colour...

Apparently all jobs in the horse racing industry need a license. This is given to you after you have filled out a form and paid a fee – surprised? Me neither. It's achieved through Racing Victoria Limited (RVL) and is needed if you want to be a strapper, trainer, jockey, apprentice or any other horse job in the racing industry so I'm told. Not sure that I'll have to worry about that piece of paper, it's been fun but I don't think the racing world is for me. Maybe once I've stumbled across a small $60,000...

May

Lise smiled as she did up the head collar on the chestnut filly, her patience rewarded by the fact that she was able to get the synthetic item onto the young animal's head and securely done up. She was in a yard of young horses, working with Declan to get a hand on the animals before the farrier turned up for a routine trim of all their feet.

"I'll take this one here. She can be a bit of a feisty thing to handle."

Feigning indifference, Lise handed the lead over to Declan.

"I just spent ten minutes convincing her to let me put the head collar on but sure, you can take the credit," she commented for his ears alone.

Declan paused, surprised. *Attitude... just like the other women.*

"I'm just saving ye from getting hurt," he bit back childishly.

"Awfully nice of you considering you concluded when first meeting me that you weren't going to like me. So why start acting like such a gentlemen now?"

Lise was three weeks into her new job, having met most of the staff except the few who were yet to come back from their annual holidays. She had already decided that she loved working with Trevor and didn't mind the redhead Kaye, or the other two women whom she had been working alongside for most of the week. That was, as long as she didn't try any pleasantries. Neither seemed that interested in general chit chat or getting to know her, just getting the job done. Lise concluded she would work with this if that's the way they wanted it to be.

The young Irishman was yet to convince her that she should be nice to him. He seemed to go to the opposite extreme, constantly being in her face or way, almost as if he felt he should carry out every task.

She looked at him pointedly as he firmly grasped the lead rope that was clipped up to the weanling she had recently caught. Declan held her gaze and frowned. *A chip on her shoulder and she's clever. Not a good mix.*

Not dignifying her comment with a response of his own, Declan unclipped the lead from the same filly he'd been holding and let her wander off while he grabbed another head collar.

"And the point of that was?" Lise questioned, working hard to keep her anger in check.

"Well ye caught her before, didn't ye? We might as well get as many head collars on these babies as we can before Stuart turns up."

Not disagreeing, Lise grudgingly encouraged a pair of weanling fillies into a corner of the yard before gesturing for Declan to give her a hand to get closer without them breaking free. Realising that he was in a better position to get a hand on one - and possibly a halter - she kept her distance, ready to discourage them if they tried to run past.

The pair both turned their sole focus to the young animals before them and managed to halter another three of the fillies before a car pulled up beside the yard, the sound of rock music creeping out from its interior.

Concluding that it was the farrier, Lise picked up a lead rope and headed for a nearby bay filly, wanting to have one ready for the two men once they had their tools together. Declan headed over to the familiar dual cab Ute, lounging against the soft top tray as the two men got out.

"How long we got ye for, lads?"

Stuart Hunter grinned, shaking Declan's hand once out of the vehicle, his gaze taking in the horses milling about in the yard.

"Couple of hours, we'll break around lunch. Will that do? Otherwise we can finish off the rest on Thursday or Friday if you have time to spare."

"We'll see how we go. There are twelve fillies in here and Trevor, Jodie and Kate will be running in the colts once they've finished feeding out."

"No worries."

Stuart finished putting on his chaps and picked up his tools before heading over to the other body in the yards. He didn't recognise her to be one of the usual staff members at Nirvana Park and was always eager to find out how reliable new staff were.

His partner in work, Dave, didn't seem to mind either. As far as he could see it, Stuart could potentially risk his own safety by allowing a stranger to handle the horse he was putting himself under. Dave was happy to do the feet of a horse that was in the hands of someone he knew to be capable. Grinning at Declan he queried in a quiet tone who the new worker was. Declan returned the smile, ducking between the rails of the fence to get to the horses, Dave in tow.

"One that's got a bit more spunk than the others here, Dave. I'm not sure if you'll like her."

"I don't have to, I'm spoken for," he winked at Declan, waiting for him to get a hold of one of the young horses.

Hunter grinned as the young worker took his hand, smiling up at him.

"Well I'll be. So you actually took my advice?"

"Why not? It seemed pretty fitting for me," Lise responded, still smiling.

The pair easily struck up a conversation as Stuart got to work, being steady and calm with the young animal who had only had its feet done a half dozen times.

Declan remained reasonably quiet as Dave worked on another, surprised to find the elder farrier chatting with Lise like they were old friends. He made a mental note to ask Hunter about her when he got a chance. He didn't want to be on Lise's off side, in fact – far from it. He'd welcome any extra information about her if Hunter could offer that, too.

He saw a chance after both men had done a couple of horses each and paused for a cigarette break. Lise was chatting with Dave about his views on whether much could be done for a horse with a club foot. Seeing she appeared to be caught up in the conversation, he leant against

Stuart's car, his gaze resting on Lise but his conversation directed toward the older farrier.

"Old friends?" Declan queried, brows raised.

"Not exactly," Stuart commented with a grin, "I did happen to enlighten Lise to the fact that Kingsley was looking for another worker. We met at the Adelaide Sales just passed."

Lise walked over with Dave, catching Stuart's comment.

"You want someone to blame for me working here, Declan? Here's your man," she commented with a smug smile.

"To *blame*? Don't tell me you aren't getting along with Lise, Declan? A bit more attitude than you're used to in females?" Dave questioned in a teasing manner.

Declan refrained from responding, instead heading into the yard, calmly walking up to the nearest filly with a head collar on that hadn't yet had her feet done. He waited patiently for Dave to finish his smoke and then join him.

"I think you're going to have a bit of fun with that one," Dave stated quietly, Declan hearing the amusement in his tone as he picked up the near fore and started cleaning it out.

"Doubtful. She's already decided she doesn't think highly of me."

"So? Change her mind," he stated simply, continuing in silence.

Declan frowned, patting the filly on the forehead, smoothing her forelock from her eyes. *Easy as that, apparently.*

The two men made short work of the small paddock of fillies and managed one paddock of colts before needing to call it quits for the day. They set up a time to meet the following week to finish off the young horses on the farm.

"Perfect. See you both then. Great to see you again Lise," Stuart ended with a smile, waving as he headed back to his ute.

"Ye sure made an impression on him," Declan commented, as he headed to the opposite end of the yard to open some gates so the colts could be run back out to their paddocks.

"Every now and again a good impression sticks," Lise commented with sarcasm, missing Declan's small smile as he continued on away from her.

The broad Irish fellow had concluded over the past two or so hours that he could indeed change his mind and more importantly, hers. He recognised that when she wanted to be, she was pleasant and not lacking in guts. Plus, she could actually handle horses, but as of yet hadn't boasted about her capabilities. *Unlike a couple of the girls here.* The gates set up, Declan gestured for Lise to let the colts out of the yard as he waited patiently on the All Terrain Vehicle, ready to travel in front of the young horses and keep them at a safe trot on their way home.

Clapping and waving her arms behind the young male horses, Lise managed to guide them through a couple of gates and out into the laneway where Declan was starting to move off on his ATV. Following suit, she climbed onto the other bike and started the engine, moving slowly behind the colts, tooting the horn at any that stopped along the side of the laneway to pick at some grass.

Between them they kept the colts at a trot and led the ten into their paddock smoothly, Declan circling in the paddock and coming back out of the gate, Lise closing it after him. He brought his bike back to first gear and paused, turning his attention back to her.

"I've got to get some treatments done in the barn after lunch. If yer able to give me a hand, meet me there at half one."

Lise opened her mouth in surprise, not having time to respond as he took off at a roaring pace on the bike. She smiled.

"Well I'll be. Did he just ask me for help?"

***

"So how did your work experience go?" Jake queried as he brushed over his gelding with a body brush.

"Great! Funny to think that just up the road are horses worth up to a quarter of a million dollars… and mum and dad bought my boy for five hundred," Wes stated with a smile, patting the invaluable gelding.

"So are you tired of mucking out boxes and filling up water buckets yet?" he questioned dryly, moving on to pick out his mount's four feet.

"Nope! Was thinking Caulfield Racecourse would be perfect for my next lot of work experience. You know, just up the road they pick out all of their horse's feet from the left hand side?" she commented, watching Jake move around to the right hand side of his gelding to do the other two feet.

"They reckon a stablehand's time is more valuable than having to waste time moving around the horse to do his feet... the horse is just expected to lift any of the four from the left hand side."

"Fascinating," Jake stated with a wink, reaching for his saddle blanket, "and are you going to be insane enough to do your next lot of work experience over the school holidays, also? What about *your* poor horse who doesn't see you at all during the week? And haven't you considered a riding school? At least you'd get to sit on those horses!"

"For the record, my horse loves being obese and is put out by any sign of exercise. Weekends work perfectly for him... well, he'd probably prefer not to be worked on even them and yes, the school holidays are the perfect time to gain more horse experience! I've still got another bout to do after the racecourse - plenty of time for a riding school! Not that I'm sure insurance would cover me riding other people's horses," Wes frowned, putting Reign's bridle on, sliding the bit into his mouth.

Doing up the throatlatch, leaving four fingers room she turned to face Jake, the reins in her hand.

"You ready?"

"Course!" Jake grinned, putting his left foot into the left stirrup and hopping up onto his horse.

"Great! Can you help me with my turn on the forehand? Reign seems a little confused about lateral movement."

"No worries. You should see how good we're getting at reinback, too! Captain is really responsive now."

"Hmmm... my horse works fine forward and we're struggling with sideward movement... think I'll pass on encouraging him to go backwards!"

"Whatever. I'm sure if it comes up in Pony Club you'll be the first to give it a go," he teased, pushing his gelding out into a walk beside her.

"Probably," Wes grinned, not disagreeing.

June

Hunter smiled at Michael, shaking his hand before putting on his chaps and picking up his farriery tools.

"How's things going with this bloke?"

"Good, thanks. I was thinking we could put shoes on Beau though... I want to go out on road rides and he didn't seem to like the stones much last time. Is that alright?"

"Fine. You'll find we will more likely have to do his feet every six weeks rather than every eight if he was just getting a trim. If he slips a shoe I'll put it back on for free, but it costs seventy for a full set of shoes to be put on. If you're happy to commit to that, I'm happy to shoe your horse."

"That sounds fine."

"Wonderful. So are you buying this guy then?"

"Not sure. I've enjoyed my weekly lessons with him so far and if he feels better on the roads then we'll be out and about more often, too. He's nice and quiet - doesn't seem to mind vehicles and is happy in a group which makes things more enjoyable for me."

Hunter listened as he cleaned out the near fore, clipping back excess growth before neatening up the hoof with a rasp. This done he grabbed a shoe and held it up against the hoof, comparing the shapes. Not quite right to fit the hoof, Stuart let go of the gelding's leg and walked over to his anvil, dragging it out the back of his ute. He held the shoe against the anvil, hitting it with a mallet to reshape it. Michael watched curiously, holding Beau as he did so.

"What are you doing?"

"Adjusting the shape of the shoe to fit the foot. I'm happy with the shape of the foot, so want the shoe to match it. If I manipulate the foot to fit the shoe, it can place unnecessary stress on the foot as it's making it an unnatural shape. Shoes will be the same but feet can be different shapes.

Front feet tend to be rounder or wider than the back pair. I believe it's because a horse carries two thirds of his weight on his front feet. It is possible to put just shoes on the front feet and leave the hinds bare, but we'll see how he goes with all four shod. If you think his hind feet will be alright we can leave them bare next time."

"Ok. Will I book in a time with you now or see how things go with his feet?"

"Let's book in a date for six week's time. If the shoes look like they're doing well, you can just let me know and we'll leave it for a week or so."

Hunter finished working on Beau shortly before the end of Madison's lesson in the arena. The young redhead said a quick hi to both men as they passed, leading the fat little chestnut and white pony back to be untacked.

The young rider for that lesson was a six year old charge whom Madison had just waved goodbye to, as her mother was rushing to get her to a party on time after her riding lesson. Generally at the end of lessons students were encouraged to untack and brush down their ponies but Maddie was happy to carry out the familiar routine by herself on this occasion. The young girl had been just adorable and kept her smiling as she removed the riding gear from the reliable pony, Peaches and Cream.

"And what's caused that grin?" Jack queried, resting his frame on one of the tie up rails as he watched Maddie.

He'd finished his chores for the day except for making up the morning feeds but didn't want to leave without first having seen the attractive redhead.

"Sara. She's the most gorgeous kid. I swear if they were all like that I'd have half a dozen."

"Scary thought," Jack stated, a brow raised in surprise.

"Oh but honey, we're going to have to have at least three, don't you think?" Madison queried with a wink, heading toward the tack room with a saddle and bridle.

Looking around to make sure no one had heard her comment, Jack grinned at her reply.

"One of these days Maddie Jamison, I'm going to hold you to that."

Heading toward the feed room that was housed beside the tack room, Jack nearly collided with Maddie as she stepped out before him, quickly followed by ducking behind his frame. He frowned, looking down at her hiding behind the door to the feed room.

"What's gotten into you?"

"Shh!" she insisted, putting a finger to her lips.

Frowning Jack paused as he heard the sound of two young girls talking excitedly, headed in his direction. They didn't spy Jack as they headed into the tack room to check which ponies they would be riding for the lesson.

"Oh Hannah, you're on Sheila this lesson... do you think we could swap? I don't really want to ride Dundee," Geordie queried her friend as they looked over the list.

"I don't know... let's ask Emmy and see what she says," Hannah replied, the pair coming to a pause outside the tack room as they spied Jack in the feed room doorway.

"Hello!" Geordie stated happily, "have you seen Emmy, Jack? We thought she went this way but can't seem to find her."

Jack looked around helplessly, not wanting to lie to the pair. Spying Melanie in the arena setting up for the lesson he pointed toward the arena with a smile.

"Looks like she's ready for you," he stated, watching the pair head toward their ponies with relief.

Madison let out a sigh as she heard the pair departing.

"How did you talk your sister into this?" Jack queried with an amused smile, looking down at the redhead.

Madison shrugged, grinning sheepishly. She and her twin taught under the name of 'Emmy' pretending to be one and the same instructor. This way they only had to teach half as often and as of yet, none of their regular clients had caught on.

"Guess Mel was having an off day when she agreed," she admitted, brushing past Jack.

"So what's so bad about those two?" Jack queried, stepping into the feed room to grab some buckets.

"I don't want them to work out that there are two of us and if they saw me, then I'd be stuck teaching the terrors. They're just trouble!"

"I'm sure you're overreacting."

"Right... you don't have to worry about the trouble makers at this level, just stick with your talented, single minded students and you'll be fine."

"Single minded?"

"Yes, single minded. Blue, blue, blue... is that all you teach them, Jack? That a blue ribbon is the only reason to ride?"

"Of course not! But don't tell me you don't like to win an event, Maddie. I know you're as competitive as the next person."

"So? That's not the point," she responded with a frown.

Jack rolled his eyes as he stepped out of the feed room, buckets in his grasp.

"Most of the time Madison, I don't get what your point is."

Not deeming his comment with a reply Madison stormed off, around the back of the feed room so as not to be spotted by the two young charges now mounted in the arena.

***

Melanie smiled ruefully, questioning how on earth she'd get her sister back for this one. She'd just had one of *the* most frustrating hour lessons, trying to keep Hannah and Geordie in check. *And I've already agreed to take them for the day program. I really am going to have to kill Maddie.*

"Please tell me that look on your face wasn't caused by my younger sister?" a resonate voice inquired as a lean tanned figure strolled lazily toward Melanie and her two young clients.

"I assure you, it's *my* younger sister causing the look," Mel stated with a grin, taking back the murderous thoughts.

She didn't say anything about a gorgeous older brother.

"Well I guess that's something," the young man returned the smile before asking Geordie how her lesson was.

"Great! Emmy let us canter lots and jump lots!" came the fervent reply.

Mel raised her brows. *Let you? I couldn't stop you two!*

"And does that just make Emmy the best instructor ever?" the figure queried with a grin, winking at Mel.

She felt a small flush creep up her face, but returned the warm smile as both girls replied in the affirmative. Both finished with grooming their horses before turning to the older male with pleading eyes.

"Have we got time to take the horses out Johnny? Please?"

He turned his gaze to Mel and upon her smile, told the pair they could.

"I'll even come out with you, if that's ok?" he put forth the question, more for Mel than the girls.

All three agreeing, he held open the gate for them as Mel kept an eye on the two leading their ponies. She directed one to the left hand side of the horse to lead and the other to have her lead in both hands and then let them be, falling into stride with Johnny.

"Are you taking them both home?" she inquired, wanting him to hold a conversation with her until he left.

"Guilty as charged. Hannah convinced her mum to let her stay and then suddenly both mothers convinced me to baby sit while *they* have a night out. I'm still not sure how I got stuck with that one," he finished with a wry smile.

Mel laughed.

"It's amazing how people can talk you into things," she agreed, opening the gate so the girls could lead the ponies into their paddock.

"Oh?" Johnny queried.

Mel only shook her head, smiling. *If I let you in on that, you'll know my little teaching secret.* With both girls facing their ponies to the fence and safely spaced out, Mel told them they could undo their head collars and step back out of the way. Happy to be free, the ponies spun around, kicked up their heels and took off across the paddock, the other occupants joining in.

"Better get out of here before they head back this way," Mel warned, guiding the girls out of the paddock and shutting the gate.

The four then stood to watch as the paddock of ponies continued their mad dash.

"Bet you could watch that all day," Johnny murmured.

"If time permitted," the redhead agreed, "only if time permitted."

July

"For your homework for next rally I'd like you to get back to me on the tendons on the horse's leg."

"You mean the extensor and flexor?" Wes queried their theory instructor.

"Now that you've done everyone's homework for them, that's exactly what I meant. If everyone could get back to me on where they are on the leg, without asking *this* student, that'd be appreciated."

"Nice one," Jake nudged Wes in the ribs as she picked up her notes before heading out of the room with him.

"It's not my fault. We studied it at my VET course a couple of weeks ago. It was sorta on the brain, you know?"

"No I don't, considering theory doesn't excite me in the slightest, but that's fine. Now we'll get onto the real horse stuff!"

Wes rolled her eyes as all the young riders headed over to their ponies located in nearby yards. As far as she was concerned, theory was the important stuff. It taught you about riding, care of the horse, rules and regulations, owning horses... everything! Grabbing a dandy brush, Wes set to work on Reign's tail, having already lightly brushed him over before their theory lesson.

"I'm not sure Reign would let me tie a ribbon in his tail," she pondered out loud, thinking over a conversation with her riding instructor.

Apparently it was pony club rules to put a red ribbon in the tail of a horse that was known to kick to warn others of this vice.

"Bah, you shouldn't have to! If someone's stupid enough to walk close enough behind your horse to get kicked, then it's their fault. Besides, all horses can kick. Should we only worry about the ones with ribbons in their tails?"

"Point taken. What class have we got now?"

"Games," Jake stated with a grin as he tightened the girth on his gelding, "and you'd better hope that you're on my team."

"Why, so I can help you win?" Wes threw back with a grin, doing up the throatlatch on her bridle.

"Nooo... so *I* can help *you* win, of course," Jake retaliated, opening the gate of his yard to lead his gelding out to the arena.

Wes followed still smiling, knowing with certainty that Jake was right. She would need him on her team, and the sole other male that attended their pony club.

Not ten minutes later when everyone had had their gear checked and were mounted, she could have audibly groaned. Both boys were on the other team and to make matters worse, Sarah was on her team. A couple of years older, the rider was very accomplished but was solely focused on dressage, liking everything to be calm and collected on her horse. *Someone should teach her extension belongs in dressage tests, too.*

Wes was certain her team would lose but was willing to give it her best shot anyway. They'd been split into two groups of five, Wes being third for her team. Each rider was to trot past the first 44 gallon drum, pop over a small crossbar, land in a canter and jump a small vertical, continue on around the end drum and trot back. It was keeping at a steady trot and not breaking into a canter while heading back towards all the other horses that would prove to be the most difficult, testing each rider's control.

Wes watched in anticipation as the first riders for each team shot forward, her teammate in front by a small margin. *Not that that means a lot, Jake and Fisher are last and will make up plenty where it matters.*

Wes was so focused on the race that she barely noticed Fisher sidle up beside her, one of her teammates Sarah on the other side of him. She didn't notice anything was up until Jake came up on the other side of Sarah, effectively sandwiching her horse between the two of them. Wes contemplated warning her teammate, but honestly wasn't sure what she should be warning her about.

Sarah remained unaware as her attention stayed focused on the second players who were now halfway through their leg of the race. Her gelding stood quietly, not bothered by the equines on either side of him.

Reaching to the left hand side of the horse, Fisher managed to pretend to pat Sarah's mount while working to undo the throatlatch. This done he nodded to Jake who quickly reached over and pulled the brow band over the same gelding's ears, dropping the bridle to the ground before quickly backing his horse up and trotting over to his lineup of teammates, Fisher in tow.

Wes only had time to spot Sarah's confusion as the weight increased through her reins. As realisation dawned on her, Wes could only laugh, turning her attention back to the race and kicking her gelding into a forward trot as it was her turn. She was going to give this her all, even if it was now guaranteed that they would lose. There was no way Sarah would be able to dismount, re-bridle her horse and get back on in time to make a closing finish. Wes was convinced the other team would have won anyway, but was questioning if the boys had considered the dangers of their stunt, or only the certainty of winning due to it.

***

Madison smiled, heading over to the hay shed with a wheelbarrow, glad to be done with her lessons for the day. Of course the last had to have been Geordie and Hannah, extremely full of energy but she'd managed to keep them entertained with race games and their parents had only turned up in time to see them come in from the paddock where they'd put out their ponies.

All she had left to do for the day was hay the hacks, putting out a couple of bales for the eight horses. She loaded one on top of another into the wheelbarrow, securing the load with some baling twine before pushing it out toward the paddock. Spying Jack in the main arena finishing up with Jacinta, she paused to watch the pair converse, Jack no doubt summing up points for Jacinta to remember for their next lesson. She was convinced the younger rider was interested in her instructor but couldn't seem to get out of

Jack if he thought the same thing. Shrugging, she continued pushing the barrow, pausing to open a gate.

"Are you coming to watch us compete on Saturday, Jack?" Jacinta queried as she walked her mare out of the arena, Jack strolling beside her.

"Sorry, Cint but I can't. I'm teaching all day Sunday and Saturday's the only day I've got free to do some study for my Instructor's Certificate."

The young girl pulled a face.

"I don't see why you need to get a qualification to teach when you already instruct."

"Having your Level 1 means you're insured to teach your own clients, wherever that may be, plus, it'll mean a better rate of pay," he commented, glancing up at her.

"I guess that makes sense. Oh well, you'll just have to make it up to me some other way," she stated with a smile as she looked down at him.

Jack let his gaze drop to the ground, not knowing how to comment. He didn't want to encourage the girl but also couldn't work out how to discourage her interest as she seemed to be increasingly suggesting spending time together outside of him instructing her lessons. For the moment he concluded he could get away with doing nothing.

Madison groaned as the big chestnut gelding grabbed a mouthful of hay from the bale balancing precariously on the wheelbarrow. It was inevitable – it didn't matter if she tied the bale to the barrow, one of the horses was going to pull it all over, causing her great frustration.

"Every time! We invest in new arenas, new horses and advertising but a laneway for me to walk the hay down to the next paddock without getting bombarded by horses in *this* paddock? No, *that* would be too hard!"

Picking up a clod of dirt she hurled it at the horse to blame, smiling in triumph as it glanced off his round hindquarters, spooking him into flight, the others in tow. Realising time was short she rushed to right the wheelbarrow and replace the hay to where it had been before jogging toward the next gate. She achieved entering the paddock just as the galloways were trotting back toward her, some snorting, uncertain. *Not uncertain enough to worry about* not *trying to take the hay.*

"You've all got issues. You're fat and so, so gluttonous," she grumped, spreading out the hay into more piles than there were horses, one big bay gelding following her around from one pile to the next.

"Stupid cookie monster syndrome. You can't just stop at the first pile I put out for you, you have to try the whole lot!"

Jack grinned, watching Madison finish up in the paddock, certain she was in a foul mood by the way she stomped about the paddock. He looked up momentarily as Melanie came to stand beside him, resting her arms on the top rail of the fence.

"You could just ask her out, you know."

"I don't know what you're talking about," he responded too quickly.

"Of course you don't," Melanie stated quietly, turning away and heading to the house.

Jack stood quietly also, staring at nothing in particular until he realised Madison was struggling at the gate with the wheelbarrow.

"You know, I don't think I've seen something so amusing."

"Hence you not stepping forward and offering to help," she retaliated dryly, putting down the barrow to step forward and open the gate before walking through; Jack falling into step beside her.

"It would have interrupted the show, yes," he stated with a grin.

"Glad to be of assistance," she muttered, dumping the barrow beside the stacked bales of hay unceremoniously.

"Your number one fan gone home already?" she queried, her dig not lost on Jack.

"Afternoon, Maddie. I'll see you tomorrow," Jack sighed, turning from her and heading to the car park.

Madison frowned, stomping into the house, shrugging off her jacket and hanging it up by the front door.

"That good a lesson, ey?" Melanie queried from beside the heater, a book resting in her lap, "I thought they were delightful girls, just full of energy."

Madison rolled her eyes at her sister, thinking her annoyed state wasn't going to help her convince her mocking twin to take on the pair for a lesson she wasn't actually assigned to.

"They were fine," Maddie stated dismissively, "listen, Mel… I've got a favour to ask…"

The other redhead sat quietly, holding Madison's gaze.

"There's a combined training day coming up in a few weeks and it falls on a Tuesday when I'm supposed to be teaching but I'd really love to take Phoenix along. I think it'd be perfect timing to test her out with others…"

"And you want me to teach the bratty pair for you so you can go."

"I want to know if you'd be willing to teach the Tuesday for me so I can go," Madison corrected her sister.

"I don't think so… the pair can be way too much trouble. I'm quite content with teaching them fortnightly, thank you very much."

"Please? It'll be some extra money for you to put toward the new dressage saddle you want," Madison pushed.

"Tell you what, sister darling," Melanie stated with amusement, "paper, scissors, rock. You win, I'll teach. I win, you leave me alone. Deal?"

Noting she didn't really have a choice, Madison held her fist out to her sister. On the count of three the pair each portrayed their choice of paper, scissors or rock with their hand. Madison let out a shriek of joy when she realised her scissors beat her sister's paper.

"Thanks Mel!" she stated, escaping from the room before her twin had the chance to change her mind.

Spotting her mother at the computer in the study room, Madison retraced her steps, entering the room.

"Whatcha doing?" she queried her mother, leaning over her shoulder to get a good look at the computer screen.

"Working out when to send you three off to renew your first aid. They run out in August. I think Mel and Jack can go on the Monday and Tuesday and you can do yours on the Wednesday and Thursday. That should keep us open for each of the lessons you teach."

Madison frowned, realising that if she were teaching this coming Tuesday she'd be in charge of Geordie and Hannah. On top of that, four days without Jack's company was totally unappealing. Inwardly she groaned, questioning how on earth she could fix that dilemma when she'd already talked Melanie into teaching them the week after so that she could take her mare, Phoenix, to a combined training day.

"Do you think if Mel agreed to it, we could switch?"

"I don't see why not. Just let me know shortly so that I can fill in the details for each of you."

"Will do!" Madison stated with more cheer than she felt as she left the room to interrupt her sister's reading in the lounge room.

"Mel... Feel like getting that saddle even quicker than you had planned?" she questioned meekly, thinking if she could convince her sister, it'd be one of her best arguments yet.

"Fine."

"Now before you say... what?" she questioned, surprised by the response.

"I said fine. I'll teach them so you can do the first aid course with Jack," she stated with a smirk.

"But... why?"

"So you'll leave me alone. Feel free to take the subtle hint," she responded, lifting her book up to her face to block out her twin.

Madison frowned as she left the room, certain that something was up, but not sure that it mattered when things had turned out how she wanted them to. However, now she was extremely curious. She made a note to get home as soon as possible after the first aid course to find out what her sister was up to.

August

"Hello gorgeous," Declan crooned, scratching the forehead of the mare enjoying the groom that Lise was carrying out.

This was in anticipation of the clients that would soon be arriving to have a look at her with the possibility of buying.

"You talking to Lise or the horse? You have to be nice to her on her birthday, you know, no teasing," Trevor stated with a wink and a smile as he strolled past.

Lise smiled to herself, focusing on brushing out the mare's full tail, her body turned away from the Irishman who was now staring at her in surprise.

"Ye didn't say! How old are ye, Lise?" he accused, waiting to catch her gaze.

"Should I have?" Lise queried, still not turning to face him.

"Indeed. One, the other girls here love to make a show of it when it's their birthday - get out of work and the like and two, ye share yer birthday with every thoroughbred in the southern hemisphere. That's great craic."

Dropping the brush into a grooming bucket, Lise picked it up as she headed out of the box, pausing in the doorway before Declan.

"One, I'm not like the other girls here, I'll work the same every day... and two? A birthday is a birthday. On this one I'm twenty."

Declan stood grinning in the doorway as she brushed past him, strolling down the breezeway.

"Happy birthday, Lise," he murmured before closing the door and heading toward the stallion boxes.

It was the end of the day and time to bring in all the boys for the evening. Coming to the first roomy box that housed one of the stallions, Declan grabbed the lead and bit that was hanging up outside the box and headed for the stallion runs that were set up alongside each other on the farm.

Each stallion had their own paddock of about two acres, enough room for a decent pick of grass and a chance to burn some energy in between breeds. At the moment each of the four boys were out all day - weather permitting - as the actual breeding side of things hadn't started yet.

The first of September marks the date that all farms in Australia are allowed to start breeding their thoroughbred stallions with mares. This set date meant that no foals were due to be born before the first of August, due to the eleven month gestation of a mare.

For commerciality, most mare owners loved to breed their mare as early in the season as possible as this meant an early foal the next year and therefore a big yearling once the sales came around. Some owners had the luxury of racing the horses they bred themselves and these weren't so bothered about when their mare got in foal but the majority of the clients at Nirvana Park bred to sell. Declan shook his head at the quirks of the industry as he reached the gate to the first stallion's paddock.

Putting his fingers to his mouth he let out a shrill whistle, being rewarded with the sound of cantering hoof beats shortly after. The big chestnut stallion came to a sliding halt at the gate, eager to get into his box and therefore to his afternoon feed.

"Bit hungry there, big fella?" Declan questioned good naturedly, letting himself into the paddock, being careful to shut the gate after him while keeping a close eye on the testosterone filled 600 kilogram animal.

Used to the stallion's movements, he dodged teeth as he quickly worked to put the bit in the horse's mouth and clip up the lead to both bit and head collar, giving him extra control for leading the animal. This done, he opened up the gate and walked briskly with the large animal toward its box, entering and turning back to the door before rugging him. He then removed the bit and lead and bolted the door shut after him.

Trevor fell into stride beside Declan shortly after and the pair headed back toward the stallion run, enjoying the clear and warm afternoon that had settled before them.

"Been down to see the first foal's yet?" Trevor queried, pausing with Declan as he stopped at the next gate.

"Nope, why?"

"The first was a nice colt, thought you might be interested. It is King's first crop after all," he responded, referring to the stallion owned outright by Nirvana Park's manager.

"Maybe I'll have a look after all the boys are put away,"

"You should. I think Lise was headed over that way... another foaled just after lunch, apparently."

Declan grinned, choosing not to respond to Trevor's not so subtle push toward Declan spending more time with Lise.

***

"There was this gorgeous chestnut mare at Caulfield Racecourse, Jake. Very clever – she knew how to get out of her stall. If you didn't close both the top and the bottom catches on the door, she'd be gone. I think she got out three times in the two weeks I was there."

"Sounds like not everyone has learnt that yet then. Bit of a worry when the equines are smarter than the employees," he stated dryly, walking with Wes out to the paddock to bring in their ponies.

Both were rugged up in jackets, planning on ignoring the drizzling rain that was creating a blanket around them. Making her way around the edge of a rather large puddle, Wes smiled as she took in the water.

"You know they swim their horses there? They have a pool shaped like a keyhole; you start at one side and lead the horse down a ramp, slowly getting them deeper in the water while you hold onto the lead and a pole that is clipped onto their head collar. It gets really heavy once the horse is fully in the water, their head just above as they're swimming. That was sorta cool to do with the horses that needed to be exercised but nothing too strenuous for their legs. Apparently it's really good for their lungs."

"So what else did you have to do? More mucking out and filling up feed and water buckets?"

"You're such a cynic. Yes, but other stuff too. I got to groom and tack up the horses and lead them out to the exercise riders at the track and bring others back and help cool them down and wash them. One of the guys showed me how to put on something called Swell Down. He said it was a poultice – it draws out heat and swelling after a horse has done a hard gallop. It was like a cream that turned hard once applied... sorta like cement."

"Sure that'd help horses run faster, cement plastered to their legs," Jake laughed, reaching Captain and putting a head collar on him.

"So what time did you have to start?"

"Well... insurance for school doesn't cover outside the hours of seven in the morning to seven at night but mum dropped me off about quarter to six every morning so that I could do more hours. I think everyone started about three each morning and worked until nine. Then they have to come back from two to four each afternoon to do the afternoon feeds, water and quick pick up of the boxes."

"So do you think you learnt much?" he asked genuinely.

"Sure, the most important being racing hours are not for me," Wes stated firmly, smiling as she held her lead rope loosely, Reign trailing behind her.

"Up for just a plod around the paddocks today?" Jake asked, glancing back at her.

"Reckon so. There's no way Reign is going to pay much attention to flat work or jumping when he'll be spending the whole time making sure the rain isn't getting in his face," she laughed.

"You're pony is such a sook."

"Yup. A gorgeous, irreplaceable, sook."

***

"How's it looking?" Declan queried, peering over the half door of the foaling box that Lise was working in.

Hearing the sudden voice she jumped and gritted her teeth. Lise continued what she was doing, rubbing her hand slowly along the belly and flank of the first time mother in an attempt to get her hand on the mare's udder to milk out a bit of her colostrum.

"It'd be fine if some moron, didn't come along and scare the crap out of me when I'm at the back end of an uncooperative mare, trying to collect some milk!" she bit back, ignoring the sound of the door opening.

Stepping into the box Declan walked up to the mare's head and picked up her near front foot, staying on the same side of the mare as Lise as she again tried to collect some milk, this time being successful.

Lise spilt a drop onto the refractometer, a device used to test the quality of a mare's colostrum and therefore the level of immunity the foal should receive due to ingesting the milk. Looking into the device, she was happy with the number that showed up.

"Thirty. Good. I'll milk out around 500mls once this filly's had a decent drink so we have some stored up for the start of the season."

She stepped out of the box, Declan behind her, the pair leaving the newborn and first time mum to further bond. Declan shadowed Lise as she headed to the small Vet lab to clean up. She rinsed the milk affected area of the refractometer under the tap before wiping it clean. Turning around she nearly dropped the said item as she found Declan standing closely before her.

"Hi," he stated with a grin, not stepping back.

"Do you know how much these things cost?" Lise ground out, stepping around him to place it on a nearby shelf.

"I think I'm about to find out," Declan quipped, leaning against the sink.

"So are ye ever going to give me a chance?" he queried casually, the underlying meaning not lost on Lise.

She continued to stand looking at the shelf, unsure how to answer his question when she'd only just started asking herself if she should consider entertaining the idea of a relationship with this man. Turning to face him she found she had more time to find an answer, as he'd left the room.

***

"Well, wasn't that awfully boring," Jack sighed, stepping out of the large building in the city, Madison walking beside him.

"Mmm... not as bad as last time! At least this guy had a sense of humour... and the company was good, so I'm not going to complain," she returned with a smile, pausing at the pedestrian crossing, waiting for the lights to change.

Jack smiled at the compliment, waiting beside Maddie. She smiled up at him.

"So are you coming to the competition on Saturday?"

"So I can see you and Phoenix compete? Why won't anyone just let me have a day off?" he questioned, shaking his head incredulously.

Madison laughed, stepping out across the road as the lights changed.

"Actually, I thought you might go along to cheer on a certain student of yours, considering she's so eager for you to spend time with her," she retaliated, smirking as a flush rose up over Jack's face.

"Stop it, it's not funny. I'm having enough trouble working out how to deal with her without you making fun of me," Jack frowned, cutting across the car park towards his stationary vehicle.

"She's such a talented rider I want to keep encouraging her but I'm worried about giving her the wrong impression or embarrassing her."

"Think it's happening the other way around," Madison joked, coming to stand at the car door, her gaze meeting Jack's across the car, "besides, it's not Jacinta's fault she's got good taste," she concluded with a wink.

Seeing Jack blush for a second time in such a short space of time kept Madison amused the whole trip back. It wasn't until they came to a stop in the riding school's car park that she remembered her curiosity about her twin.

"Melanie!" she stated eagerly, hurrying to get out of the car.

"What about her?" Jack questioned in confusion, locking the door after them and hurrying to keep up with Madison.

He followed her as she took the long route around the feed and tack rooms, coming to a sudden stop at the edge of the building. Jack complained as he slammed into Maddie, his protests being quietened with her warning glare.

Peering around the corner, Madison spied Melanie tending to Geordie and Hannah, a fourth figure with them, chatting with Melanie.

"Guess that answers that question," Madison murmured, a large grin spreading across her face.

"What?" Jack whispered harshly, pushing past Maddie to get a look.

"Who's the guy?"

"Who? I don't know... but I do believe he's the reason my twin agreed to take on a few extra lessons with the girls."

"Because...?" Jack queried, confused.

"Hello – he's gorgeous! Why wouldn't she?" Maddy bit back, taking in the lean, tall figure with a grin.

"I don't see anything that special," Jack muttered, turning away from the tie up area.

"Please, anyone would find him attractive!"

"Well sorry to say, but he's not my type," Jack muttered sarcastically, stalking off.

Madison grinned, ignoring his annoyance.

"Lucky for me he isn't, otherwise I'd be wasting my time, Jack Brown."

September

Lise opened the door in response to a hesitant knock, smiling at the young woman on the other side.

"Kate?" she queried, opening the door wider to usher her in.

The young woman was from a local TAFE (Tertiary and Further Education) facility and to be staying in Lise's quarters for the next four weeks while carrying out work placement which was due to finish mid October. Lise had been told a few days earlier that because she had a spare room in her two bedroom house, the student would be staying with her and was to join Lise at the broodmare stables in the morning to work.

Lise ignored the stories going through her head that Declan had told her the day before about "disaster tafies", instead focusing on showing Kate around the house and which room was hers.

Once happy the student was settled and knew what time she had to be ready for work the next morning, Lise headed out of the house and to her car. Hunter was due to do the feet of a gelding she'd just taken up a lease for and she didn't want him to have to do the horse unattended.

***

Smiling, Wes waved goodbye to her mum who had dropped her off at the property where Reign was agisted. She was on a mission this afternoon. This Wednesday just passed at VET they had each had a go at instructing horse riding, having the week before been told to pick out one aspect of riding a horse and to research it to teach to a small group of riders. Although all knew the basics of riding, each student as the instructor had to pretend their class knew nothing about the topic and teach it as if teaching a first time rider.

Wes had chosen the rising trot, thinking the balance required to rise to the trot a difficult task for a first time rider. She had had fun explaining to the four riders before her the importance of learning to rise to the trot and how to tell if you were on the correct diagonal – that is, rising in time to a particular leg of the horse. She had had a lot of fun teaching and it had shown with her receiving the second highest score out of the students in relation to her teaching.

Next week she would be marked on her riding. She thought it a bit frustrating that she rode one horse while at VET and her own any other time. Normally it wouldn't matter but each student was being assessed on a freestyle dressage test – that is, a test to music. It was up to the students to design a dressage test (to their capable riding level) and pick out music to fit in with the horse's footfalls at the walk, trot and canter.

Wes' dilemma was that during VET hours, she rode a 16 hand high thoroughbred gelding that had a big stride and all other times, she rode Reign who reached barely 15 hands and had quite a short stride. If she practiced the music with her horse, it would be almost guaranteed that the music wouldn't be fitting to the larger gelding she rode during the week. It seemed ridiculous to her to have to get her parents to hire a float to transport her gelding to the VET property to be able to perform the ride on Reign but it made things difficult to fit to music.

Concluding the best she could do was practice the routine on Reign and have it memorised, she pulled the scribbled test out of her pocket, glancing it over while heading out to the paddock to bring in her gelding.

Twenty minutes later she had him brushed and tacked up, giving her a short amount of time to practice before her mother would be returning. She mounted and quickly warmed up her gelding at a walk, trot and canter before heading for one of the 'arenas' on the property. It was a grassy area of about 60 metres by 20 metres with large wooden logs placed around the perimeter.

She entered the arena at the letter A at a walk, halting at the letter X which was situated in the middle of the arena between B and E, a spot where students were expected to halt on their horses and bow to the judge. This done she continued on at a walk, carrying out half of the routine she'd written before having to stop Reign and check her piece of paper for the next movement.

Uncrumpling the piece of paper with one hand, the other lightly on the reins she had not much to hold herself in the saddle when Reign reacted with fright to the sound of the paper, letting out a buck which sent Wes through the air, over his shoulder and to the ground with a hard thud. She lay for a moment, catching her breath and waiting for her heart to slow from the fast thudding in her chest. She sat up with a groan, looking at her gelding standing apologetically beside her.

"Guess reading something on paper while on horseback is out of the question, ey?"

Not feeling any real damage she placed the piece of paper back in her pocket and remounted, eager to complete the dressage test before heading in to untack. *As long as I have it memorised and Sultan doesn't throw me off while carrying out the test at VET, I think I'll be happy.*

***

"Have you given one of these before?" Lise asked of Kate, holding up an Ovuplant.

Kate shook her head, affirming that she wasn't familiar with giving the ovulating drug to a horse.

"I know it looks a bit like a harpoon," Lise grinned, "but it's given subcutaneously, which is under the skin. I like to think this hurts less than a needle going into the muscle of the horse's neck. The idea is to grab a pinch of the neck and insert the needle into the skin fold. I do so from the top of the fold, pushing it down and then inserting the tablet. This way the tablet can't fall out. Once you've removed the needle, you should be able to feel the tablet in the neck just below the surface. If you can't feel it, it's gone too far."

"Is that an issue?" Kate queried, taking the Ovuplant handed to her.

"I don't think so, you'd have to ask the vet but I believe it may work slower if put intramuscular. Give it a try," Lise instructed, holding the mare for her.

Kate looked at the needle uncertainly. Lise questioned if she was just unsure or had something against needles.

"Will I do this one and you can do another after seeing how it's done?" she offered, noting the girl's relief as she nodded in reply.

Switching positions, Lise took the Ovuplant, offering the lead rope to Kate. Grabbing a fold of skin she inserted the needle, depressed it and then felt for the tablet after retracting the needle. She had Kate feel for the tablet in the horse's neck before instructing her which yard to let the mare go in. Lise frowned as she headed to the opposite yard to catch another horse for the vet, questioning if the 'tafie' actually knew what the drug she'd just given was administered for. She decided yes, but made a note to query Kate about it the next time a horse needed to be given an ovulating drug.

Catching a mare from the yard after making sure it was on her vet list, Lise headed toward the vetting crush, lining up behind the few already in front of her. All staff once finished with particular morning duties were required to help out with the vetting which started around 9am and continued up till lunch, sometimes afterwards also.

Nirvana Park was one of Victoria's largest thoroughbred farms, vetting around one hundred mares a day. They were looked at on a regular basis to determine the best time to breed a mare and achieve conception.

Lise stood quietly with her mare in line, watching curiously as Tony slowly stepped down from his perch on a rail, handed his lead to Lise with a wink before heading toward the horse Kaye was holding in front of him. Focused on the vet who was scanning a mare in front of her, Kaye was loosely holding onto the end of her lead ignorant of the mare standing behind her.

Tony smoothly unclipped the lead rope, reattaching it to a clip on a nearby post. Grabbing the mare by the head collar, Tony put her in the nearest yard, closing the gate after her. This done, he retrieved his lead from Lise, winking in response to her amused smile. Kaye was ignorant until required to bring her horse into the crush to be looked at. Tugging at the lead rope she nearly fell to the ground, turning around in surprise. Tony brushed past her in the line, effectively skipping one spot. Angered by his laughter, Kaye looked around, storming toward her horse once she spotted the docile brown mare nearby.

Lise pretended to be focused on her mare, having pulled out a comb from her back pocket to shorten and neaten up the horse's hair. She said nothing when Kaye cut in front of her, taking Tony's previous spot.

Lise grinned when she spied Kate watching the episode, brows raised in surprise. She chose not to respond however, not wanting to incense Kaye further. Vetting continued for the next couple of hours, Trevor and Declan joining in once finished with the stallions. The vetting had resulted in the discovery of a couple of mares that were in need of covering that day to produce the best chance of conception.

Declan fell into step beside Lise as they headed over to the covering shed where the lunchtime breeds would be carried out. Declan slowed his pace, holding onto Lise's elbow to encourage her to do the same. Once happy Kate was ahead and out of earshot, he asked Lise how the 'tafie' was doing.

"She was given a chance toward the end of vetting to do a PG shot but requested not to have to touch the drug," he stated, referring to a common hormone given to mares during the breeding season.

"I guess that's fair enough - PG can be quite harmful..." Lise responded diplomatically.

"But?" Declan queried coming to a standstill.

"She wasn't eager to give an Ovuplant either. I don't think she's overly impressed with the idea of giving needles."

"Not helpful in this industry."

"Agreed. It's only her first day though. She's got four weeks to get used to jabbing horses."

"Not to mention the rest. And we're about to introduce her to the wonderful world of breeding horses... that is, if she's not familiar with it already," he concluded with a grin, making Lise smile.

They parted ways at the covering shed, Lise entering just behind Kate who was with Trevor. The same staff member who had been helping out with vetting – Kaye, was holding the mare while Trevor talked Kate through the procedure of bandaging the mare's tail, wiping her down behind, putting a bit in her mouth as an added restraint and a pair of kicking boots to restrict the damage to the stallion if the mare were to kick out. Lise smiled, not surprised once Trevor had done all the work and talked Kate through it that Kaye palmed the mare over to him. Rolling her eyes, Lise walked over to Trevor as Kaye left the shed.

"Want me to hold the mare while you grab Harry?" she queried, referring to one of the few pony stallions on the property.

Trevor smiled his thanks, leaving the covering shed after handing the mare to Lise. Lise turned her attention to Kate, questioning if she had seen any breeds before.

"A couple at TAFE. We have one stallion and about a dozen mares but that's all."

"Trevor has gone to get our teaser. Normally we wouldn't worry about teasing mares that are vetted on farm once up in the covering shed as they're put up to a teaser stallion when the vet makes the call to breed them. But, because this girl's a maiden, we're unsure how she'll react to a stallion. To prevent her kicking our expensive stallions, poor little Harry gets to be the potential punching bag instead," Lise said with a wry smile as a loud roar could be heard from the small stallion feeling the need to announce his presence.

Lise took the twitch that Kate handed her and put it on, her focus on the uncertain mare, the young animal's ears flicking back and forth being a sign of her nervousness. Pushing thoughts of the TAFE student from her mind, Lise stayed on the left of the mare near to her shoulder while the small stallion was being introduced to her. She could worry about Kate's interest in the industry later.

The young mare jumped as the teaser's nose reached her flank, sniffing excitedly. Lise stayed as she was to the side of the mare, away from potential strikes from front legs.

She kept a firm hold on the lead rope and the handle of the twitch as Trevor positioned the small stallion to mount the mare. There was a minimal reaction from the young animal but they carried out the procedure once more before Trevor left with the excited animal. Shortly after Declan came in with one of the farm's thoroughbred stallions to carry out the cover.

Lise was pleased to find that things went well and the young animal handled the new situation fine. They had one other cover before all staff headed to lunch for the day, the focus quickly moving to afternoon chores that needed to be completed before the day could come to an end.

October

Melanie frowned as she watched the young rider and pony once again come to a standstill in front of the small crossbar. Quickly Geordie turned the pony away from the jump and headed toward Melanie in the middle of the arena. Maddie had informed her that Geordie had had a fall the week before and her confidence seemed to be shaken. Despite the young girl's protest, Melanie had insisted that she ride the same pony this week. The last thing she wanted was for Geordie to think her riding was limited to only the ponies that willingly jumped every obstacle put in front of them.

Riding wasn't about just hanging on while the horse worked, it was about convincing your mount to do something even when it wasn't sure. She instructed Hannah to continue down the long side of the arena and over the crossbar before looking up at her other client, smiling softly.

"Just not happening today, is it?"

Geordie shook her head sadly.

"I could do it on Dundee, I know I could!"

"Geordie... do you know that getting Sheila to jump over this would prove to me that you're a better rider than if you jumped something twice this height on Dundee?"

The young girl shook her head, obviously not convinced. Melanie sighed, opting for another tact.

"Do you sing at all?"

She grinned at Geordie's surprised look, happy to have her full attention.

"I want you to go back out there and sing for me, the whole time around the arena and as you're going over the trot pole and crossbar. Do you think you can do that for me?"

"What will I sing?"

"How about... Mary Had A Little Lamb?"

"Will you sing with me?" she queried, eyes wide.

"Of course! Come on, it's your turn," she grinned as Hannah walked over to them on her mount after clearing the crossbar easily.

Her face marred with a determined frown, Geordie gathered up her reins and kicked her pony into a bouncy trot, heading toward the outside of the arena as she lined up the jump. Melanie started singing loudly to encourage the young girl to do the same. They both got through the first couple of lines of the song before Melanie found herself singing alone as the young girl tensed up and the pair came to a sudden stop before the jump.

"I was singing by myself there suddenly, Geordie!" Melanie called out, ignoring the dejected slump of the girl's shoulders.

"This time I want you to sing even louder and focus solely on the song... don't worry about your position, just sing!"

Nodding, the young client turned her pony around and started again, singing even louder to be heard over her instructor. Melanie let out a scream of excitement when the young girl popped over the rail and crossbar with her pony, still singing.

"Brilliant! Well done!"

Geordie was grinning from ear to ear as she trotted toward Melanie.

"Oh, I don't think so! You've got to do that for me once more to prove it wasn't a fluke," she teased, glad to see the pair once again head toward the jump.

Geordie forgot to sing this time but made it clearly over for a second time, causing Melanie to not mind as she sent out Hannah to have one last go before the lesson finished. Both managing this, Mel decided to end on a high note and told the girls they could cool down their ponies by riding them around the outside of the arena. She smiled as she spotted Johnny standing at the said gate, smiling at both young girls as they rode toward him.

"Did you see me, Johnny? Did you see me and Sheila jump?" Geordie asked anxiously, pulling her pony to a stop before Johnny who opened up the gate for the pair, smiling widely as he watched them each pass.

"I did! I saw you both make that jump look so small by the massive height you jumped over it," he replied enthusiastically, winking at Melanie.

"We've just got to cool out our horses before untacking them," Hannah informed him with grave importance.

"I'll wait over at the tie up area then," he returned with the same level of seriousness before turning his gaze to Melanie, eyes alight.

"That was a pretty neat trick."

"What was?" she asked, walking back with him to the tie up area.

"Distracting Geordie from her nervousness by making her focus on her singing. What a brilliant idea... and, it didn't half sound bad," he stated, a small chuckle escaping his mouth.

"What? The sound of Mary Had a Little Lamb?" Melanie asked incredulously, leaning against a rail.

"No. The sound of your voice," Johnny stated quietly, cutting the conversation short as the two young girls headed toward them, now out of the saddle and leading their tired mounts over to be tied up, untacked and brushed down.

***

Lise smiled as she raced outside, excited by the tone of the TAFE student, hopping onto a four wheeler bike she'd kept parked outside for this particular purpose.

Kate had rung a minute ago stating excitedly that one of the mares was lying down and had started foaling. After instructing Kate to move the mare into a single foaling yard, she'd thrown on a jacket and her boots and headed down to the foaling unit that was well lit up for the evening.

During the day a staff member was to check the heavily pregnant mares each hour. Staff were assigned on a rotational basis. Once it hit six in the evening, the checking increased to every half hour due to the average mare foaling in the evening hours. Someone carried out "dog watch" from six to nine and then the night watch attendant worked from nine that evening to six the next morning, checking the mares every half hour.

Lise had suggested to Kate that she do dog watch as when all the mares had been brought into yards and sorted that afternoon, there'd been a couple that Lise thought were very close. Kate had had the chance to see a lot of covers in the near four weeks that she'd been at Nirvana Park but not foalings. She'd caught the end of some while others were on duty but not seen the first stages of labour through to the delivery of the foal.

Lise applied the brakes to the bike and brought it to a stop, killing the engine before heading over to Kate who was in the small yard with the mare lying flat out pushing.

"Got the foaling kit?" Lise queried, climbing through the rails.

Kate nodded, gesturing to it, her focus on the mare.

"Great. Grab a couple of gloves."

Kate looked up, surprised.

"Why?"

"We're going to have a feel of what's going on inside."

"But I can see one hoof and the nose and I'm sure we'll be able to see the second foot soon. It looks like the foal's presented correctly."

"I like to confirm that that's the case and the best way to do so is feel how things are positioned inside the mare. The second leg is coming now just behind which is great but how do you know they are both front legs?"

Kate nodded, mimicking Lise by putting a pair of shoulder length gloves on. Squatting down, Lise slowly put one hand inside the mare, following the path of one leg, then the other.

"I'm happy they're both front legs. Have a quick feel and see if you can feel the foal's knees."

Kate did so, pulling back with a smile, recognition crossing her face. Lise smiled to herself, stepping back to give the mare some room while thinking she might have just discovered Kate's passion. Up until now, she'd shown mild interest in all other stud areas, but she seemed focused while foaling and interested.

"Look, here she comes," Kate stated in a hushed tone.

"She?" Lise queried with another smile.

"I think it'll be a filly."

"Well, we'll find out soon," Lise commented, watching as the mare continued pushing, the shoulders of the foal passing through and the rest of the young body following shortly after. Lise looked to Kate with a cheeky grin.

"Well? Is it a filly?"

Helping the foal, Kate removed the amnion sack, watching its nostrils flaring rapidly. She placed her fingers at the top of the nasal bone, one on either side and ran them down the nose, ridding the newborn of excess fluid to assist it with breathing. This done she removed the rest of the birth sack, lifting the tail of the foal to check its gender.

"A filly," she confirmed with a smile.

Lise reached into the foaling bucket and pulled out a spray bottle filled with diluted iodine. She handed the bottle to Kate while lifting one of the filly's hind legs, exposing the umbilicus which was bleeding due to the separation of the umbilical cord. Kate sprayed it with the iodine which acted as a cauterising agent to stop the bleeding. Lise instructed Kate to hold the stub between her thumb and forefinger for a minute or two to help the process.

"I'm just going to check the other mares. I'll be back shortly."

Kate nodded, watching the now mother as she nickered to her foal, watching the filly take in gasping breaths that were slowing to a normal rate.

Lise hopped back onto the ATV after having taken the high powered torch from Kate. She turned on the head lights of the vehicle and started checking over the closest mares first, those that were in nearby yards. She noted one pacing around one of the yards and made a note to check her again on the way back to Kate and the mare and foal.

Ten minutes later Lise had shone the torch over each paddock, counting bodies to make sure that she hadn't missed any snoozing under the shelter of a tree or lying flat out, dead to the world. Those in the paddocks were generally resting peacefully, a couple grazing, looking up curiously as she shone the torch off their frames, checking the coat for signs of sweat and each back end to see if any tail was raised, anything out of the ordinary. Finding nothing amiss Lise came back by way of the yard that housed the mare that had been pacing. Her double checking was rewarded with the sign of heat rising off the mare as she continued pacing up and down the fence line.

"Two in one night. Kate is going to be ecstatic," she said to herself, again stopping the bike and turning it off before grabbing a lead from the handle bars and heading into the yard toward the anxious mare.

She started at first at the sight of the strange light headed toward her but quietened down when Lise switched the torch off, concluding she'd just have to find her way in the dark. As her eyes adjusted to the evening light she came up beside the mare, patting her on the neck in a reassuring manner.

"Hey, sweetie. I'm just going to bring you into a yard by yourself so you can have your baby in peace. How does that sound?"

The mare snorted in return, standing quietly while she clipped up the lead rope, walking briskly with the young woman as they headed to the gate and out of the yard, double checking the gate was shut before heading toward one of the foaling yards.

Kate looked up in surprise upon hearing the sound of footfalls – those of a person and a horse.

"Not another one?" she asked in wonder.

"Indeed," Lise replied with a smile in the dark, letting her go in the yard next door.

The mare immediately took up her pacing of the fence line, steam still rising off her body. Lise let her be, leaning on the fence rail beside Kate, watching the newborn filly struggling to make sense of her long legs.

"She was looking pretty worked up when I headed out, pacing a lot and really sweaty so I thought I'd better check her again after looking over the others. Everything out in the paddocks is pretty relaxed which is great to see. I'd hate to think we missed something in the afternoon and a mare ended up foaling out in a large paddock unassisted."

"Especially considering how much some of these are worth. I just checked out the tag of this mare, Ebony's Wings. I hadn't realised she was in foal to one of Danehill's better performing sons."

"Pretty cool, huh? At least being a filly she should have residual value. Even if she doesn't make it to a track, she'll have the breeding to be kept on as a broodmare. Sometimes I think fillies get it easier."

"So we should," Kate stated with conviction.

Lise laughed, watching as the young foal made her way to standing very unsteadily on her four legs.

"Amazing, isn't it? Half an hour in this world and she's already to her feet. Once she's had a good drink we'll make further use of that foaling kit by getting the refractometer and testing the quality of her mum's milk."

Kate agreed, her focus suddenly turned to the yard next door as the other mare dropped to the ground with a grunt, a large amount of water bursting forth from her vulva. Lise positioned herself so that she was still out of the yard but could better see how things were progressing.

Lise waited ten minutes and upon seeing no further movement again armed herself with a pair of gloves, heading to the back end of the mare. She had a quick feel before telling Kate to do the same.

"Feels like one of the front legs is bent around, somehow stopping things from progressing."

Kate pulled her hand out, stating that she could feel the difference between this foaling and the other.

"All I'm gonna do is reach in again and try and find the hoof, lift the leg a little and pull to try and right things. I think it'll be pretty simple but because I'm pushing against the natural force of contractions, the mare will probably strain against me. If it was a more complicated problem like the foal being upside down, it'd be best to have the mare walking to encourage the repositioning of the foal inside."

Kate nodded, listening intently as she watched Lise adjust the limb, the two front legs consequently making their way into the world as another contraction gripped the mare and she continued pushing.

Things went well until the shoulders came to rest in the birth canal and again things seemed to be stuck. Lise let the mare try by herself for another set of contractions but seeing no progress, directed Kate to grab one leg, the best point being at a joint. She herself grabbed the other, holding on tightly around the fetlock joint. As the mare contracted, both young women pulled on the two legs, directing them toward the mare's hock in a downward movement that was the natural progression the foal took as it was expelled from the mare.

After a couple of contractions the shoulders unlocked and came free, the body and hind end of the foal following in a very quick procession.

"Well, two foalings in one night. Do you think that's enough?" Lise joked, turning to Kate.

"I'll let you know once I've done another check of all the mares," Kate returned with a smile, heading over to the little Tonka truck that'd she'd been using for foal watch.

Lise squatted down beside the newborn, lifting the tail to find that a colt foal had just been born.

"Guess that about makes things even," she stated quietly, stepping back from the pair to just watch for awhile.

November

"I cannot believe that woman!" Trevor muttered, barely containing his rage as he stormed down the breezeway, reached the end and started pacing back the other way.

"Who?" Lise queried with concern, sitting on an upturned bucket as she finished oiling one of the stud's leather show halters.

"Miss Cline. The woman that owns Jade's Mystery?"

Lise nodded, confirming she knew who he was talking about.

"What's happened?"

"Four days ago she came down to take a look at all the stallions to make a final decision on which one she wanted her mare to go to. Money isn't an issue *of course,* so she wanted to see which caught her eye. She decided on King and now she's just rung Kingsley to say that she's changed her mind. She'd love to give the freshman sire a chance instead."

"Well that's good for Rocket, isn't it? It won't hurt a first season sire to have as many mares as possible and King isn't exactly lacking in bookings."

"It *would* be fine but we covered her over the weekend, with *King.*"

"Oh..." Lise frowned, realising Trevor's frustration.

"So what did Kingsley say? Are you going to let her go to fifteen days and do a pregnancy check or wait the nine or so days and give her a PG shot and try again?"

"Kingsley's discussing it with her at the moment and by the sound of his raised voice in the office, things aren't going too well. It's already late in the season and she could jeopardise the commerciality of the mare's progeny by making it an even later foal!"

"Well I guess you can't do much about it until you find out what the owner has stated they want to do. It's for Kingsley to worry about, Trevor."

"I know. I'm just sick to death of the breeding season and more importantly stupid owners!" he ground out, exiting the stables.

Declan passed Trevor on his way in. He raised his brows as he headed toward Lise.

"End of season blues?"

"Definitely seems that way," Lise confirmed with a smile, standing to hang up the head collar so that it could air out.

Declan picked up the saddle soap, bucket and cloth she had been using, heading with Lise toward the tack room.

"Have ye any more to do?"

"Nope. All done. With any luck we won't have to use any show halters again till the Premier Yearling Sales."

"One can hope. How many mares are left to foal down?" he queried, emptying the bucket outside the stables on a garden bed before rinsing each item under a tap and leaving them to dry in the sun.

"We've still got fifty to go... and to think that'd be the sum total for a smaller stud."

"Ye sought out working at this place," Declan warned with a grin, leaning against a wall as Lise put away some halters she'd cleaned earlier.

"I know. And for the record I'm quite happy to be working here. It's great to get so much experience with the newborns but I'm just recognising there's still quite a way to go before the season is officially finished."

"Indeed! It may be over for ye once the last foal is on the ground but it isn't over for me until we've bred that mare three weeks later!"

"And the owner doesn't change their mind after you've covered and ovulated her off."

"I thought that was rather amusing, honestly. The weekend went really smoothly, like. Isn't it amazing how an owner can make a mistake of correctly carrying out a routine?"

"I'm sure that's exactly how Trevor would word it," Lise replied with a grin, heading out of the stables.

"You going to bring the boys in for the afternoon?"

"Shortly. Got any treatments ye need a hand with first?"

"That'd be great."

***

Wes grinned as she used the fifteen minutes provided to read over the exam set before her. There were questions about the horse's vital signs, exercise, normal weight, colours, markings and points of the horse that made her smile. *Too easy.*

Flicking to the last page she found a choice of three questions that required a detailed answer. Marking the question regarding a mare's stages of labour she was eager to start as this was a topic fresh on her mind. She'd looked it up specifically as a fortnight before their teacher had been telling them possible topics they'd need to answer detailed questions about. Currently Wes was leaning toward the idea of breeding horses for a living although instructing was high on the list too.

Glancing up at the clock she waited impatiently for the few minutes to pass so that she could start writing.

An hour and a half was allocated to doing the exam and within the hour she had answered most questions with confidence, flicking back through the pages to read over her answers, making an attempt at the few she really wasn't sure about. She'd come up short on her memory of the digestive system which she was supposed to provide a drawing of each of the organs, listing them in order from mouth through to stomach through to rectum. *I should have made a mental note of how many things made up the digestive system at least then I'd know if I'd missed something.*

Seeing no point for pondering the digestive system further, she gathered her papers, handing them in to the teacher keeping an eye on the class, before grabbing her things and heading outside to wait for her mum.

She smiled, content with how she'd answered her questions but frowned at the realisation that this marked the end of her course. The following week they'd be given their results, have one last riding lesson and be awarded their Certificate II in Horse Studies. She loved that she was able to acquire a piece of paper relating to horses within a twelve month period, but questioned what would keep her sane in her final year of high school. She didn't need to drop any of her subjects due to her Certificate II finishing in 2001, meaning she'd be left with five very general topics, none of which covered her passion or afforded the chance to do work experience with horses.

Maybe I should have done the course via correspondence... at least it spans over two years. But then I wouldn't have gotten the hands on with horses every week – tough call...

To make things worse, she wasn't sure she'd be able to keep up pony club alongside year twelve. She frowned, suddenly not looking forward to the following year.

A blue falcon pulled into the drive, capturing her attention and Wes ran for it, forgetting her foreboding for 2002 and eager to tell her mum about how she thought she'd gone on her final exam.

***

Trevor bolted upright in bed, his breathing coming out in ragged gasps. He groaned, running his hands through his hair and across his sweaty face. For the fourth night in a row he'd awoken from a nightmare concerning things going wrong at Nirvana Park.

It was the same every year at the end of a busy breeding season. Owners started to get to him what with constantly changing their minds, purchasing mares and sending them to a stallion that is completely wrong for the mare or just constantly turning up and wanting to be able to visit their 'investment' out in the paddock – where a dozen or so other pushy, hungry mares would be all too happy to make even the most comfortable people around horses careful of where they were to tread.

Broodmares were rarely in Trevor's mind aptly described as 'cute' as many owners leant toward as a description for their beloved equine. They were 500 kilograms - sometimes more - that deserved to be respected, especially those with less appealing attitudes. They could kick, bite, step on and even maim or kill - not necessarily on purpose but it had happened. He couldn't think of anything scarier than taking an uneducated owner into a paddock full of mares that had a pecking order, horses that they liked and horses that they didn't.

Tonight his dream had consisted of this and he'd woken up only as one mare had turned on another, letting fly with a kick while the ignorant owner was stuck in the middle, Trevor powerless to do anything about it.

With a sigh he pulled back the covers from his bed and tread barefoot across the carpeted room to the kitchen. Pausing at the sink he grabbed a glass from the drying rack, filling it up under the tap as he thought over the other dream that had been a little more persistent. A dream he was certain he could blame on owners like the young Miss Cline.

Finishing his glass of water he glanced across at the calendar he knew to be hanging in the dark room. Although he couldn't see it, he knew the date to be the twentieth of November. His psychologist and he had a deal each year in which the second half of November for Tuesday and Thursdays an hour slot was saved in the event that Trevor would need to have a talk. He concluded that with the following day being a Thursday, it'd be wise to head down to the office for a visit, rather than having to endure the nightmares until the following Tuesday.

***

Wes smiled at her mum as a group of parents wandered into the quarters that were housed above the stables; the area where she'd been taught along with thirty other students, the theory of her Certificate II in Horse Studies each week. It was lunch time and their day had technically finished with the afternoon being the presentation of each student's certificate and a general well done talk from the teachers who had presented the course throughout the year.

"I can't believe it's finished already. The one subject I have a total interest in and it's over in a matter of less than a year."

"You mean that in less than a year you've managed to acquire a qualification in relation to horses?" her mum rephrased the statement.

"Sure, that," Wes replied with a grin, sitting down on the couch with her mum.

"The presentation shouldn't go for too long if all they're doing is giving us our certificates... and of course mine will be toward the end. Dad should change his last name to Abbott or something so I can get mine first!"

Her mum laughed as she glanced around the room, taking in the posters on walls and looking out curiously at the one side that was made up of glass so you could look down on the large indoor arena below. She knew that one day her daughter would be running a place like this.

Before too long the students were called to take seats at a cluster of tables set up facing the teachers who were standing together at one end of the room. They gave a general speech congratulating all on passing their Certificate II before handing out each one individually. Wes frowned as when it came to her turn to go up and receive the certificate the introduction took a different turn to the other students.

"Not only is this student getting her Certificate II but we want to also award her with the Certificate of Excellence for achieving the highest average score over the duration of the course..."

Wes tuned out as they mentioned her name, standing with a start when a student beside her elbowed her in the side. She stumbled up to the teachers, shaking the hand offered to her before receiving the two pieces of paper and ball point pen with the property's name engraved on it. Thanking them automatically she returned to her seat, staring at the pieces of paper, a smile making its way onto her face as the last couple of students were awarded their qualification. *Certificate of Excellence... brilliant!*

***

Trevor stood in the doorway, stepping into the room only when the psychologist – Mackenzie Taylor – gestured for him to enter. Mackenzie quickly turned his attention back to the phone as someone answered on the other end.

"Hello there. Have I caught you at a good time? You're not about to paint your house, are you? No? Oh, good..."

Trevor relaxed on the couch, resting his eyes, tired from the previous night's lack of sleep. They'd had a busy day at work too with three mares for each King and Rocket, meaning covers at half past six in the morning, twelve noon and five thirty that afternoon. At least things had gone well, even if the working day had been eleven hours in length. He opened his eyes upon hearing the phone conversation come to an end and turned his gaze to the psychologist.

"So, old chap – how goes the wonderful world of horses?"

Trevor told the psychologist of his trouble sleeping and delved into the two dreams he'd been having. Mackenzie sat quietly, listening to him tell of his fears of a client being hurt by a horse. He didn't open his mouth until Trevor moved onto the second dream which he'd had on more than one occasion.

"So I'm there, surrounded by all these young and old girls who are obviously in season and I don't know what to do."

The trained psychologist cleared his throat, his brows raised.

"Girls... in season?" he questioned dubiously.

"Yeah... and they're all backing up to me and I just know that if I let them fall pregnant the boss'll kill me, but I'm stuck."

"Umm... what exactly are we talking about?"

"My dream: me holding the teaser and all the clients' expensive mares-"

"Oh! So these *are* horses. Tell me, what's a teaser?"

"A teaser is a stallion used on the farm to assess the receptiveness of a mare to a stallion. He helps us to judge if she'll be submissive to the stallion we want to breed her with."

"And if not?" Mackenzie asked curiously.

"We'll be able to tell by her reaction – biting, kicking, ears pinned back, squealing..."

"And this... teaser, he has to put up with it?"

"They're used to it, I guess... or just so eager to be near a mare that they put up with it."

"And why so eager?"

"Hormones," Trevor stated simply, "we don't breed with these stallions so I guess they're eager to get as close to any mare that they can."

"Well starve the lizards! How cruel for a stallion. Tell me, do they spend their whole life as a teaser?" the psychologist asked, leaning forward eagerly in anticipation of Trevor's response.

By the end of the session Mackenzie was a lot more enlightened to the 'wonderful world of horses' but Trevor questioned as he made his way down the steps out the front of the building, if they'd actually managed to come up with a way to stop his nightmares. He did feel better for having talked them through but questioned if that would be enough. Thankfully he had another session booked in with the 'Doc' for the following week, just in case the nightmares didn't cease.

December

Melanie smiled; glad to see the kids partaking in the day program having so much fun in their theory lesson. Today they were learning about preparing horses for competition. Melanie had discussed and shown them three different ways to do the horse's mane or tail and now some were fish plaiting, starting plaits to be turned into rosettes or attempting to braid tails. She smiled at the annoyed look on one of the young girl's faces.

"What's wrong Josie?"

"It's done... but it looks bad. How can I make it better?" she queried, frowning at the plaited up tail of her pony.

Melanie ducked under the rail, approaching the front of the animal before working her way to the back to view the tail. She smiled as she took in Josie's handiwork.

"I know of only one thing that can make it look better, but it will make a big improvement."

"What?"

"The braid just needs to be tighter. So the bad news is you'll have to undo the whole braid and start again."

"And the good news?" Josie asked hopefully.

"You tell me if there is any once it's finished," Melanie replied with a smile, heading over to another student who had finished their fish plait.

"That looks great Sarah! I always prefer a fish plait for a palomino horse... do you know why?"

The young girl shook her head, shyly looking at her feet. Melanie squatted down to be level with her.

"Most people that have palomino coloured horses let their manes and tails grow *really* long. The fish plait is the quickest. Could you imagine Snowy here with a mane and tail all the way down to the ground?"

The young girl looked at her with wide eyes, again shaking her head.

"That would be hours with a hairbrush," Melanie joked, eliciting a small smile.

"How about you get some practice in on Snowy's tail?"

Sarah nodded, finding a dandy brush in the grooming bucket before heading back to her pony. Noting that a couple of others were nearly finished with their ponies' manes and tails, Melanie pulled a couple of stencils out of her competition bag. The stencils had stars or diamonds cut out of them and were great to put on a pony's rump and brush the hair in the opposite direction against the stencil. This left star or diamond markings on the horse's rump, something she was sure the kids would love.

***

Trevor stepped into the office in the yearling barn, needing to make a quick call now that he'd agreed to fill in for Kaye and do her foal watch shift for the following evening. He sat down at the desk as he dialed the familiar number, waiting for someone to pick up.

"MacKenzie speaking."

"Doc, it's Trevor."

"Oh! Trevor. Have I got you at a good time? You're not about to skip the country, are you?"

"I rang you..." Trevor stated in confusion.

"Oh, yes... yes you did."

"But no, I'm not about to skip the country. I hate flying."

"You could take a boat."

"I get seasick."

"Oh... a shame. How about a train?"

"I don't need to go anywhere," Trevor stated with a frown. "I was ringing to say that I can't make our appointment on Thursday evening. I'm filling in for one of the other workers, so I've got to be on foal watch."

"Foal watch? Tell me, what are you watching the foal for?" Mackenzie Taylor queried in surprise.

"Umm... it's not exactly watching foals. Should be called mare watch, I guess. We've got a lot of heavily pregnant mares left to give birth and each evening someone has to keep an eye on them before the night attendant arrives."

"And what do you do if they start giving birth?"

"Generally leave them to it. We only have to step in if there's a problem."

"Well isn't that a different kettle of fish! Assisting a mare give birth! Well no bother about your appointment. We'll just reschedule for next week unless you call in and state you need to talk earlier. How does that sound?"

"That sounds great. Well, I'd better get back to work, we've got a barn full of yearlings."

"Yearlings?" Mackenzie questioned, causing Trevor to roll his eyes.

"I'll tell you all about them in our next session."

"Indeed. Have a lovely afternoon Trevor."

"I'll try."

Trevor sat quietly at the desk, realising there was a voice in the barn he didn't recognise. It dawned on him that the new TAFE student must have arrived and not wanting to have to deal with introductions at that point in time he stayed where he was, certain all would move on shortly to show the student around the property.

Before the breeding season even ends we have a barn full of yearlings to prepare and sell. When does it stop?

***

Declan smiled and offered his hand to the young man that stood before him.

"Scott? Pleased to meet ye. Ye'll be staying in the stallion handlers' quarters with me self. I'll show ye them now and then perhaps I can show ye around the farm."

"Already you're a lot nicer to Scott then you were to Kate, what gives?" Lise questioned with raised brows, arms folded across her chest as she leant against the stable wall.

"Kate was a tafie," Declan shrugged.

"*Is* a tafie as is Scott," Lise replied.

"No... Scott here is a man looking to secure a job in the thoroughbred industry."

"Typical. Here I was thinking they were one and the same. Silly me," she commented with a hint of sarcasm, making her way down the breezeway.

Declan grinned at Scott, gesturing for the male to follow him.

"It's no fun if all the women here like ye. It's great craic if ye get them riled up."

Scott laughed, walking with Declan down the breezeway, patting curious heads that peered over doorways as the pair strolled past.

"I think for the benefit of my personal health that I should disagree with you."

"Perhaps... but the males are in the majority on this property, live a little," he replied with a laugh, opening the door to Scott's quarters.

"Just the basics - bed, wardrobe, heater - not that ye'll need it at this time of year! We share the living room and kitchen and the best phone reception is down the driveway beside the fountain: lots of fun in the dark. I think the torch I bought is the second best investment I've made while in Oz."

"And the first?" Scott queried, looking over the room.

"A pair of sunglasses," Declan replied with a grin, "the summers here are something else! Now... how about I show ye the stallions we've got here and ye can see some of their progeny that ye'll be helping out with prepping over the next couple of months?"

"Lead on McDuff."

"It's McAlister, actually," Declan stated with a laugh.

"And how long have you been outside of Ireland, Declan McAlister?"

"That depends on yer idea of time… I was there for the first six months of last year before getting a job here with the stallions. Before that I was doing seasonal work in Ireland, then Oz and back again. I've been here for the past twelve months and will be staying through the yearling and weaning season and the breeding season again but I'd like to head back home sometime in the near future. I don't mind yearlings but honestly I prefer to do the breeding season all year round."

"And why's that?" Scott asked as the pair strolled back down the driveway, past the fountain Declan had mentioned earlier.

"I think it's just because I love me stallions, ye know? Most of the ones I've handled have been really well educated, a lot more fun to deal with than uneducated yearlings. Plus there's something thrilling about looking after an animal that was a great racehorse and is now being given the chance to pass it on to his progeny. We had a lovely breeding season just now with Rocket covering his first book of mares. I can't wait to see what his foals will be like next spring. Now, ye might as well meet the boys while I'm talking about them," Declan concluded, turning away from the main barn and heading down a tree lined laneway toward the separate stallion boxes.

He introduced Scott to the two stallions owned outright by Nirvana Park and the other two that were owned by clients but housed on the stud.

"I tend to handle Rocket and the grey fella over there. The two that don't belong to Kingsley are kept here all year round and during the season he gets a fee to manage the boys and their advertising as well as half a dozen or so nominations to each of the stallions. This way we tend to have foals from each of the stallions for the coming year as well as any outside stallions that appeal to the boss and are in his price range. If ye end up working at a big time stud, chances are if ye stick around long enough, this'll be a bonus that'll be given to ye.

"It's not uncommon for studs to provide their staff with a nomination to one of their cheaper stallions each year after they've been there for an extended period of time. Tis a great way to make some extra money by selling it on for a slight lower price ye see. Or, ye can find yerself a mare and do the whole breeding thing and race the progeny or hope to make something from it at a yearling sale. Nice way to bring in a little extra cash."

"So do you get nominations to the studs here, then?" Scott queried as they moved away from the stallion boxes.

"To the two owned by Nirvana Park but not the other two. I'm sure Kingsley could work out a deal so that staff would get access to the stallions at a cheaper rate but I don't have any mares of me own. I tend to sell off me nominations at a cheaper price and make quick work of the money. Now, let me show ye some of King's babies that are up in the barn."

The pair walked through the stables discussing pedigrees and conformation of each of the animals as they made their way from box to box. Declan found Scott to be well informed when it came to pedigrees and not too bad on picking up faults or strong points of a horse's conformation either. The young Irishman quickly concluded he was going to like working with this particular tafie.

***

Maddie grinned as her client correctly executed a rollback – a sharp turn shortly after one jump, the horse and rider effectively doubling back toward a second jump, in the matter of a small amount of strides. She called out congratulations as the young rider approached the second jump at the correct point, rose over and continued on across the arena at a forward canter, bringing his horse back to a trot at the letter A and then a walk shortly after.

"That was brilliant! Did that feel as good as it looked? It's wonderful when everything comes together and the horse does as you ask."

Her client, Alex, grinned and nodded in response, still trying to catch his breath as he came to a halt in the middle of the arena, facing his instructor.

"That did feel awesome, Emmy! I can't believe how much difference it makes to be able to so quickly pick up if I'm on the correct lead and then focus on the next jump."

"Definitely! I believe the most difficult part is recognising if your horse is on the correct leg at the canter and if not, to be able to adjust that. We'll go through once more Alex and finish on that note. This time I want you to land and have your horse continue at a canter on his left leg, rather than his right. Do you know how to ask him to do that?"

Alex nodded.

"Put more weight in my left stirrup as we're going over the last jump."

"Perfect! Show me how it's done," she grinned, her stomach doing an unpleasant jump when she realised Jack was watching their lesson, paused with a wheelbarrow full of hay to take out to the hacks.

She turned her attention back to Alex, in two minds. She really wanted him to execute the small course as well as she knew he could, but she feared if Jack was noting his skill, he'd be pushing to take over the promising young man. Jumping was his specialty after all and generally Jack took on clients that were capable at 75cm jumps or higher. Alex was just reaching this point and his technique was better than some of the kids who could jump higher.

She watched with apprehension as the young male pushed his mount into a working trot before heading him through the short course, his timing and judgment of strides between jumps carried out perfectly, the pair looking amazing even to Madison's eyes as they went through the course completely focused.

Alex's smile was as big as his instructor's as he pulled up beside her, giving his pony an enthusiastic pat.

"I'd ask how we went but it felt so good and you're smiling so much I'm not sure I need to," Alex teased good naturedly.

Madison laughed, strolling toward the end of the arena where she opened the gate to allow Alex to exit and cool his pony out before tying up to untack.

"I think you did too well this lesson and I'm just going to have to try and find something harder for you to do… perhaps I should find you another horse…"

"Don't you dare!" Alex cried, looking back at her in alarm.

"I wouldn't dream of it, Alex. The next horse you ride in a lesson is going to be one you've bought or are considering buying for yourself. Until then I couldn't think why anyone would want to separate a pair that work so well together."

Madison let him continue on at a free walk while she headed toward the tie up area. She noted that Jack was gone but couldn't help but feel that he'd somehow find a way to mess things up. *Well, not intentionally mess things up… but Alex is going so well I don't want that to change.*

Alex was quick to cool his horse down and chatted amiably with Maddie as he untacked and brushed the young gelding down before putting him out and telling Maddie he'd see her the following week for his next lesson. Jack came in from the paddock just as Alex was heading off.

"That was some pretty good riding going on in that lesson."

"Well when you put together a pretty good horse, rider and instructor, what else can you expect?" Madison questioned with a smirk, not shaking her feeling of unease in regards to Jack.

"Apparently not modesty," Jack replied with a grin, putting the wheelbarrow away and walking with Maddie up to the house.

"Got much planned for the afternoon?" Madison questioned as Jack followed her inside.

"I've got to brush up on some of my horse management theory. My exams are coming up in a few weeks. How about you?"

"Phoenix needs to be ridden and I think Mel's going to be riding one of the new geldings that mum and dad bought in November so maybe I'll go for a ride with her. Now tell me Mr. Brown, if you're so keen on getting some study done, what are you doing hanging about here?"

"I just needed to catch up with your mum about the date of my exams and some lessons that may need changing around. I guess I'll see you tomorrow," Jack stated dismissively, causing Maddie to frown.

Why do I get the feeling I'm about to lose my best student? This may just mean war, Jack Brown. Realising if Jack was going to suggest that Alex be moved up a group that she wouldn't succeed in convincing her mother otherwise while in such an annoyed state, Maddie let Jack be, instead heading to her room to put on her half chaps and grab her helmet. A ride was definitely on the cards.

Year 2

January

Melanie sat straight in the saddle, her seat moving with the horse's stride. As she approached the next letter in the arena she sat deep in the saddle and stopped the movement of her seat that naturally moved from side to side with the horse's stride. The stilted movement of her seat told the horse that she wanted to stop and they executed a square halt at the planned letter.

Melanie smiled and allowed the reins to relax; leaning forward to pat the young gelding she was working with.

Before getting in the saddle she'd done some work on the ground with him, using the end of a whip to apply pressure to just behind his brisket and when he stepped away from the whip, she left the pressure off. If he didn't respond, she increased the pressure, insistently tapping his side with the whip until he moved away from the pressure. It didn't take long for him to understand this and move away from the pressure on either side.

While Melanie had worked with him on the ground, she'd been applying the pressure just behind the girth where her leg would be once she was sitting in the saddle. Now that she was in the saddle she turned down the three quarter line and rode him in a straight line until they were halfway down the long side of the arena before applying pressure with her right leg to push him across to the left, toward the fence that marked the perimeter of the arena.

He responded and moved across, Melanie rewarding him with a pat and continuing walking on, asking the gelding to again stop, this time at the letter A.

Again the pair cut down the three quarter line, the young redhead this time moving her right leg a little further back before applying pressure. At the same time she kept a firm hold on her outside rein to encourage him to move straight across.

Commonly, when horses were taught a lateral movement they tended to move the front half of the body toward the destination but not the hind end at the same time; resulting in a diagonal movement rather than sideways. Moving her leg further back and applying pressure to her outside rein should help to counteract this. Again she found the young horse to be responsive and he moved correctly away from the pressure applied by her leg.

Having already warmed up at a walk, trot and canter in both directions she attempted the lateral movement a few more times, getting the young animal to move away from her left and right leg at the walk before pushing him into a trot and trying the same movement down the long side.

At first the gelding increased the pace of his trot due to the pressure of her leg but Melanie steadied him with her hands and seat and brought him back to a walk, asking for the sideways movement again before moving back into a trot. The second time she asked at the faster pace she was rewarded with the lateral movement and gave him a pat once they'd executed it correctly, telling him he was a good boy.

***

Wes smiled, taking in the sight of the small acreage surrounded by a large rounded track, the surface appearing to be sand. A lone pair were at work on the track, driver and horse each connected to a sulkey as they paced around the perimeter. *Very cool. I want a go!*

Turning her attention from the pair at work to the rest of the surroundings Wes spied the reason she was there: three figures were in a large sand arena with half a dozen horses, a couple grooming while the other gathered bits and pieces of tack from a nearby building. As Wes strolled toward the bodies at work she recognised some saddle and bridles but found herself unfamiliar with some of the equipment she saw.

She introduced herself, meeting the others that volunteered their time to helping out at one of the branches of Riding for the Disabled of Australia. Wes had decided to help out every second Saturday to get more hands on with horses and see a different type of work or service that was provided with these gorgeous animals. She was quickly introduced to the horses and given one to groom and tack up.

The staff told her of the work they did fortnightly with kids and the horses. Riding for the Disabled was used to help people with Down Syndrome, Spinal Bifida, Cerebal Palsy and other physical or mental restrictions.

Most of the horses were quite aged and extremely quiet, having been donated to the association.

Wes found her day consisting of getting to know the workers and helping to keep people stabilised while on the horses or leading the horses around obstacles in the arena or out on a trail ride around the trotting track she'd been admiring earlier.

The area was surprisingly green and lush, showing the fruits of not over stocking a property with horses.

As Wes walked she daydreamed about the property she'd have - 300 - 500 acres in size, full of gorgeous thoroughbreds, quarter horses and arabs and of course a friesian or two to take people on carriage rides around the property. She wasn't sure where she'd find the money to set up a place that would offer many different disciplines (or the time to learn about them) but figured as long as she was always doing something with horses then things would be alright.

***

Madison strolled out to the main arena of the riding school to watch Jack's lesson. Mel was out for the rest of the day so there was no fear of the twins being found out by clients. Taking advantage of this, Maddie wanted to see if Alex went ok in Jack's group lesson.

She was furious with her mum for agreeing to change him over and even angrier with Jack for taking a promising client from her. As angry as she was though, Maddie was going to leave things be if Alex went alright. She recognised that he could do well in the class but firmly believed Jack's change of mount would be detrimental to Alex whom had established a strong bond with the 14.3hh pony, Fuzz that he rode in her lessons.

Jack's argument was that as Alex progressed to higher jumps he'd need a bigger mount - something around 16 hands in height. Maddie believed once Alex had progressed to this stage, he'd purchase a horse for competing and be able to establish a relationship with a horse he owned rather than one ridden by half a dozen different students throughout the week.

Jack's lesson for the more advanced group focused on technique over small jumps which worked well for Alex to get used to his change of mount. Maddie realised grudgingly that Jack had put some clever thought into the lesson with his new client in mind. It didn't surprise her either that Alex went well in the lesson though she could see that although he executed the exercises proficiently, he wasn't doing as well on a different horse. Then again, he was a good rider and after another lesson or so, Maddie could see that he had the potential to be back to the level he'd pulled off in their last lesson.

She frowned, cynically questioning if Jack had pushed things because he wanted another student that would compete well and be able to say that Jack Brown had taught him or if it was to do with having another paying client and therefore more money in the pocket of the instructor. At the East Riding School each instructor was paid an hourly rate of twenty dollars and then on top of this they were paid an extra two dollars an hour per student. Obviously it was more appealing to be teaching a class of six at thirty two dollars an hour than an individual at twenty two dollars an hour. Maddie questioned just how angry she'd make Jack if she accused him of either of these things.

As the lesson drew to a close she decided to leave things be for the moment and retreated from the area, heading back inside to watch a video she'd recently bought about cross country.

***

Lise warily entered the wash bay, not liking the cheeky smile that was once again on Declan's face as he held the hose. He'd already 'accidentally' gotten her wet twice while washing down some of the yearlings for the first time and she feared that by the end of the afternoon she wouldn't be dry at all. At least it was a warm day.

A few weeks into the yearling prep and they were nearly through having washed each animal for the first time. The general idea was to get them used to being washed when they had the time so that when the horses had to be cleaned before the sales it wouldn't come as a rude shock to them. For the moment they were just getting introduced to being hosed down, something every young equine without fail had resented at first; a few still unhappy by the end while others concluded it easier to put up with being wet rather than walking round and around the wash bay with one person attached to their head, the other staying pinned to their side with the evil green snake that was spitting water out at them.

Lise had managed on a couple of occasions to switch with Scott and have he and Declan wash a couple but other than these few times, she'd been stuck with the task of getting saturated for the day.

Somehow Kaye and the other girls managed to stay out of sight after the morning work of exercising the horses and mucking out their boxes. Lise still wasn't sure what Kaye did in the afternoon. She knew that Trevor and Scott were working hard to get through the number of horses that needed to be groomed each day to bring out the best in their coats for the sales. She rarely saw another female form wandering the stables later in the day however, only spotting them when it came to feeding up for the afternoon or on the odd occasion grooming a horse.

Turning from her questions about the staff she focused on the young filly that she had positioned close to one wall near the hose.

Declan turned the water on and patted the filly reassuringly, letting the water run over her feet, slowly moving it up her leg. Unimpressed by the cold or just the unusual feeling, the chestnut filly stomped her front foot and upon finding this didn't work, switched between taking steps forward and back, trying to avoid the fall of water.

Lise kept a firm hand on her shoulder to keep her in place while Declan ran his hands gently over the young animal, talking to her in quiet tones as he slowly let the water run up to her shoulder.

"There now darlin'. That's not so bad. Surely ye don't have a problem with some cool water on such a hot day."

Lise smiled as she watched him work, still focused on the young animal and where the three of them were positioned, but tuning into the soft Irish accent, admitting that she didn't mind spending this time with Declan but she also didn't want to find herself on the receiving end of any complaining from other members of staff for not helping out with other tasks that needed to be done each afternoon. *Then again, if no one's around to switch with, they can hardly complain now, can they?*

Moving from the near fore to the hind leg, Declan started again at her hoof, the filly kicking out angrily at the annoying water. Lise brought her forward a step after the first kick met with the brick wall of the wash bay. She cringed at the sound.

"That sounded hard enough for her to be a bit sore on that foot tomorrow."

Declan nodded his agreement.

"She's just going to love me when I try and wash up around her flank and between her legs. This one may be a bit of fun to rug also. It'd be just luck wouldn't it that the day we introduce her to being washed is the day Kingsley concludes that we'll start rugging them all."

"Indeed it would - bad luck," Lise concluded with a grin as Declan brought the hose higher up the filly's cannon and to her hock.

"Ye going to help me rug this one or should we leave her to Kaye and one of the other girls?" he queried, glancing her way with a smile before focusing again on the young horse.

"That McAlister, would be too cruel. I'll give you a hand with her."

"I'd say fair play to ya, but she may be the quietest one of the lot."

"Doubtful. You'll be congratulating me on my bravery after we've achieved getting a rug on her through all the kicks."

"So I'll hold and ye'll put the rug on, right?"

Lise could hear the smile in his voice, aware he was teasing.

"As long as you're happy to take me to hospital afterwards due to a kick that you could have prevented if you'd held her properly while I put the rug on, sure."

"Noted. Ye hold, I'll put the rug on," he stated with a grin, quickly running the water over the filly's back before getting Lise to turn her around so he could start on the other side, all the while believing he still preferred the breeding season over yearlings but if he could do this each day with Lise, it would be worth it.

February

Scott rushed into the stable block with his horse, working quickly to remove the head collar and bit as Lise was putting one on the horse in the stall beside him.

"Is it always this hectic at the sales?" he asked in surprise.

"Generally," Lise replied, brushing some shavings out of the colt's tail before heading out of the stall to parade to a client who had asked to see the whole draft of twenty yearlings.

King's progeny were popular and Kingsley had sent some of his Group 1 mares to some freshman sires that also seemed to have sparked interest. This was the third full draft parade they'd had to do for the morning and Scott was getting a good feel for parading young animals and avoiding kicks, bites and strikes as the young horses got fed up with being dragged in and out of boxes and up and down for clients.

Many would just watch the horse; observing its movement and makeup while others poked and prodded at unusual lumps or bumps, checked jowl size and depth of bone.

The past few days had been full of parading for clients and the actual sale would start the next day and run for two days. Around 500 horses would be going through with thirty lots an hour being the average number to go through the ring. Some would have reserves set and not be sold unless this predetermined figure was met while others would sell for whatever was offered in the form of bids.

The parading was pretty consistent from about nine that morning until half past four when Kingsley told the staff to start feeding and rugging the horses for the night.

"Only half four and we're feeding up... Kingsley must be fed up," Declan joked as he and Scott got out the rugs and sorted them, leaving them folded beside each door.

"You won't hear me complaining," Scott replied, handing a rug to Lise as he came to the same box she was in.

She smiled her thanks as she took it to put on the occupant of the stall. Declan stood quietly watching until she was finished and exited the box.

"Why is it ye get a large smile and all I seem to elicit are death looks?" He asked Scott, loud enough for Lise to hear.

"Because I actually like Scott," Lise bit back, causing the TAFE student to laugh.

Declan smiled also, brushing up against Lise as he handed her the rug for the next stall.

"Honey, ye may like him but I know ye-"

"Can't stand you at times, McAlister?"

"At times! She said at times! That means there're times when she can stand me," he replied with mock cheer, causing Lise to smile.

Quickly she turned away from the Irishman, catching another yearling to rug. Kaye entered the stall beside her, tipping a feed into the corner feeder and avoiding a lazily aimed kick from the occupant of the stall.

"That was a bit nasty!" Lise commented as she did up the front buckle on a rug.

"Thankfully only half-hearted. I think I'd kick back if I survived a decent kick!"

Lise smiled, silently in agreement although she could understand that the young horses – although adult in stature, were still babies and prone to be tired and cranky when in a new environment and forced to be on show constantly. Clipping up the last leg strap she returned to the head of the young filly and removed the head collar before exiting the box. The filly next door had quite an attitude and required two to safely rug and unrug her. Scott came to her aid, smiling.

"Time for trouble?"

"You bet," Lise replied with a grin.

She put a head collar on the filly and held her while Scott rugged her, Lise staying on the same side as Scott for safety. Scott glanced at Lise before placing the rug quietly over the filly, doing up the front strap before pulling the rug back into place.

"He likes you, you know?"

"He likes to tease," Lise responded, knowing the tafie was talking about Declan.

"He likes to tease *you*."

"And if this were kindergarten I'd consider taking that as a compliment," she replied with a smirk, switching to the offside as Scott did up the other leg strap, looping it through the first.

This done, Scott exited the box and Lise released the filly while she had the equine facing the door. As Lise exited the box the filly spun around and let fly with a kick, a loud bang resounding as her shod feet connected with the door.

"Well, wasn't that fun," Scott stated with a grim face.

"I couldn't think of anything I'd prefer," Lise replied, moving on to the next box while Scott chose the stall opposite.

By five o'clock the four staff and manager had every horse rugged, fed and waters topped up. Double checking the doors on the way out, Lise told Kingsley it was her turn to come back and check all the waters and horses before bed.

The staff rotated this routine check at the summer sales to top up waters in the hot weather but also to make sure all horses are resting peacefully before staff retired for the night.

Declan decided he'd help Lise but didn't voice the opinion for fear she'd try to dissuade him and he wasn't about to let her off that easily. He figured he'd just offer to drive after they'd finished dinner. The socialising at the sales was one of his favourite perks. He loved having dinner with staff, catching up with old friends and establishing relationships with people he could bump into anywhere around the world. That was the joy of thoroughbreds and stud work – it was seasonal and most workers had the travel bug.

***

Wes grinned, looking through the list of possible courses related to horses. She wasn't interested in racing or being a trainer and now her focus had moved to the idea of breeding racehorses; the hours just slightly more appealing than that of working at a racetrack.

She was required to put in her preferences for after year twelve but had only found two, three less than what their teacher had suggested they put in. Of the courses available through university and TAFE, there were only two that applied to focusing on breeding horses.

Perhaps to make things even more infuriating for her careers teacher, both courses were the same, just in different locations. Shrugging, Wes entered the details of these courses on the computer, doubting she would be changing them in 10 months time when she received her results for her Victorian Certificate of Education.

Apparently come the end of the year when all students received their results, it was common practice to login to their accounts and change preferences to suit what they would be able to get into based on their overall score. This seemed pointless to Wes who felt that even if she managed the score of 75-85 that she was aiming for, it didn't matter.

The course she was applying for required that she completed year twelve or had relevant working industry experience. Due to not having the latter, Wes was happy enough to complete year twelve even though the subjects she covered seemed completely irrelevant to what she wanted to do later in life. She was aware that doing a broad range of topics including math kept doors open if the impossible happened and she decided she no longer wanted to pursue working with horses.

***

Declan smiled as the two young women stepped out of their room. He'd like to think it was in response to his tooting of the horn but considering he had beeped on five separate occasions he couldn't prove it. Lise caught him staring and self-consciously ran her hand over her hair.

"What?" she asked defensively.

He just continued smiling as he replied.

"Nothing. Now get in the car, both of ye!"

The smile was due to seeing Lise slightly dressed up. She looked lovely any day as far as Declan was concerned but he wasn't going to complain seeing her out of work clothes.

Declan drove the five of them down to the local pub that served meals to the stud hands and managers who frequented the sales. It was well positioned, being stumbling distance from the motel and many workers caught up over a drink or game of pool afterwards.

After winning three games in a row against Lise, Declan queried if she had had enough of losing.

"I think I'd better check on the horses and call it a night," she replied with a smile.

"I'll drive ye."

"I'm quite capable of driving myself."

"Ok, ye can drive. I'll sit in the passenger seat," Declan stated with a grin.

Lise nodded, an amused smile crossing her face.

"Ok... are the others staying or did they want a lift?"

"Let them walk. It'll do Kingsley some good," Declan joked, glancing at his boss to see if the older male had overheard the jibe.

"Don't let that Irishman corrupt you!" he called out to Lise as she exited the room, Declan in tow.

He paused at the door to wink at Kingsley.

"Spoil all me fun. I nearly had her convinced that was a good idea!"

With that statement he ducked out the door, jogging to get to the car before Lise drove away without him.

"Ye do know yer going to end up going to every sale, right?" Declan queried as they drove down the highway toward the sales.

"And why would that be?"

"Because Kingsley likes ye, ye handle the horses well and... yer short," he finished simply, causing Lise to laugh.

"A positive for working with yearlings."

"Exactly. Why did ye move from yer last job?"

"I'd learnt a lot and felt it was time to move on and try another stud and see things perhaps done differently. Also, there was no chance to specialise or move up on that stud. Many workers had been there a lot longer than I and the managers and assistant managers weren't going anywhere and I didn't want to be a stud hand all my life. I'd rather focus on foals and get paid well because I do my job well."

"And do ye think Nirvana Park is going to be a place where ye can get this?" Declan asked in curiosity, trying to work out if she'd be staying put.

"I think so... Kingsley is great and I'm getting on fine with all the workers and the pay's good and I've had lots of responsibility with the foals but that doesn't restrict me from being in the covering shed or being picked for horse sales so unless something were to change for the worse, I could see myself here for awhile yet," she replied, pulling into the complex and putting the car in park before killing the engine.

Declan smiled to himself as he got out of the passenger side, falling into step with Lise as the pair wandered between blocks of stables until they got to their barn. He checked the horses to the left while Lise checked those to the right, both making note of any waters that needed to be topped up before they left.

"Declan – we're going to need a lead rope, maybe two," Lise said suddenly, catching his attention.

The young Irishman rushed to her side, looking in the box to find a horse cast in the corner under its feeder. Grabbing a key off his belt he went to the spare box that was used to store all the stud's gear, pulling out a couple of lead ropes. Lise was already entering the stall.

"Don't get too close until ye have a rope," Declan warned, knowing that this was the same filly that required two people to put on her rug to avoid getting hurt.

Lise nodded, taking the rope offered to her before heading to the horse's head while Declan went for the hindquarters, both working with their leads folded in half, trying to catch the two legs that were further away. Both achieving this they were able to pull the filly over, quickly letting go of one end of either rope to be able to untangle them from the young animal's leg's as she struggled to stand. Not happy with ropes flapping against her legs, the chestnut filly let fly with a couple of kicks, Declan grabbing Lise to drag her out of the way.

Both stood quietly in the doorway, watching as she righted herself, their hearts racing. Lise looked up at Declan who still had a hand protectively on her arm.

"I thought she was going to get ye a good one."

"Me too. Thanks," she smiled, pushing against him to get out of the doorway, closing it after her.

She then turned away from him to check the other horses down the right hand side. Declan stood quietly for a moment, waiting for his heart to slow down as he watched Lise continue her check of each animal. He frowned, not liking the fear that had hit him when he had thought Lise was going to get kicked.

It's fine to look out for her... but I hope I don't get so caught up in this that I'm worried for her safety just because she's working with horses. Shaking his head as if to clear such thoughts, he continued down the left side of the breezeway, checking horses and waters as he went.

March

It dawned on Madison that this was the first time she'd met Johnny... and he thought she was Melanie. A large grin making its way to her face, she greeted him warmly as he strolled over to the tie up area. He said hello to the two young girls before asking Madison how she was.

"Suddenly the day has improved," she stated cheekily, winking at him before helping Geordie to undo the girth on Sheila.

"That's good to hear," he returned with a large smile, turning his attention back to the two girls, asking them how their lesson went.

This was Maddie's last lesson for the day and she was amused to think that finishing with the troublesome pair could brighten her day.

"Can we stop by McDonald's on the way home, Johnny?" his younger sister asked as she brushed over her pony, focusing on the mane and tail, ignoring the sweaty back and girth area.

Madison went to say something to her but was interrupted by Johnny's reply.

"Sure... perhaps Emmy would like to join us if she is finished for the day," he stated with a smile, his gaze seeking Madison's.

She returned the smile.

"Extremely tempting but I haven't finished for the day, I'm sorry to say."

Johnny nodded, striking up another conversation with the girls while Maddie brushed over the parts of the pony that Geordie had missed. The three left shortly after putting the ponies out, Johnny saying he'd be back next week to pick up the girls.

Maddie smiled saying she would look forward to it. And in truth, she was looking forward to not teaching the girls the following week and she was sure Mel would look forward to seeing Johnny so she saw no harm in saying so. Albeit, in a roundabout way.

The smile was still on her face when she strolled inside. Jack had given all the horses hay and checked their waters while she was teaching so she was actually done for the day.

Mel was reading a book in the lounge room, her curiosity roused when she spotted her sister.

"It's a rare Tuesday afternoon that you come in here smiling."

"It's a rare Tuesday arvo I find you inside reading when I am finished for the day... oh, wait – it's not!" Maddie finished as she walked out to the kitchen to get a drink.

"Why so happy?"

"The girls just behaved well today," Maddie replied as she strolled back into the room.

"Who picked them up?" Mel asked.

Maddie smiled at the question, leaning against the doorframe.

"Oh, some guy... Jamie? No, maybe Jimmy..."

"Johnny," Mel corrected, taking the bait.

"That's it! Johnny. Talkative guy," she commented with a grin, lounging opposite Mel who had put her book down, her focus fully on her twin.

"So talkative in fact, he wanted to continue conversing over dinner!"

"What?!"

"Tempting... it really was but I've come to the conclusion he must have thought I was you... It'd be an extremely confident male to invite out someone he'd just met to dinner, don't you think?"

"What did you say to him, Maddie?" Mel asked quietly, not amused that her sister was having so much fun.

"That I had work to do and that I was looking forward to seeing him next week when he came to pick the girls up. And you are, aren't you?" she questioned with a smug smile.

Mel sat quietly, a smile finally making its way to her face.

"How could I not? He's gorgeous!"

Maddie rose from the chair laughing.

"Now how are you going to get away with this? You'll have to tell him you have a twin to avoid complications but we can't let the girls know."

"I'll find some way," Mel stated, picking up her book and finding her page.

"If you say so. I'm going to work Phoenix. I'll be in, in time for tea."

She couldn't be sure her twin had heard her for there was no response from behind the book she was reading. Rolling her eyes Maddie went to her room to grab her helmet and half chaps.

In five minutes she was back out at the stables, grabbing a head collar and lead rope and a handful of pellets to grab the attention of her cheeky mare.

Phoenix was her six year old thoroughbred mare that had been deemed not fast enough as a racehorse and sold at three before Maddie bought her from an older woman when Phoenix was rising five. The woman had wanted a dressage mount and found the young mare rushed too much and wouldn't settle for competitions. Maddie had taken an interest in her at a one day event she'd gone to see Jack compete in.

Phoenix's dressage test had been anything but controlled but she handled the show jumping and cross country extremely well considering her previous owner wasn't big on jumping. Chatting with the woman after the event, Maddie was delighted to hear that she was considering selling Phoenix as her passion would always be dressage.

Maddie had been working with the young horse now for nearly eighteen months and found that although she was too slow to be a good racehorse, she was a promising jumper and had enough speed to carry out cross country.

Rushing between jumps could still be a problem and Maddie knew the pair of them would continue to benefit from controlled work in the arena between cross country sessions.

After tacking up Phoenix, Maddie set up some poles down either long side of the arena, four in a row and walked and trotted Phoenix through them before cantering on the circle at either end of the arena. Once warmed up she adjusted the four poles on either side, making the last two poles into a crossbar and a straight on the other side. She then remounted and took Phoenix through the two lots of trot poles and jump, the poles beforehand working well to keep the horse at a forward trot but not rushing.

It wasn't until Maddie had set up all eight poles into four jumps with room for a few strides in between that the young mare started rushing.

Maddie used the letters A and C at either end of the arena as a point to put the mare on a small circle at the canter and then a second even smaller circle at a trot before heading into the second lots of jumps at a forward trot.

After a few goes of repeating this pattern the mare recognised that they would slow between each set of jumps and she started to settle, not rushing into the jumps or between each pair.

***

Hunter pulled up to the side of the stable, a large grin directed at Kaye as he said hello. She paused from raking with a smile, stepping closer to his Ute to peer into the cab.

"Hello to you both. Cute pup. What's his name?"

"Please."

"Seriously? Ok, what's his name *please.*"

Hunter grinned, barely holding back a laugh, Dave sitting beside him with a large smile also.

"Oh, I'm going to have so much fun with this."

"With what?" Kaye asked with a frown.

"The name of my kelpie," Hunter replied smoothly.

"You mean with not telling people the name of your kelpie?"

"But he did," Dave replied with a chuckle.

"No he didn't."

"Sure I did! His name is Please!" Hunter clarified, stepping out of the car.

"Excuse me?"

"That probably would have worked just as well," he chuckled, patting the young canine that moved to his seat, peering down at the ground and then up at the farrier as if asking permission to get out of the car.

"Now I am completely lost."

"I've named the dog Please. It just sounds so polite. Hop out of the car, Please. Drop, Please. Roll, Please. See?" Hunter finished with a broad grin, rewarding his pup with a pat for being obedient to his requests.

Kaye rolled her eyes, turning her focus back to raking up stray bits of hay out the front of the stables.

"You're both insane."

"Me? What'd I do?" Dave asked, incredulous.

"You encourage him. Trevor and Declan are in the stables ready when you want to do some work," Kaye stated gruffly.

Hunter winked at Dave, stepping past the fiery redhead and into the darker stables; the pup following at his heels. The pair found the two men in one of the stalls, looking at the front foot of a yearling.

"Our first victim?" Dave queried, peering through the bars of the stall wall.

"Reckon so," Declan muttered as he stood up from being bent over the leg Trevor was holding up.

"He's got a decent crack and is a little sore."

"Sure we can fix that up with a trim and some shoes. Is it alright to bring the Ute in here? Park it in the middle of the breezeway?"

"That should be fine. We can start on the colt next door, Dave," Trevor directed, getting out of the box.

He paused to kneel down and say hello to Hunter's latest acquisition.

"Cute pup, what's his name?"

Hunter smiled, finding it hard to ignore Dave's pained look.

"I've named him Please," he stated, winking at his coworker who looked relieved to not have to repeat the conversation they'd had not two minutes ago with Kaye.

Declan laughed from inside the box, keeping a hold of the horse with the cracked hoof.

"That's great craic! I love it!"

"Very clever," Trevor replied with a smile, heading into the box next door while the pair of farriers headed back to the car to relocate it inside the stables.

As the two farriers were finishing up for the day, Kingsley made an appearance at the stables, leaning against the doorframe as he stood watching Hunter twist the end off a nail, clip it back and clench it down.

"That you boys done for the day then?" he queried, his gaze on the older farrier.

"Indeed! We haven't got any other farms booked in for the day."

"So you'd be free to help me out with some soldering then?" the older male queried innocently, his arms folded across his chest.

"You bet!" Stuart replied with enthusiasm, wiping some sweat from his brow.

Standing up from underneath the horse he stepped out of the door, following the manager down the breezeway.

"Lead the way! Come on Dave, time for some soldering."

Trevor grinned as he watched the three stroll down the breezeway.

"I do wonder why he still claims he's working when we all know he goes down to the back shed to knock back a drink or six."

"Guess he's just gotten into a habit of pretending," Declan replied with a grin, removing the head collar from the yearling he'd been holding before stepping out of the box and securing the door.

Kingsley paused at the exit to the stables and looked back at the two men.

"You got a problem with us doing some soldering?"

"Not in the least," Declan replied with a grin.

"Good! Then I expect you'll be joining us once all the horses are fed."

Declan let out an amused laugh, saluting his boss before heading into the feed room to collect the buckets that the girls had been making up for the afternoon feeds. Ten minutes later the team of workers had finished and Trevor hopped onto one of the four wheeler bikes, Declan sitting on the back as the pair drove down to the back shed where Kingsley, Hunter and Dave were already onto their second beer.

Kingsley stood from the esky he'd been sitting on just long enough to extract two more bottles, tossing them to the two new arrivals before returning to his makeshift seat. Declan found a bucket and turned it upside down to sit on while Trevor stayed on the bike, sitting sideways to face the other men.

"I was just enquiring after the other properties where the boys are doing some work. Sounds like those riding schools are giving you more work than the thoroughbred studs!" Kingsley stated with a teasing tone.

"Nearly. I almost feel obliged to return the favour."

"How so?" Declan queried.

"They provide me with so much work I feel more like going out of my way when they're looking for something. The owners of East Riding School are looking for more hacks to re-educate and introduce to the business. Let me know if you hear of any thoroughbreds that'd be quiet enough to be passed on to a riding school. I'd like to help them out."

"Taidem," Trevor spoke up suddenly, his gaze going to Kingsley.

"What about him?" the manager queried, looking at the older male.

"He's spelling at the moment but didn't Asterly say that he wasn't sure it was worth putting the gelding through another prep? That you'd be spending more money in stabling and training fees than you'd make?" Trevor replied, referring to the stud's trainer.

"True enough. There's one for you, Stuart. Just ask Trevor here and he'll happily sell you all my racehorses for a cheap price," the manager joked.

"Is the gelding quiet?" Dave asked, taking another swig from his beer bottle.

"Extremely. And I think I'll take Asterly's advice. He probably wouldn't be worth investing in for another prep and seeing as he's a gelding he'll no longer be making us money. Trevor's probably right, it wouldn't hurt your riding school friends to invest in him and it sure wouldn't hurt us. He's a seven year old gelding, is that young enough to 're-educate'?"

Stuart Hunter smiled, kicking at the dirt with his feet.

"I'm sure that'd be fine. Will I give you their number?"

"Nah. Just tell them about the horse and if they want to chase it up, get them to get in contact with me. I'm not interested in chasing up owners for retired racehorses," Kingsley shrugged, his gaze turning to Declan.

"Speaking of chasing things... when are you going to catch a hold of that girl?" he queried with a smirk, causing the other men to laugh.

"Me? How on earth am I supposed to convince her I'm worth stopping for when ye keep on encouraging her to run?!"

"I don't know what you're talking about," his boss replied with such innocence that Declan almost believed him.

April

"So tell me something good about this paddock," Madison stated, standing at the fence line with half a dozen students.

"There are horses in it," the sole male in the group answered with a cheeky grin.

Madison returned the smile. It was school holidays again and Jack was taking the week program for the two riding lessons of the day and Madison was filling in for the afternoon, providing the theory lesson while Jack taught his regular afternoon lessons.

Being Thursday, Madison was glad that she only had to come up with one more thing to teach the kids before it was the end of the week program but she was amused by the young male in the group who was obviously shining in amongst so many females.

"And something bad about this paddock, then?" she asked the group, letting his comment slide.

"There's not enough horses?" a young girl stated hopefully.

"I'll second that! Now, let's look at some other things: water, grass, size of the paddock, shelter and fencing. Can you all see the water trough in the middle of the paddock?"

The majority nodded their heads, a couple vocalising that they could.

"Good. Because it's in the middle of the paddock and not up against a fence, it means that the horses can get to it from any side of the trough. This is a good thing; especially if two horses that don't get along want to have a drink at the same time. Now what about shelter, is there anything in the paddock that the horses could use to keep out of rain or wind or even the hot sun?"

"Trees along the fence and a shed in the middle," Jennifer, one of the girls spoke up.

"Great! Can everyone see the trees? They're planted in a good spot where they are as when the sun gets high in the afternoon, they cast shade into the paddock. If we had them on the other side of the paddock, all the shade would go to the property next door."

"What about the fencing?"

"I like it," another student spoke up, causing Maddie to smile.

"For any particular reason?" she prompted.

"Ummm... it's high."

"Good. Is it easy to see?"

The group nodded.

"I'd agree with that. It could be easier if the whole fence was made out of post and rails, but having posts and a top rail means the horses can see it from far away and shouldn't run into it. If the whole fence was made out of wires with no rails, do you think it'd be easy to see? Can you see the wires across the other side of the paddock?"

They shook their heads.

"Some people choose wire because it's cheap and post and rails is quite expense. That's why we use a bit of both. It's more cost effective for us to set up the fence with wire but we wouldn't be saving money if the horses couldn't see the fence and they went through it! Now what else did I mention we should have a look at?"

"Grass."

"Ah! Very important! If our horses have nothing to eat, we're in trouble! There's enough grass in the paddocks at the moment, but what if there wasn't? What could we put in there to stop them from going hungry?"

"Hay," James spoke up, offering a sensible answer this time.

"Perfect. Because there are six horses in this paddock, how many piles should we put out when we put the hay out?"

"Six," he replied.

"Can anyone tell me why?" Madison looked at the rest of the group.

"So they don't fight over it," Lily stated quietly.

"Exactly! We'd want to put out at least six piles, perhaps more and have them well spaced apart so everyone can get to a pile to eat in peace."

The group went on to discuss sizing of a paddock and having gates big enough for vehicles to enter and people and horses to get in and out of before Madison took them back to the office where parents were waiting to collect children.

Jack was just finishing his lesson as Madison saw the last child off. She wandered over to the tie up area toward him and Jacinta.

"Good lesson?" Maddie directed the question to Jacinta, her eyes on Jack.

"Great! Jack's the best," Jacinta stated with conviction as she started to take off the saddle, Geira already tied up and standing quietly.

"And how was your mare?" Maddie queried, not managing to hold back an amused smile.

Jack muttered something about going to get Geira's feed and headed off to the feed room. Maddie watched as Jacinta gave the mare a good curry over, working over the sweaty girth area and across her back.

"So I hear the pair of you managed another blue at the show last week. Well done!"

"Thanks. Geira was really well behaved and things just seemed to go right. It was awesome! We had a brilliant round on the show jumping course. Jack is a great teacher."

"He also has some talented jumping students," Maddie replied, frowning as she thought about Alex.

He'd not been around over the Christmas holidays due to going away with the family and had now had a couple of lessons back and wasn't riding as well as Maddie knew he could and she felt it was because Alex just hadn't clicked with the gelding he was now riding.

Jack had concluded it was just because Alex was a bit rusty due to having had a reasonable break from riding. Maddie was going to give it one more week before suggesting to her mum that Alex switch back to Fuzz. She wasn't going to push to teach him again but felt that he would excel back on the pony that he'd connected with so well.

Wandering into the house that same evening she found that she didn't have to make any requests as her mum called her into the kitchen while chopping up some vegetables as part of tea.

"I got a call from Alex's mum today and had a chat with Alex as well."

"Oh? What did they have to say?"

"Alex doesn't feel that he's doing as well in the group lesson and has requested to have you back as his instructor."

"What do you think, mum?"

"I want to do what makes the client happy but there's no room for you to take Alex this week so I've told him that if he wants to ride this week he'll have to do a group session with Jack."

"Which horse have you got him on?"

"Barry. The same gelding he's been riding in Jack's lessons."

"Can you put him back on Fuzz? I can understand Jack's logic for a larger horse but Alex has such a connection with Fuzz and I don't think he should change mounts until he gets his own horse. If he rides on Fuzz in Jack's lesson, he may decide to stay in the group sessions. I think it'll make the difference," Madison stated in earnest.

She frowned at her mum's amused smile.

"What?"

"I'm just pleased to see you offer something that is solely in the interest of the client, even if it means you losing out on teaching someone you love to teach."

Madison rolled her eyes as she strolled out of the room.

"I know the whole world doesn't revolve around me."

"Of course you do daughter darling," her mum replied with a laugh as Madison left the room.

***

Wes threw a pair of shoes on and raced out the door with her parents, wanting nothing more than to be with her horse at that very second. The owner of the property where Reign was kept had just called to say that the palomino gelding had gone through a fence during the storm the night before and cut up his leg. She'd cleaned it up and bandaged him and put him in one of the few stables in the pony club paddock but thought Wes would want to know and come see him if she could.

When Wes was dropped off she found the woman who had called her and then went to inspect the damage, not familiar with treating wounds but aware that Reign was lucky he hadn't damaged an extensor tendon as he'd cut up his near fore cannon. She realised it'd mean not being able to ride for awhile but was glad her parents had agreed to drive her each day so she could clean out his stall and clean up the wound with the help of the property owner. She'd made them promise before they'd even finished the trip out to her gelding.

Not even twenty four hours later and Reign had managed to rip at the bandage and half pull it off.

"Probably been biting it. We may have to put something bad tasting on the edges to stop him doing that again but at least it gives us a chance to have a look and we can re-bandage it then it should be fine for two to three days. You can come get me each time you want to change the bandage and we'll do it together."

Using some sharp scissors the older woman cut down the side of the bandage and peeled it away from the cannon. Wes leant forward to get a closer look, taking in the sight of the bone, tendon and cut skin. Horses are unusual in that they don't have muscles below their knee and it was this fact that made Wes realise how lucky Reign truly had been.

"It's not too bad but let's get him out to the hose and give it a clean and wipe down before bandaging again."

Wes nodded, leading her gelding out of the dim stables into the slightly brighter overcast day, the older woman following with a bucket of items for cleaning the wound. Reign paused indecisively leading up to the hose, ears pricked and nostrils flared, his sore leg raised off the ground.

"Come on pretty boy," Wes crooned, tugging on the lead and then releasing the pressure.

The older woman slapped her hands against her thighs from behind Wes' horse, scaring him into moving forward. Wes shook her head, continuing on slowly toward the hose, her arab cross high stepping the whole way despite his sore leg.

"You can't be feeling too bad handsome man," she muttered, putting a hand to his chest to hold him in place while the proprietor turned on the hose, running the water over his hoof and then up the cannon.

Wes watched as she brushed away any debris, loose scabs or blood and then wiped down the leg with a towel before showing Wes how to apply the antibacterial cream, cotton wool and then wrap the wool with a crepe bandage, securing it in place with some Elastoplast at either end. Wes watched with interest, querying if there was a particular direction to wrap the bandage and how tight to have it. She wanted to make sure she knew how to wrap the bandage for the next time it had to be changed.

Wes had to continue this process every few days over the next few weeks, the bandage shortly after being removed for good with Wes hosing the leg when she was visiting with Reign, removing scabs to encourage closure of the wound. She was instructed to throw lime on the face of the wound where proud flesh was forming to fight this extra growth.

Wes was relieved to find that over the duration of the wound healing, Reign didn't show signs of lameness and it wasn't too long before she was back on him. Not knowing a lot about wound management the end result was a large scar on Reign's near fore cannon but no signs of lameness and Wes concluded that the pair hadn't done too bad in relation to injuries considering she'd had him for five years. Now if they could just keep it that way.

May

"Got everything?" Maddie asked her twin as she waited impatiently in the doorway of the garage.

"I think so... let's go," Melanie replied.

"Finally."

Madison exited the garage, her sister in tow. It was a Monday and they were making use of the quiet day by cleaning out the water troughs on the property. The East Riding School wasn't open on a Monday, giving horses and staff a break after the hectic weekend. So, their mother had suggested the two girls clean up the troughs. Maddie wasn't impressed but figured it shouldn't take too long. She hadn't factored in Mel wanting to change her clothes and locate some long boots and gloves, however.

They started at the closest paddock to the house, Maddie using a shifter to undo the plug on the large cement trough and let some of the water out before they commenced cleaning the trough.

"This is disgusting," Melanie frowned, eyeing off the slime that lined her gloves with distaste.

"And yet, strangely satisfying," Maddie replied with a grin, scrubbing at the side of the trough with a dandy brush.

She'd let out two thirds of the water and the girls were using the remaining water to splash up on the sides of the trough, scrubbing away dirt and algae that had accumulated.

"We should put something in here to keep the troughs clean... yabbies or something," Maddie declared, using the shifter to loosen the plug and let some more water out.

"I can just picture the horses taking a drink and leaping back in fright with a yabbie attached to their nose by a claw. Great idea," Melanie stated with sarcasm.

Maddie laughed at the image.

"That'd be a Kodak moment! Now, tell me about Johnny," she looked at her twin with a large grin, "have you gotten a chance to tell him you're a twin yet?"

"No. He hasn't been about and the one time he was he arrived just when the girls had put the ponies away and apologised for having to rush off."

"Well that's something," Maddie declared, scrubbing at the base of the trough.

"He apologised. The least he could do for not having time to talk with you!"

Melanie smiled, amused.

"I hardly think you should be telling me how a male should be behaving. How's Jack going?"

Madison shrugged.

"Fine, I assume. Perhaps he's out and about with Jacinta," she finished with a conspiratorial wink.

"You need help, dear sister! She's a bit young for him, don't you think?" Melanie paused, eyes wide.

"You don't make suggestions like that to Jack, do you?" she asked, incredulous.

Maddie cracked up laughing, flicking water at her sister.

"You should see your face! So what if I do?"

"That's some way to treat a guy you're interested in."

"It's just teasing, Mel. He'll be fine. And he knows I'm interested, so what's the problem?"

"He's interested, you're interested... you're not involved!" she replied, exasperated.

"And?" Maddie queried, amused by her sister's annoyance.

Melanie flicked some dirty water back at her twin.

"We sure don't share the same thought process! You make no sense."

Madison laughed, letting the rest of the water out, sweeping it toward the plug hole with her dandy brush. This done she returned the plug, tightening it with the shifter while Melanie untied the float, letting water back into the trough.

"Got time to do another trough before lunch?" she asked her sister.

"Unfortunately," Melanie replied, trudging toward the next paddock.

"We'll check that trough has filled properly on the way back."

***

Lise frowned, taking in the sight of one of the rising two year old fillies standing far off by herself. Kingsley had four fillies and three colts in separate paddocks that he was hoping to send off to be broken in soon. Some had been bred on the farm and a couple had been purchased at the recent yearling sales and then put out in the paddock to grow out a bit more before being put into training. Lise was sure the manager wouldn't be so rapt to know something was up with one he was planning on sending to the trainer.

She left Declan to divide up the feed into the feeders and headed over to the dark brown horse, not liking the lowered head or the fact that she wasn't eagerly heading for the feed trailer as the other young animals were.

"Hey girlie, you not feeling well?" she queried as she got closer, noting as the filly slowly looked up at her that one eye was puffy and half closed, she had hair missing in a couple of spots on her neck and her near hind was swollen to twice its size, the indents around her back leg looking to be the work of a piece of wire.

"Got a bit too friendly with a fence, did we?" she asked, reaching out to pat the young animal reassuringly as she did a quick scan of the property, looking for any fence that may be bent out of shape or a wire down.

Not being able to see any without taking a closer look, she stood a distance behind the young horse and clapped her hands, trying to encourage her to move forward so she could inspect the damage. The filly did so, taking a few painful steps toward the feeders before stopping.

"At least you're putting weight on it. Guess we'll be bringing your feeder a little closer and I think we'll be back to clean you up a bit, too."

Declan drove the bike over to Lise, pausing before the filly to get a closer look. Lise smiled when she realised he'd had the same idea when it came to the feeder and took this off the trailer to put before the sore animal.

"Verdict?"

"I don't think it's too bad, she's putting weight on that leg which is a good sign but we might want to cover bases with some penicillin. We'd better take a trip around the fence line too and see where she's had a run in. I can't see any loose wires from here and we might as well get one of the maintenance guys onto it. They were complaining today that they're sick of raking up the leaves from all the maples that Kingsley has planted down the drive."

Declan laughed as he drove forward again, Lise sitting on the back of the four wheeler as he made a quick trip around the perimeter of the paddock. The pair found two top wires down on one side of the paddock. Stopping the bike they both hopped off and found the ends of the wires, wrapping them around a post to keep them out of the way, not wanting any horses to get further hurt before maintenance had a chance to clean things up.

"Are all the others ok?" Lise asked as she hopped back onto the bike, Declan not far behind her.

"Indeed. We'll check the other three paddocks and then get onto the boys about that fence and see what Kingsley wants to do about treating that filly."

"Sounds like a plan."

Lise and Declan finished the feed run for the morning and Declan went to find Kingsley to check that he was alright with treating the filly and to see if the manager wanted to take a look personally.

Declan also made a note to tell the maintenance guys about the fence. Lise had agreed to head back to the stables to see if the others needed a hand with the weanlings. Once the yearling season was finished with, weaning started.

This involved bringing the mares and foals in, in groups of ten, introducing the foals to having head collars on and a couple of days later taking away the mares.

The young horses were then handled daily for around ten days, getting used to being led, having legs picked up and at the end the farrier came in to do their feet before they were put into paddocks based on gender. They stayed in these groups until brought in at the end of the year for their yearling preparation and the sales.

Declan grinned as he passed the driveway leading out of the property. Two maintenance men were still raking up leaves and piling these into bags that were then loaded onto the back of their work ute and unloaded at the dumping area on the property.

Declan headed toward the pair, telling them of the fence in one of the fillies' paddocks that needed repairing.

He could have laughed out loud at their relieved looks as they hurried to the ute, leaving bags behind in their haste as they drove off toward the maintenance area. Declan paused for a few seconds, questioning if it would be too cruel to kick up the piles of leaves that had been so carefully raked up. Deciding he couldn't do it he headed on to find Kingsley.

***

Melanie laughed as she watched her client bounce about in the saddle down the short side of the arena.

"That looks very uncomfortable, Wendy!"

Coming back to a rising trot down the long side, Wendy managed a smile, breaking her frown of concentration.

"It is! Do I really have to manage this before I can canter?"

"I'm afraid so. You sit to the canter so it's good to establish your seat at a sitting trot in anticipation of the canter. I want you to try again down the short side of the arena. We'll do that a couple more times then I'll put you on the lunge to try a canter."

Melanie watched as the older woman relaxed more and consequently found it easier to sit to the trot. Once she was happy with her client's capabilities, Melanie directed Wendy to one end of the arena where she clipped up the lunge line to the horse's bridle.

"We're going to go around to the left first at a trot and when you're ready, I want you to go into a sitting trot once you pass the letter A and I'll ask Cody to canter. Does that sound alright?" Melanie queried.

At Wendy's affirming nod she flicked the lunging whip behind the older gelding and he started trotting a twenty or so metre circle around her. Melanie instructed Wendy to keep a hold of her reins but to also hold onto the pommel of the saddle to keep herself sitting deeply. Once the pair passed the letter A, Melanie flicked the whip again, encouraging Cody into a canter. Already holding onto the front of the saddle, Wendy managed to keep herself sitting deeply and not thump on the gelding's back.

"Excellent! Now if you'll just lean back a bit Wendy, you'll be more balanced in the saddle. That's it. How does that feel?"

The older woman smiled, her face flushed.

"Wonderful! Much more comfortable than the sitting trot."

"Great to hear. I want you to bring Cody back to a trot and then walk and we'll change direction before I take you off the lunge."

They repeated the process before Melanie took Wendy off the lunge and sent her out around the perimeter of the arena at a working trot before directing the older woman to try a canter by herself upon reaching a corner of the arena. Her client did so, pushing her mount into a canter and going down the long side of the arena, coming back to a trot at the next corner.

"Well done! That was excellent!"

Wendy came back to a walk on Cody, turning the gelding in toward Melanie, a large grin across her face.

"Emmy darling, that was wonderful. Thank you."

"My pleasure. You can cool Cody out and then untack him. I'll be over at the tie up area."

June

"Emmy! Come quick! There's an old man stealing all the horse poo!"

"How old?" Madison queried, looking at the young boy running toward her.

"Ancient. Like a hundred."

"And what do you think we should do about it?"

"Call the police! He's stealing!"

"I'm sure my parents know he's there."

"No! You've got to call the police!"

"And what would we tell them?"

"That someone's stealing the horse poo and to get here quick. Their trailer is already half full. What if they leave before the police get here?"

Madison smiled and knelt down so that she was eye level to the young boy.

"What do you think would happen if no one came to get manure? If the horses keep eating, they're going to keep making manure and it needs to go somewhere. We can't let it all pile up. So, do you think it might be alright for someone to take some of the manure?"

Leighton nodded.

"So we won't call the police," Maddie clarified.

"No... we won't call the police."

"How about while we're waiting for your dad to arrive, we go find out what the man's using the manure for?"

"Ok."

The pair wandered around the back of the stables toward the manure pile where an older gentleman was shoveling it from the pile into his trailer.

"Afternoon, Mr. Briggs. How are you today?"

The older man smiled at Maddie.

"Well thank you, darling. How are the horses?"

"Still eating."

"I see," he gestured to the pile of manure with a grin.

"Mr. Briggs, this is Leighton. He'd like to know what you use the manure for."

"I have a large garden at home that I put it on to help things grow. I bring in some of the vegetables for the Jamison family in return for them letting me use the manure. Would you like to see what I grow?" he asked, leaning against the shovel as he stood beside the trailer.

Leighton nodded, looking up at the older man in surprise. Resting his shovel against the trailer, he ambled over to the car and opened the passenger seat, pulling out a bag of vegetables. He lowered the bag, opening it wide for Leighton to see inside.

"You put horse poo on the food that you eat?" Leighton asked, incredulous.

The older gentleman burst out laughing.

"When you say it like that it does sound insane!"

Maddie grinned, turning her attention from the pair to an older male that was strolling towards them. It was Leighton's father. He made his way over to the three, taking in his son's face before turning to Maddie for an explanation.

"Leighton doesn't seem to think that Mr. Briggs here should put manure on his garden."

"Daddy, do we eat food that has had horse poo put on it?" he asked in a grave manner, reaching up to take his father's hand.

The older male waved goodbye to Maddie and Mr. Briggs, holding back a smile.

"No, we don't. Would it stop you from eating the food if it had at one time had manure on it?" he asked the young child, trying to be sincere.

Maddie laughed as she headed back toward the tie up area to tidy up. Her smile continued as she spied Johnny heading toward her. He returned the large grin, coming to pause in front of her frame.

"I didn't expect to see you today!" Madison stated honestly, looking up at him.

"I just couldn't seem to stay away... do you think I need help?" he asked with a grin.

"Hmm... nope. I do seem to have that affect on people," Maddie joked as she went to step past him to grab some brushes that needed putting away.

Johnny put his arm out to stop her, leaning forward quickly to kiss her.

Having been mixing up feeds for the following morning, Jack stepped out of the feed room in time to spot the pair and he paused in surprise. Madison's gaze went from Johnny to Jack, and back to the male before her, fighting surprise of her own.

"Sorry, excuse me, Maddie," Jack muttered, continuing on past the pair, heading brusquely for his car.

Madison grinned, staring up at Johnny.

"As pleasant as that was, I think you've got the wrong girl," she stated cheekily.

"Sorry? Why did he call you Maddie?" he frowned in confusion.

"It's short for Madison."

"And Emmy?"

"Is the name my sister and I use for teaching."

"Your sister?"

Madison refrained from rolling her eyes as Johnny repeated her words, even less eloquently.

"Yes. My twin sister. Melanie. The one who doesn't stop talking about you. The one who you thought you were kissing. She's in the house… and I must be off. Catchya!" she stated cheerily, questioning if she wanted to explain this one to Jack or not.

I wonder if he'll pretend he's not bothered…

Jack frowned, starting up his car. *Great way to finish the day!* He sighed as he drove down the driveway, keeping to the twenty kilometre speed limit. Often he was convinced the redhead was flirting with him and then he walks in on her kissing another guy!

He couldn't work out if she was flirting, if that's how she acted around any male or if he'd read things wrong. Not coming to any conclusion that satisfied him, he continued on home.

Melanie paused on her way out of the house, surprised to see Johnny striding toward her. She was even more surprised when he bent to wrap his arms around her, kissing her firmly. Relaxing in his embrace she wrapped her arms around his neck, returning the kiss. He pulled away with a smile.

"This one kisses back," he stated cryptically, causing her to frown in confusion.

"Meaning?" she queried, not sure she liked the feeling that quickly settled in her gut.

"I'm thinking I should make sure you respond to Melanie anytime I want to kiss you. Heaven knows you both respond to Emmy," he muttered wryly.

Melanie held a hand up to her mouth, working to contain her smile as she realised what he was saying.

"You didn't?"

"Kiss your *twin sister*? No, why would I do that? After all, I was fully informed you had a twin," he continued with chagrin.

"I'm so sorry... it's all Maddie's fault. She came up with the teaching under one name idea and it appeared harmless enough to me."

"No offense, but I believe it could be harmful to me to be carrying on *one* relationship with *two* women. What do you think?"

Melanie laughed, nodding.

"So what are you doing here? Your sister doesn't have a lesson today."

"Which means I can see you without your focus being on her," he replied with a wink, taking the hand Melanie offered, following her inside.

***

Lise grinned as the car pulled up outside her house. Racing toward the vehicle, she enveloped her friend in a hug as soon as she got out of the car.

"Boy is it good to see you!"

Her friend Skye returned the hug just as enthusiastically.

"This place is gorgeous, Lise! You should have told me how gorgeous and I would have come for a visit sooner!"

"I'm not sure if asking sooner would have been a smart move. As much as Kingsley agreed to let me have you stay for a week, I get the feeling he isn't totally keen on staff having housemates that aren't working on the property."

"Well, that hardly matters now, does it? He said yes and here I am! Show me where I can dump my stuff and then I want to see the babies you foaled down last season, meet your workmates and learn a bit more about the thoroughbred world!"

Skye Harrison and Lise used to ride together when they were both in their early teens. Lise had taken to riding Skye's ponies and eventually leased a horse of her own. She wasn't as passionate about riding as Skye, more being interested in handling them on the ground whereas her friend loved competing at events, especially cross country. As far as Skye was concerned, speed and high jumps were a great mix.

Lise grabbed a bag out of the car, leading the way toward the house, pointing out certain things in the house to Skye as she headed to the spare room where her friend would be staying for the next seven days.

"How's Toploader going?" Lise questioned as she dumped the bag unceremoniously on the floor, sitting cross legged on the bed.

Skye grinned, sitting on the edge of the bed as she leant down to unzip her back pack, pulling out a folder.

"I thought that'd be one of your first questions. Considering you've missed our last few events, I made sure I got copies of these," she replied, opening the folder and pulling out a couple of photos and articles.

"You guys are really going well!" Lise stated with pleasure, taking in the photos of the pair clearing different jumps from recent competitions.

"Things are going well. We came second in our last show and first the one before that. Ben keeps on telling me we should be going up a class but I'm happy sitting for awhile and getting a few more events under our belt," Skye spoke seriously, referring to her instructor.

Lise smiled to herself, leafing through the last few articles. This was perhaps the one thing in Skye's life that she was serious about. Apart from her horse, everything else was about fun, testing limits and no consequences. It was nice to see her grounded and being responsible about this gorgeous animal with heaps of potential.

"Enough about my boy for now, show me this farm!" Skye said suddenly, jumping up from the bed, "take me to the stables, first! I want to see what you've got nearby."

"Hardly the best place to visit at this time of year. If they're in a box, they're sick considering its not weaning time, dry mares aren't in under lights and we're not preparing a draft of yearlings for a sale," Lise stated dryly, leading the way despite her comment.

"Party pooper," Skye stated with a grin, taking in the property around her with awe.

"I think I ride some gorgeous horses and get to see awesome competition facilities but this place is another kind of wonderful. I love the plaques down the driveway listing all the winners that have been bred on this farm."

"It is something," Lise smiled, heading into the darker interior of the stables and stopping at the first stall to peer in through the bars.

"Very cute," Skye commented, looking at the young horse soon to be a yearling.

"Agreed but I'm not so keen on having to give them oral medications three times a day when the poor babies have had minimal handling."

"Three times a day? Better you than me! So what's wrong with her?" Skye asked, pressing her hand up against the rails where the young filly was sniffing.

"Rattles. Generally they have a cough and lesions on their lungs and a high temperature. They're getting treated with a medication that unfortunately results in them not being able to regulate their temperature and so they have to stay inside during the day and can go out at night. We're only putting them into one of the smaller yards near the stables though so that they're not too hard to catch and get back inside each morning."

"Poor babies," Skye crooned, moving down the stable block and patting the few bodies that came over to say hello.

"If you feel so sorry for them do you feel like helping to put them out later so they get their freedom for the evening?" Lise queried with a smile.

"Sure! Just make sure you give me one of the quieter ones when we do so."

Lise promised that she would and the pair continued on out of the stables, Lise directing the way toward the main house and the gardens that were a favourite to clients.

"I'm sure you'd kill me if I didn't show you where the manager stays, the pool he invites staff to freely use and the gardens below."

"Lead the way!" Skye replied with a smile, glad to see her friend working on a property that seemed to care about its appearance and more importantly, its horses.

The pair wandered the beveled gardens for twenty minutes or so with Lise catching up on what her friend had been up to since they last talked. They wandered back toward the stables, passing the stallions that were coming toward the end of their season rest, Lise explaining that the stud had an open day for clients the following week to show off their stallions for the season. Kingsley was big on keeping clients happy and giving them a personal display of each of the stallions that the farm stood and clients sent their mares to. It was common in the month of October to invite them all back to show off the first lot of foals for the season.

Skye's gaze wandered from the stallion boxes toward a broad frame that was headed for the stables. She casually started back toward the stables, Lise following.

"There is something I haven't been enlightened to about this place," she commented with a smirk, glancing at Lise.

"How is it that you seem to be safely enquiring about where I work and yet I feel that you're up to something?" Lise questioned warily, emitting a laugh from her friend.

"Who knows? You haven't told me about the people you work with. Are there many staff here? Who handles the stallions? Is your manager around much?"

Lise smiled at the sudden barrage of questions.

"Plenty of time but you'll meet one of the stallion handlers and a couple of the other workers now. Let's get the babies outside."

Skye agreed happily, leading her friend toward the brick building. She paused inside the door, blinking at the lights that had been turned on due to the day darkening. It took her a short time to recognise the broad frame she'd seen heading to the stables and quickly she wandered after him, figuring she'd find out more from the person himself rather than pressing Lise for information.

Declan was surprised as he stepped out of the tack room, nearly colliding with a dark haired young woman. The surprise turned to a cheeky grin when he saw the interest on her face.

"Now I'm sure we weren't on the look out for another worker but I think I could find someone you could replace if you're after a job," he said to her, all the while smiling.

Skye returned the grin.

"I'm a friend of Lise's. I've come to annoy her for a week or so. I'm Skye."

"Declan," he replied, offering his hand.

"Now that the introductions are over," Lise stated with sarcasm, strolling up to the pair and brushing past Declan to get into the tack room.

"You helping us take out the horses, Skye?" Declan queried, his gaze on Lise as she picked up a couple of lead ropes.

"She kindly volunteered herself, yes," Lise replied, handing her friend a lead rope and heading up to the end of the stables, Skye in tow.

Kaye arrived shortly after, introducing herself to the young ebony haired woman and the four worked quickly to put the nine weanlings out into two paddocks.

Skye managed the babies well but was thankful that Lise had directed her toward the quieter ones to handle. This was especially true when she witnessed a young colt rear up and strike out, nearly getting his foot over the lead. This in turn caused Lise's weanling to balk and start running backwards, Lise working hard to keep up with the young animal. Despite the unpredictable behaviour, all were put out into the paddock safely.

The four walked back from the paddock together, Skye surprised to find herself suddenly on the ground, having tripped on some uneven ground. Declan quickly came to her aid.

"A bit of competition for you, Lise," Kaye commented with a smirk as she walked past.

Skye looked up at her friend in surprise as Declan helped her to her feet. Lise just shrugged, pretending to not know what Kaye was talking about.

She knew however that as soon as Declan was gone, Skye would be pressing her for answers.

July

Madison smiled, recognising Jack's figure as he stepped out of the feed room, brushing his hands across his jeans in an attempt to rid them of the horse feed that had clung tightly to his skin.

"Finished for the day, then?" she called out from astride Phoenix, her young thoroughbred mare.

Jack looked up, his eyes taking in Maddie's form on the mare before resting on the second horse that stood quietly beside the pair, tacked up and waiting. *For whom?* He asked himself, frowning at the thought of the male he'd seen with Maddie. *Guess I'll not be asking her out, then.*

Madison smiled, noting the annoyance on Jack's face.

"You'd better not be so annoyed while riding Marlin," she stated, referring to the older gelding, "he doesn't like attitude and I'd rather have a cheerful person accompany me out riding."

"And who's to say I've the time to join you?" he replied, ignoring his shock.

"Beats me. Guess I was just expecting. Tends to work for me most of the time," she stated cheekily, sticking out her tongue.

"Real mature," Jack replied, taking the reins from her to mount.

"It's more fun this way," Maddie stated simply, smiling softly as she asked her mare to walk on.

"Plan, then?" Jack queried, feeling himself smile.

"Hack out, bit of a chance for her to do a decent trot and canter. Might pop her down the jumping lane on the way back... she's not been ridden for a week so might be a bit fresh. Oh... and she seems to think her own shadow's out to get her."

"So this sunny afternoon will be perfect for her then," he stated sarcastically, causing Maddie to laugh as they rode side by side.

"Great weather, lovely company. I won't complain."

And with that statement she pushed the bay mare out into a working trot, rising easily to the big stride. Jack sat parallel to her, his mount keeping abreast at a collected canter. He watched the young mare for signs of nervousness before his gaze lifted to Maddie.

If I hadn't seen her kiss that guy, I'd swear she was flirting with me... like I thought she had been for the past few months. Maybe she was... maybe that's just her... or maybe she's just trying to be nice. Perhaps it doesn't matter either way... I won't be pursuing something now. Not if she's with that bloke.

Feeling Jack's gaze, Madison glanced his way, aware that he was looking through her at that point in time. Collecting her reins she prepared to increase the speed.

"Up for a faster pace?" she queried, pulling him up out of his thoughts.

"Sure. Seems she's going nicely for you."

For now, Madison agreed mentally, all too aware of the mare's changeable behaviour.

They cantered a few strides, Maddie relaxing just enough for Phoenix to throw her head down and buck, the reins slipping through Maddie's fingers. Grabbing some mane for support, Madison held on while leaning back and sitting deep, gathering up her reins and pushing the mare forward.

"Absolute charmer," she stated with a grin.

The pair continued on, the redheaded young woman pushing Phoenix out into the lead and circling back round toward some jumps, giving the young mare time to establish a rhythm at the canter before heading her towards a small cross bar. This cleared, she circled back towards a related double, keeping her focus beyond the jump as her mount easily cantered towards and over, took four strides and then leapt over the last jump. Jack smiled as Maddie sat up tall, putting her weight deeper into the saddle, encouraging the mare to slow to a trot, then a walk.

"Reckon you should keep her more collected coming up to the double. She could do five strides between and not have to leap over the last one."

Maddie nodded, pushing Phoenix out again, establishing a canter before going over the crossbar and then sitting a little deeper, using a half halt to check the mare slightly. A little more collected, the pair went through the related distance, putting in five even strides between the jumps and clearing the final nicely, before slowing to a trot and then a walk.

"Excellent!" Jack rode over, offering a high five which Maddie accepted.

"Once more and we'll move on, ey?" she stated with a grin.

Jack nodded, pushing Marlin into a trot as he called back over his shoulder.

"You can't have all the fun. Think we'll go over too."

Maddie smiled as she watched him clear the first and then pushed Phoenix forward as the pair headed for the other two jumps. Clearing them just as well, Maddie let Phoenix canter on, pointing her up a hill as Jack followed behind. The pair slowed to a trot on their mounts upon reaching the top and continued single file down the other side of the hill. A gust of wind picked up some leaves, brushing past Phoenix and Maddie, causing the green horse to dance on her toes.

Maddie sat deeply, talking softly to her mare. Jack watched from behind, his gelding keeping up a steady jog. From here he had a perfect view of the bay mare taking a wrong step and falling forward to her knees and rolling to the side. Maddie was thrown onto her neck before sliding over the horse's shoulder, the pair tangled as Phoenix tried to right herself.

This done she broke into a nervous trot, legs stepping high and reins dangling free from her neck. Jack ignored the mare, swinging his leg over Marlin as he hurriedly dismounted.

"Mads? Maddie?" he asked hesitantly as he jogged over to her lying form.

"Can you sit up?" he questioned, falling to his knees beside her.

"Sure," she croaked out, slowly sitting up.

"Are you hurt?" he queried, checking her eyes for a sign of concussion.

"No," she lied, knowing with certainty that she'd broken her wrist.

"Jack, get Phoenix, please. I don't want her tripping on her reins."

"I'm not leaving you."

"If you don't get that horse Jack Brown, I will never speak to you again!"

"So life will be peaceful for me then," he muttered, rising to his feet and remounting; taking another look at her before heading adjacent to the now walking mare, planning to cut her off.

"Don't move," he ordered before trotting off.

"Not far," Maddie muttered, standing and cringing as pain shot through her wrist.

She slowly and stiffly headed to a nearby tree, using its trunk for support as she sat against it. Shortly after she heard hoof beats headed her way but refused to open her eyes.

"I told you not to move," Jack growled as he hitched up Marlin to a branch; Phoenix tied to the reliable gelding.

"Wasn't far," Maddie murmured, gasping as she felt hands on her arms, pulling her to her feet.

Jack frowned, noting her cringe.

"You are hurt," he commented, lifting her chin so she would look at him.

"I'm fine. Let's head back."

"Fine. But I'm riding Phoenix."

"As you please," Maddie sighed, letting Jack give her a boost into Marlin's saddle before he untied the gelding from the tree.

She felt tears build up as her hand connected with the saddle.

"Get your reins, Maddie."

She looked at Jack, unseeing due to the pain.

"Huh?"

"I said grab your reins."

She picked them up in her left hand, the movement not lost on Jack.

"What's wrong with your right hand?"

"Nothing," she responded simply, avoiding his gaze.

"Maddie..." Jack warned.

"It's my wrist; not my hand. It's broken."

"Stupid woman. Why didn't you say something?" he cried, pushing her left foot out of the stirrup.

"Lean forward."

She did so, surprised to find Jack suddenly behind her, sitting behind the saddle as he reached around her to grab the reins.

"Phoenix," she argued, already relaxing into his arms.

"She's hitched to Marlin. She'll be fine," he murmured against her cheek, as he looked over her shoulder steering the gelding home.

The ride back was long and painful and Maddie concluded she'd happily sleep on Marlin's back rather than have to go to the effort of getting down. Jack brought the gelding to a stop and sat quietly, his arms firmly around her waist.

"Anyone home?" he questioned softly, not certain she'd let him dump the horses to race her off to the hospital.

"Dad. Mum and Mel were planning on being out for the afternoon."

"Ok. We'll find your dad and then I'll tend to the horses," he decided, releasing his hold on her to dismount.

"Can you get down?"

"I think so," she stated shakily, sliding her right leg over the horse's rump, but staying bent over his back as pain shot through her right arm.

Frowning, Jack stepped forward and gripped around Maddie's waist, pulling her from the horse and holding her to steady her. Maddie didn't really want to leave his embrace but her wrist throbbed, demanding attention.

She headed toward the house. Jack tied up the horses before running after her, the pair finding her father in the living room. Mr. Jamison looked up from the lounge, his paper momentarily forgotten when he saw his daughter's face.

"Broken wrist," Jack stated before the older male could ask.

"Right. I'll grab some ice and my wallet and we'll head to the hospital," Maddie's dad stated, rising to his feet and heading out of the room.

"You'll tend to the horses?" Maddie questioned softly, turning to Jack.

He sighed, nodding slowly as she stepped closer, standing in front of him.

"I'll go deal with them now."

"Not *now,*" she commented, smiling softly at his confused face.

Leaning forward she kissed him, capturing his mouth softly before placing another kiss to his forehead.

"*Now* you can," she stated simply, looking up as her father came into the room, keys in hand.

"You coming, Jack?"

"He's agreed to see to the horses," Maddie murmured, heading for the door.

"Alright then. On the way you can give me your version. I'll get the truth off Jack later," he stated dryly, following her out to the car.

Maddie smiled, wishing she could head back in to Jack. *He'll probably be gone by the time I've got this thing in plaster... I wonder if he'll work Phoenix for me while I can't...*

***

Lise and Skye raced childishly out of the house, running toward the stables where the stallion parade would surely have started by now. Technically it was Lise's weekend off but the pair had decided to stay close due to wanting to see the stallions on parade. Lise couldn't help but think that Skye just wanted to stay nearby because Declan was involved in the parade. She held back a smile, not arguing with this line of thought.

The pair slowed to a walk as they reached the stables, walking casually around the corner and putting themselves on the end of a line of clients watching as Trevor walked King past the assembled group of people before turning him to the right and heading back past the group, this time stopping to stand up the stallion so they could look him over.

"He looks good. They're doing a great job with them," Skye whispered, earning a nod from Lise.

After walking the stallion out once more, Trevor headed back toward the stallion boxes while Declan came in from another direction with the young sire, Rocket. Again the stallion looked wonderful but Lise found her gaze traveling to the handler.

An older woman beside the two girls nudged Lise in the side, excitement evident in her voice.

"Look at that gorgeous boy; in his prime, well built, fit. He's absolutely stunning."

Mmmhmm, Lise thought, and then there's the horse.

"And look at those hindquarters, so well muscled... I can't wait to see the foal by him out of my mare this year."

Lise smiled as she realised her mistake. Skye giggled, leaning in toward her friend.

"For a minute there I was unsure if the old bat was talking about the handler or the horse," she whispered.

Lise smirked, feeling a slight confidence in the fact that she wasn't the only one. For all the good taste in *looks* that Skye had, Lise knew her friend had actually noticed a good one this time. As much as he liked to tease, Declan was genuinely nice, laid back and with a great sense of humour. Lise wondered if she should just give the guy a break and return the attention.

August

Wes frowned as the young girl ran toward her, panic evident.

"You've got to do something! My pony's sick. I don't want her to die!"

A group of less than six was down at the agistment stables for the afternoon with the owner out running some errands. Wes had arrived not too long ago wanting to spend some time riding Reign as she hadn't done much since his leg had fully healed. She realised she was the oldest and perhaps the most informed about horses, which didn't leave her feeling too great. After all, even with her Certificate II finished, she still felt she had so much to learn.

"Where is she, Katie?"

The young brunette pointed out toward a nearby paddock where a blue roan pony was standing dejectedly, head not far from the ground.

"Grab your head collar and we'll bring her in to the stables and see if we can get her to eat or drink something. I can have a closer look when she's in here."

The young girl nodded and the pair headed out to the paddock to fetch the mare. Wes noted with alarm the dried sweat across her body and the way the horse seemed extremely fatigued, not wanting to walk despite Katie's insistence.

With a great deal of effort they got the mare out of the paddock and into the tie up area. Wes instructed the younger girl to get some food and water to see if they could persuade the roan horse to eat or drink. Katie ran off to do so.

"I don't think I know this horse," Wes stated in confusion, standing watching her tremble in the stall, the back legs of the mare moving almost without her consent.

"She's been out in the paddock for a long time and Katie brought her in for her first ride in a long time yesterday. They barely warmed up and spent the afternoon hooning around the paddock before Katie turned her out, not taking the time to cool her out," one of the other girls informed Wes quietly.

Wes took in the information, looking over the horse with further concern. Stepping forward she lifted up the lips of the horse to check the colour of her gums, something she'd been taught about in her course. She noted their yellow colour; the term jaundiced being used to describe this. This meant that she could be suffering liver damage. Wes couldn't remember what could be done about this but watched as the mare took no interest in the food or water that was offered to her by Katie. Every now and again she turned to look around at her gut.

Suddenly the mare seemed to lose control of her back feet, them sliding out from under her and she struggled to right herself. Katie let out a squeal, throwing herself to the floor in distress.

Wes directed one of the other girls to walk the pony in case she had colic while she ran inside to grab a vet's number and make a call. She managed to get a vet on the phone and described the mare's symptoms as best she could, receiving the diagnosis over the phone that it sounded like the mare had colic. The vet said they'd be on their way as soon as they could.

Wes hung up the phone and walked over to the pair that was keeping the mare walking. She'd thought colic but wasn't so sure, thinking she could have better described the mare's symptoms to the vet and perhaps gotten a different diagnosis. She watched in alarm as the mare dropped to the ground, Wes yelling at the pair to get out of the way incase she struggled to stand again.

Wes frowned as she saw the mare urinate, the fluid coming out a deep brown colour rather than the normal pale yellow colour. *Something's seriously wrong.* With a big sigh the mare lowered her head to the ground and promptly passed away. Wes half tuned in to the distressed cries of Katie but turned her focus back to the phone, realising she should cancel the vet so as to avoid a fee for the owner when the horse could no longer be helped. She made the call before passing the phone on to Katie's older sister, instructing her to call their mother and tell her what had happened and find out when she'd be able to get home.

A dreadfully slow half hour passed before the owner of the property came home, tending to her upset daughter. She commented that based on what Wes had told her, it sounded like stress colic that had caused the sudden death of the roan mare.

It wasn't until Wes got home that night and logged onto the internet that she was able to do a search based on the symptoms that mare had displayed. She soon discovered that the darker coloured urine was a high concentration of protein due to muscle break down.

Azoturia or Tying Up was what the mare had actually died of. The sudden and extreme amount of exercise after such a long period of rest had caused an extreme build up of lactic acid in the mare and the resulting muscle breakdown had caused the incoordination and eventually, the death of the mare. Wes realised this was an extreme case and that not all Tying Up was a life or death case, but concluded that the lack of a warm up and cool down with the mare would have helped to cause the problem.

She questioned if Katie would actually learn that due to ignorance, she had cost a horse its life.

***

Madison smiled, thankful to see that Melanie had brought in Phoenix for her amongst the other horses that had been in for the dentist to see to. She greeted the equine dentist, Mick before heading to her mare, making use of the couple of brushes she'd carried over in her left hand.

"This horse new?" the dentist inquired, putting the gag on the young gelding, working quietly and pausing if the animal resisted in any way.

Once he'd settled he continued on with his work. On an annual basis, the owners of the East Riding School got the horse's teeth seen to and filed down if need be by an equine dentist. When horses graze, their teeth brush against each other from side to side as they chew and consequently high edges build up that need to be rasped down so the horse can best chew and digest his food. Madison nodded, catching the eye of the older male.

"Yeah. Not sure if he's going to make a riding school horse, though. He's too flighty. I was thinking mum and dad should sell him on to someone who wants a youngster or lease him out to one of our more experienced riders but since last week I'm not so sure."

Madison finished brushing her mare, putting the brushes away in the bucket between the tie up yards.

"What happened last week that changed your mind?"

"He seems to cope fine with walking and trotting while on the lunge and being ridden but once asked to canter, he fell over with a rider on him last week and when being lunged this week he's only been able to keep a few strides of the canter before breaking back into a trot and even then it's a short, choppy stride or disunited. He doesn't seem to know where to put his legs."

"Bingo."

"What?"

"Ever heard of Wobbler's Syndrome?" the older man asked, rasping away at the young horse's teeth.

"No. What is it?"

"A dangerous horse, that's what. They can become uncoordinated at any time and cause serious harm to themselves and anyone around them. What you need to do is blindfold him – use a jumper or something to wrap around his eyes and push down on his head to make him walk backwards. Watch his legs. You'll know if he has trouble doing it."

"And if he does?"

"Sure sign of being a wobbler. Put down job," he replied simply.

Madison frowned, her gaze going over the young animal as Mick removed the gag, doing up the head collar and tying the horse back up to a piece of baling twine. He moved onto a chestnut mare beside the young gelding and started the same process.

"Will I tell you her problem or are you likely to deem her a put down job too?" Madison asked, putting the saddle on her mare rather awkwardly with the use of one good hand.

"What's wrong with this one, then?" Mick asked, ignoring the jibe.

"She's fine out in the paddock but when she's being ridden she salivates the whole time. She seems fine otherwise but alarms clients."

Mick grinned.

"You changed her bridle recently?"

"Yeah..." Maddie replied, surprised.

"Switch her bit."

"Excuse me?"

"Some horses hate copper and a lot of bits are made out of copper. I bet you she's got a copper bit and if you switched it, that'd solve your problem."

Madison grinned as she did up the girth on the saddle, ready to take her mare out to be lunged.

"Simple as that."

Mick laughed.

"I get the impression you like that answer better than the previous."

"You bet."

Maddie left her mare saddled and walked over to the young gelding, untying him.

"I'll put him back in his paddock and bring you another," she told the dentist.

He nodded, looking at her right wrist in interest.

"You're not riding that mare you just saddled up, surely?"

"No, she's too flighty. I have been riding a couple of the other quieter ones in the arena though. A broken wrist won't stop me! But I can lunge this girl with one good hand and she's not going to get out of exercise just because I can't be in the saddle."

The older man laughed, turning back to the chestnut mare and Madison left the tie up area with the young gelding, making a note to look up Wobbler Syndrome, switch the bit on the chestnut mare and *if* this made a difference, to consider carrying out a test on the gelding to see if he didn't have issues with coordinating his legs when walking backwards.

Until then maybe she could introduce some pole work to make the young horse pick up his legs and hopefully be more aware of where he was placing them.

September

"So what's the verdict?" Declan asked, peering over the door of the foaling box.

Lise looked up from where she was sitting with the foal that had been born in the early hours of that morning. She had the baby's head resting in her lap while the proud mum stood quietly over the pair, keeping guard.

"John said to wrap the legs to give them support and he'll assess again in twenty four hours to see if something else needs to be done," she replied, referring to the vet that resided on the property and tended to all of Nirvana Park's horses.

"So he's left that for you to do?" Declan queried, resting his arms on the top of the door.

Lise nodded, preparing to stand up.

"Stay there. I'll grab what we need and give ye a hand."

Lise smiled her thanks, relaxing against the stall wall. The foal was what the staff termed as 'down on it's bumpers'. This meant that the tendons in its legs underneath the pastern joint – otherwise known as flexors – were extremely slack and consequently the foal couldn't stand upright properly. Because it was such a young animal, it was possible to support the legs with firm bandaging and sometimes this was all that was needed to strengthen up the legs and they would sort themselves out in a short space of time.

It was amazing how twenty four to forty eight hours could see a huge strengthening in the young horse's legs.

Five minutes later Declan returned with the cotton wool, crepe bandages, Elastoplast and some scissors. Lise held the foal firmly while Declan applied first the cotton wool, wrapping this firmly with the crepe bandage and securing it in place with the Elastoplast. Once done the pair exited the box, standing in the doorway to watch the foal as it attempted to stand. Lise grabbed at the door when the young colt got to his feet and promptly fell down again. Declan put a hand to her shoulder, stopping her.

"Has he had a feed recently?"

"Yeah. I held him up while nursing when John was assessing him."

"Then leave him be. It's not essential that he get up now but if he does do it by himself, then great. If not, you can come back in half an hour and help him up to feed."

Lise smiled, realising she was going into overprotective mode. She looked at the young man before her and released her hold on the door. Unsure why this time of wanting should be any different to the others, but willing to go with it anyway, Lise leant forward, kissing Declan soundly. Needing breath, she reluctantly pulled away, finally daring to catch his eye. She wasn't sure what she read more in his gaze – amusement or wonder.

"That was unexpected," he stated carefully, refusing to enlighten her as to how he was feeling.

For all that Lise had so carefully analysed and put under the category of flirting, she was suddenly finding that these moments could be moved to some new categories – 'being nice' and 'teasing'. How could she have gotten it so wrong? Unable to find something to say and uncomfortable by the silence she spun on her heel and walked away, rushing around the corner of the foaling boxes and through the trees toward her house.

It took Declan a minute or so to digest that she had actually kissed him... and then ran. Following in the direction he'd seen Lise go, the young Irishman raced toward her house.

Pausing at the door he knocked tentatively, this quickly turning into a loud banging when he received no reply.

"Lise, lemme in. C'mon, open the door."

"Why?" she called out from the other side, sitting on her couch as she hugged a pillow to her chest.

"Because I want to see ye."

"Because..?" Lise prompted, not sure what she expected as a reply, but wanting some confirmation that she hadn't made a fool of herself.

"*Because*, I want to talk to ye."

"About?"

"About why ye should open the door when I first ask."

"Well, it sounds like I need convincing as to why I should open the door, so if I do so to let you in, then that defeats the purpose – doesn't it? You're gonna have to convince me from out there," she stated in all seriousness.

Declan didn't reply and she waited a few minutes before treading quietly to the front door to open it, revealing the fact that he had gone.

***

Trevor smiled, his gaze moving from the misbehaving young horse to the person holding on. Charlie refused to let go despite the rears and lunging forward.

"That's one for the long paddock," Trevor stated as the horse quietened down, allowing the older man to get closer with the hose, letting cool water run over the swollen knee.

"The long paddock?" Charlie queried.

"Now I'm feeling old if you don't know what the long paddock is. It's the road. When I first had ponies we turned them out on the road to graze if there wasn't enough of a pick in the paddock. It was quieter on the roads back then though and in a small country town. I'd let this guy out cause it'd hardly be a loss," he finished dryly, avoiding the set of teeth that were aiming for his arm.

Trevor growled at the colt, being mindful of the fact that the horse's ears were still pinned back as he continued to hose the leg. The young horse was a speller being agisted at Nirvana Park in between racing preps. He had been found with a swollen knee on the feed run that morning.

Charlie – the current work placement student – and Lise had checked the perimeter and within the paddock to try and find something that could have caused the cut knee but found nothing obvious.

Kingsley had agreed to keep the colt outside and the knee didn't require bandaging but the colt was being put on a course of penicillin to cover bases. After hosing the knee for a period of time Trevor turned off the hose and wiped down the knee. This done he collected a syringe that had been resting in a bucket away from the misbehaving horse.

Taking the cap off the needle, he drew some air into the syringe and returned the cap before shaking the syringe to mix up the penicillin that tended to set at the bottom of the syringe. This done, Trevor pushed out any excess air in anticipation of injecting the fluid.

"You given many needles?" Trevor asked Charlie, his attention turning to the student who was patting the colt and talking to him quietly.

"A reasonable amount of intramuscular," Charlie replied, looking at Trevor.

Satisfied, the older male nodded.

"If this boy behaves well enough perhaps you can carry out the rest of the course of needles. We'll see how he reacts to this one," he stated, standing beside the horse and grabbing a skin fold with his left hand before inserting the needle with his right.

Drawing back with the syringe, he made sure that after injecting the needle into the horse's neck that he hadn't hit a blood vessel or vein. If this were the case, blood would seep into the penicillin that was residing in the syringe. Instead nothing traveled through the needle and Trevor was satisfied that he'd inserted the needle correctly into the neck. Expertly he pushed the twenty milliliters of white fluid into the neck, withdrawing the needle and rubbing over the area where he'd inserted the fluid, telling the colt what a good boy he was as he did so.

"Have you ever seen a horse have a reaction to penicillin?" Charlie asked of the older worker as he made his way back to the paddock where the colt was spelling.

"Yeah. Not pretty at all. It's scary to see a horse so completely out of control and then drop dead. I've heard some horror stories too. Honestly, I'd rather let a tafie loose with oxytocin than with some penicillin. As it is, legally we're not supposed to be giving these drugs but it's ridiculous to have to get out a vet every time you need to give a horse an injection, especially on a horse stud when there's hormone manipulation with many of the mares. It's just not viable so it's more effective for us if we teach students coming through how to do things properly.

"When you're doing this guy over the next few days I want you to make sure you've got someone with you. You'll need the extra hand anyway, I suspect. I don't think this boy will make things easy on one person trying to jab him with a needle each day. I'll help you out tomorrow but over the weekend you'll need to get Lise or Declan to help you."

Charlie nodded, saying he would do just that. Trevor smiled as the pair headed toward the smoko room for their morning tea break. This TAFE student was working out very well.

***

Madison frowned as she watched Jack put Phoenix through a series of two and a half to three feet high jumps. The mare was going very nicely by the looks of things. *Would help if he actually told me when he was going to work her.* Since she'd broken her wrist, Jack had agreed to keep Phoenix exercised and school her over jumps but otherwise, he'd not spoken to her at all. Unhappy with this arrangement, Maddie watched him tie up the filly before heading into the feed room to make up a mix for her.

Once done he headed back out to the young mare and untacked and groomed her over. Madison slipped into the feed room to grab the bucket for him but rather than heading out to the pair, sat herself upon one of the feed barrels, waiting patiently.

Jack paused in the doorway when he spied the redheaded woman sitting with the bucket of feed he wanted. She held it out to him, holding tightly when he tried to take it from her.

"Why are you mad at me?"

"I'm not," he responded tersely, tugging at the bucket.

"Well, I'm convinced, thanks for that!" Maddie replied sarcastically, holding on tighter.

With a mighty tug Jack managed to free the bucket from her grip but sent her sprawling from the barrel in the process. Dropping the bucket he caught her, breaking the fall.

"Well I guess someone who was mad at me wouldn't have done that," she stated quietly, looking at him.

"I told you I'm not mad at you," Jack murmured, refusing to meet her gaze.

Smiling Maddie wrapped her arms around his waist, stepping in toward him. Quickly Jack's hands came to rest on her arms, pulling himself out of her embrace.

"What's wrong?"

"I'm just trying to work out how I fit into the equation when I saw you kissing another guy not too long ago."

Madison frowned, lost.

"What guy?"

"Tall fella, lean... dark hair..?"

"Oh, Johnny! We had a bit of a mix up - he thought I was Mel... I kindly informed him otherwise... think they've got everything sorted now," she stated quietly, watching Jack's gaze fall to his feet.

She bent at the knees so that she could look up at him.

"Have *we* got things sorted now?"

"Almost," Jack responded, leaning down to kiss her.

Maddie smiled against his mouth, her arms coming to embrace his figure as she returned the kiss.

"I should have done that a long time ago," Jack murmured, tucking some hair behind her ear.

"*You* should have? I don't think you would have made any move if it weren't for me Jack Brown! I can't believe you're taking the credit for-" she was cut off as Jack kissed her again.

"Maddie?" he queried when he pulled back to look her in the eye.

"Shut up," he grinned, cutting off any further protest with another kiss.

***

Lise walked out of the stables and waited as her eyes adjusted to the bright sunny day. She paused indecisively when she spied Declan with Kingsley and Jordan Smith, one of the stud's bloodstock agents. The three had their attentions focused on a recently turned two year old colt that Declan was handling.

Kingsley had high hopes for the young horse, anticipating him to be a two year old racer and had decided he wanted to syndicate the young colt, while keeping the majority share in the hopes of being able to stand him at Nirvana Park in two to three years time.

After a walk away from the manager and bloodstock agent, Declan headed back towards the pair, standing the horse up for inspection, facing the young animal on the left-hand side as the bloodstock agent checked over the colt under the eye of Kingsley. Curiosity overriding her feelings about Declan, Lise joined the group. She'd loved the colt from the night of his birth and couldn't wait until he was racing. She knew Kingsley was trying to think of a name for him as well as finding the right owners to take part in the syndication.

"How about Anticipation?" she offered as a name, moving to the right hand side of the horse, giving him an affectionate pat.

"Not bad..." Kingsley commented, his gaze not leaving the agent.

"Unless of course someone else interprets it as excessive waiting," Declan commented, a glint in his eye when Lise caught his gaze.

He's referring to last night, she thought, returning her attention to the equine before her.

"Then again anticipation can be good," he murmured, surprising her as he came to stand beside her figure on the right hand side of the colt.

Ignoring the shivers that had been caused by the soft tone of his voice she moved aside so that the bloodstock agent could view the rest of the colt. She tried to ignore the confusion, the voice that was telling her she should have stuck around after she'd kissed him to find out how he really felt. Especially considering he was acting like he hadn't minded. But why couldn't he just say so?

October

Trevor frowned, pulling up the work Ute beside one of the spellers' paddocks. It housed the chestnut colt that had cut open his leg a week or so back. He looked fine now, Trevor noted as the young horse cantered around the yard, one of the maintenance men in hot pursuit... barefooted.

Confused, Trevor called out to the man named Glen. Pausing in his run, the older male bent over, dragging much needed air into his lungs. He glared at the colt that was now stopped at the other end of the paddock, watching the two men, something hanging out of his mouth. Trevor's eyes widened when he recognised the item.

"How did Djanibi get one of your socks in his mouth?" he questioned, amazed.

"I was fixing the float in the water trough and took off my boots and socks to get in there to fix it and I turned around to get the shifter and there he was, sniffing at my things! I tried to shoo the bugger away and he picked up one of my shoes and trotted off with it. Well, I went after him see, and he dropped my shoe and came back for a sock!"

Trevor bit his lip hard to avoid laughing at Glen as he looked to the colt that was still standing in the opposite corner, shaking his head up and down, the sock in his mouth. Not managing to hold in his laughter, Trevor chuckled as he strolled up to the playful equine, putting a weathered hand on his neck and giving him a pat while reaching up with the other hand to pull the sock out of the colt's mouth. Djanibi protested, not wanting to open his mouth.

Trevor moved backward with the colt and with his right hand reached up to his jaw, placing a finger in the side of his mouth toward the back of the jaw where no teeth were.

The colt opened his mouth, releasing the sock and Trevor headed back to Glen, keeping an eye on the playful colt in case he decided he'd like a piece of a staff member as well as their clothes.

"Is the trough fixed?" Trevor asked as he handed over the damp sock to the maintenance man.

"Nearly. I've got to adjust the float and untie it," he stated grudgingly.

"Can you do so from outside the trough?" Trevor asked with as much sincerity as he could muster.

Glen stated that he could and proceeded to put on his soggy socks and shoes before going back to work on the trough. Trevor headed out of the paddock, ambling between the rails and pausing to look at the chestnut colt still down the far end of the paddock, watching the maintenance man curiously.

"If someone doesn't point you toward the long paddock boy, I do fear you're going to end up gelded. You'll want to be an impressive racer to stop that from happening," he murmured heading back to his Ute and on toward the feed room to collect the afternoon feeds.

***

Wes grinned in the sunlight, enjoying the warmth on her back as she worked the shampoo through Reign's coat with her fingers, massaging and cleaning his body. The palomino gelding fidgeted under the flow of cold water, eager to be done with. Wes held him with one hand, using the other to work the rest of the shampoo through his coat before turning the hose back on and rinsing the cleaning product out of his coat, mane and tail.

She inhaled deeply, the smell of the horse shampoo appealing to her senses. Her eyes took in the welcome sight of Reign's now peroxide blonde mane and tail, a stark contrast to the green/brown that the dirty tail had been before the wash.

Having rinsed out the shampoo she turned off the hose and got the conditioner, putting a dollop on her hand before putting that through his mane and tail. While she was working with the conditioner, another friend had picked up the hose to rinse out their shampoo while another sat on a nearby rail of a post and rail fence, holding onto the end of a lead that was attached to her pony's head collar. The fat pony was happily grazing along the fence line.

"Come on you two! Hurry up already," she grinned, kicking her feet impatiently against the lower rail.

"Ellie and I have almost finished, Jodie. Patience is a virtue," Wes replied.

The younger girl rolled her eyes, sighing when the pair had each finished rinsing out the conditioner.

"Finally!" she exclaimed, jumping off the rail and dragging her placid equine friend up the driveway toward the large expanse of overgrown nature strips that marked either side of the road.

Wes and Ellie followed, their ponies only too eager to fill their bellies while drying off in the sun. Wes and Ellie sank down in the grass beside Jodie, also enjoying the sun.

"I think I could do this every day and not grow tired of it," Ellie stated, content.

"Agreed. But in the future it'll be on my property," Wes replied.

"I think I'll have to agist my horse at your property, you make it sound so good. You'd better make sure it's nearby," Ellie warned, Jodie nodding in agreement.

Wes smiled, her eyes moving over the golden coat of the horse drying before her.

"I found a property in Lancefield for an assignment as part of my Certificate II and it looked good to me! Perhaps there'll be one in that area when I'm looking for land... one big enough to agist a hundred horses and have a big indoor arena... and jumps."

"I'm there if you get the indoor. That's what we need here for winter."

Wes smiled, not disagreeing. She'd loved the lessons that she'd had at TAFE in the large indoor that had a mirror down one side so you could see your position as you rode. It was great to help spot faults and improve but would be awhile before she had the two hundred thousand needed to set up an indoor... never mind the cost of the land!

For now, Wes was more interested in daydreaming about her property and gaining as much experience as possible with the horses rather than worry about how she would be able to afford it.

***

Lise stumbled, working quickly to right herself. She looked up in surprise at Declan who had just purposely bumped into her as he passed to get to the feed room in the stables. Rather than apologise, he just winked as he passed Lise, a smirk crossing his features.

Frowning, the young brunette trudged toward the feed room, getting sick of his arrogant and cheeky behaviour that had been on full display for the past two weeks.

Even Kaye and a few of the others had noticed the difference in him and Lise wasn't sure she liked it, especially when she wasn't seeing any other difference in him. He wasn't making a move, but he sure wasn't holding back from suggestive comments or finding ways to make her blush. Truth be told, she was sick of it.

Choosing to ignore him she headed for a group of buckets, each being full of feed. She picked up four to take out to the mares in the stables. Declan stood in the doorway, looking down at her.

"Are you going to move?" Lise asked him while looking past his figure out to the stables.

"Mmm... nope."

Sighing, Lise put the buckets down on the ground and stepped closer to Declan, peering up at him.

"Don't tease me," she stated simply.

"Sorry?" he frowned, confused.

"I kissed you..." Lise stated tentatively.

"Recently? Because I'm sure I would have remembered that happening," he mocked her, his whole demeanor changing.

She persisted.

"I kissed you not that long ago and you seemed surprised... but I was reasonably sure then and am almost certain now that you're flirting with me."

"And..?"

"Not *and*, so. *So*," she emphasised, "if you're intentions *aren't* to flirt with me, then you should know that it appears that you are... but," she struggled to continue.

"But... if I *were* flirting with ye..." he continued for her, taking a step toward her small form.

"Then, I... I..."

"Then..," he leant forward, his lips resting at her ear, "ye wouldn't mind?" he inquired, noting her shiver with a small smile as he leant back.

"Don't tease me," she whispered this time, her eyes closed.

Smiling, Declan leant in toward her again, his tone quiet.

"I'm sorry it *appeared* that way," he whispered sincerely.

Confusion crossed Lise's features and she frowned, questioning how she had gotten it so wrong... again.

"I meant for it to be *obscenely* obvious that I was flirting with ye," he continued calmly.

Immediately her frown deepened, her eyes flashing angrily as further confusion clouded her judgment.

"Damn you, McAlister!" she all but growled, giving the young man a sharp shove and towering above him as he fell back, supporting himself on his elbows.

"Do you treat all relationships like a game?" she cried out, containing herself quickly she continued quietly, "I really shouldn't bother."

He watched her storm off, presumably toward the foals and grinned despite the predicament he'd put himself in. Well, it was simple to solve really. A lot of apologising and groveling would probably break down Lise's resolve, though secretly he hoped not. Although he was keen to issue a relationship with Lise beyond that of friendship and learn more about her, he was having fun discovering what made her tick and learning her small insecurities that made her all the more attractive to him.

He was achieving this by testing their friendship boundaries. At the moment, anything could happen – and it amused him to no end.

November

Lise frowned, unhappy with how much the mare seemed to be straining without a sign of a foal. She hadn't seen the water break yet and was reasonably sure she hadn't missed it, making her question if something was wrong. Her fears were soon confirmed when rather than the white birth sac expelling from the mare's vulva, she saw a rich red colour.

Quickly putting on a pair of gloves and grabbing a scalpel blade out of the foaling kit, she entered the yard where she'd put the mum to be and went to her tail end, talking soothingly to the mare on her side. Lise first tried to break the placenta with her hands but not being successful at this, she cut it with the scalpel blade, making a tear which she made bigger with her hands, effectively breaking the mare's waters. This released the foal, allowing the mare to continue pushing and expel it fully.

Quickly Lise broke the birth sac and pushed out any fluid from the newborn's nasal passage, helping it to draw in its first gasps of breath. She watched the baby's breathing, looking for any signs that she should be worried.

Lise had just helped with what was known as a red bag delivery. The placenta didn't burst at the cervical star as is supposed to happen, releasing the foal in the amniotic sac. When this break didn't happen, the mare's water's didn't break and the foal was starved of oxygen until the birth sac was broken and the foal delivered.

If this happened and the mare was unassisted, there was a high probability of death for the foal.

Luckily, red bag deliveries weren't common but Lise was glad she'd experienced a few and was getting used to recognising the warning signs; like a mare in distress – getting up and down, straining with no sign of a foal and the big one – the mare's water not breaking which marked the second stage of labour and the impending arrival of the foal. A red bag delivery couldn't happen after the mare's water breaking.

Lise focused back on the pair as the exhausted mare raised her head and whickered at her baby that was throwing its legs about, trying to make sense of things.

Lise knew that she'd have to keep a close eye on the newborn over the next twenty four to forty eight hours just in case it had been compromised during birth due to a lack of oxygen. Lise loved working with the newborns but was aware of the numerous things that could go wrong with the neonates in their first seventy two hours of birth; things that could result in death.

This put a large responsibility on night staff and those working with newborns but she loved it.

In twenty four hours she'd take a blood sample from the foal to find out its immunity level. This was given to the foal through the mare's colostrum and if the reading didn't turn out to be of a good level, there were things the staff could do to help prevent the foal getting an infection due to a low immune system.

Noting that it was nearing midday she sighed, concluding it'd be a long day keeping an eye on this baby amongst the afternoon chores. Leaving the pair for the time being, Lise wandered off to get the mare they were covering that afternoon.

***

"Have ye done any bandaging before?" Declan queried the TAFE student, smiling when she shook her head, stating that she hadn't.

"Ok. First ye want to make sure the wound is clean which we've done with the saline water and this one we're going to put some prednoderm on to reduce swelling and keep it clean. We put that on the gauze swabs and then directly onto the wound," Declan instructed the young woman, doing so as he explained.

"Next we want to pad the leg for support. We use cotton wool for this. When ye wrap a leg, the cotton wool and the vet wrap should go in the same direction. Always. And ye want the pressure to be the same the whole way around. I'll let ye feel how tight it is once I've wrapped it, ok?"

Noting her nod of affirmation, Declan wrapped the cotton wool around the mare's leg, covering the cut on the cannon bone. He worked his way down toward the fetlock joint and above, just below the knee.

"Now for a cannon wound, ye don't want to wrap over the knee or the fetlock if ye can help it. We don't want to restrict movement of any joints. Because it's the near side, we wrap the bandage anticlockwise from the inside around the front to the back. With the cotton wool covering the wound, we then wrap the vet wrap in the same direction and this sticks onto itself," he continued while wrapping the leg.

Preempting his need for the Elastoplast next, the young woman grabbed a roll off the stable ledge, holding it out for Declan. He smiled his thanks, pulling a pair of scissors out of his back pocket to cut the heavy duty tape after he'd wrapped it around the top of the bandage. He mimicked this for the bottom before standing to admire his handiwork.

"There! C'mere, take a look at it and have a feel how firm it is to give ye an idea of how tight to do it. When we replace it in three days, ye can have a go," Declan directed, taking the lead off her and holding the mare while she inspected the bandage.

"Now if it was an offside leg, the bandage would go clockwise."

She nodded, taking it all in as she put a finger between the bandage and leg to feel how firm it was.

"How many times will you have to change the bandage?"

"The first week or so we'll change it every three days unless it comes loose. It's not too bad a cut so it should only be a few weeks and we can change it less as it heals. I think the cannon is probably the easiest to learn to bandage so ye lucked out there. Ye'll be a pro by the time ye leave this place!"

She laughed, saying that would be great before taking the mare off Declan and leading her out of the stables to a day yard so that the mare could stretch her legs and get a pick. If the leg looked good in three days when the bandage was to be changed, they would put her back out with the other mares rather than leave her locked up and away from companions.

Declan left the student to it, heading down to the stallion paddocks. Rocket had a lunchtime cover and a possible breed that evening. With this in mind, he bypassed the covering shed, making sure someone was setting up before he went to get the young stallion.

Trevor would tease the mare and then Declan would bring in Rocket. He grinned as he thought about how well the stallion was doing in Australia. He had a full book for the season. In fact, they had to turn people away whom were now enquiring about sending their mare to the popular stallion. After all, the stud didn't want to tire the young stallion out.

He had one hundred and twenty mares booked in for the season which potentially meant two hundred breeds if mares didn't get in foal due to not breeding at the right time, or health issues with older or 'dirty' mares. Probably ninety of the mares were full fee paying clients which meant at $11,000 per mare, the stud would be bringing in close to a million dollars for the season.

This wasn't unusual for a medium or larger stud in the racing industry. In fact, some studs made in the tens of millions and higher each breeding season.

A good stallion was worth a small fortune. Of course, a stallion was only as good as his fertility and consequently, his foals. With the money made in foaling fees on the property, the stud probably made enough over these five months to cover the annual wages of one to two staff.

Of course, expenses were high - staff fees, feed for the horses, maintenance of the property, vetting and numerous drugs and first aid supplies and accommodation for staff. Still, Declan knew Nirvana Park was well managed and he looked forward to being a part of the successful operation for years yet.

***

Wes glanced over to the folder beside her, her hand brushing over its surface almost as if to convince her that it was on the seat beside her. She and her parents had just entered the town of Wangaratta and her father was navigating his way out to the TAFE property where she'd be having an interview for one of the horse course's she'd applied for. Her mum had suggested she bring a folder with details about her previous horse experience/qualifications. This was what the folder contained: her three lots of work experience at two racing stables and a riding school; the short stint she'd done at Riding for the Disabled, volunteering fortnightly, her Certificate II in Horse Studies and the Certificate of Excellence she'd received and her D Certificate she'd gotten at Pony Club.

In a short time they pulled into the driveway of the property, Wes noting a bulky chestnut in a yard by himself, looking more quarter horse than thoroughbred. They drove down a poplar lined drive and pulled up beside a white sedan, stopping here.

Mirroring her parents, Wes stepped out of the car and headed toward the well marked office, being greeted by a staff member who ushered them inside, carrying out the formalities before offering to take the three for a walk around the property. Wes agreed immediately, taking in the setup of the property with much interest, her parents interjecting with questions now and again. The four strolled down a terracotta coloured laneway, brown paddocks either side; their guide pointing out the importance of fattening up the mares in the spring growth so they were sustained throughout summer when the grass dried off.

"Of course they get fed and checked daily and we've put a round bale in each paddock which is topped up when eaten. Ahead is a heap of dry mares for the season. Most are in foal although a couple are yet to be covered, late for the season. See that mare?" he asked of Wes, pointing out a dark brown figure away from the others but in clear view.

"How's she look?"

Wes frowned, glancing her over. She thought the mare's 'udder' looked a bit big but otherwise she looked well.

"Fine, I think."

"How can you tell? She's stationary."

Wes nodded, comprehending that the mare could be lame and she'd only know through watching her walk.

"She lost her foal a couple of days ago – the one I mentioned before, hence being by herself – she's not yet buddied up with another horse."

Hence the udder full of milk too, Wes thought, mentally kicking herself. They turned around here, a few mare paddocks being pointed out as the perimeter of the property. Wes wasn't sure how big the place was but figured it was equipped and big enough to teach her about the industry. They finished the tour at the paddock they'd driven past when entering the property, Wes being introduced to the education facility's stud and his racing history. *So he is a thoroughbred... go figure.* This done, they returned to the office, Wes and her parents sitting opposite their tour guide and another teacher they'd previously been introduced to.

Wes answered questions about herself, her horse experience and why she wanted to do the course before handing over the folder containing her certificates, work experience records and pony club experience as well as a photo of her and Reign. Their guide closed the folder with a smile and looked at Wes.

"We can't officially say this yet, but welcome to TAFE. You'll be starting in February."

Wes grinned, shaking the hand offered to her as she stood, her parents mirroring her movements.

The three headed out to the car, her mum already marking a list provided by the TAFE of possible places for her daughter to live while studying. Crossing out those too expensive and those only offering four days live-in a week, she suggested they get lunch and then visit a few of the possibilities. Wes and her father quickly agreed, ready for a celebratory lunch.

***

Declan called out to Lise as he spied her across the yard. Excited he ran toward her, slowing enough to catch her up in his arms rather than knock her off her feet. Surprised, she held on tightly even when he let her feet return to the ground.

"Good news?" she queried, curious at how excited he was.

"Great craic!" Declan confirmed with a grin, "Kingsley just got a call from Park Grove Stud in Ireland. They want to stand Rocket over their breeding season because he's a three quarter brother to their top stallion. They feel they'd be able to cover a decent book of mares and have offered the owners a deal. They told Kingsley and he's happy to not have to worry about another stallion here in our off-season so was only too eager to agree."

"But won't you miss him?" Lise queried, still not sure why he was so excited.

"Miss him? I'm going with him! Kingsley mentioned how well he'd been going with his first covers last year like, and he's looking just as good this year and all and he said they'd be stupid to not have me continue to handle him and look after him. They're paying me way over and he's covering the cost of me return flight. I'll get to catch up with the family while I'm there. It's brilliant!"

"It sounds very exciting. Congratulations," Lise smiled lightly, finally releasing her grip on his arms, suddenly eager to get out of his embrace.

Having other plans, Declan grabbed her wrists, refusing to let her walk away.

"Ye don't sound too impressed," he stated softly, catching her gaze.

"Why wouldn't I be? It's wonderful news, honest."

"I'll be back. It's only for six months."

Lise raised a brow, a smirk making its way onto her face.

"I promise I won't miss your annoying habits, Declan. Enjoy yourself in Ireland," she retaliated, pulling herself out of his grip, eager to leave his questioning gaze.

December

Maddie frowned, looking at the long list of riders and the comparatively short list of available horses.

In two weekends time the East Riding School would be hosting their annual show that ran at the end of each year, tying up all the skills that riders had been learning each week. The show was the last day the school was open before things closed up for the school holidays giving workers and horses alike a rest for about a month.

There were classes to cover show jumping for those that loved to jump high and fast, jumping equitation for those more focused on style and striding, over and between jumps, dressage, games and bareback classes.

Things worked well during the week with a specific number of classes available each day but when it came to everyone riding on the same day for a competition, it became all too apparent how many clients made use of the riding school and how few horses. It was Maddie's job to sort out the timetable now that her mother had assigned particular riders to horses. Half the fun was fitting all the kids into the timetable for each class they wanted to participate in. What further complicated things was that some ponies had two or three different riders who were competing in two or three different classes.

She'd already sorted them into riding capabilities for each of the classes as the school was making available to its students three different levels of jumping as well as three different dressage tests dependant on the rider's capabilities.

Maddie felt this was supposed to make things easier when it came to organising times for riders, but looking at the list she now wasn't so sure.

Sighing she started with the list of youngest riders, making sure that as she marked down each child for a class, she left room in between for them to be able to get to their next class. The older riders she'd decided to leave until last, assuming they'd have fewer troubles with getting to classes on time.

A couple of hours later she'd had more than enough and had nearly finished, feeling quite proud at having set out a feasible timetable that gave the ponies that were to be used multiple times, a bit of a break at least twice during the day.

Having worked out the times on paper, she now started entering the information into a template her mother had created.

It listed the name of the horse and had a column for times, events and their location and the rider. This was to be printed out, laminated and pinned to the horse's saddle blanket so at any time during the day, all the rider had to do was look down to find out where they were due next and at what time.

"So are we going to be able to have a smooth running competition?" Jack queried as he stood in the doorway, smiling at her.

Madison returned the smile, gesturing for him to enter the room. Jack came up to her, placing a kiss on her cheek before sitting down beside her, looking over the timetable.

"And more importantly, who's judging the jumping?" he asked with a cheeky grin.

Madison rolled her eyes.

"There's no way you're judging both classes I'll have you know. Of course Mel is judging the dressage which will go practically all day so that leaves one of us to take jumping equitation and bareback while the other takes show jumping and games. I think mum's going to take half of the games while show jumping starts and at that time you or I will be taking the bareback classes in groups. That should be finished in time to start the equitation class. So which do you want?"

Jack shrugged.

"Honestly, I'm happy to judge either - most of my students are doing both jumping classes," he stated with a grin, ignoring Maddie as she rolled her eyes again.

"So I'll judge whichever class you don't want to."

"Stop being so accommodating, it doesn't suit you," Maddie chastised, looking at the list before continuing to enter the data onto the computer.

Shortly after she turned her attention back to Jack who was watching her quietly, obviously amused.

"I'll take the show jumping and games."

"Sounds good. Now, Miss Jamison, do you think there'll be time for a couple of instructors to go for a ride after the competition is all finished with?" he queried, standing up from his seat.

"Thanks to daylight savings, I think that should be more than possible," Maddie replied with a grin, allowing Jack to kiss her before leaving the room.

Refusing to let herself be a gushing girlfriend she turned her focus back to the competition timetable, concluding if she finished it in time, she could catch Jack before he headed off for the day.

***

Lise stared at the horse before her, brushing out the caked mud on the yearling filly with all her energy. She reasoned that if she focused entirely on her work there wouldn't be time to ponder the fact that Declan was on his way out of the country. *And what a mess I've left things in.* She'd managed to avoid him the couple of times he'd sought her out to talk before heading to Ireland for the Northern Hemisphere's breeding season. Pushing back thoughts of him choosing to stay in the country he called home, she switched to the other side of the young animal, brushing again.

"You going to leave any hair on that horse?" a soft tone inquired from the other side of the door.

Not recognising the voice, Lise looked up in surprise, wiping some hair off her brow.

"If I don't, will you hold that against me?" she asked, hands on hips.

The young male smiled, shaking his head.

"What smart person would choose to make enemies of someone they'd just met?"

"I know a lot of males that claim to be smart but would do just that," she replied, turning back to the bay filly who was nudging at her arm.

"Sounds like you've been hanging out with the wrong kind of males. I hope you find one that changes that opinion," he commented softly, stepping away from the box.

"You wouldn't happen to be the extra pair of hands that Kingsley's just hired, would you?" Lise called out after him, curiosity getting the better of her.

"That would be me. I'm Jeremy," he called back as he walked away.

Lise smiled, hoping for his sake that he was right. She really wasn't in the mood to put up with another male that thought the world of himself. It'd only make her think of McAlister. Frowning again she turned back to grooming the filly, moving on to the body brush once she'd removed all the dirt with the curry comb. Using this softer grooming tool she swept it over the young equine's body, flicking up dirt and grit as she worked, pausing every few strokes to wipe the brush against the curry comb to clean it and then going back to brushing, working from the neck to the tail.

This done she stepped out of the box in search of a towel. She wandered down to the wash bay remembering having seen a few hanging up to dry earlier in the day.

"Meet the new worker?" Trevor asked as he stepped out of the wash bay, handing Lise a damp towel.

She smiled her thanks.

"Jeremy? Yeah... when did he arrive?"

"Only half an hour ago or so... seems very eager to check out the farm rather than unpack. Reminds me of someone else I know."

Lise smiled, looking up at the older man.

"Are we rugging the yearlings today? I'm not sure I can handle another day of grooming animals covered in mud. It'd be different if the weather weren't so changeable but they all seem to be making a point of going for a roll just before they're due to come in."

"I did mention it to Kingsley and he agreed. It wouldn't hurt to keep them that bit warmer, anyway. It'd sure help their coats for the sale. Will I give you a hand once I've finished grooming this last one?"

Lise nodded, looking down the breezeway.

"We'll need to sort through all the rugs first."

"No need. Kaye and the other two girls are. They've already got the sizes out and are working out which would fit which horse."

Lise looked back at Trevor, brows raised in surprise. The older man just smiled before heading back to his horse. Lise did the same, using the damp towel to wipe over the filly's face, cleaning eyes and nose after having done the rest of her head. Finishing shortly after, she removed the head collar, giving the young horse a pat on the cheek before going to find Trevor.

The pair started down one side of the stable block and Lise noted with surprise that Jeremy returned to help Kaye to start rugging on the other side while the other two continued to sort through rugs. Tony was out on the afternoon feed run, checking the spellers, broodmares that were still on the farm and any other horses out in paddocks.

Lise stayed focused on holding each yearling as quietly as possible while Trevor introduced them to being rugged for the first time. They always started off this task in pairs, one holding the horse while the second worked first from the near side, with the rug folded into thirds, sliding it over the horse's wither and letting it rest gently over their back. This proved to be difficult at times because it was in a horse's make up to resist things on their back. Once managed, the front strap was done up and the rug then gently opened up until it covered the horse's whole body.

Generally this was managed relatively easily on each horse as long as the pair worked quietly. The real trouble was more likely to show up when the leg straps had to be done up. Trevor worked his way quietly down the filly's rump, lifting the side of the rug to undo the clip before looping it around her back leg and doing it back up to the clip. Lise praised the young horse, patting her on the neck before the pair both moved to the right hand side so Trevor could do up the second leg strap.

This achieved he exited the box quietly, Lise heading to the door with the young animal before quietly letting her go and quickly slipping out of the box. They both grinned when the filly let out a squeal and started bucking around the box, protesting her new item of clothing. A couple of minutes passed and she quietened to walking around the box.

"Think she'll take it alright," Trevor murmured.

Lise nodded and walked with him to the next box, her attention moving to the opposite stable where Kaye was chattering incessantly, having a rather one sided conversation. Lise smiled to herself as she watched Jeremy working quietly with the young colt who was kicking out each time he tried to put the leg strap around the animal's back leg.

"You'd think Kaye would shut up at least until he's gotten that strap done up," Trevor muttered, pausing with Lise to watch.

Jeremy didn't seem bothered by the noise however, rubbing his hand over the horse's leg and up the inside to get him used to the idea of something moving around his leg. Eventually the colt stopped kicking out and let Jeremy do up the strap.

"Looks like he's got a lot of patience and he knows what he's doing."

"Does that mean we can let him work with Kaye all the time?" Lise asked hopefully, emitting a chuckle from Trevor.

"Not if we want him to stay working throughout the season. He may appear patient but no one's that patient."

"Guess not," Lise replied, moving toward the next box, Trevor following.

***

Wes grinned as she brought Reign in from the paddock, watching the three agistees that had ignored saddles for the day and were currently in the middle of one of the property's dams, sitting on their horses that were knee deep in the water. As she watched, one slid off into the water and started collecting mud from the bottom, placing it on her rotund mare's back.

Laughing she concluded she might as well ignore the saddle for the day and join them. It was already hot and the day still had to reach its top of 35 degrees. Why not enjoy a splash in the dam?

It didn't take her long to pick out Reign's feet, brush him over lightly and put his bridle on although he did protest for a few minutes, working hard to keep his head out of reach so she couldn't put on the leather contraption with the metal bit.

Tiring quickly from having his head up in the air he eventually lowered his neck, letting out a breath of air as he did so. Wes rolled her eyes.

"You really don't know how to stick things out, do you?" she queried, patting him lightly on the neck.

Ten minutes later she feared she'd have to retract that statement, having found that it was true - you could lead a horse to water...

Reign wasn't interested in drinking it, pawing at it, rolling in it or anything else that involved him getting his hooves or any part of his body wet, it seemed. Wes frowned, thinking back to the Pony Club session they'd had off site and the water jump her gelding had been so against considering. Eventually one of the parents had managed to lead him in but Wes feared he was going to be a lot more obstinate about this murky water.

She watched as the others stood in the middle still giving their ponies a mud bath while a couple of others were astride their horses, cantering through the dam, doing a lap around at a canter and coming back through, flicking up water as they continued their mad dash. Laughing Wes scooped up some water in her hand, flicking it at her horse. Unimpressed the palomino gelding pulled back against the lead, shaking his head as Wes continued to flick water at him.

Finding that it wasn't working, he lunged forward, splashing Wes as he connected with the water. Amused by his antics she moved further into the dam, pulling him with her now that he'd decided he could afford to get wet.

The rest of the afternoon consisted of lots of mud, squealing and giggling before the day started to cool down and each rider took their beloved equine over to the hose to be rinsed off before the weather got too cool. Wes was tired by the end of the day but very happy to have gotten Reign into the water and to have had a relaxing day splashing about and riding bareback. What could beat summer time and playing with horses? If something could, she couldn't wait to find out what it was.

Year 3

January

"Hi Jackie, how are you today?" Melanie asked the young rider, smiling at her as she checked over the tightness of the girth before allowing her client to mount.

"Very well, thanks Emmy! Ready to try and get this girl onto the correct lead at the canter, though! We've been progressing really well in our rhythm and straightness but it's so frustrating to think we can't do a simple twenty metre circle at the canter."

Melanie had had a quick chat with Madison about Jackie and realised that they both had different ideas about how to go about solving this problem.

The young mare that Jackie was working with she'd recently been given from a work colleague who didn't have the time to invest in educating her. Jackie who was an accomplished rider was only too happy to take on the challenge of educating a young horse - especially when it was for her own horse. Last week she and Maddie had been working on getting the mare Indi to pick up her right canter lead. They'd had a small amount of success and Melanie was ready to try another approach. After all, every horse was different and different methods produced different results.

Jackie floated her horse to the riding school for her lessons so it was important to both of the twins that they equipped her with ways to go about working on improving her horse while she was riding at home by herself.

"Remind me how we were going about things last week," Melanie stated casually, wanting to find out exactly what Madison had been teaching and to see how much of this exercise Jackie had understood.

Swinging into the saddle Jackie found her right stirrup and picked up her reins, pushing the mare into a walk to warm her up as she talked to Melanie. The young redhead walked with them around the arena, telling Jackie to stop at every third letter to ascertain that Indi was listening to 'whoa' as well as 'go'.

"We were using the corners to ask for the canter lead as the horse is already bent in the direction we want to go, making it easier for them to pick up the correct canter lead. If she picked up the incorrect lead, I would bring her back to a trot on the long side and try at the next corner."

"This didn't really seem to work so we moved onto working on a twenty metre circle at the sitting trot and asking her again in a corner and cantering down the long side. She got the idea once but then continued to pick up her left lead so by making the circle smaller, we made it harder for her to balance if she picked up the incorrect lead and this seemed to work. We finished after she picked up the correct lead twice in a row and just popped over a few jumps to give her a bit of a break before the end of the lesson."

"Good. Have you had a chance to practice over the past week?"

"Yes and I'd say we managed the correct lead using that exercise about fifty per cent of the time."

"Well, that's a start. How about we pick up the rising trot and I want you to do some leg yielding down the long side after we've warmed up in both directions. When you're warmed up at the trot I want you to turn down the three quarter line and leg yield back to the outside rail, really getting her to move sideways and forward off your leg."

Jackie nodded, pushing her young mare into a trot, picking up the correct rising diagonal and completing a lap and a twenty metre circle on the right diagonal before changing rein across the arena from the letter B to E and repeating the process on the left rein, changing the diagonal she was rising to as she crossed over the letter X, situated in the middle of the arena.

After warming up at the trot, she followed Melanie's instruction, turning up the three quarter line and with Indi's nose pointing slightly toward the inside of the arena but keeping pressure on the outside left rein, Jackie applied pressure with her right leg, sliding it just behind the girth as she did so.

Responding quickly, the young mare continued moving forward at the trot but also to the side, moving away from the leg pressure. Jackie gave her horse a quick pat before continuing on down the long side at the rising trot. Reaching the short side of the arena she again turned her mount up the three quarter line, repeating the process and finding Indi just as responsive.

"Excellent, Jackie! She's really listening to you. How about we change rein and see if she's just as responsive to moving off your left leg."

Changing direction produced the same results and Melanie smiled with pleasure as she realised how far the pair had come in the few months that Jackie had been riding Indi. She instructed Jackie to have a canter around on the left lead before getting her to stop in the middle so Melanie could explain her plan for picking up the right canter lead.

"Today we're going to try something a little different. As the saying goes, there's more than one way to skin a cat and we can use a lot of different exercises to encourage Indi to pick up the correct canter lead when going around to the right. I want to use leg yielding today and the fact that she's so responsive to moving off your leg means that we should be able to try out this exercise and produce the right result. I wouldn't suggest using it if Indi was unclear about what was expected from her in the leg yielding, does that make sense?"

Jackie nodded.

"Perfectly. We can hardly use an exercise she doesn't understand to try and get a result from something else we haven't quite mastered yet."

"Exactly. We're going to pick up the rising trot again and I want you to trot her around on her right rein, again turning up the three quarter line and leg yielding off your right leg. I want you to try it at a sitting trot this time. You'll have to keep a tight outside rein on her and bring her back if she ever mistakes the leg pressure to mean to go into a canter. I want her moving off your leg to the outside. Once you've reached the outside, I then want you to apply your canter aids. Does that all make sense?"

"Yes... do I wait until we reach the corner to ask for the canter or ask for the canter sooner?"

"As soon as she's reached the outside rail I want you to ask for the canter. So you're going to be applying pressure with your inside leg to push her to the outside and as soon as she's hit the outside rail straight away ask her for the canter. I want her to be used to bringing her inside hind leg underneath her which she does for the leg yielding and as she's doing so, the canter aids should be applied to encourage her to strike off on her left hind leg which will give us the leading right foreleg."

Jackie smiled, nodding.

"Gotcha! Let's give that a go."

The pair moved out into a sitting trot and as she came up to the three quarter line, Jackie directed Indi to turn up it and started leg yielding, pushing her to the outside with pressure from her inside leg. As they reached the perimeter of the arena she applied her canter aids and Indi struck out with her right foreleg landing further in front. Instantaneously Melanie and Jackie let out an excited cry.

"She did it!"

"Perfect, Jackie! Let's try it again to make sure the timing is right and that Indi will do it again."

The pair repeated the exercise three more times, only once Jackie not quite getting the timing which resulted in the young mare picking up the incorrect lead. The rider recognised this to be a fault of her own and accepted the incorrect lead.

After repeating the process again and this time getting the correct lead, Jackie directed the mare in toward the centre of the arena where Melanie was standing. She stopped just before the young instructor.

"That felt great, Emmy. Thanks so much!"

"You're very welcome. Now you've got two different exercises to use when you come across that problem in a horse that you're riding. Now that we've got the hard work out of the way, how about a little fun for the rest of the lesson? Some jumps?"

"I thought you'd never ask," Jackie replied with a grin, taking her foot out of her left stirrup to shorten it a couple of holes.

***

Wes looked at the closed door, suddenly feeling at a loss. She turned to face the older woman who was in the kitchen with her.

"They're gone."

"Yes, dear it appears that they are. It's a long drive back to Melbourne."

Wes nodded, turning toward the living room door and making her way through the room to the bedroom that would be hers for the next two years.

Her parents had just left after helping her put all her belongings into the house that had been opened up to her in Wangaratta. Of the living possibilities that they'd checked out late the year before, Wes' parents hadn't particularly liked any of the possibilities for their daughter to live in.

Some only offered four or five days a week when there were weekends that Wes would need to stay in Wangaratta as part of her TAFE course. Others were asking too high a price in rent or were older single men offering a room which wasn't at all ideal in her parents' eyes. Wes could understand that and was glad that her mum had gone to the trouble of seeking out possible accommodation elsewhere.

In the end she'd advertised in the churches in the town, looking for someone who had a spare room that would be willing to take in an eighteen year old for a two year duration while she completed her Diploma of Horse Studies.

An older woman, similar in age to Wes' grandparents had agreed to take her in, providing a home including meals, not just a place for her to sleep each night. Wes was very grateful for the accommodating older woman but at that point was feeling like she'd just seen off the two people that she actually knew and now was in a town of 25,000, all strangers.

Taking a deep breath she turned her attention to her computer that her tech savvy parents had set up for her and opened up a music program, playing some John Mayer as she went about unpacking her clothes and sorting out the books and writing utensils she'd need in a couple of days time for her first day at TAFE.

She was excited about starting the two year course but also very nervous. She knew it would be smart to ride out to the complex that afternoon to get an idea of how long it would take her to get out to the school and consoled herself with the fact that maybe she'd be able to find someone that could give her a lift in the following days.

Apparently the majority of the students that attended the horse focused education facility came from Melbourne, New South Wales and some as far as South Australia and Queensland. Rarely were there students who were actually from the town of Wangaratta or surrounding areas. At least this meant everyone else was in the same boat of having had to acquire and get used to a new place to live as well as starting a new course. That fact comforted Wes as she went about making herself feel at home.

Two days later she set out on her bike at eight thirty with the view to get to TAFE in time for nine o'clock when all the students would be assembled together for the first time.

As the students gathered Wes noted with relief that she wasn't the only student to be arriving on a bike rather than driving in through the front gates. The majority of cars that did come through the front gates had a P plate up high in one corner of their windscreen, telling Wes that most would be around her age. As it turned out, of the eighteen students – 3 male, 15 female – only a handful were over twenty and the majority had come straight from high school.

Some had horses of their own and a few had even been working with horses in racing stables alongside school but there were also those who had next to no experience with horses, making Wes feel that although the main experience she had was with her own horse, she wasn't going to be out of her depth.

Shortly after nine, the eighteen students were introduced to the four teachers that would be imparting knowledge to them over the next twenty four months. After being introduced, one of the teachers took control, directing the students into one of the portable classrooms where she introduced herself properly, going over the experience she had acquired over many years in the equine industry. She then turned the focus to each of the students, asking each one to introduce themselves, what experience they had had with horses and why they were doing the course.

Wes' was surprised to find at the end of the day that they were informed of an assignment that would be coming up but relaxed when she found out it was to be done in groups on an excursion that the whole class would be attending the following week. The Melbourne Premier Yearling Sales were on over the month of February and this seemed perfectly timed to introduce the students to the world of thoroughbreds that the majority would end up working in once finishing their diploma.

Wes looked forward to seeing this horse sale as she'd never been to one before. Until then, she realised she had a week to get to know some of the students and potentially find a ride to and from TAFE each day.

February

Lise smiled gratefully at Jeremy as he handed her a salad roll, taking a seat beside her. There was a lull in clients wanting horses to be paraded and Jeremy had taken advantage of the quiet time, making his way up to the cafeteria to get lunch for the staff that were attending the sales. It was just after two in the afternoon, a bit late for lunch but when it came to sale days, this wasn't unusual.

Lise had been in a foul mood for most of the morning and quite thankful for being so busy so that she could try and distract herself from thoughts of Declan.

Kingsley had mentioned that morning that he'd received an email from the Irishman, detailing how well Rocket had been going overseas. The young stallion had settled in well and was focused on the job. Declan was enjoying being back in his home country too, it seemed.

So much so that he'd not bothered to email Lise or pass on a message through Kingsley.

Lise knew she'd avoided Declan just before he left but figured this just confirmed what she'd feared - he was toying with her. Jeremy seemed to sense her unhappy state and avoided asking Lise if something was wrong, instead helping her out if he saw that she needed it but otherwise leaving her alone.

Lise was thankful for his sensitive observation of her, this heightening her like for the young man.

She looked up from undoing the plastic wrapping on her roll, her gaze drifting toward the sound of scuffling shoes. In front of the pair a young filly was spooking at a stroller that was being pushed along the bitumen parade area designed specifically for walking out horses for clients. Lise sighed, amazed at the owner's complete ignorance.

"Do they honestly think that the pathways are so they can push their prams around with their young children? What sane person brings a baby along to a horse sale anyway?"

she muttered, watching as the handler of the filly managed to get her under control and lead her back to her box.

"Almost as bad as all those TAFE students milling about, getting in the way," Kaye mused, seating herself on the edge of the seat beside Jeremy.

"You're kidding, right?" Lise replied, looking at the redhead in surprise.

"Why would I be?"

"The TAFE students do have a purpose for being here, even if it is sorely obvious which ones don't have the equine experience... yet," Jeremy replied, taking Lise's side of the argument.

"Well I think they should learn how to handle and be around a horse safely before they are let at large at a yearling sale. Fancy a group of them getting in the way earlier and expecting me to parade a horse for them in the middle of a full draft for an actual client!" Kaye replied, standing and heading back down the breezeway.

"I'll bet she scared the group when it came to her refusal to do so, too. She's probably just made it extremely hard for them to do an assignment that a teacher set," Jeremy muttered, his gaze going to a group of students sitting quietly on a grassy rise, watching a few yearlings parade up and down.

Putting his roll down beside Lise, he strolled over to the group.

"Did you guys still need to see one of our horses? Sorry about before but we've got the time to show you one now, if you'd like," he offered, smiling softly.

Wes stood up quickly, smiling.

"That'd be great! It's lot number 259, the grey filly by Made King," she told him, turning back to her classmates with a smile.

She'd been paired with another girl her age and one of the guys who was quite a bit older. The girl seemed to know quite a bit about the thoroughbred industry, but not a lot about conformation which Wes had read up on before coming to the sales. She'd also studied it a bit for her Certificate II.

The whole class had been put into groups of three and been given two horses to look at and compare. How were they presented? Were they well groomed; free of shavings from their box? Were they clipped or not? Had their manes been pulled and neatly presented, hooves painted black or clear or left alone? Did the staff wear uniforms and present themselves well? Was it easy to identify a horse while it was being paraded if someone walked past and the animal caught their eye?

Wes found that through this short assignment she was learning a lot already about the thoroughbred industry and how the horses were presented to potential clients and this excited her. She watched eagerly as the older male brought the stunning chestnut filly out and stood her up before the three TAFE students.

Wes directed the male in their group to note down her brands and any white markings before asking Jeremy to walk the filly out for them. Thankful for the second chance they'd been given after being rudely told to go away earlier in the day, she was eager to get as much information about this horse as possible to fill in for their assignment and she wanted to do it all and move on before there was a chance of running into the redhead who hadn't been at all happy with their presence.

Jeremy walked the filly out well, a numbered tag clipped onto his jeans so that any passersby could look up the filly's number in the catalogue if they so desired. Wes made a mental note of this before turning her attention back to the horse when Jeremy again stopped before them, standing the young horse up for further inspection.

"So do you know this filly is part of King's oldest crop?" Jeremy directed his question to the male in the group.

"I didn't, actually," he replied, making a note on the assignment sheet.

"Because he was a sprinter it'll be really exciting for the stud next year when his first two year olds start to race. They've been well received at the sales, or at least really popular when it comes to people wanting to look at them. We'll find out truly how popular when they go through the ring this afternoon."

"How much is his stud fee?" Wes queried, thinking this would help them to estimate how much the filly would receive in the ring which was another question for their assignment.

"He was $13,000 for the 2002 season but I believe Kingsley's going to be raising it... to $16,000 the rumour has it. He had a full book last year so it looks like he can get away with raising the fee," Jeremy replied, patting the filly that was standing patiently.

The three moved to stand in front of the filly, Jeremy applying pressure at her chest to get her to take a step back so that she was standing up squarely in front. With her standing evenly on both front feet, the TAFE students were able to assess if the legs were straight. Wes thought that maybe the filly was a little offset and made a note to ask the other two what they thought afterward. A horse that was offset rather than having a straight line through their forearm, knee and cannon bone, tended to have the cannon set slightly to the outside of the knee, which could put extra pressure on the leg. Wes had learnt that although not desirable, it wasn't a trait that tended to turn buyers off a horse.

She did some quick math in her head, concluding that even if the filly didn't make that particular price, technically the owner would want to make at least $30,000 on her at the sales to make a profit.

The students had been informed that a yearling preparation of eight weeks in duration which was the general length for any sale prep cost around $5,000 per horse. Including the stallion fee plus agistment costs for the mare and vetting costs when first getting her in foal and foaling fees, Wes' guessed that at $30,000, the owner would be making a $10,000 profit. For the sake of this new stallion and the owner, she hoped the filly made even more and more importantly, went on to race – and well.

The three moved to the right hand side of the horse and then behind, Jeremy again moving the grey filly, this time forwards a step so that she was standing square behind. Once finished, Wes thanked him before moving on with her two classmates, eagerly discussing what they'd seen.

"That was really nice of him!" she stated as they headed up to the parade ring, noting that the first horse they'd assessed would be heading up to the outside ring shortly where they could see the young colt being led around before going into the ring to be bid on.

Lise watched the group walk away, chattering excitedly. She followed Jeremy as he walked down the breezeway, putting the filly back in her box, patting her before exiting the stall with the head collar and lead in hand.

"Is that your good deed done for the day?" she queried with a smile, latching the door after him.

"I only get to do one?" Jeremy asked with alarm, hanging the head collar and lead up with the others that were stored in a spare stall.

He winked at Lise as he picked up a bottle of drink, taking a swig.

"I'm liking you more every day," Lise stated, laughing.

"You know, me too!" Jeremy replied, earning another laugh in response.

The pair managed to finish their late lunch just before another client turned up, wanting to see all the fillies. Kaye and Kingsley got one of the colts ready that was due to go up to the ring very shortly while Jeremy and Lise were kept busy taking out and bringing in each filly that they had available.

***

"So are we agreed on $35,000, then?" Wes asked her two classmates.

They were up at the ring having just watched lot number 257 go through the ring. The young colt had been passed in at $18,000. Wes had been told that most of the studs set a reserve for their yearlings and if they didn't reach that reserve while in the ring, they were taken back home and either sold privately or the owner kept them and raced them. She wandered how far off the reserve the colt had been.

"Agreed. I think it might be a bit high, but she was a lovely looking filly," the young woman replied, her gaze flitting to Wes and then back to the ring where 258 was pronounced sold for $11,000.

The three stood quietly, making sure not to scratch anything or buzz away any flies for fear the gesture would be counted as a bid.

The young horse entered the ring with ears pricked and eyes wide as she pranced on a tight lead, Jeremy working to get her to walk properly rather than prance.

"Lot number 259, a grey filly by Made King out of Bella Babe. This is King's oldest crop of foals and we have high hopes for them as two year old racers. Will we start the bidding off at ten thousand?" the auctioneer queried, looking around the auditorium.

The filly snorted, her tail sticking up like an Arab but stepped out well, showing off her ground eating walk.

Wes knew this to be a good thing as her teachers had informed the class that a horse with a ground eating walk would more likely catch the eye of a buyer. If they had a nice walk, it was assumed they had a free moving gallop.

The filly after doing a lap was stood up by Jeremy. He halted her at each side of the ring and in the middle, making sure all could get a good look at the filly while she was in the ring.

The bidding faltered at $25,000 and Wes thought it was all done when suddenly another buyer put forward a bid and the bidding went back and forth between the new bidder and the first bidder. The fee was eventually settled at $41,000 with the newest bidder receiving the final bid.

Wes grinned when the gavel hit the auctioneer's desk, announcing the sale of the filly. Jeremy led the grey yearling toward the exit, leading her out when a staff member opened the door. Upon her exit the next yearling entered the ring from an opposite door. Wes looked at the two with her who were obviously ready to head back outside. With a nod the three walked around some bidders, heading for the exit.

Wes smiled as they ended up outside where Jeremy was leading the filly back to the block of stables where Nirvana Park's draft was kept. *I think I'm going to like working in this industry very much.*

March

Lord, can I really do this? So we weaned the foals today – that is, removed their mums from the equation. Thank God that doesn't happen to humans at six months of age!

For the past few weeks at TAFE we've been bringing the mares and foals in out of the paddock, putting each pair one at a time into the crush, one person holding the mare while a student stupid enough to be standing around gets 'volunteered' to go into the foal crush and magically put a head collar on the bub before being released, resembling something like the exit from a chute on a bucking brute at a rodeo. Can you say fun? Neither can my crushed foot, or my bruised knee... or the side of my chin that feels rather tender after it collided with a foal's head.

I know, I know… those parts of my body can't talk but if they could, fun wouldn't be in their vocabulary!

The rodeo act continues as the (lucky) holder of the mare walks around in calm circles while the (hmmm… so many words to put here) person who is in charge of the foal (reading that statement while switching the words 'person' and 'foal' would have a better effect) rush about in a haphazard daze, pretending to go in a circle.

Baby lunges forward and back, stops suddenly and takes off trotting which is hilarious for any of the so-called teachers as the attached student tries to stay with the young horse! Extreme sports… hmmm, we should set up teams and make it an Olympic event.

So over a few weeks things have been improving and the foals have been learning to be led with a handler beside them and walk where directed. Today the teachers decided to add in something to spice things up a bit.

I thought they were getting all healthy on us when they introduced the oranges but soon realised the more awful truth. The oranges were accompanied by injections (I know, what a likely pair, right?)

The injections were tetanus and strangles vaccinations to inject the foals with a small dose of the disease with the aim to prevent them from getting either in the future. The first couple of foals were done by our teachers and then with the empty injections we got to practice jabbing an orange. All kinds of weird.

Then we got to actually administer an injection which I got perfectly the first time, aiming, quickly inserting it into the neck and just as quickly pushing in the dosage before pulling the needle out. It felt good to be able to get it right the first time! Pity the second time didn't mirror the first. Very bent needle on the way out!

So after they got the joy of a needle in the neck, we all pondered what else we could do to annoy the babies. The teachers obviously already had a head start as they'd planned to wean the young ones that day.

So in pairs, the band of students and small herd of horses headed into the stables and then we each exited the box, those holding onto the mares exiting with their horse, leaving the foal behind.

The next job was walking the 500 metres or so (read: 5km hike) to the farthest paddock where the 500 kilograms of sudden energy were to be housed, without their young. On return to the stables we discovered one of the teachers had turned on the radio full bore to drown out the anxious cries of the young, now without their mothers. A painful noise... seriously, can I do this?

The next day we had a day focused on being in the classroom to allow for the young ones to settle in their new environment without mums.

The morning's theory was based on safe fencing and we discussed checking a fence line before putting horses out into a paddock that hadn't been used in awhile. Makes sense and is relevant considering the weanlings will be getting put out in the paddock by themselves in a couple of days. I did find it amusing that the emphasis seemed to be the fence line – never mind the rest of the paddock!

Mentioned this to Kat, a classmate and she was suddenly scribbling furiously on a piece of paper. I tried to ignore her, to focus on the teacher who was droning on about the excitement that is droppers and spacing them out well for visibility.

It was very difficult to hold in the laughter when Kat handed me her finished work, a sketch of a group of Tafies scouring the fence line, looking for any possible hazards while the bunch of weanlings stood huddled together in the middle of the paddock – right next to the pile of nails, needles, broken pieces of wire and wood that were piled in the middle.

This was rather amusing but the extremely random tiger also in the paddock had me working rather hard to hold back a laugh. Teacher caught me smiling and returned the large grin. Why not let her think I find fencing interesting?

The afternoon came and we got down to something a bit more interesting – the bones of the horse's leg and the tendons. After going through the theory, teacher took us all out to the stables where a freezer was storing a heap of legs for dissection.

Oh yeah, gotta tell dad about the teacher that keeps legs in a freezer in the stable. Apparently they'd gotten them from the knackery so we could at least have a look at the actual bones in a horse's leg and the tendons.

The whole seriousness of the situation was lost on me when another classmate faced me, looking at the leg with focused attention before very gravely stating.

"I'm sorry, but I don't think she'll ever race again."

***

Melanie excused herself from chatting with the mother of one of the East Riding School's students and followed her mum into the feed room.

"You haven't got a gap between lessons anymore. A pair that were supposed to ride yesterday and didn't show up obviously got their dates confused. The young girls and their parents are here now and I'm not eager to turn them away. I've sent out one of the weekend staff to get the horses ready if you can give her a hand and I'll talk them through the run of things and get the waiver agreement signed. Neither has riding experience so it should be a basic lesson for you."

Melanie nodded, grabbing a head collar and running after the worker to help her catch horses and tack them up.

Fifteen minutes later two ponies were tacked up and Melanie was finding out how little experience and confidence her clients had with horses. She talked them through moving around the horses safely and instructed the pair on how to untie their horses and lead them over to the arena.

The younger of the pair had trouble leading her pony and quickly found herself trodden on. Unaware that she was causing any pain, the pony stood quietly, still on the young girl's foot.

The screaming stopped when Melanie managed to move the pony off her client's foot but quickly she was handed the reins and her client moved far from the horse. Melanie frowned, continuing on into the arena, shadowing the first, older girl. Not seeing any other way to check over the first pony and help her client onto the horse, she managed to convince the younger client to take the reins back and stand quietly with her pony, albeit sobbing as she stood.

The lesson continued at this nervous, slow pace with neither girl wanting to ride by themselves, even at a walk.

Consequently Melanie worked with one at a time, leading the ponies and eventually getting the girls to weave between cones, practice lots of stopping and going and by the end they were doing a little bit of walking by themselves. Melanie considered this a big step for the extremely nervous pair but it was the first lesson in a long time where she hadn't had first time riders having a bit of a trot. Accepting that this may have to wait another lesson or two, she congratulated the pair on their control of the ponies at a walk and taught them how to dismount correctly and lead their ponies back to the tie up area.

Although still wary of the horse's feet, the younger girl had managed to forget about her sore foot while riding, showing Melanie at least that she'd had fun and been kept occupied.

The afternoon continued in a similar fashion for Melanie however, as a lesson plan she'd put a lot of time and effort into went out the window when her class deemed it boring and just wanted to do lots of cantering and jumping.

The end of the day couldn't come soon enough and Melanie was happy in the afternoon wind as she threw hay out to the hacks, even when it flew back in her face if she was standing in the wrong spot. All it meant was that she was nearly finished for the day.

As she headed back out of the paddock with the now empty wheelbarrow, Melanie spied a familiar figure at the gate, awaiting her return.

"What are you doing here?" she asked with a smile, pushing the barrow through the gate that Johnny held open for her.

"I feel like I haven't seen you in ages, especially when I didn't have my younger sister having lessons over the school holidays as an excuse," he replied with a wink, following her over to the hay stack where Melanie placed the wheelbarrow.

She stood with a smile as he reached out to remove some hay from her hair before leaning in to give her a kiss.

"Hi," Johnny stated softly, grinning.

"Hi. You got time for a coffee?"

"Sure. Can I take you out for one though?" he questioned, walking toward the house with her.

"If you can handle waiting for me to shower and change, then absolutely," she smiled back at him before heading into the house.

"I believe I can manage that," he replied, sitting himself in the lounge room to wait for the young redhead.

***

A few days after the twelve young horses had been weaned, Wes was starting to get used to the idea of walking with these six month old horses, doing laps around the shed with the tanbark floor that the education facility used throughout the year for varying reasons.

Now that they'd been handled and seemed to have accepted the fact that they were suddenly without a mother, the weanlings were ready to be put out in small groups in a yard to kick up their heels for a bit. The TAFE facilities included a group of four large yards that could contain groups of horses for a short amount of time.

Each year these yards were used to introduce the weanlings to their 'nanny'. The nanny was usually an older mare or gelding that was known for its quiet and unflappable nature and was put out in the paddocks with the young horses to act as a guide and to provide discipline if needed. The education facility used the yards to put the weanlings out and put the nanny in the yard next door so they had a chance to meet each other over the fence.

Wes observed this with the other students for fifteen minutes or so after all the babies had been put out with access to their future nanny. The older gelding spent some time sniffing at a few of the babies before turning his attention to the dirt yard he was in, sniffing at different areas of the enclosure.

After getting the students to ensure that all yards with horses in them had water, their teachers informed them it was time for lunch. In the afternoon they'd have theory focused on the care of stud horses before finishing early so they could all head out to bring the babies back into their stalls for the evening.

Wes recognised that now that they'd been weaned, the foals would be spending each evening in the stables, out of the cold as in less than eight weeks time they would be getting sold at the June Weanling Sales near to Melbourne.

Wes looked forward to the idea of taking part in the sales by working in them this time rather than just observing and doing an assignment but questioned if it was possible for these barely handled babies to be in sales condition in less than two months. She concluded it had to be possible considering the TAFE turned out weanlings for the sale each year. Wes smiled as she headed inside for her lunch, picturing parading one of the young horses around the ring while bidding hands went up everywhere in the auditorium, elevating the price it would be sold for. *I wish.*

April

"I'll be back in a minute. Just wait here."

Wes stared after her TAFE teacher as if she had grown two heads. *Why is she trusting me with this young excitable animal?* Not convinced her capabilities would be able to withstand holding onto a green weanling if it suddenly found itself frightened, she nervously eyed the animal as it fidgeted impatiently.

It seemed an eternity to Wes before the teacher returned and informed her that the young horse could be put in its box. She then instructed Wes to follow her out to the house paddock where a group of weanlings were being walked while their boxes were mucked out.

Wes did so and then stood with the TAFE teacher as a group of her classmates walked the perimeter of the paddock, leading the six weanlings around at a prompt walk.

"If you look at each one closely, you should be able to see which are walking well and those that are dragging. See how the Desert Sun filly is powering along?"

Wes nodded, talking in the little chestnut filly that despite her small size covered a lot of ground at the walk. One of her classmates who was also small in stature was doing a great job of walking out the filly. Wes watched in interest as two handlers were switched under the instruction of the TAFE teacher. This resulted in both young horses walking better. This was the main focus as when the students were at the Weanling Sales, they wanted their horses to be walking forward at a brisk pace to best show off their movement and build for potential buyers.

"Some partnerships just don't work so it's worth seeing if a change of handler works for the horse."

Wes nodded before her attention was suddenly turned back to the small chestnut filly that had reared up, the pull putting pressure on her handler's knee, popping it out of place. Wes and the teacher hurried over.

"Can you take the filly?" Wes was asked.

She looked hesitantly at her friend on the ground and then nodded slowly.

"You're sure?"

"Yup."

Wes took the lead off another classmate who had been holding her filly as well as the chestnut. The student who had fallen was helped out of the way and after she was checked over and deemed ok, the walking continued, the teacher not wanting to disrupt the other students and horses. Half a lap around the small paddock and the chestnut filly lunged forward before rearing up suddenly, spinning and striking out with her near fore.

Wes fell to the ground as the hoof clipped beside her left eye, just above her temple. The young horse ended up loose in the paddock and tore around with the lead streaming from the head collar. The students came to a hurried stop as she tore about but didn't manage to prevent the young horse from slamming into the front end of another before continuing on.

Wes sat up slowly as the teacher rushed to her side to inspect the damage. She looked to the young horse that had been hit as the teacher called out to the handler.

"Don't let her move! I think she's in a bit of trouble, looking at that shoulder," she called out, noting the filly didn't want to put weight on the leg that had been slammed into.

"Two students in a short space of time! Are you ok?"

Wes nodded, putting her hand to her head.

"It hurts but I think I was pretty lucky."

"Maybe but we'd better get you checked out by a doctor," she stated, looking back at the rest of the group to see that the loose filly had been caught.

She rose to check on the other horse and directed all the students back toward the barn, walking slowly with the filly that was now putting weight gingerly on her leg. Wes noted that the teacher looked relieved and concluded that it wasn't as bad as first thought if the young horse was bearing weight on the sore leg.

While the horses were getting put away the teacher pulled Wes aside and cleaned up her cut, concluding it wasn't too deep.

"I think we'd better get you checked for a concussion though at the local hospital."

"Ok... I fell off a friend's horse yesterday and blacked out, so maybe a hospital is a good idea," she stated with a small smile.

The older woman rolled her eyes.

"Are you trying to get yourself hurt?" she questioned with a small smile.

"No, I promise."

"Good. Now have you got someone that can take you to the hospital?" she questioned.

Wes nodded, slowly standing.

"Ok. Well it's time for everyone to finish anyway, so make sure you get checked out before tomorrow."

Wes stated that she would before she headed toward the stables in search of her lift for the afternoon. She sighed, thinking it'd been an eventful afternoon and questioning if young horses were really for her.

***

Lise ran her hand down the young filly's near foreleg before moving her hand across her back and down her near hind leg, talking quietly as she went. This was the last weanling that she and Jeremy had to work with and Lise was more than ready for lunch and then the afternoon feed run. She'd had enough of the babies for the day although she usually loved working with them and seeing them slowly come to trust and respond to humans.

The stud started weaning about February of each year, starting with the older foals that had been born August of the previous year. With the number of staff they had, they worked through lots of ten or so, box weaning them by taking the mother's away and relocating them on the other side of the farm in a large paddock. The foals were then worked with and introduced to being handled over the duration of two weeks before being put out into paddocks based on gender.

They'd had nearly sixty foals to wean this season and had one group left that had been born late November and over December. These wouldn't be done until mid May however so that the youngest foals were at an age where they could live independent of their mothers. Studies showed that the age of five months was a good time to wean a foal as at this point the mare's milk was at its nutritionally lowest value and the foals had been introduced to eating solid foods and their stomachs could handle a substantial amount of this on top of grass and any other roughage.

Lise was thankful to know that they would get a break from the repetitive work once this group was put out. As the filly she was working with protested at her hand moving down the left back leg, she kept on talking, trying to soothe her.

"Whoa there darlin', it's alright."

"There you go again," Jeremy murmured quietly as Lise managed to run her hand down the filly's leg and pick up the hoof.

She patted the hoof with her hand before slowly releasing the leg and letting the filly stand on all fours. Happy with how things had gone, she now turned to Jeremy with a questioning gaze.

"There I go again?"

"When you are reassuring them, especially if you call them darling, your voice takes on an Irish lilt," he commented with a smile.

"Too much time hanging around an Irish jerk," she muttered, stepping out of the stall as Jeremy removed the head collar before following her.

"Jerk? I'd heard you got along quite well with Declan. Aren't you looking forward to him coming back for the season?"

"He's an idiot," Lise replied simply, waiting for Jeremy as he did up the head collar around the metal rack that was attached to the stable door.

An idiot who doesn't know how to keep in touch, she thought. Jeremy paused beside the door with a smile.

"What?" Lise asked, managing a small smile of her own.

"Want to do something tonight? Go out for a movie or a drink?" he asked, standing quietly awaiting her reply.

Lise smiled.

"That sounds like a great idea."

***

Pointing her gelding toward the next jump, Wes looked ahead, trying to keep her gaze up rather than on the jump below the pair that were moving toward it. Reign lifted in time, rose over the jump and landed, throwing in a buck for good measure. Caught behind the movement of her horse, Wes went flying through the air over his shoulder and landed on her side, her body crushing her hand. Laying for a moment she stared at the gelding grazing contentedly beside her before slowly sitting up and then rising, awkwardly pulling the reins over his head with the right hand while she carefully held her left against her body.

"Damn it... this isn't good. Thanks very much, buddy."

Taking a steadying breath she headed out of the jumping ring and toward the older woman who ran the property, thinking it was just her luck that on the weekend when she'd taken the effort to make the three hour train trip home she also managed to get on her horse and promptly come off and hurt herself.

"Think I'm in a bit of trouble here," she stated casually holding the enlarged hand out for the older woman to inspect.

"I'm going to have to agree with you. Better ring your parents and head off to the doctors for an x-ray."

Back in Wangaratta on Sunday night and off to TAFE the following morning, Wes sighed, frowning as she looked at her hand, tears welling in her eyes at the pain caused due to carelessly knocking it against the half ajar door in her haste to get to the car waiting out front. She opened the door to the spluttering vehicle and dumped her bag before jumping into the passenger seat.

"What happened?" the driver asked, glancing at her before reversing rapidly down the drive.

"Reign threw me. It's not broken, just huge," Wes replied with a grin, catching her classmate's eye.

"Not sure how I'm going to write in class."

"Never mind lead the weanlings," her friend interjected.

Wes nodded, secretly relieved that she wouldn't be expected to handle the excitable animals. She realised for her confidence she needed quite the opposite but was happy for a break.

Half an hour later she wasn't so sure she liked the way she'd gotten the break as she struggled to take notes in class and therefore to stay awake as she sat idly in the classroom. She welcomed the change of pace when the teacher split them into groups to start an assignment on developmental diseases and she and two other young women from the class had been given Wobbler Syndrome to research.

Wes liked learning about new topics but didn't look forward to organising times to meet up with classmates and complete the assignment on top of two others. She sighed, thinking it'd be a long afternoon of one handed typing.

That afternoon the first year students were due to bring in the weanlings from the paddock, do a lap around a small holding yard and then stand them up before putting them in their boxes. Wes watched with the teacher again, surprised to find herself frustrated that she couldn't walk one of the young horses herself.

Wes was amazed to see the change in them already now that they were a few weeks into the preparation. Most had the hang of standing still and moving forward or backward a step when asked by their handler. This was important when at the sales and a client was looking at them.

Wes observed a switch made by the teacher and frowned as she recognised that one of the pairs of horse and handler didn't seem to go well together. The stubborn filly refused to walk no matter how much the student coaxed her.

"One of the boys might be better suited to her," she suggested to the teacher, making note of the filly's long legs.

Another switch was made and Wes smiled at the results.

"Good job," her teacher commented before telling the students they could stand the horses up and then head in.

While a group had gone to catch the weanlings out of the paddock, the remaining students had been putting feeds in feeders. Hay and waters had been topped up that morning after the boxes had been mucked out.

Wes liked that each Monday, Wednesday and Friday morning and afternoon she had work with the horses and a class in between. Tuesday and Thursday afternoon from April when the second years had come back from holidays, the more seasoned students handled the stable duties while the first years had theory for the whole of these two days. For those who didn't have a lot of hands on experience, it meant that at least every second day they were given many opportunities to handle horses, muck out boxes and look after the young horses' wellbeing.

Once all had been brought in for the afternoon with the view to spend the evening in the stables, the students were dismissed for the day. Wes suggested to her driver who also happened to be paired up with her for the assignment that they get started on the piece that night if she had nothing else planned.

May

Lise smiled, agreeing with Jeremy that she would see him later that afternoon when the farm was due to be fed and weanlings brought in from their paddocks for the evening. The pair had disappeared into town a few hours earlier, after finishing the morning chores. Both needed to do some food shopping and being a Saturday they had to rush to get into town before the local supermarket closed.

Jeremy had suggested they go in together and get some lunch while they were there. Lise had had a lovely time chatting with him while they ate. She was thankful for the male's friendship and the fact that he seemed to genuinely enjoy her company and not want to play games.

"You're making Tony one very unhappy man," Kaye commented as she strolled past Lise, bringing her out of her thoughts.

"Excuse me?"

"Well first you accused him of being gay and involved with Declan," she commented with a smile, causing Lise to emit a small grin of her own.

"And then you obviously blow that out of the water by giving the impression that you're involved with the Irishman and now that he's gone, you're spending all your time with Jeremy."

"*All* my time? An embellishment on Tony's behalf if that is indeed his perception of how things are. But even if I were, I don't see how that's any of his - or anyone else's business," Lise responded simply, smiling at Kaye before turning toward her house.

Unsure whether Kaye was trying to stir up trouble or not, Lise wasn't happy with the idea that the staff would be talking about or making guesses about her relationships with particular male members of staff. She sighed, closing the door after her, questioning indeed which sex it was easier to befriend.

Settling down at her computer she turned it on, glancing at the calendar that hung on the wall beside the monitor while she waited for the machine to boot up. Her gaze drifted over the month of May and the small top right hand corner where the dates of June were listed.

She still missed Declan but recognised that in the short space of a couple of months he would be home, Rocket arriving shortly after him once he'd spent some time in quarantine under observation. With the computer now whirring away softly she opened up the internet and put in the web address of Park Grove Stud, curious to know how the young stallion was going.

The main page of the site listed the six stallions available at this stud set in Ireland and showed a head shot of each as well as any pressing news. There were some photos available of foals that had been born to their stallions during the current breeding season and an article titled Rocket Takes Off.

Lise let her mouse hover over the title, the cursor changing to the image of a hand, showing her that it was a link. Clicking on this Lise was taken to a page that housed the article and quickly she read of the warm reception the stallion had received from Irish breeders and how the young horse had settled in well and had a first cycle conception rate of 85%. Lise recognised this information - if 100% correct - to speak volumes of the management of the stallion and the mares that were being sent to him. The fact that he'd gotten 85% of the mare's he'd been bred to in foal was a very positive thing and this percentage could only improve as those that didn't conceive were bred again as the season progressed.

Lise realised she was looking forward to both Declan and Rocket getting home. She also realised with a smile that she couldn't wait to see his second lot of foals that would start arriving early August.

Although the season wasn't far away - a matter of a couple of months - she couldn't wait for that time to pass.

***

"Who's finished their lunch and is up for helping put some horses back into a paddock and getting them off the road?" the TAFE teacher called out from her car that had just come down the TAFE facility's driveway.

Wes looked up from her conversation with a couple of mates, discussions of the upcoming weanling sale that they would all be taking part in quickly forgotten.

"Loose horses?" someone questioned, the group quickly rising to their feet.

"They belong in a paddock at the end of this road and for some reason are wandering. Grab a couple of head collars and get in," their teacher replied quickly, waiting impatiently as the group ran toward the stables to do just that.

"I wonder how they got out," Wes stated, more to herself than the others.

"Or where the owners are," another interjected, causing her to nod.

Indeed. Where were the owners? Quickly the three had a head collar each and clambered into their teacher's vehicle before she drove them out of the property and down the road.

Wes spied two older mares and a young chestnut horse – perhaps a couple of years old. The three were quite happily standing on the corner nature strip, picking at the plentiful green grass.

The group of students and teacher quietly exited the vehicle, being careful not to slam doors before casually strolling toward the three escapees, talking quietly as they did so. It was a non eventful saving, with the horses accepting the head collars and random strangers leading them across the quiet road and into the paddock where a gate was hanging open.

Quickly the gate was closed over, the horses released and the students exited the paddock, their teacher holding open the gate for them. The small group stood to inspect the gate, noting the chain and padlock which were hanging open.

"That's weird... maybe the owner thought they had locked it but they hadn't?"

"Who knows," their teacher replied, clicking the lock shut and checking it just to be sure.

"Perhaps if any of you see someone in the paddock in the near future you can tell them that their horses got out and we returned them. Hopefully it won't happen again."

The group murmured their agreement, heading back to the car and on toward TAFE for the afternoon's classes.

The very next day Wes found herself riding to school, her usual lift not available due to that friend being at home sick. She didn't mind however, now that her hand was feeling a lot better and with the weather being warm, it was nice to be outside.

On her way home she came to a stop at the end of the road where the TAFE was housed, noting that someone was in the paddock with the three horses they'd rescued the day before.

"Well what do you know."

Checking that there were no cars, she pedaled across the road, parked her bike beside the gate and clambered between the wires, being careful not to get caught on the top wire which was barbed.

The body was that of an older gentleman, perhaps in his seventies, Wes concluded. She said hello and introduced herself as a student from up the road, studying horses at the local TAFE. The older man smiled and offered his hand, telling her his name was Pat.

Wes mentioned about the horses having been out the day before and noted that the older male was quite surprised to hear this.

"The chain wasn't broken, the padlock just appeared to be unlocked and they were happily grazing on the opposite nature strip. Our teacher got us to come help her and we put them all back – they didn't seem too bothered about it all."

"Did you have any trouble catching the chestnut fella?" Pat queried, his gaze wandering to the young animal.

"No, he seemed happy to follow the others."

"Good. He's unbroken, you see and can be a bit difficult to lead."

The pair chatted some more, Wes suddenly curious about the paddock arrangement Pat had and how much it was costing him to agist his horses. She mentioned that she had a gelding she wanted to bring up from Melbourne and keep in Wangaratta for the next eighteen months while she completed her course.

"Well this property is full at the moment but it would cost you about twenty dollars a week per horse here. I know a few other people that have horses and some land, so I'll keep a look out for you and let you know if I find something. You're at the school there five days a week, are you?"

"Yes, and some weekends at the moment because we're preparing the weanlings for a sale."

"Wonderful. I'll let you know if I find something."

Wes thanked the older man before saying she'd better get home. He waved her goodbye, staying with his horses as they ate while Wes went back across the paddock and through the fence to her bike.

***

Melanie smiled, watching one of her students once again go through the course of nine jumps. She had a class of only two on this Sunday afternoon which was very unusual – there were normally five or six in the lesson.

The day's constant winds and persistent rainfall Melanie deemed to be the underlying factor. She was almost tempted to tack up a horse herself and carry out the lesson on horseback in a form of follow the leader just to keep moving rather than stand in the middle of the arena, shivering under her many layers.

She had started off the lesson as usual by getting her students to warm up their horses at a walk, trot and canter in both directions, focusing on quiet hands, a steady lower leg and a bit of work on their jumping position, otherwise known as two point. Both riders were quite established in their seat and position on the horse but Melanie believed that any rider could benefit from this foundational work.

Now warmed up, the riders and their mounts had gone through each set up jump individually before riding them as a whole course.

Melanie had it set up so that they first went over a double with a stride between the two jumps before cantering around to the right and going over two that were set up in a bending line, then left around the outside of the arena, changing direction across the centre of the arena and once back on the right coming down over a set of three jumps and finishing with a bounce – two jumps placed close enough together that the horse jumped, landed and took off again right away, without any strides in between.

A bounce and even three jumps in a row with a stride in between gave good practice for staying in your jumping position and keeping the horse moving forward. In the case of the three jumps with the stride in between, the focus was on the rider returning to their upright position or 3 point before going back to their jump position once they were again headed over a jump.

Both riders were managing the course well on their mounts but Melanie was frustrated to see that rather than looking past each jump and toward where they were to go next, each rider was looking down at the jump they were to be going over. This could throw both the rider and horse off balance and if the horse stopped suddenly, it wasn't uncommon for a rider to continue over the horse's shoulder and end up on the ground of the arena.

Especially in this course where there were a few changes of direction after jumps, it was important for the rider to always be focused on where they were going next, rather than the jump they were currently going over.

Melanie called the two into the middle once they had completed the course, complimenting them on keeping their horses forward, approaching each jump from a good line and getting over clear. She then went on to express her concern for where their gaze was fixed, explaining again the importance of looking forward, past the jump, not down at it.

"We're going to go over the bending line again and after you've jumped the crossbar and are headed toward the vertical candy stripe, I'm going to stand a few metres away in front of the jump and hold up my hand. I want you to tell me how many fingers I'm holding up. The only way you'll be able to tell me is if your focus is beyond the jump and toward where you're riding next. Amy, you can go first and then Belinda can follow along, remembering to keep a safe distance."

The pair nodded, urging their horses into a walk and then trot before Amy headed toward the first jump, Belinda aiming for the crossbar once she saw Amy jumping the vertical.

Melanie held up two fingers for Amy and was rewarded with the correct answer from the rider and the sight of her focus being ahead of her, rather than down at the jump.

"Great! Give your horse a walk for a bit."

She repeated the process for Belinda and found the result to be the same - a rider that was no longer looking down at the jump. Finding this to be successful, she asked the pair to go through the exercise once more and then sent them around again, this time not holding up any fingers for them to count.

Both went over the bending line pair, their focus each time beyond the jump they were currently going over.

"Excellent!" Melanie praised them as they again brought their mounts back to a walk.

"We'd better stop there as we've run out of time but next week I think we should do another course and really focus on where we're looking as we go around the course. Good job, both of you. I'll let you out of the arena and you can cool your horses down before unsaddling them."

June

Wes tuned out from the plentiful conversations surrounding her, her gaze instead going to the world that was traveling by the window at around one hundred kilometers per hour.

The class of eighteen students plus three of their teachers were headed down the freeway toward Oaklands Junction where the June weanling sales were to be held. Wes was excited and nervous about the sales this time around. For one thing she wouldn't be looking at the horses; she would be parading them to clients - potential owners. She questioned how the young horses would go with a new environment and new stresses on them over the next few days.

Her thoughts moved from the young horses to what the facilities would be like that they would be staying in while working at the sales. She already knew who she was sharing with and that they were all to be staying in the motel not too far from the sales complex but was eager to get settled in before they were all due out to the complex to water and feed the weanlings for the night.

The young horses had been loaded up on a couple of transport vehicles before the students left for the same location. They would have been unloaded by staff at the sales complex and put in their allocated boxes on arrival. The students along with the teachers then had the responsibility of seeing them settled for the night.

Wes knew she'd need to get a decent night's sleep that night but questioned how, when they were all so excited about the sale and likely to be chattering late into the night. It was almost a guarantee that all too quickly the time of five am would arrive when they would have to arise, get dressed, make a quick stop at McDonald's for breakfast and then be on their way to the Oaklands Junction complex.

This became the routine each morning and Wes was amazed at how organised the teachers were and how smoothly everyone got ready - even those who had been drinking heavily the night before. She was thankful when mucking out boxes or walking the weanlings in the early morning preparation that she didn't have a hangover to deal with though and didn't find herself pitying the few who were groaning and complaining about something they could have prevented in the first place.

She smiled when one of the young women ended up with a particularly dirty box to clean the third morning in and the smells were obviously upsetting to her stomach.

"Perhaps all those Bundy's last night weren't such a good idea," she mused quietly, picking up droppings in the box next door.

Her neighbour just grunted in reply, continuing to clean the box. One thing Wes did find different with regards to mucking out boxes at the sales was that the students were instructed to only pick up the droppings and rake over the boxes, making them as even as possible. They didn't have to turn over the shavings or remove any wet spots, as they'd been informed the boxes were to be completely stripped once the sale had finished.

The morning work routine was quickly established by all students. While half walked horses, the other half tidied boxes, topped up waters and hay and put feed in feeders. The roles were then reversed.

Once all horses were fed and watered the students and teachers took a break and came back shortly after to groom the young animals before the day's parading. Wes quickly became familiar with the term 'parade out of your pocket' and was amazed at how closely the filly she was in charge of stuck by her side any time they left the stabling complex to parade up and down on one of the many bitumen areas designed for walking the horses before a client or clients.

It was pointed out to her by a friend that the clients in themselves had preferences too. Some were noted to want to look at only the fillies while others were only interested in purchasing a colt. Still others were after foals by a particular stallion or out of a particular mare. The ones that fascinated Wes and her friend the most however were the few who came through and wanted to look at the whole draft.

On their few breaks throughout the days of the sale, as they wandered around they came across a young man who seemed to be looking at each draft and each individual horse on sale. Wes was amused by his casual attire of a shirt that wasn't tucked in, long cargo shorts and a pair of thongs on his feet – hardly safe attire around horses. Especially young unpredictable thoroughbreds.

"Bet you he's got more money than we can poke a stick at," Wes whispered as they wandered past on their way back from having purchased lunch up at the ridiculously priced kiosk.

"I wonder if he is going to look at every horse here."

"Well he looked at all of ours and it looks like that farm is showing off their whole draft, too," Wes replied.

"Out of the hundreds in the sale, I hope he finds one he likes."

"If he does I'm sure he'll buy it without any qualms of how much it costs."

Nodding in agreement, the smaller blonde followed Wes back to where a few of the students were sitting on one of the benches parked at the end of an aisle. It was always occupied by a few student bodies that were taking a break and watching the rest of the goings on at the sales.

There had been quite a bit to watch, too. Earlier in the day one horse had gotten loose and it had taken quite a few people to catch the scared filly. Wes had watched in fascination, expecting someone or the horse to get hurt and was thankful to see someone catch her before this happened.

A couple of the students had accidentally lost their particular horses due to sudden movements, a rear or someone coming around a corner suddenly and spooking the animal.

Wes was thankful she hadn't lost hers although there'd been a couple of times when she'd been holding on to the end of the lead with one hand. She realised it was possible however, as the actual sale started today and would continue until late into the afternoon the following day. Anything could happen over the next thirty six hours.

Her filly was one of the TAFE's earlier lots to go through the ring and before she knew it, Wes was holding the young horse while a couple of students finished brushing her over, painting hooves, making sure the mane was all on one side and that the numbered stickers were sitting at the same point on each of her hips.

Each of the horses when they went through the ring had to have their lot number displayed on them. This was generally placed on the horse's hip and the stickers were provided by the complex.

The TAFE weanlings also had another sticker that sat above the lot number. It was a Super VOBIS sticker, standing for Victorian Owners and Breeders Incentive Scheme.

Wes had only since seeing the stickers, come to be familiar with this term. One of her teachers informed her than any foal born out of a stallion that was bred to mares in the state of Victoria was eligible to be part of this scheme – at a small fee. The VOBIS qualified foals when raced in particular TAB races in Victoria were then eligible for bonuses if the horse placed or won. These bonuses went to the owner and the breeder of the horse.

Some buyers were only interested in VOBIS nominated horses and it worked as an incentive to encourage breeders to send their mares to Victorian based stallions rather than look out of the state for a stallion to breed to. Wes thought this a great idea and learnt that the same was for other states too.

Ten lots before she was due to be in the ring, a white coat – one of the complex's staff, named by the long white jacket they wore – arrived at their stable block to let her know it was time to head up to the first outside ring.

At the complex there were three parade rings, one outside where horses were walked before being invited to the inside ring where a lot of buyers congregated to get a last look at a horse. From here they were ushered into the auditorium and the sale ring one at a time. All up about ten horses would be in the three rings.

Wes had her hands full while in the first two rings, working to keep her filly walking at a nice pace and not stopping, propping or shying. She also had to work hard to keep a decent distance between the horse in front of her and the one behind her which was difficult if one in front suddenly propped and shied at something. She was almost relieved when it was her turn to head down the laneway that led to the auctioning ring.

Quickly she heard the gavel slam down; announcing the sale of the lot before her and immediately after a large door was slid open to allow her into the ring. Wes took a step forward and immediately felt a pull on the leather lead attached to her horse. She looked back at the young filly that stood legs splayed and eyes wide.

"Come on, sweetie. It's nearly over," Wes stated quietly, pulling at the lead before looking up to the auctioneer with an exasperated expression.

"This one seems to be having a bit of stage fright," the auctioneer stated over his microphone, "quick, someone make a sound like a chaff bag," he joked, gaining a ripple of laughter from those in the auditorium.

Wes continued to tug at the lead and had to jump to the side when someone got behind the filly and made a loud clap, causing her to leap forward. Quickly Wes started walking around the ring, after a couple of laps reminding herself to stop the filly and stand her up so that everyone could get a good look at her. She was visibly relieved when the filly stood quiet enough – although whinnying rather loudly – and then walked forward when Wes asked her.

Very quickly the bidding was over, the gavel slammed down and suddenly Wes was heading out of the ring and back toward the stable block in a daze. She was only vaguely aware of two students shadowing her, talking about the price the filly had made.

Once back at the stable block, she placed the filly into her box which had been raked over, hay refilled and water topped up while they were away. Wes removed the head collar and bit and exited the box, bolting the door after her.

As much as the students had bonded with the young animals over the duration of the eight week preparation, they'd been informed that once the young horses were back in their box after being in the sale ring, they were to be left alone and not touched again. They now belonged to someone else and unless specifically asked by the buyer to bring them out, the students weren't to touch the horses.

Wes watched the bay filly play with her hay, realising with a smile that she'd survived the weanling prep and the young horse had been sold. *I'm not sure I want to do that again any time soon!*

July

Madison frowned, her gaze focused on Dundee as she walked into the paddock, closing the gate after her. The mare was painfully moving from one patch of grass to another not wanting to bear weight on her near fore. Because it had been raining a lot the past few days and some of the paddocks were rather muddy, Madison was willing to bet that the buckskin coloured mare had an abscess.

Walking up to the mare, she laid a hand on her shoulder, talking to her as she ran her hand down the left front leg. She felt around the coronet band at the base of the pastern for heat, a sign of inflammation.

She placed her hand on the right foot at the same place, comparing the two and finding the left to be quite warm. Picking up the foot, Maddie looked at all the mud caked into the hoof thinking with a frown that she had nothing to remove it with. Putting the foot down, Maddie gave Dundee a pat before heading out of the paddock to grab a head collar and lead, concluding it'd be easier to bring her in, clean up the foot and poultice it if need be.

Jack met her as she was headed back out to the paddock.

"Who are you getting?"

"Dundee. She's got an abscess. I thought it might need poulticing."

"Want a hand?"

Madison's smile worked as a reply and Jack strolled out with her, looking to the cream and black pony as they got closer.

"Not a happy pony," he observed, closing the gate after them.

"Indeed," Maddie replied, placing the halter over her nose, putting the long strap behind her ears and doing up the buckle.

"You may have to help encourage her to move," the young redhead said with a smile.

Jack nodded, moving behind her but out of kicking distance before he started clapping his hands and stamping his feet, making noises that would encourage the mare to move away from him and toward the tie up area.

Once at the tie up area Jack went to collect the items they'd need to apply a poultice and Maddie tied up the mare, using a hoof pick to clean out the hoof and a dandy brush to scrub off mud that had collected around the outside of the hoof. Jack came back with a bucket of water shortly after as well as an animalintex poultice, some vet wrap and gaffa tape as well as a pair of scissors.

Jack soaked the animalintex in the bucket of warm water before removing it and placing it over a rail. Madison picked up Dundee's left front leg, allowing Jack to place the bucket beneath it where her foot was lying. Releasing her grip on the leg, Maddie carefully guided the mare to put her foot in the bucket of warm water.

Unsure, Dundee lifted her leg quickly, nearly knocking the bucket. Jack righted it as Maddie again encouraged the mare to lower her leg, more slowly this time. Once in the bucket, she gave the mare a reassuring pat, encouraging her to stand for a minute or so to soak the foot. After this short length of time she lifted up the leg, finding the foot to be nearly as clean as she wanted. While she scrubbed at the foot with the dandy brush, every now and again dipping the brush into the water before scrubbing again, Jack went in search of a towel.

After cleaning the hoof, Maddie dried it off with the towel and held the leg up while Jack placed the animalintex over the sole of the hoof, making sure it covered the whole foot. This done he got the vet wrap out of his pocket and wrapped it around the poultice and the hoof, using one hand to hold the poultice in place while the other wound the crepe bandage around Dundee's hoof, being careful not to bring it up too high past the coronet band, or too tight around the top of the hoof.

This done Jack moved onto the gaffa tape, repeating the process. The gaffa tape helped to keep it all together and worked as a tough barrier as a horse walking on vet wrap very quickly wore through the bandage, causing it all to be a waste of time.

"All done," Jack stated, checking the pressure around the top of the hoof when Maddie released the leg to the ground.

"Guess we'll check her tomorrow and see if the poultice has helped to draw out the abscess. If not, Stuart is here on the weekend and maybe he can have a poke around and see if he can find it and open it up so it can drain."

Jack nodded, seeing no other option.

"She's pretty sore, really only putting weight on the toe. I wouldn't be surprised if the abscess bursts out on its own in the next day or so. I don't think Stuart will need to look at her."

"Guess we'll know by Saturday," Maddie replied, poking her tongue out at Jack as she untied the buckskin coloured mare.

Jack rolled his eyes, collecting up the left over items and placing them in the bucket after emptying out the dirty water.

"How do we come to agree on anything when you have so much fun treating every thing like a game where we're on opposing sides?" he muttered, shaking his head.

"Hey! We both agree that we like me," Maddie stated cheekily, ducking as Jack threw the end of the gaffa tape roll at her.

"And we both agree that you're not modest," he threw back at her, heading into the stables while Maddie started back toward the paddock, Dundee in tow slowly behind her.

***

"There's one missing," Lise commented, her gaze going over the numerous bodies of dry mares that were getting heavier with foal as each day passed.

"On the other side of the dam," Jeremy replied, pointing to the far end of the paddock.

Lise nodded, switching the bike back on as he climbed on the back. The pair headed across the muddy paddock, Lise working to not get the bike bogged or pass through any suspicious patches of mud that could cause trouble. Shortly after they arrived at the mum to be that had her head hung low, a foreleg resting on its toe as she tried to keep weight off the foot.

"Abscess," Jeremy observed, hopping off to get a closer look.

"Agreed. She looks pretty swollen, is her leg very hot?"

"Pretty warm," Jeremy replied, lifting up the hoof and cleaning it out with a hoof pick he kept in his back pocket.

Lise noted this fact with a small smile. She'd been working with horses for years and hadn't considered carrying the small handy tool on her even though it made complete sense.

She hopped off the bike and trudged through the mud to get a look at the hoof that Jeremy had finished clearing of mud. Now he was digging around with the pick, trying to distinguish where the abscess was situated in the hoof.

"Maybe we should get Hunter to look at her and have a bit of a dig around with a hoof knife."

"I don't think so. I think he'd disagree with opening up her foot, especially if there's the potential that it could be deep in the hoof. If she wasn't in foal I think he'd do so but he'd probably be happy enough for it to burst out on its own accord rather than make a decent hole in her hoof that could get infected. Once its burst out we can always put her on penicillin if the leg stays swollen."

"Fair enough. Will we move a feeder over here or try and get her over to where the others are?"

"I'll go grab a feeder," Lise stated, returning to the bike to do just that.

Jeremy waited with the mare, talking to her quietly and rubbing his fingers over her forehead, watching her close her eyes with a smile.

"It won't be too long now honey before that baby comes out and you can get your figure back," he joked, squatting down to check the size of her bag.

As the mares got closer to foaling, their bag filled up with milk, especially within the last month of their gestation. It was a good way to tell how far away a mare was from giving birth. This one still had a while to go.

Lise dropped the feeder and a bucket's worth of feed before the mare and then she and Jeremy headed back toward the gate, having the rest of the farm to feed before they stopped for their morning tea break.

***

"We're going to focus on what needs to be checked out in relation to a newborn's health today. Once they've been delivered by the mare and their nostrils have been cleared, you've checked the gender and that the navel stump isn't bleeding profusely, we need to check for abnormalities. Does anyone know what entropion is?"

Now in July, the weanling sales completed and successfully having given each student a first hand look at what is involved in a sale preparation and what is expected of them at a sale, the focus was very quickly turned to the impending breeding season.

The teacher looked around the class, noting the unsure or bored looks of each individual.

"I'll take that as a no. Entropion is the technical term for an inverted eyelid or eyelids. Generally it is possible to manually fix this by just flipping the eyelid to the correct position. You'll find that it's usually the lower eyelid that is inverted and if left for a couple of days or not noticed right away, the eyelashes rubbing against the eye can actually ulcerate the eye and cause damage to the cornea."

"What happens if you can't manually fix the eyelid?"

"I'd suggest over the course of the night trying a few times and once it's a reasonable hour in the day, to look into getting the vet to assess the situation. Our vet likes to stitch the eyelid in the correct position and it's possible to use dissolvable stitches so that no removal of stitches is necessary down the track."

"Is it difficult for them to stitch the eyelid?" another asked.

"It's a pretty straight forward procedure for a vet but because it's working close to an organ, the foal needs to be well restrained to avoid damage to the eye. Once newborn foals start to arrive, familiarise yourself with what their eyes look like normally so that you'll be able to better pick up if something isn't quite right. What else might we need to look at?"

"Their mouth?" another interjected.

"Good. Anything in particular?"

"To see if there is anything that could restrict them feeding properly..." the same student guessed.

"Yes, more to the point you can see if they are parrot mouthed - have an overbite or have an under bite - sow mouth. Once they are actually nursing, if there is a sign of the milk flowing from the foal's nostrils you need to determine if they've just had milk spray on their face or if they actually have something wrong with the palate in their mouth. It's unusual, but possible that there's a hole causing the milk to run out their nasal passage rather than go down the oesophagus. Does anyone know what this is called?"

"A cleft palate?" Wes interjected, causing the teacher to smile.

"That's the one. Unfortunately prognosis for the foal isn't good as it isn't possible to fix and because the foal can't properly nurse, they have to be put down."

"Just what you want," Wes muttered to herself, making notes.

Moving on from problems to check for immediately after birth, the class started to learn about issues that could arise within the next seventy two hours. Wes was amazed to learn that so much could go wrong in so short a time and came to appreciate how important it was for a foal to nurse early in life to gain antibodies through the colostrum produced by the mare.

If this didn't happen, the foal wouldn't be able to build an immune system and therefore would be susceptible to many possible infections and death. *Maybe it's just easier to buy them as a yearling ready to race with someone else having put in all the work and money to keep them alive…*

August

Wes paused from turning over the shavings box she was in. Upon returning from the sales, the property had quickly turned its focus to breeding. As had been the case since early July, the stables were currently full of dry mares, that is – mares that weren't in foal and were to be bred in the upcoming season.

Horses are polyoestrous breeders, meaning that they have multiple cycles over a particular season of the year. For mares, this tended to be in the spring and summer months. In the Southern Hemisphere this caused the breeding season to be focused around September through to the end of December while in the Northern Hemisphere it was focused around the early months of the year.

The mare's body starts to cycle, causing her to come into season every three weeks or so once daylight hours increase, temperatures rise and there is growth in the pastures. All of these things indicate to the mare's body that spring is on its way and so her system comes out of anoestrous – winter shutdown – and she starts cycling, having periods of being in season and periods of being out of season.

There was a link between the amount of daylight hours and a mare starting to cycle so thoroughbred properties had taken it upon themselves to stable dry mares, rug them to increase warmth, increase feed levels to coincide with the usual spring growth and they left lights on in the stables over particular hours of the evening, effectively lengthening the daylight hours with this artificial light. The lights were set up on a timer allowing the horse to have 16 hours of 'daylight' in total.

Wes was amazed at the way they were able to manipulate a horse's system and have them come into season quicker. This was valuable in the thoroughbred industry as it meant mares could be bred earlier and foals born early the next year.

One downfall – at least for the students – she concluded, was the cleaning out of boxes that housed in season mares. The strong smell of ammonia attacked her senses, and she found tears falling from her stinging eyes each time she worked to rid the box of damp spots. She paused from one particular spot, turning away from the urine soaked shavings and sticking her head out the doorway to get some fresh air.

She paused to take in a conversation that was going on between two students who were mucking out boxes opposite.

"So then these herd of sparrows flew past and I-" one continued on with her story, quickly being interrupted by the other.

"Herd? You idiot, it's not a herd of birds."

"Well what is it?"

"You know... I can't remember... a swarm?" the other pondered, propping herself up against the rake as she mulled the question over.

"Flocking idiots," Wes muttered to herself with a grin, turning back to the box and the offending dark patch of shavings.

"A flock, that's it!" the second concluded with a proud tone, also moving back to finishing off her box.

All the manure and wet shavings were emptied into wheelbarrows or out into the breezeway if there weren't enough wheelbarrows around. Other students then double handled the removed materials, emptying them into a wheelbarrow and taking this out to the rapidly growing manure pile.

Once all boxes were done, many students donned a broom and started at one end, sweeping their way toward the other while other students topped up water buckets and put out hay for each horse.

The end of cleaning the stables marked the time for a short morning tea break – or smoko as it was more affectionately known by the majority that were nicotine addicts.

Twenty minutes later the students were back in the stables, fighting over who got which head collar before heading out to the large paddock that housed the mares that to Wes appeared enormous in stature in comparison to the weanling's they'd so recently sold. And a couple were enormous. There were two particular mares that stood on 17 hands high, causing Wes to have to reach up while on her tippy toes to be able to get a head collar on either of them.

The students had been learning in class about the tell tale signs of when a mare was receptive to the stallion and therefore ready to be bred.

Today they were learning about putting this information to use and into practice. The TAFE had two stallions on the property – one thoroughbred that they used for breeding and a Welsh Mountain Pony that was used for teasing the mares. The mares were first introduced to this teaser stallion to judge their interest level. If they were receptive to the stallion, that is, they stood quietly with ears forward, they raised their tail and straddled their hind legs and urinated, then the mare was obviously in season.

If she had flattened back ears, tried to kick and bite at the small stallion or didn't want to be anywhere near him, it was deemed that she was out of season.

The students had learnt in class that a mare's oestrus cycle was around 21 days in length and over this time, she tended to be in season 3-7 of these days with 5 being a common length of time.

Based on this information, the first years brought in the mares Mondays, Wednesdays and Fridays to assess their interest levels and mark it down on a piece of paper. Noting each mare's response meant they were able to over a length of time distinguish a pattern of behaviour and work out the best time to breed the mare.

This all made sense to Wes but she found herself petrified at the idea of leading a 600 kilogram animal toward a stallion that she may not even want to be near.

This fear intensified when she watched another student lead a mare up toward the teaser who was housed on the other side of the post and rail fence. As soon as the mare's nose met with the small stallion she let out a squeal of rage, half reared up and struck out her front leg.

By the time she'd landed, she was side on to the stallion and suddenly striking out with both front feet. The handler had a hard time keeping out of the way of her striking legs and quickly worked to drag her away from the teaser stallion.

"Off," the teacher commented simply to another student who was keeping the teasing records for the morning.

Off? You don't say! Off! Wes looked at the teacher in surprise, amazed that she hadn't asked the student handling the mare if she was ok.

The offending teacher turned her gaze to Wes, directing her to grab a small chestnut in the left yard and take her up to the teaser. Wes bit her lip, fiddling with her hands to make sure the mandatory helmet was firmly on her head.

She entered the yard, closing the gate behind her before catching the mare and placing the head collar on her. The small mare stood quietly, walking with the unsure student up to the teasing rail where she sniffed at the grey stallion on the other side.

Wes made sure she was standing off to the left hand side of the mare and tried to tell herself that if the mare moved suddenly, she was in the safest possible place. *Not true, out of this yard would be even safer...*

The chestnut mare was obviously in season, she stood quietly while the stallion sniffed at her and her tail was raised. On the teacher's instruction, Wes angled the mare so that she was standing side on to the teaser and was rewarded with further signs that the mare was receptive to the stallion.

Even though the mare was in season, there would be no chance of breeding throughout the month of August due to the legalities of the thoroughbred stud book. At the moment, the teasing was about establishing a behavioural pattern and giving the students a chance to practice teasing mares and recognise signs of oestrus behaviour and dioestrus – when they were out of season.

Wes was very much thanking God that for today, she had been given a mare to tease that was obviously in oestrus. She didn't want to think about the teasing they would do in two days time and the potential for a mare that was out of season. That worry could wait until Friday arrived.

***

Lise laughed as she walked down the driveway toward the main barn with Jeremy. He seemed to have sensed that she was distracted earlier that morning and had suggested that once they'd finished the work expected of them for a Saturday morning that they get out for a walk.

Lise was reasonably sure that Jeremy knew her distraction was due to the fact that Declan was due back that weekend. Either way, she was thankful for his pleasant company and found herself quickly involved in the stories he told of other horse properties he'd worked at and the situations he'd found himself in.

"The most fun was when I had started working on a stud in South Australia and there was a mob of yearlings that were supposed to come in for the farrier. Eager to show that I had no problems with running in a paddock of young horses, I raced for the bike and entered the paddock, flying across it toward the young horses that were herded together at the far end.

"I'd not been in that particular paddock before and someone failed to mention the two massive ditches located one and two thirds of the way across the paddock. Before I knew it I was airborne on the bike and panicked that I wouldn't be in one piece when I landed... so of course to add insult to injury, I'd just gotten the bike under control when I came across the second ditch. Needless to say on the way back the yearlings were run in at a slow trot... I don't think I could look left for the next week due to jarring something."

"That's indeed a classic," Lise replied with a large grin, patting Jeremy on the shoulder.

Jeremy stopped suddenly, causing Lise to do the same, looking at the male in surprise.

"What?"

"I think your stallion handler's back," he responded simply, gesturing to an unfamiliar car parked out the front of the stud's office.

Lise would have stayed where she was but Jeremy started forward again, headed toward the office. Unsure, Lise followed his footsteps, the pair entering the small building where laughter was heard.

Kingsley was sitting at his desk, Declan and Trevor in chairs opposite as the Irish fellow finished his story, emitting further laughter from the other two men.

"It sounds like your stories might rival my own," Jeremy stated from the doorway, grinning.

Declan looked up at the unfamiliar male, his gaze quickly going to Lise who stood closely beside him.

"Jeremy, I take it?" Declan queried, rising to shake his hand.

"Thanks for filling my boots while I was away," he stated with a wink, his gaze traveling to Lise.

"Filling your boots implies you taking them back over and me leaving. I'm pretty sure I'm staying put," Jeremy replied, taking Declan's hand in a firm shake.

The stallion handler turned back to Kingsley, brows raised in surprise but a smile on his face.

"That so, boss?"

"Indeed. Jeremy drives a hard bargain. He agreed to initial employment only if I agreed to employ him at least until the end of the breeding season. We'll have even more mares to Rocket this year so I don't see how it can hurt to have another staff member."

"I've got to go check on a mare that was looking restless this morning," Lise suddenly interjected, gaining the attention of the four men, "welcome back Declan."

Quickly she exited the room, not interested in having four pairs of eyes on her, four pairs of eyes that each seemed to hold a different question. Questions that she wouldn't have been able to hear over the thudding of her heart.

She walked briskly toward the foaling area, running her gaze over the half dozen bodies that were housed in a paddock close by as their due dates implied that foaling was imminent. Noting that all were pretty settled, Lise strolled on toward the Vet lab, wanting to see the results of some blood she'd taken that morning from a foal born the day before.

"I leave ye alone for half a year and ye go and find yerself a new beau! What is the world coming to?"

Lise turned to face Declan, her stomach fluttering at the sight of seeing him propped up against the doorframe.

"Excuse me?" she questioned, annoyance taking over due to his assumption that she was involved with Jeremy.

"I told ye I'd be back for the season."

"And that can be translated to 'Don't get involved with someone else while I'm away'?" Lise queried in surprise, not ready to tell him that she wasn't.

"Ummm..." Declan faltered for a second, leaving the doorway and heading toward her.

"Exactly," Lise stated emphatically.

"So I should have started something before leaving?" he queried with a smirk, stepping into her personal space.

Lise looked up at him, eyes wide.

"No..." she stated slowly, stepping back into the corner of the room.

"Then I'm not sure how I could have won this one either way."

"Maybe you couldn't have."

"So this whole conversation is a waste of our time?"

"You brought it up," Lise stated defensively, finding nowhere to go as Declan took another step toward her.

"Yes, I did. And I don't think I like how it's finished."

"I'm not sure I can help you with that McAlister."

"Perhaps you could help me with something else then," he stated with a smile, leaning in closer.

Lise put her hands up to his chest to stop him from getting any closer. Seeing his chance, Declan covered her hands with his own, keeping a firm hold of hers.

"Before I left, ye kissed me," he started, tightening his grip when Lise tried to escape, "and I was stupid enough to play games but I'm sorta thinking ye only did so because ye wanted something to eventuate from it... am I right?"

"Yes," Lise responded quietly, glancing up at Declan.

He let one hand release hers to reach up and rest a finger under her chin, keeping her gaze focused on his.

"And has that changed?" he asked sincerely.

Lise faltered, her gaze dropping to the ground. Declan looked over her face, allowing his finger to run across her cheek.

"I don't think it has," he stated quietly, grinning when Lise looked up at him in surprise.

"And I don't want it to either," he commented, leaning forward to kiss her quickly before promptly letting her other hand go and stepping back.

He made his way out of the room, pausing in the doorway.

"Let me know if things change between ye and Jeremy, Lise. I'll be here."

September

"Argh, stupid frustrating, idiotic-"

"Irishman giving you trouble again?" Trevor interrupted Lise's tirade with a knowing grin.

She looked up in surprise at the older figure that was headed toward her, a head collar in one hand, lead hanging over his shoulder. She rolled her eyes and nodded. Trevor paused to hang up the gear on a hook at the end of the stable block.

"It seems to me he's competing with Jeremy whenever I'm around."

"And not, otherwise?" Trevor asked, curious.

"Well, no... Jeremy's told me they get on great when I'm not around. He finds the whole thing very amusing."

"Of course he does. You're an attractive young woman who's letting Declan think Jeremy and you are involved. Where's the downside for him?"

Lise smiled, shaking her head.

"I'm sure it's not smart but Jeremy doesn't seem to mind, nor does he seem to expect anything from me. Declan on the other hand... I can't bring myself to tell him that I'm not involved with Jeremy. He'll just expect to jump into a relationship never mind the fact that I didn't hear from him for six months."

"Give him a break, Lise. You know he's been interested from the start."

"Maybe," she shrugged noncommittally, "enjoy your afternoon off, Trevor. I'll see you tomorrow."

He watched her stroll out of the stables and across the sunlit lawns toward her house. Hearing Declan heading toward him, Trevor turned away from watching Lise, suddenly annoyed.

"You're all kinds of stupid," Trevor muttered, stalking past the younger male, down the breezeway.

"I – what? Hey, c'mere! How many kinds of stupid are there?" Declan called out, rushing after him.

Trevor turned on his heel, looking up at the young Irishman.

"You know... I don't know. I thought I did and then I met you and they just keep on coming," he replied with a grin, sitting on an upturned bucket that had been left outside to drain.

"Now that's hardly fair, what have I done to ye?" Declan asked curiously, lounging against the wall of the stable block.

"Not me. Lise."

Trevor plucked at a long strand of grass, twirling it around a finger.

"You get annoyed with her for not reciprocating your interest but where was that interest while you were back home? Half a year is a long time to not receive a call, an email, a letter even. And yet she got to hear all about how well you were doing over there. You sure didn't seem short on time to stay in touch with Kingsley."

"That's not fair – most of the time Kingsley was in touch with the manager of the farm there, see and they'd communicate to me through each other. I rarely talked to him."

"I didn't know that and I doubt Lise does either. Why would she consider a relationship with a guy who all but ignored her for six months?"

"Just because I didn't talk to her doesn't mean I didn't think of her."

"You're going to have a fun time convincing her of that," Trevor replied, slowly rising to his feet.

"Just ye watch me. Now are ye going to help me get this mare ready for the lunch time cover or not?"

"Not," Trevor stated simply, walking away.

"Ye can't be serious?"

"I can too. Don't you remember I have Tuesday afternoons off along with Lise and Kaye? I hope she's a real wranger too, Declan. Maybe she'll knock some sense into you."

Declan stared after the disappearing older man in disbelief, thinking it was too early in the season for Trevor to be getting so uptight. Pushing the conversation from his mind he wandered down to the triangle paddock where the lunch time cover was housed.

Jeremy had already beaten him to it so Declan ambled along behind as the other male walked the mare up to the teasing yards. When presented to the teaser she laid her ears flat back and tried to bite at him. Jeremy held firm, keeping her beside the small stallion, eventually turning her side on so that the small horse could tease her properly.

It took a few minutes but she quietened down and stood still, tail elevated and urinating.

"Guess that's a yes," Declan muttered to himself, heading back toward the stallion boxes.

***

Wes rushed in the door, dumping her bag in her room before gathering up some fresh clothes to change into after having a shower. She was on foal watch for the evening, slowly getting used to the idea of a full day's TAFE and then some. The routine followed the day's study, getting home, changing and heading back out to the facilities for 5pm.

She would then be on foal watch until eight the next morning, go home and sleep until twelve and be due back at TAFE for one when the afternoon classes started. The one thing that made it doable was the fact that foal watch was done in pairs or threes and on a rotational basis so each member got broken sleep over the course of the evening.

But then again, sleep was sleep.

The students while on foal watch were to check the heavily pregnant mares every twenty minutes throughout the course of the evening. They generally worked two hour shifts, rotating using alarms on phones to get some sleep in between.

So far a few foals had been born but Wes was yet to be listed as one of the attendees at a birth. She hoped her favourite mare GG would foal while she was on watch.

As one who was constantly snacking, she packed a meal supplied by the older woman she lived with as well as snacks, drink, something for breakfast and some fruit. She'd managed to gather this up as well as shower and pack one of her assignments to work on before hearing the familiar sound of a friend's Ford utility pull up in the drive. As a last thought she also grabbed her guitar.

"Bye Rosie! I'll see you tomorrow morning," she called out as she raced for the door.

"Have a lovely evening, dear," came the reply.

***

Lise rapped at the door, impatiently waiting for it to be opened. She frowned as she heard the muffled sounds of someone awkwardly making their way to the door. Declan opened the door, his hair a disarray as his focus slowly targeted her.

"I woke you up," she stated simply, taking in the singlet and track pants.

"Mmmhmm," he yawned, opening the door wider so she could enter the room.

"How are you?" Lise queried, sitting on the edge of his couch.

Declan closed the door and made his way to the couch with a reasonable amount of pain. Lise had been out due to her afternoon off but had been met by Jeremy when she came back to the farm.

He quickly informed her of the average cover they'd had that afternoon and how the mare had kicked when the stallion mounted her and Declan had copped the majority of the blow.

He sat down slowly, turning to face her with a cringe.

"Doing great," he stated, smiling slowly.

"I should let you sleep rather than wake you up and make you more aware of the pain. I'm sorry," she stood up, finding herself quickly pulled back down onto the couch.

"Ye got me up already woman, the least ye can do is stay a bit longer."

"Ok, ok. Can I get you anything?"

"Mmmhmmm... something to keep me warm in bed. I'm freezing."

"Have you got a hot water bottle or something?" Lise queried, looking around the room.

"Nope," Declan replied, his gaze firmly planted on her.

"Then what- oh..." Lise pulled her arm out of his grip, trying to ignore the cheeky smile that was now lighting up his face and causing her own to redden.

"You can't be feeling too bad, McAlister. I think I should go."

"On one condition," he stated in earnest, aware that he'd probably crossed the line but not caring at that point.

"What?" Lise asked, resignedly.

"Let's do something tomorrow after work. Kingsley has me on light duties tomorrow and I'll be particularly bored. Let's go see a movie or something."

"You can hardly drive in your state."

"I make a great passenger. Ye can drive," he replied simply, grinning again.

Lise rolled her eyes, slowly getting off the couch.

"I'm glad you're feeling fine, Declan."

"Is that a yes? I can hardly chase ye down at the moment to make sure ye stick to yer word."

"I'll come by with the Ute at seven, ok?"

"Perfect."

***

The trip out to the TAFE was quite quick for Wes as she discussed with her classmate some things they'd been learning in class with regard to a mare's cycle, getting her in foal and the gestation period.

It had surprised her to hear that a horse was pregnant for just over eleven months, around 345 days. Now that she considered the newborn had to come out ready to run, it didn't seem so surprising that the pregnancy was close to a year for the foal to fully develop.

They'd been taught a clever little formula to work out a mare's due date. All the pregnant mares at TAFE were tagged with their name on the front, their due date on the back and the stallion they were in foal to.

The idea was you took the date that the mare was bred to the stallion and take away one month, add a week and add a year. For example, if a mare was bred on September the first, she would be due on August the eighth the following year. Wes had also been amazed to learn that mares generally came into season nine days after they had foaled and some people chose to breed them again at this early stage.

She wasn't so sure about this idea, preferring to let them rest a little longer before considering breeding again. But it was common in the industry for mares to have a foal each year and maybe have a year off every three or four years.

Because it was still early in the foaling season the two first years were accompanied by a second year student for foal watch and they spent the first few hours accompanying each other when going out to check the mares. Both first years fired questions at the more experienced second year and were glad for the available extra experience.

Mares generally foaled in the early hours of the morning but the three lucked out that evening with one mare showing particular signs of being uncomfortable, sweating and pacing around nine that evening.

As was protocol when these signs were prevalent, the students were to phone whichever teacher was on call for the evening and it was twenty minutes later that she arrived to observe the foaling.

At this stage the mare was still pacing, not yet having reached the second stage of labour which was determined by the breaking of her waters. Both first years were rapt that the dark brown mare they were watching was their favourite GG.

Having switched on the foaling lights that lit up a couple of yards close to the stables, the four sat quietly on chairs, watching as the mare continued pacing the fence line, a gush of water being released down her back legs.

Wes was amazed to see a big white bag, much like a balloon protruding from the mare's vulva. This was the birth sac that contained the foal.

Things moved quickly from here with the mare lying down and straining to expel the foal. Once the shoulders were through there was a gush and the foal was suddenly out in the real world.

Wes marveled at how the whole process had taken less than half an hour.

"That's a good sign," their teacher interjected quietly, the four pairs of eyes still on the mother and newborn.

"If she was still straining at this point and the shoulders hadn't come through, we would need to get in there and help by pulling as she is pushing. Thankfully it was a straight forward delivery."

"You might as well get in there and find out whether we've got a colt or filly and check all looks good," she said to the two first years with a grin.

The students rose slowly and climbed between the rails, walking quietly toward the pair and squatting down beside the young nickering mother.

Careful not to distress her, they worked quickly and quietly, Wes removing the amnion from the foal's body and her classmate pushing out excess fluids from the foal's nostrils to help it breathe.

Wes lifted the tail of the newborn and grinned.

"Bay filly," she stated quietly, stepping back from the pair.

"Lovely. A white snip and two white socks," her friend interjected, also smiling.

The two exited the yard and went back to the second year and their teacher.

"Thoughts?" the older woman asked with a grin.

"Awesome," Wes replied.

"If only they were all that straight forward," her mate responded.

"I'll just be thankful that this one was and hope the many to come are also," Wes replied, sitting down again to watch as the newborn started to make sense of her long legs.

"You'll be seeing plenty alright on your placement next month," her teacher chimed in.

Wes grinned at the thought.

***

Lise paused at the front of the stallion quarters, putting the car into park. She applied the handbrake and left the motor idling; stepping out of the car at the same time Declan limped his way through the door.

He closed it after him looking at Lise with a cheeky grin.

"Stop it," she replied, ducking into the car so he couldn't see her smile.

"Stop what?" he asked, opening the passenger door.

"Thinking whatever it is that's making you smile so."

"And where would be the fun in that?" he replied, easing his way into the passenger seat.

"How's your leg?"

"Change the topic, smooth like. It's bruising nicely. Want to see?"

"Considering that would require you removing your pants," she stated dryly, putting the car into drive and ignoring the young man's amused grin, "no thanks."

"No fun at all, are ye?"

"And yet you insist upon being in my company, McAlister?"

"It does seem rather odd, doesn't it?"

Despite his teasing and flirtatious behaviour on the trip into town, Lise found herself amazed that the young Irishman toned himself down for the evening, engaging her in serious conversation.

She was relieved to hear that he had had a good time while in Ireland but considered Nirvana Park to be home.

After a meal the pair drove back to the stud in companionable silence, the headlights of the utility vehicle shedding light on the dark twist and turns of the road that marked the way home.

Beyond the rows of trees that lined the bitumen road lay paddocks on either side containing cattle, sheep and the odd stockman's horse.

The acreage afforded perfect grazing for kangaroos and it wasn't uncommon for them to be seen in the paddocks at dusk or dawn. The drive was suddenly interrupted by a large figure keeping pace with the vehicle as Lise traveled along the otherwise quiet road.

Not wanting to swerve and risk a run in with a tree she applied pressure to the brakes, slowing the vehicle down gradually.

"It's keeping up with us," Declan murmured, almost incredulous.

Not managing to safely slow the vehicle down to a stop in time, Lise had to slam on the breaks when the large roo took off across the road in front of the car.

Although it registered that they hadn't hit the native animal, Lise sat quietly, waiting for her heart to quiet down. Declan reached across to rest his hand on her arm.

"A run in with something that size could have written this Ute off," he stated quietly, catching her eye to see that she was ok.

She nodded slowly, taking her foot off the break and applying it again to the accelerator. They continued on in silence, both relieved to see the familiar stud sign and driveway marked by the dark shadows of trees on either side.

Lise pulled up outside Declan's quarters a couple of minutes later, turning off the car and walking with Declan to his door.

"Ye did a great job missing that kangaroo. Are ye ok?"

Lise nodded, giving him a small smile.

"Are you going to be working tomorrow or is Kingsley allowing you some time off to rest your leg?"

"Rocket has three covers tomorrow and no one else is touching that horse," he stated with a smile though Lise was pretty sure he wasn't joking.

She nodded slowly, glancing at the Ute before her gaze fell back to Declan. He smiled down at her, not wanting to head inside without her, but also realising he'd only offend her if he asked her in. He wasn't about to reestablish himself as *Enemy Number One.*

"Can I, just..." he hesitated for a fraction of a second before leaning forward and pecking her on the cheek.

Surprising him, Lise leant toward him, embracing his figure.

"Thank you," she whispered.

Finding his face resting in the crook of her neck, he inhaled deeply, taking in her fragrance before grudgingly pulling back.

"Yer welcome," he murmured, turning to his door and heading inside without looking back.

I don't know what for, but yer welcome.

Turning slowly Lise headed for the work vehicle, unsure what to make of their relationship but happy enough to focus on the fact that she'd had a great evening with him and wanted things to continue that way.

October

Wes looked between the trees lining the drive, grinning at the sight of the numerous sleek bodies grazing or dozing while standing, tails flicking at annoying flies.

She was in the station wagon with her parents as they drove at the 20 kilometres per hour speed limit down the wide driveway of Nirvana Park. For the next four weeks she would be working on the property, carrying out her first lot of work placement. The idea in itself emitted nervousness and excitement.

As they continued on down the sandy coloured drive, plaques with the names of group winning or placing horses caught Wes' eye. Some she was familiar with, others not at all. It stood to reason that they were bred on this property though.

Her parents murmured appreciatively as the driveway ended, bringing them outside the weatherboard, cottage like office.

To the left lay an old weather beaten house and to the right, two sets of stables, paddocks, a large shed and what appeared to be private stable blocks, four in a row.

The three stepped out of the car and headed to the office, Wes' mother rapping on the door before opening it and leading the way into the simply set up room. A woman in her fifties or so greeted them with a smile. She finished typing something on the computer before turning her full attention to the three.

"I take it our work experience student for the month has arrived."

At the affirmative nod from Wes she informed the three that Wes would be staying in the house just outside the office that was located to the left of the drive. She told them that they may as well start unloading anything they'd brought along and that Mr. Kingsley, the farm's manager would be over shortly to introduce himself to Wes and her parents.

Wes was amazed to find upon entering the house, that no one was home although the place definitely looked lived in. She'd been told she was living with one other person, a female member of staff and that the room beside the living room was to be hers.

Not seeing any reason to wait, her parents helped her to take things from the car and set them up in the room allocated to her.

Wes' father continued to bring in bags and her guitar while her mother helped to place things, giving the room a more homely feel.

By the time they'd finished, Wes' housemate still hadn't arrived. Concluding she should see a bit of the farm before it got dark, she exited the old house with her parents. Kingsley was heading in their direction and gave them a smile as he approached.

"Pleased to meet you," he said, shaking first Wes' hand and then her parents.

"I always like to meet the parents and rest any concerns they may have. I have a young daughter, myself," he stated.

Wes tuned out as the parental figures talked, her gaze taking in the large property, neatly mown lawns, pruned roses bushes and other flora.

Shortly after, Kingsley was departing, telling Wes that she should check out the gardens behind the main house and that the swimming pool was available to all staff if she liked to swim.

"Are you likely to want to go back to TAFE?" he father questioned with a grin.

She returned the smile and shrugged.

"I'll let you know in four weeks time."

Giving each parent a hug goodbye she waved as they departed down the long drive. Making a full circle, she took in the property and opted to check out the gardens that Kingsley had mentioned first.

The gardens were indeed worth a look, as Kingsley had said. Wes stood at the base of them, staring up at the main house. It was an old bluestone building and the gardens were beveled, being in layers with the same bluestone marking each layer.

There was a myriad of colours with bright roses, different coloured maple trees, poplars and many perennials.

The wisteria draped across the balcony of a room of the house was what most caught Wes' eye and she made her way up the levels of the garden to get a closer look.

The pool was of a reasonable size and clean, looking inviting despite the cool day. Smiling she turned around to look back over where she'd walked and found the downward view from the house to be even more stunning.

Making her way slowly back down the levels of beveled garden, she paused at a particularly appealing wattle, the blue leaves, yellow flowers and purple seed pods aesthetically pleasing. Reaching up to the tree she extracted a handful of the pods, concluding that on her place it'd be nice to have a plant from this gorgeous property.

Exiting the gardens she wandered back toward where she'd be staying, moving past the old building out to a large set up of many yards.

Quickly she spotted the crush and looking at the large floodlights on tall poles, concluded the area was used for foaling. Proving this to be the case a number of heavily in foal mares were gathered in a couple of the yards, standing nose to tail to keep flies from each others face with a well timed swish of the tail.

A Ute pulled up beside the yards and a rough looking older male jumped out, dragging a rolled up leather case out from the tray at the back. Spotting Wes he waved her over. She approached uncertainly.

"Afternoon. You working here?"

"Yeah. I start work experience tomorrow."

"Wrong. You start now. Care to hold that old mare over there?" he pointed toward one standing by herself, a front leg resting on its toe.

"Ok," she stated uncertainly, taking the head collar he offered.

She climbed between the wooden rails and walked over to the side of the mare, putting the head collar on and securing it before giving her a pat and heading back toward the man who was also climbing between the rails.

He put the case down, extracting a hoof knife and rasp from within.

"I'm Rob, by the way. Do night duty here a couple of days a week. Saw this mare was sore last night and figure she's got an abscess. Thought I may as well have a dig around and see what I can find," he muttered from underneath the horse.

Wes nodded and then smiled, realising he couldn't see her non verbal response.

"Do many mares foal down here?" she asked curiously, holding a hand out to the muzzle of the dark mare who breathed in her smell.

"About a hundred or so, so a reasonable amount."

One hundred! Wes stood quietly, stunned.

"Gotcha!" Rob exclaimed, obviously pleased with himself.

He moved out from under the horse, holding the foot out so Wes could see the pus from the abscess draining to the dirt ground below.

"She'll be a lot happier tomorrow."

Wes smiled and nodded, watching as he picked up his tools and started back toward the Ute.

"You can let her go. Drop the head collar in the back of the Ute and enjoy your placement," he called back over his shoulder, already climbing into the cab.

Wes did so quickly, racing across the yard to deposit the head collar before he drove off toward some other yards. To check the rest of the mares, she presumed.

Shaking her head in wonder, Wes headed back toward the house, thinking she'd better make something for tea from the groceries her mum had carefully picked out for her.

Her housemate was inside watching television, eating a hot meal when she got there. Lise looked up at Wes and smiled.

"Been out for a wander around the farm?"

Wes nodded.

"This place is so big!"

"One of the bigger studs in Victoria, definitely. I'm Lise."

Wes introduced herself and set about making something for tea while she asked Lise what would be expected of her over the following weeks and at what time they started in the morning.

She smiled at the response of six, knowing that time would come around way too quickly.

***

Melanie headed out to the paddock, a head collar and lead rope draped over her shoulder. It was a typical Monday morning, the riding school being empty and things therefore a lot more laid back around the property.

Her mother and Madison had gone out for the day and her father was at work so the young redhead deemed this morning the perfect time to get in some work with the young chestnut gelding, Red.

Maddie had suggested that he may just need to spell a while out in the paddock and maybe in another six months after he'd done some more growing he might be better with his coordination. Melanie was surprised her mother had agreed but didn't see how her doing some work with the young horse would be an issue, either.

Considering the way a horse moved, Melanie was planning on doing a bit of work with Red over elevated poles, hoping to raise his awareness of where he placed his legs while in the trot and canter. She also planned on doing a lot of transition work, encouraging him to increase the pace to a trot, decrease to a walk and repeat the process. The idea was to build up strength in his hindquarters.

When horses cantered, the gait started first with one hind leg shortly followed by the opposite hind and foreleg and finally the last foreleg.

Because it was a gait that started with the driving power of the hind quarters, Melanie felt it important to build up this area of the young horse's body. She concluded that if this area was strengthened, he might find it easier to keep up the canter for longer periods of time. The pole work was to try and help him put his feet down in the correct order so that he wouldn't be disunited.

She'd already set up one side of the sixty by twenty metre arena with four slightly raised poles - otherwise known as cavaletti - and left the opposite long side free of any obstacles in the hope of pushing him out into a canter.

As much as lunging meant he could consistently go around in a circle at a particular pace, the young redhead thought the twenty metre diameter lunging was carried out on was too small and therefore tough on the horse to keep up a canter for any length of time.

Also, it'd be easier for him to be balanced going down a straight line rather than in a small circle at a high speed.

Bringing the gelding into the tie up area, she tied the lead rope in a quick release knot before picking out some brushes to give him a good groom.

She worked methodically, using the rubber curry comb in circular motions to bring up any loose hair and dirt. This was followed by the body brush which was also used over the more sensitive parts of the horse's body - his legs and face.

Lastly Melanie used the hoof pick to clean out the build up of mud and stones in the young horse's feet.

She worked from the heel of the hoof toward the toe, picking out the unwanted matter in a downward motion, being careful not to press the sharp pick into the sensitive frog. The frog - the softer part of the horse's hoof - acted as a shock absorber and when it hit the ground it pumped blood up through the horse's legs.

It was important to make sure there were no stones pressing into this tissue area that could bruise, and that mud wasn't left packed in between the clefts where it could cause rotting of the frog.

This done she headed out to the arena with the young horse attired in a head collar and no other gear.

Having set up barriers down each long side, Melanie had made it relatively easy for herself to let the horse go loose and just drive him forward with a lunging whip. Because he had been lunged on a regular basis, the gelding was reasonably responsive to voice commands. She used these to steady him or change the pace and very quickly the gelding seemed to understand what was expected of him.

"You're too smart a horse to not have as a viable riding school mount," she muttered to herself, watching the young horse really elevate his legs at the trot as he passed over the cavaletti.

"We might just have to work a bit harder with you to harness that intelligence."

***

Alarm set for half past five the next morning, Wes dragged herself out of bed, dressing quickly in the too cool morning.

After breakfast she shadowed Lise out to the main stables, quickly being introduced to the idea of mucking out boxes while the inhabitants were still inside.

She worked on one side of the box while the mare and foal occupied the other. It seemed to work for the first few minutes and then she found a very curious baby beside her, sniffing at her clothes and the rake she was using to pick up and discard unwanted manure and wet shavings.

She struggled to keep at work without having curious teeth checking out her shirt.

Having headed out of the house with four layers on, she had already discarded two, finding the physical work had quickly warmed her up.

"Listen here, little man," she stated trying to shoo him away with a hand, "if you get too close I'll accidentally catch and bruise a leg with this rake or poke out an eye or something. It's safer to stay away."

The pep talk didn't seem to have much effect and Wes concluded with a smile that the box would be done in half the time if she wasn't fighting off a serial pest throughout.

The shavings were thrown out into the breezeway of the stable, wet patches on the stall's concrete floor covered with lime and then the sides pulled back down and the box evened out with fresh shavings being added if the need arose.

At the end of the muck out, a small bobcat truck came through and picked up and disposed of all the shavings, Wes had been informed.

The morning moved quickly with so many boxes to get through easily taking the staff to morning tea time or the aptly named smoko.

After their short break, some continued with the few remaining boxes while others ran paddocks of horses into yards for vetting or went to catch the odds and ends that were kept in boxes due to questionable health or in smaller paddocks for various other reasons.

As Wes followed Lise across to the vetting yards and crush she was amazed to see one of the other staff overtake her on a four wheeler bike, a mare and foal trotting along behind. The driver of the bike steered with their right hand, the left holding onto the lead that was attached to the head collar on the mare.

"Guess that's one way to go about things," she commented to herself in surprise, hurrying up to get to the vet shed.

The vetting went by in a whir, constantly catching horses, lining them up for the vet, going through the crush where they were assessed by the form of a rectal examination with a scanner. They were then put in other yards corresponding with which stage of their cycle each mare was up to.

Wes wasn't sure she'd be able to follow the whole procession by the end of her time at Nirvana Park and questioned how anyone had come up with an effective way to run such a large property. It was like a production line... for horses.

Lunchtime arrived at a racing pace and went just as quickly.

Lise informed her over lunch that the afternoon was more laid back and today she'd be holding horses for the farrier who was due out at half past one. The pair left the house and headed for the yearling barn as he pulled up the drive. Lise paused to greet him as he exited the car.

"Hi Hunter. How's business?"

"Hey there, Lise. Goin' well thanks. Picked up a new client yesterday. Runs a property full of show jumpers - some nice horses there... Owns that gelding Kingsley used to race... big bay fella, offset at the knees."

"Taidem?"

"That's the one! Going quite well he is... What have we got on for today?"

"A couple of the mares and foals in the yearling barn. Most are straight forward but there's one young filly in particular that toes in a bit on the off fore."

"No worries. We'll straighten that out. How many foals for today?"

"Six, I think."

"You'd better meet our current work experience slave, Hunter. She'll be giving you a hand."

The farrier smiled and held out his hand.

"Stuart, pleased to meet you."

"Likewise," Wes replied accepting the hand that offered a firm shake.

Lise departed, leaving the two for the rest of the afternoon. Wes quickly ascertained that she liked the knowledgeable farrier and asked him questions relating to his work when the opportunity arose.

They were discussing the value of corrective trimming on young horses when a figure's head appeared in the doorway.

"No Dave today, Hunter? And where's your dog?"

The farrier glanced up from where he was rasping a mare's foot and smiled at Tony. The male whom Wes guessed to be in his late twenties rested against the half opened door, one hand holding loosely to a broom.

"No Dave today. Just the better man of the two - myself. Dog's at home with the wife and kids today. I have to sneak him into the Ute if I want him on the road with me. Honestly... have you met the farm's latest work experience slave, Tony?" Stuart asked, noting the male's open curiosity.

"Another slave! This farm seems to run on work experience kids," he stated, causing Wes to grin.

"It seems to be running pretty well, so I'll take that as a compliment."

Tony laughed.

"You do that, kid. Speaking of compliments, I was chatting with Irish before, Hunter... have you heard of the compliment sandwich?"

"The what?" the farrier queried, "and haven't you got work to do?"

Ignoring the second comment, Tony grinned.

"It's a compliment sandwiched between two insults, the compliment sandwich."

"Insult, more like," Hunter cut in from underneath the horse.

"It's ingenious. The theory is if you insult someone followed by a compliment and then an insult, they will focus on the compliment."

"Note – you said *theory*. As a rule people are so insecure that they don't hear the compliment and gain a *complex* about their new found flaws," Hunter muttered, Wes nodding in agreement.

"That's not true! You're just no good at it."

"Insulting people? Woe is me," he rolled his eyes, finishing the off fore of the mare with a flourish of his rasp.

And yet you just did it beautifully. Wes smiled at the pair.

"Observe," Tony conspiratorially whispered to Wes, suddenly finding use for the broom he had been leaning on.

He quietly watched the approaching figure. Wes half focused on the mare she was holding and the man working underneath her. The rest of her attention went to the young woman now walking up the breezeway.

"Afternoon Kaye. Are they new work shoes?"

The redhead smiled and nodded, propping herself up against the wall of a stall, looking down at the pair with apparent contentment.

"Not sure about them... I like your hair today – it covers your earrings," he stated simply, holding back a grin.

Wes did the same, a hand covering her mouth as she witnessed the changes from annoyance to pleasure to anger before the young woman stormed off.

"Well, I'm convinced!" Hunter smirked.

Laughing, Wes followed the farrier out of the box and the stables, waving to the sheepishly smiling figure they were leaving behind.

November

Second Thursday on placement:

Got kicked today. Hurt! We were vetting and as the mares and foals were going through the crush, mum got scanned and baby got to get wormed. Now if I were a foal, I think I wouldn't be complaining... unless of course you're a filly and you know that the paste is just a lead up to later in life when you meet the vet - hand to... err, rear. Whatever happened to face to face?

I mean seriously, would you prefer some paste in your mouth or a human's hand up your rear end? I think it's a no brainer. But still... I got the distinct impression that baby didn't agree. And I have the knee to prove it!

Got handed some worming paste by one of the guys and was told to worm the young rascal. Easy! Right? ...right? Unlocked the crush door, ambled in and promptly got kicked in the knee. Ouch! Paused for a moment, reassessed the situation and concluded I had more brains and therefore should be able to achieve a different outcome. Built self up so much that I pushed forward and ouch! Got kicked again! There's something wrong when you're seeing stars in the middle of the day. Paused a little bit longer and the Irish one came in to give me a hand. (Read: took the paste from me, wrestled with foal and gave it the paste orally in a matter of seconds).

It happened so fast that I couldn't take note of how he achieved it although I did see some pretty stars fluttering about while he was doing it.

Inspected the knee tonight - starting to look blue. Not impressed... if there's pain there should be a bruise to show for it! Will look again tomorrow.

Two days later and bruise still the same. Rather put out about it all really. To add salt to the wound I was on dog watch tonight - covering the shift from 6-9pm. No foals.

Still debating over whether I'm happy or disappointed. Was rapt when the night watch person called me about nine thirty and said to get out to the foaling unit quickly as a mare was foaling down.

Raced out of the staff quarters in the dark (without a torch) and ouch! Slammed into the barrier around the fountain, hitting my other *knee on one of the posts and doubling over the chain between the posts as I hit it full force.*

Convinced self that the stars this time were actually up in the sky and that was fine because it was night. Orientated self and then trotted off toward the foaling unit, still in the dark but a little more cautiously. I don't think I had a noticeable limp this time as I was equally hurt on either knee.

Success! Made it there without any further injury and didn't feel the need to mention my mishap. Foaling attendant did seem surprised that I was out of breath and laughed when she realised I'd been staying in the quarters farthest from the foaling area. Told me if I'd said so she would have come got me. That was another grain of salt.

Got to see the mare foaling anyway which was rather cool. My fifth foaling. Can't ever imagine seeing a total of one hundred which appears to be the amount of mares that they foal down here every season. Insane!

Wes groaned as she heard the shower running in the room next door.

"Stupid early mornings, stupid nights that seem to be on fast forward and stupid coworker who has her showers in the morning."

Knowing she wouldn't like what she saw, she picked up her phone anyway to find out that the time was as she expected - about fifteen minutes before her alarm would go off, insisting she depart from her warm covers into the cool chill of the bedroom. The bedroom that just happened to be covered in wooden floorboards, to encourage her want to get up at half past five in the morning, obviously. Groaning again she rolled onto her stomach, dragging her pillow over her head as she mumbled.

"Who chooses to work with horses, honestly?"

As she lay in the darkened room she stretched her left hand out from under the covers, flexing it slowly. Since the fall from Reign in April it wasn't fully healed and in the cold mornings it seemed to have the same reservations as Wes did with regards to functioning so early in the day.

She concluded with the full on days as well as getting back into her guitar, her left hand was just protesting against the continual use. She didn't deem it time to yet worry about the fact that when she awoke each morning it was extremely difficult to clench and unclench.

With a large groan she sat up, reaching out for the day's clothes which she had kept close to the bed so she didn't have to fully escape the warm covers before putting on warmer layers.

In the half hour she allowed before work each morning she rose, dressed, ate and brushed her teeth before heading out to the closest block of stables to start the familiar routine of mucking out boxes while trying to fight off extremely curious young foals.

As she mucked out a box she smiled over the pay slip she'd received the day before, the third lot of pay she'd received so far, showing her the amount wasn't indeed a fluke. As a student on work placement, Nirvana Park – and any other stud on which she did placement at for that matter – only had to pay her $20 a day. She'd been excited the first week to read that they'd actually deposited $275 into her account rather than the $120 expected.

It did occur to her that this fee was a saving for the stud as they would be paying their full time workers quite a bit more and she was doing as many hours as they. This didn't stop her from being grateful for the larger than expected sum though.

Finishing her second box she moved onto the next, knowing they had a big vetting day ahead of them. After all it was Wednesday. Monday, Wednesday and Fridays were the busier vet days, busier being a total of 100 or so mares to vet. It amused her to think that on a quiet day like a

Saturday they still did in excess of 60 mares; perhaps six times more than a big vetting day at TAFE.

She couldn't believe how long it took all the students – herself included – to do ten mares at TAFE. It occurred to her that they'd all be that much more efficient after completing individual breeding placements.

Especially if they'd been doing as much vetting as she! Wes was amazed that she'd handled in excess of one hundred different horses – a sum she couldn't fathom ever achieving in her lifetime and yet it had happened on her first placement. She could only conclude that nothing could beat practical experience and looked forward to her other two placements that she had to partake of before finishing her diploma.

Finishing in the stables she sighed, realising it was only another week before she was back at TAFE. She wasn't sure she wanted to go back to the classroom and knew it would come by in a rush.

Smiling to herself she headed over to the two foaling boxes with her rake. She was more than ready to clean them out if they hadn't already been done.

***

"So do you have any specific riding goals, Gary?" Maddie asked of her new client as they made their way out to the arena.

Jack was out in the cross country paddock with Jacinta and her gaze wandered that way, taking them in before focusing again on the older male. He smiled down from the tall chestnut gelding he was on.

"Not particularly... However, I've actually taken an interest in the Great Australian Cattle Drive and seeing as it's not that far away, feel that I should get back into regular riding so that I don't end up too sore after the five days of constantly being in the saddle."

"Sounds like a wise move," Maddie conceded with a grin, closing the gate to the arena after them.

She talked Gary through the general riding position and how it helped to keep you balanced over the horse but suggested that when riding over the five days, position may not be listed at the top of his priorities.

"Because it's such a long ride, perhaps we should focus on the difference between the rising and sitting trot and what best works for you. I'm guessing you'll be riding in a stock saddle which is rather different to the general purpose you're in now. It'll be a bit harder to rise to the trot in a stock saddle because of the way it's put together, so it'd be worth your while being established at the sitting trot."

Gary nodded, stopping his mount at every second letter as Emmy had previously instructed, counting to three and then asking the gelding to move on again at a forward walk.

"It'd be good to establish the rising trot too as I think over a long distance this can be easier on your seat and easier on the horse's back. So we'll focus today on both and constantly changing between them. Does that sound ok?"

"Sounds like a plan," he replied with a smile.

As Maddie directed him, he shortened his reins and pushed the chestnut horse into a trot, focusing first on establishing the up down rhythm of the rising trot. This came relatively easy for the client who had ridden previously, just not for a long time.

After Maddie felt they'd covered enough for the day, she directed Gary out of the arena for the last ten minutes of the lesson, talking him through the position needed as a rider went up and down hills.

"I don't know what the terrain will be like on your ride but again, it's all about balance. On the way up a hill we lean forward a bit to help take the weight off the horse's back. On the way down a hill, we need to lean back but be sure not to pull on the reins and therefore the horse's mouth. It's best to trust your mount and give them a loose rein. You can hold onto the pommel of the saddle if you need to, to keep balanced."

They finished their lesson on this note, the older man apologising for having to leave without tending to the horse but thanking Maddie all the same and telling her he'd book in for the following week.

As Maddie led the gelding back to the tie up area, she spied Jack and Jacinta already back. She struggled to hold back a grin as Jacinta was talking earnestly to Jack, her hand on his arm.

"Seriously Jack, you should know better," she commented to herself cheerfully.

She approached the pair casually, asking Jacinta how her ride was. The young girl turned her attentions back to her horse with a grin.

"Great! As always. I was just telling Jack he should come out riding with me sometime."

"What a lovely idea!" Maddie replied enthusiastically, putting a head collar on her horse and removing his bridle.

"I wasn't so sure my girlfriend would agree," Jack muttered, turning his attention to cleaning out some brushes.

"You're seeing someone?" Jacinta asked with surprise, the brush pausing just above her mare's sweaty coat.

"Yeah... an instructor, redhead, rather on the talkative side," he replied with a glance in Maddie's direction, before looking at Jacinta with a small smile.

Her gaze also went to the young redhead, brows raised in surprise.

"Really?" Maddie asked, pulling off genuine surprise, "You know another person like me? Fancy that. I'd love to meet her."

Jack threw down the brushes in frustration.

"When I tell *other* people that we're going out, are you going to act surprised then, too?" he queried, picking up Geira's saddle and heading into the tack room.

Jacinta followed with the bridle, her curious gaze resting on Maddie until she'd passed. Maddie laughed to herself, thinking the whole situation to be too amusing.

"Perhaps you should consider pursuing someone who's actually interested, Jack," Jacinta stated on her return from the tack room, untying the lead rope and taking her mare out to the paddock.

The young man stared after her in surprise. Eventually his gaze fell on the laughing redhead.

"You keep this up Maddie Jamison and I'm going to have to convince your twin to act like part of a couple. After all, it is *Emmy* that I told Jacinta I'm involved with."

"You wouldn't dare!"

"I need to get it through to the girl that I'm not available so just keep pushing and you bet I will," he muttered, storming off toward the hay shed.

Grinning to herself, Maddie continued brushing the gelding that Gary had been riding. *Too amusing, indeed.*

***

Wes had decided it was definitely good to be back at TAFE. The second lot of students were a week into their breeding placement and consequently student numbers were lower at the TAFE facility.

Her first placement had convinced her she wanted to stay with thoroughbreds and focus on breeding. She was rapt when one of her teachers told her they had a breed that afternoon and she was to be handling the stallion.

"That's what happens when you turn up consistently to TAFE," he'd said in response to her surprised look.

The excitement was currently being piqued by nervousness however as she worked to put the leather head collar on the TAFE stallion – he was obviously excited by the familiar routine.

Her head was protected with a helmet but Wes had to work a bit to keep her hands from his nipping teeth. Once the head collar was on, bit in mouth and lead clipped up to the pair, Wes walked with brisk strides, her teacher beside her as they made their way to the covering shed.

They entered the breeding shed where the mare was waiting, a handler at her side.

The mare had a bit in her mouth as a form of restraint, a tail bandage to contain the tail hairs and keep the area underneath clean and breeding boots on her hind feet to minimise damage to the stallion from a kick.

Wes followed the teacher's instructions, leading the stallion to the near side of the mare, close to her flank.

This way he wasn't right behind her where he could cop a kick if she wasn't receptive to him. The students had been told that just because a mare was receptive to the teaser stallion, they could be intimidated by the larger stallion used for breeding. She thought the idea interesting but wasn't about to ignore the advice.

Following the teacher's instructions, Wes put pressure on the lead rope, effectively putting pressure on the bit in the horse's mouth to encourage him to move back a little from the mare as he was pushing the mare around a bit.

Listening to this form of discipline he stepped back a bit, looking at the young woman. Wes smiled at the question that seemed to be on his face – *when are you going to tell me it's ok?*

The breed went smoothly with the mare well receptive to the stallion and Wes was amazed to find such a difference in the stallion on the stroll back to his paddock.

"All the energy's suddenly gone, ey?" her teacher queried with a smile, seemingly reading her thoughts.

Wes nodded as she took the head collar off and released the chestnut figure, closing the gate after her.

"Wasn't so scary now, was it?" his grin widened.

"Well, I managed it, that much is true," she replied with a grin.

December

Lise ran a hand threw her hair, the other fighting to cover a large yawn. After such a long and distressing evening, a day's work wasn't high on her list of interests but she felt it'd be unfair of her to sit the day out just because she was tired.

Declan raced after her slowly disappearing figure once he'd put out his stallions. Being near the end of the breeding season there weren't as many mares left to be covered and consequently the stud wasn't breeding so early in the morning. The staff were now starting at half past six rather than six, which was appealing too.

"I hear ye had a rough night," the young Irishman commented, calling out to her.

"You can say that again," Lise replied, smiling softly as he came up, offering her a quick hug.

Lise accepted it, walking with Declan up to the barn.

"So ye spend all night up tending to a mare with a bad foaling and then ye conclude yer going to work all day? Kingsley should've told ye to go to bed."

"He did," Lise replied with a shrug, "I was supposed to work today though and just because the evening ended up being eventful doesn't mean I should shirk on today's work."

"Lise, it's the end of the season and things have really quietened down. Besides, the yearlings come in, in two day's time and then things will be back to full on. Take advantage of the quiet while ye can."

"I must be tired," Lise muttered, pausing outside the stables.

"Why's that?"

"You're starting to make sense, McAlister," she replied with a wry grin.

He grinned, leaning forward to peck her on the cheek quickly before putting his hands to her shoulders, turning her back toward her house and away from the stables.

"Well while I'm making sense, I'm going to push because ye may just listen. At least get some sleep until lunch time. Ye can come back for the afternoon feeding if yer so worried we can't survive without ye," he joked.

Lise waved his hands away, trudging slowly toward the house telling herself she at least needed the sleep so that the world would make sense again and the Irishman would stop talking logically.

***

Wes opened the car door with a grin, unsure if she should consider sitting in the back.

She was on her second placement, now focused on yearlings for the first time. The owner of the boutique stud said she'd like to show Wes around and explain the run of the property before the young woman physically started working.

Noting her dilemma the older woman directed her oversized poodle into the back seat rather than up front where it had been resting its paws on the dash, staring out the front windscreen.

Shortly after the pair set off, Wes being asked questions on what she wanted to do with horses in the future and more amusingly, her exact height and weight. There was no explanation for these questions but she concluded logically that it might have to do with her uniform at the sales and what horses she could parade for clients.

Smaller staff tended to be preferred by studs when it came to showing off yearlings at the sales. This gave the appearance of a more filled out, taller yearling which was appealing to the buyer.

Wes' placement was technically five weeks long whereas the full yearling preparation consisted of eight weeks and the actual sale.

This placement was the end of the first year's TAFE year and consequently it was common practice for the students to stay on the full eight weeks and then attend the sales. They had the choice to only do the five week placement but were expected to attend a yearling sale as part of their practical work in order to pass.

Wes concluded that unless she really disliked the work – which she figured was highly unlikely – she'd do the extra three weeks work, especially considering this would be at a full wage rather than work experience pay.

The property that she was taken around consisted of a little over a hundred acres and mainly housed beef cattle which is where the owners made their money. The horses were a passion and consisted of around a dozen well bred mares and as many weanlings.

Only six yearlings were being prepared for the Melbourne Premier Sales and Wes was rather thankful for the smaller number, thinking it'd be an easier introduction to the large but uneducated animals.

There was one potential downfall to the small number of yearlings – because the farm never prepared more than half a dozen at one time, there hadn't been the need to invest in an automatic horse walker.

This meant for Wes as she quickly found out over the next few days that she was going to get a lot of exercise.

The routine consisted of starting around seven in the morning and first putting the two colts out into one paddock and then the four fillies into another. Wes was generally working with two other women – the manager and another staff member hired for the yearling preparation.

There was also an older man in charge of the cattle and maintenance of the property who helped with putting out the four fillies and later walking them.

Once the young horses were out, boxes had to be mucked out which Wes found to be just as physically exhausting in the height of summer, as walking the horses. This was especially so as the walks were increasingly lengthened to further exercise the young horses.

With a couple of boxes left to do, two staff would walk the colts while the third member finished off the boxes.

Once this was done, feeds were made up for the afternoon feeding of the farm. The three then borrowed the maintenance man and went out to the fillies paddock to catch them and walk them for a half hour or so. This time increased over duration of the sale preparation and Wes found herself walking up to two hours a day, humming songs in her head to help pass the time of walking the paddock perimeter.

This brought them to lunch time in which the hour and a half off seemed torture to Wes as there was nowhere really cool to rest and she often ended up stretched out in the shade of a tree fighting to ignore the copious amounts of flies.

The afternoon consisted of thoroughly grooming the young animals, feeding up the yearlings and others on the farm, checking water troughs and fence lines before making up the feeds for the following morning.

Knock off happened around half past four and Wes wearily climbed into the manager's well air conditioned car for the half hour drive back to her house where she was living for the duration of the placement.

The first couple of weeks she found to be the hardest, getting into the routine of such a physically demanding job and working to handle the two colts, one of which was particularly difficult.

She'd already decided in these two weeks that perhaps the breeding season was more for her but couldn't wait to reach the end of the preparation and attend the sale.

***

"Are you and Irish involved yet?" Jeremy asked of Lise, pausing from mucking out one of the many yearling boxes.

Lise looked around in alarm, checking that no one else was within hearing distance. She sighed in relief noting that the others that were in the barn were up the other end. Jeremy laughed.

"Paranoid much?"

"Shut up, you! The last thing I want is people gossiping about me and Declan behind our backs..."

"Good thing I'm doing it to your face then!" he stated cheekily, ducking as Lise threw a piece of dry manure at him through the bars of the stall.

"Delightful. Now seriously, he's been back near on five months and I find it hard to believe that you're not an item. Correct that, I find it hard to believe he hasn't made a move!"

Jeremy ducked as another piece of manure flew past his head.

"Should I assume that this topic is off limits?" he queried with another smile, going back to turning over the shavings box.

"Catch on quick, don't you?" Lise muttered sarcastically, turning her back on him.

Finishing the box Jeremy picked up his rake and headed to the other end of the stable block, concluding that if he couldn't get an answer out of Lise, perhaps Declan would be more helpful. Noting that most of the boxes had been done and Declan wasn't in sight, he paused at the door to another box.

"Declan over doing the stallion boxes?" he asked Kaye, watching her level out the shavings as she finished that particular stall.

"Think so. Tell him once he's done it'll be time to get the second lot off the walker," she replied.

Jeremy nodded, turning and exiting the dark boxes, pausing in the bright sunlight to let his eyes adjust before heading down to the separate stallion boxes. He found the Irishman alone, working on the third of the four stalls.

The stud didn't officially stop covering mares until December 31st so despite having a stable full of yearlings, the stallions were still boxed overnight and being put out during the day. Rocket wasn't heading for the Northern Hemisphere's breeding season again for which Declan was grateful.

He would have gone with the horse but didn't fancy the idea of leaving Lise for another six months.

"Kaye says it's nearly time to take the yearlings off the walker. Will I do this last box?"

"Thanks. That'd be great. Are ye nearly finished up in the barn?"

"Yeah. There's a couple left to do but I thought I'd leave Lise to do them, use up her energy rather than throwing manure at me."

Declan laughed, pausing from his work to catch Jeremy's amused gaze.

"I thought I was the only one who got her aggravated. What'd ye do? Or say?"

"I just asked her, out of genuine curiosity whether or not you two were involved yet."

Declan roared with laughter, leaning against the wall for support.

"Quite the opposite reaction to the young brunette, I must say," Jeremy stated with a chuckle, "good thing opposites attract!"

"Perhaps," Declan replied with a small smile, "but if she asks, tell her I had the same reaction - much annoyance and telling ye to mind yer own business."

"Hmm... still trying to get in her good books I see. I'm thinking that answers my question of whether or not you're involved but seriously man, why are you taking so long?"

Declan just smiled at Jeremy before turning back to finish the box he'd been working on. Jeremy rolled his eyes and started on the last box, thinking he'd have to try a different tact.

Declan concluded he was saved when Lise came roaring up on one of the four wheelers, announcing that Kingsley wanted them to check over the weanlings and do the morning feed run. That was, safe from the face to face questions. He was sure a bit of talking would be going on while he and Lise were elsewhere. Not that he minded... not at all.

With a grin he left his fork propped up against the stall door before hopping on the back of the bike beside Lise, holding on tight as she took off to the first paddock.

As they were feeding out in the last paddock Declan supplied Lise with the information that Kingsley had mentioned a mare was arriving late that morning to be covered by Rocket and she'd be staying on the farm to foal down the following year.

"Someone is sending their mare this late in the season to be bred?" she asked in surprise, looking at Declan from the other side of the trailer as they each scooped out feeds to hungry weanlings.

"Apparently she foaled down about three weeks ago. They've short cycled her as they didn't fancy her chances of conceiving on foal heat. She's an older mare."

"But why not just give her the year off and breed her early next year? Or if they're not so bothered about what time of year they breed her, wait to go to Rocket for late next year when he's got progeny racing and we know whether he's a good producer or not."

"Ye can't always talk sense into racehorse owners. She should be turning up shortly," he commented, glancing at his watch, "will we finish up and head toward the loading yards? I'm sure the others will be tied up with the last lot of yearlings."

Lise nodded, getting back on the bike and relaxing into Declan's side as he sat to the left and behind her, one hand holding onto the right hand side bar of the rack he was seated on; effectively resting his arm around her.

They pulled up at the side of one of the stable blocks, stopping in the shade, Lise concluding she couldn't be bothered moving to unhitch the feed trailer.

She leant back as Declan's arms came to embrace her, his hands closing together over her stomach. She glanced back at him and smiled, resting her head against his shoulder. Declan squeezed her gently, debating if his advance would be welcome, telling himself he'd had enough of playing games. He wanted this woman. He hesitated before kissing her on the cheek.

Lise only responded by relaxing further in his arms, telling herself off for feeling a pleasant tingle run over her body. She didn't want to move but knew that they should at least deal with the feed trailer while waiting for the truck to arrive.

Not having really analysed Declan's movements – after all he'd more frequently been wrapping her up in hugs – she felt herself jump when his lips brushed her neck.

Not convinced that her shock meant his movement was unwelcome, Declan rested his lips at her ear, his warm breath tickling her. When Lise made no move to leave his embrace, he returned his lips to her neck, moving slowly as he kissed her repeatedly, his lips traveling under her jaw and down her throat as she tipped her head back, exposing the bare skin leading down to her covered chest.

"Ye hear that?" he queried softly, resting his lips at her ear.

"Hmmm?" Lise responded, not fully focused on what he'd said.

"That'll be yer truck," he muttered, releasing his hold on her.

Lise sat up quickly, watching Declan as he hopped off the bike and went to remove the trailer for filling up later.

Her gaze on the truck coming down the drive, Lise stepped off the bike, waiting for it to stop. She then helped the driver to let down the large door that served as a ramp for the mare and foal to exit.

She frowned when she took in the sight of the thin mare, a large amount of her ribs visible. *Don't know how anyone can expect to breed from a horse in this condition... I'm surprised she's even cycling.*

She moved her gaze over the foal as she stepped up the ramp and unclipped the mare. Her frown deepened as she attached a lead rope to the mare's head collar.

The young foal had one badly conformed leg, the off fore being what was termed as carpus valgus. This meant that the deviation involved the foal's knee and resulted in a knock kneed appearance.

Noting that in this shape the foal really needed to be locked up to restrict movement, Lise called out to Declan saying that they'd better put down one of the foaling boxes. The Irishman nodded, heading toward the hay shed on the bike.

Lise put the mare and foal in a holding yard and checked they had water before handing the head collar and lead rope back to the truck driver, thanking him.

She then strolled toward the set of double boxes, rolling her eyes at Declan who came roaring up behind her as he blasted the horn before slamming on the breaks.

"Want a lift?"

"The whole hundred meters to the foaling boxes? I think I'll survive," she stated dryly as his face broke into an amused grin.

"And where would I be sitting, hmmm?"

The front and back of the vehicle were loaded two high with bales of straw.

"I was going to offer this small spot, right in front of me... of course, it'd be a bit cosy and I'd have to wrap me arms around ye, but for the sake of saving ye the walk, I'd sacrifice me comfort," he responded seriously.

Lise laughed, walking past the vehicle only to have Declan rev the engine and hoon past her, supposedly offended by her lack of interest.

She smiled to herself as she watched him fling a loosely tied bale into the box, effectively breaking it from its bailing twine hold, flakes scattering about the box. He quickly came back for the second bale, leaving the blue twine resting over the handlebars of the four wheeler bike.

Coming to an amusing conclusion, Lise followed Declan's broad frame closely. Indifferent about the weight of the bale of straw he was carrying, he easily dropped it in the box and knelt on the square frame, working to loosen its bind - two pieces of bright baling twine. Striding forward, Lise gave Declan a small shove, grinning as the plan to catch him unawares worked and he fell to the floor of the straw box chuckling.

"That's cheating ye know," he grinned as he made to stand.

Pushing him back down, she stood over his figure before dropping to her knees, straddling his legs as she leant over him, placing a light kiss on his lips.

"And you have a problem with that?" she questioned in mock sincerity, smiling as he propped himself up on his elbows to sit face to face with her.

Reading his amused and yet surprised gaze, she smiled to herself as she leant forward to softly kiss him again, her body shivering with the pleasant feeling of his arms embracing her, hands traveling over her back as Declan returned the kiss, pulling her down with him.

"Yer something else, ye know that?" he questioned softly after they pulled apart, his fingers reaching out to tuck a strand of hair behind her ear.

"Hmmm, as long as it's a good something else, I'm fine with that."

"It is," he responded, leaning forward to kiss her again before jumping to his feet to finish putting out the straw.

Lise grinned and rose also, grabbing a pitch fork to shake out the flakes of straw.

Year 4

January

"Another tafie!" Declan stated in surprise, finally reaching to shake the hand that was being offered to him.

"Of course. At least two for the breeding season, each for around a month and then one to two during the yearling season. You've been here longer than myself Declan and it's not surprising to me," Lise stated dryly, stepping sideways quickly when the Irishman made to poke her in the side.

The young male smirked when his gaze caught Lise's. She smiled in return.

"So which TAFE facility are you from then, Clarke?" she addressed him.

"NMIT in Epping."

"Lovely. And we've got you for up until the end of this yearling preparation and the sales?"

"Definitely... and Mr. Kingsley mentioned that it should be possible for me to stay on longer, until I'm due back at TAFE for my second year. He said there were a lot of horses for the following sales and weaning to be done and wouldn't knock back an extra pair of hands."

"Definitely not!" Lise agreed, excusing herself from the two males to go load up the trailer for the feed run.

"So what can I do?" Clarke asked, looking to Declan for an answer.

"C'mere, ye do start tomorrow, right?"

"But I'm here now," the male reasoned with a grin.

Declan laughed.

"I like ye already. Tell ye what. I was going to do the feed run with Lise but how about ye go offer her a hand so ye can get a look at the farm. I'll make up some afternoon feeds for the stabled horses."

"Sounds good. Just point me in the right direction!"

Declan headed to the end of the stable block, Clarke walking alongside him. The young man paused outside the stables, his gaze suddenly elsewhere. Declan grinned.

"Ye know what they say about redheaded fillies, right?" he questioned with a knowing tone.

Clarke caught the Irishman's eye, his gaze momentarily off Kaye.

"That they're worth the trouble?" he replied in a hopeful tone.

"Ha! Great craic!" Declan laughed, patting Clarke on the back.

"I'm warning ye, she's the worst of the lot. C'mon the feed shed's in the other direction."

"Just my luck," Clarke muttered, following the taller male.

"Indeed. Good luck that I warned ye, take my word for it."

Declan wandered back toward the stables after telling Lise of the change of plans. Personally he would have preferred to be on the feed run with Lise to himself but figured he wouldn't have shaken Clarke's company and at least this way the afternoon feeds were getting made.

He was going into town for lunch with Lise anyway so he wouldn't have to wait that long to have solely her company.

A large grin lit up his face when he came across Kaye in the feed room, sorting buckets into groups for the stallions, teasers and yearlings. Spotting the grin immediately, Kaye eyed him warily.

"What's gotten into you, Irish?"

"The poor taste in the TAFE students these days," he replied cheerfully, taking the lid off the first feed bin and using a scoop to dish out Lucerne chaff accordingly to each bucket.

"We have another student? What, she took a liking to Tony? I'd better have a good chat with her then."

"It's a *he* and *he* has taken a shining to the redhead that he saw briskly walking across the grounds. I think you'd better have a good chat with him, warn him of the dangers of pursuing such a person," he joked, ducking when she threw a bucket at him.

***

Melanie sighed, pulling out the incident book for what felt like the millionth time that day.

"Not another one, surely?" her mother asked from her station at the desk.

She was going over the list for the upcoming competition and consequently hadn't seen the most recent fall - even with her vantage point of being seated before a window that looked out over the arena.

"Indeed, another one. It's not windy today, there's not a sudden change in weather coming that we know of and the horses haven't had changes in feed, nor has it been a big holiday break where people lose time for practicing riding. As much as I couldn't explain the other falls though..."

"This one you can..." her mother stated with a knowing smile.

"Well, when your horse goes into an unexpected canter, holding the saddle and screaming just doesn't seem the best reaction now, does it? It's hardly conducive to staying on."

Mrs. Jamison let out an unexpected burst of laughter, her daughter looking at her in surprise.

"Oh Melanie, every now and again I realise that you do have some of the qualities that Maddie seems to thrust in everyone's face."

"Meaning?"

"It's just the sort of thing your sister would say, that's all. You've only one more group for the day... do you think we could finish with no falls for the last lesson?"

"I sure *hope* so."

Generally Melanie really enjoyed the days that were devoted to preparation for the East Riding School competition. She tended to take the students through their flat work first and enjoyed seeing them execute movements together, forming a dressage test or part of it. This was followed up by some practice jumps and a short course.

It was a great way to pay individual attention to each student and see how they'd progressed over the previous year. She was aware that Maddie loved the days because they required little effort on her behalf – she didn't have to plan for a lesson, just talk them through a pre-written dressage test and then over a show jumping course that had already been set up and the cross country which was permanently in position.

The girls still managed to pull off their Emmy stint with Melanie and Jack taking the morning classes and Madison taking the fewer afternoon lessons.

Melanie frowned as she started to write out the situation in which the latest rider had fallen off. She wasn't sure she liked when her mum noticed particular qualities that the pair shared. Especially when she wasn't sure they were good qualities. Her sister seemed to believe life was one big game and Melanie was convinced there were times in life where things should be taken more seriously.

Maddie was indeed having a ball of a day.

"I almost wish all lessons were devoted to practice for competitions," she commented to no one in particular as another of the intermediate students started off around the cross country course.

With less than an hour to go, the weather had been perfect and the majority of clients were riding extremely well with only one near mishap over a spread in the show jumping course.

Once all six riders had gone through the cross country course, Madison ran once more through the rules of each jumping event before sending them off to cool out their horses.

Spying Jack she strolled over to where he was watching from the other side of the fence.

"Want a hand with haying the horses this afternoon?" she offered, deciding she was in a helpful mood.

He smiled, nodding.

"Madison number two I've got this afternoon, is it?"

"The helpful, cheerful redhead?" she offered with a grin.

"As opposed to the opinionated, infuriating, redhead."

"The one that shows up ninety percent of the time..." she dragged out with a grin.

"I'll take her while I can. I'll just have to put up with the other one."

"Please. She's the one that does all the flirting and kissing, you love her," Maddie winked before turning back to focus on the half dozen riders that were coming her way.

***

Lise was thankful for the extra pair of hands, concluding that Declan would be making up feeds with Kaye and she silently thanked Clarke for saving them a half hour's work. It was always appealing to finish earlier when the opportunity arose.

They worked together to get through the farm feed run before Lise parked the empty trailer in the shed, telling the TAFE student they'd fill it up shortly. First they had to take the last bucket of feed to a lone mare and foal that were housed nearby the feed shed.

Clarke gazed at the young foal as Lise climbed between the rails to empty the bucket into a nearby feeder. As was the routine she checked over the pair, checking the mare's bag to make sure it wasn't too full of milk – a sign the foal was unwell and not drinking. She also checked legs, eyes and their bodies as a whole to make note of any unusual lumps, grazes or swellings.

"How old is this foal?" he queried, resting his arms against the top rail, peering out from underneath.

"She's a couple of months," Lise responded, gazing at the leggy animal.

"She's tiny," Clarke commented, surprised.

"She had a rough start to life... she's slowly catching up to the others. I'm just glad to see that she survived," Lise smiled, reaching out to scratch the filly on her wither, smiling at the natural response of the foal moving it's upper lip in pleasure.

"What happened?"

"She's a haemolytic foal."

"What happened?" he repeated, grinning wryly.

Lise laughed, stepping away from the pair and climbed through the rails.

"It's not overly common in horses, but the general idea is that the mare's colostrum produces antibodies that actually fight against the foal's system and kill off blood cells. If unnoticed and untreated, it'll result in death," she told him as they walked back toward the feed shed.

"But she's out in a yard able to drink whenever she likes, isn't she?"

"Now she is, absolutely. If you know that the mare has this condition then you can easily manage it as the problem is only in the colostrum. Once that's out of her system, you're fine. Generally we muzzle the foals and keep them in a large stall with their mothers but put a barricade between the two so that they can touch, but the foal can't nurse.

"The mare is milked out to get rid of her colostrum and the foal is fed from our store that is collected from other mares. After 72 hours they're right to go together and it's just a question of making sure the foal can latch onto the mare's teat after it's become so used to bottle feeding."

"It's absolutely gorgeous getting to bottle feed them," Clarke commented with a smile, collecting up the empty buckets and piling them together as Lise was doing.

"Oh, it is! As long as the foal is healthy. Generally once we know about the condition we can manage it and the foal does stay healthy and you wouldn't know there was an issue a couple of weeks down the track.

"We weren't aware that this mare had that particular problem though and nearly lost her little filly because of it. It's not guaranteed to happen each time the mare has a foal, it depends on the stallion's genetic make up also, but from now on we'll just manage her foals as if they could be haemolytic and things should run pretty smoothly. It can be frustrating having to deal with hourly feeds though and milking out an aggravated mare," she commented with a smile, getting one from Clarke in return.

The pair quickly had a new batch of feed made up in the trailer for the next feed run before heading back to the barn to see how Declan and Kaye were faring.

It didn't take Lise long to recognise Clarke's interest in the redheaded woman and she smiled to herself, questioning if Kaye would do anything with the obvious interest.

Not sticking around to find out she climbed into the passenger seat of the Ute that Declan had left idling beside the barn, asking the pair left in the stables if they needed anything in town. Declan had put his foot to the accelerator almost before they'd both replied in the negative.

Lise laughed at his eagerness to get off the farm, shaking her head in wonder.

"Ye might well have invited them along with us!"

"I doubt you would have let them get even a foot into the car," she replied as they exited the drive and turned onto the main road.

Lise looked to Declan in question as he put the handbrake on and the car into park.

"Forget something?"

"Ye betcha," he replied with a grin, reaching over to kiss her soundly.

"I wouldn't have been able to do that with them in the car," he muttered, putting the vehicle back into drive and continuing on into town.

Lise just smiled, in complete agreement.

February

Wes sighed and smiled as she lay on the bed in the room they were staying in for the Melbourne Premier Yearling Sales. They were two days into being at the complex with the two colts and four fillies and she was exhausted.

She was so excited to know that she was getting paid one hundred dollars a day for her efforts, have her meals covered and that the roomy accommodation had also been paid for by her employers. Apparently that was normal for workers of the sales and the studs they were employed by.

The yearlings seemed to have settled after 48 hours, slowly getting used to the fact that the complex was underneath many flight paths of the Tullamarine Airport.

Wes was pleasantly surprised that she hadn't yet let go of one of the horses. They had reacted quite badly to the constant planes and sudden movement of people coming around corners of stable blocks.

One of the colts she wasn't parading due to the fact that he was over 16 hands high and she made him look even taller. She was getting practice at parading the other five though and was relieved that she wasn't having too much trouble with the other colt. He'd caused her frustration and tears over the duration of the preparation as she just wasn't sure about the bold male horses that liked to act up and tower over her.

She concluded with a grin that she was getting so used to hanging onto these babies, as she'd had so much practice on the farm in Nagambie that they were previously housed at.

She didn't think that the small stud farm had that much grass that needed mowing over the duration of the eight week yearling preparation and yet in this short time, the maintenance man had often appeared out of nowhere on his noisy ride on mower, always managing to time his work in with when the babies were being led out to their yards or back into their boxes after their hour long walk.

Personally Wes would have thought that he'd time the mowing for when there wasn't likely to be excitable young thoroughbreds about who were inclined to take off. But he seemed to have such a knack for mowing at this time that she'd just learnt to hold on when they jumped sideways suddenly or reared up in surprise.

It had been a lovely place to work and she was convinced the smaller number of horses - a lot of friends were dealing with the preparation of thirty odd on larger studs - had been a good way to introduce her to these almost full grown but not so educated young animals. She was still convinced however that broodmares were of much more interest and easier, too.

Wes listened to the sound of the water running in the room next door where her manager was having a shower and bit her lip to stop from laughing at a memory back on the farm.

The owners relied on rainwater tanks. On the first day when they'd been driving around, Wes working to not get crushed by the large poodle that was convinced it should be in the front passenger seat, she was introduced to the joys of such a water source.

They'd driven past the house where the maintenance man was on the roof, sweeping.

"It rained here yesterday," the driver and owner of the property had said as if in explanation.

Wes had later learnt that the leaves that gathered in the gutters go through the pipes and into the water tanks apparently making the water taste funny. She took great joy in the future months to ask - "been raining again, has it?" anytime she saw that same gentleman with a broom in his hand.

Her attentions turned to the darkening sky outside, blue solar lights throwing a magical glow over the small garden beyond the glass doors that made up one side of the room. Closing her eyes Wes concluded this was indeed like a fairytale as she listened to the dulcet tones of Josh Groban coming from her CD player that was plugged into the wall.

Why would I want to do anything else?

***

Maddie almost grudgingly admitted that summer was starting to grow on her. She wasn't particularly fond of Australia's hot summers, especially in the warmest month of February but to be able to go out for a ride in the cooler hours that came about around half past eight in the evening, well that was something. It was wonderful to know that it was still light enough to consider going for a ride.

She watched a total of three planes heading in different directions across the azure of the evening sky while she waited for Jack to turn up. He'd said he would come by after he'd eaten and tended to his two horses and they could go for a ride before it got too late.

The riding school was located close to the Moorabbin airport, many planes crossing over the perimeter of the property and Madison loved to watch the different lights consistently on or flashing in sequence as the large vehicles traveled across the sky to who knows where.

Maddie decided not for the first time that she really should consider traveling, perhaps teaching or riding over in the UK. Melanie seemed content to stay in Victoria and at the East Riding School for the rest of her life but Maddie didn't see why she shouldn't see how things were done over the other side of the world and potentially bring those experiences back home.

If she was to seriously consider it she realised she should start saving some of that which she earned through teaching... and possibly tell Jack she might be skipping the country.

These thoughts left her mind as a pair of arms came to wrap themselves around her slight form.

"I didn't hear your car or anything," she stated with a smile, leaning back against him.

"I was hoping so," he replied softly, pressing a kiss to her cheek.

"So that you could sneak up on me and scare me, Jack Brown?" she questioned, turning in his embrace to face him.

"Perhaps. It's a rare occasion that I get the better of you, Miss Jamison," he replied lightly, placing a kiss to her lips, "now are we going for a ride or not? I see you've concluded I need the exercise to go and get our horses."

Maddie smiled at his dry tone, kissing him.

"Sook. So I haven't gotten the horses in yet. It'll take a few minutes to catch them and tack them up."

The pair each grabbed a head collar and lead before strolling out to the paddock to catch Phoenix and Marlin.

The young mare was grazing near to the gate, Marlin not much further away. Shortly after they were being led out of the gate, Jack closing it before giving Maddie a boost onto the young mare. He then leapt onto the tall gelding's back, the pair using the lead rope to steer their mounts at a forward walk across the paddock and to the tie up area.

"We could just ride them bareback," Maddie suggested lazily, leaning forward to hug her mare once they'd stopped in the yards.

"Only if you're going to put some more fat across this guy's top line. He's a little light on top to be comfortable for me," Jack stated with a look of longsuffering.

Maddie laughed as she slid off the younger mare.

"Knowing you if you're tacked up it'll suddenly turn into a jump off rather than a relaxing ride. I guess I'll be needing my saddle too, then."

Jack smiled, trailing after the redhead as she made her way to the tack room. She wasn't far wrong, he hadn't done anywhere near enough jumping of late.

***

"One day to go," Lise muttered to herself, searching through the tack box for some baling twine.

One of the Nirvana Park signs was flapping in the late afternoon breeze, and – not surprisingly – scaring any yearlings that had to parade past it. It was half past four in the afternoon and Lise was sure Kingsley would soon be telling his staff to pack it in for the day but until then she was making it her mission to fix up that sign.

Jeremy was in the wash bay with the buckets of feed, adding water to the chaff and grain mix so that they'd be ready to be fed out.

The TAFE student Clarke had worked out well for the farm and Lise had enjoyed working with him and had no doubt about Kaye liking him either. The pair had hit it off but Lise questioned if the relationship would continue with him finishing up in a couple of days.

She pondered this as she sat on the tack box, having found the bailing twine and now in search of a pair of scissors she was sure should be in with the grooming kit.

"Hey gorgeous. Kingsley's getting restless – reckon we might as well start placing rugs out the front of each door so that we can get out of 'ere quickly."

Lise smiled up at Declan.

"Works for me! It'll be wonderful tomorrow morning to have a half hour sleep in. I wish we'd had more that were to go through the sale today."

"Ye aren't the only one," Declan replied with a smile, sitting down beside her, watching as she continued her search through the grooming bag.

"Looking for something?" he questioned with a large grin, holding up a pair of scissors that had been living in his back pocket.

Lise rolled her eyes, leaning forward to take the pair from his hands. Declan pulled them back from her reach, leaning forward instead to kiss her.

"For someone who didn't want to inform others that we're an item, you're sure having fun providing opportunities for them to find out," she smirked when he pulled back.

"Too true!" Declan replied, leaning forward again, a hand resting on her jaw as he kissed her again.

"I should have sent Jeremy in here," Clarke commented smugly, interrupting the pair.

Lise looked up at the young man and smiled as she rose to her feet.

"And why's that?" she asked innocently.

"Because he's so obsessed with the idea of you two becoming an item and he need not worry, obviously."

"Who's an item? Apart from a certain redhead and a TAFE student, I've seen no proof of any other couples in the Nirvana Park staff," Lise replied with a wink, stepping past him with the scissors and bailing twine.

"You'll deny it also, won't you?" Clarke asked with a shake of his head, the question directed at the Irishman.

Declan stood also, stepping past the younger male.

"Deny what?" he replied with a grin and a wink, whistling away as he strolled in the opposite direction.

March

"Hey there. Are you nearly done for the day?" Johnny asked Melanie as he entered the covered area between the tack and feed rooms where a few stalls were set up.

Melanie placed the girth over the saddle before removing it from the back of the horse that she'd been working. She smiled at Johnny, placing a kiss on his cheek before heading into the tack room.

"I promise this is the last one. What were you thinking of doing tonight?"

"Dinner and a movie? There's a couple on at the moment that look like they could be worth watching."

"Sounds good to me," Melanie replied, heading out to the hay shed to grab a hay net and some Lucerne.

Johnny looked over the different piles of hay, noting a difference in colour but not much else.

"Why the green over one of the other types of hay?" he asked.

"This one's Lucerne. It's higher in protein than the others and they tend to like the taste better than the grass hay over there to the left," she pointed.

He nodded, a frown marring his features as he watched her fiddle with the awkward looking rope net – the hay net.

"And why are you putting it in there?"

"I can hang this up to the horse's head height and they can pick at it slowly. A hay net is a good way to keep them eating but it can take longer to eat because it's not so easy to access. It's a good way to slow them down and keep them eating longer, especially if the horse isn't getting fed a lot. Their digestive system copes better if they're continually eating. The hay nets are an interesting thing for someone to have invented," she replied with a smile and a shake of her head.

"And why is that?" Johnny asked, following the young redhead back into the covered area where she tied up the hay net before the eagerly waiting horse.

"Well I'm sure they're just supposed to be used to fill with hay but back when Maddie and I were really young - like one or two years of age - mum used to exercise and train a lot of horses. Dad worked in town so to be able to keep an eye on us; mum used to use the bigger hay nets and place us in them with food and drink and hitch them up to a tree. I doubt whoever invented them had that purpose in mind when they did."

Johnny stared at her, incredulous. Melanie stopped from grooming over the sweaty horse with a grin.

"Her argument was that this way she knew exactly where we were and that we were out of harm's way. I'm surprised the horses didn't react badly to two noisy redheaded babies hanging in hay nets from a tree."

"She seriously did that?"

Melanie nodded her head, indicating yes. She laughed at Johnny's worried look.

"I think you can argue it didn't do us any harm," she stated dryly, winking at him before going back to brushing the equine that was contentedly munching on the Lucerne hay.

Johnny shook his head, questioning if the little 'stunts' the two young women got up to - such as pretending to be the same person when instructing - were perhaps reflections of the sort of person their mother was when younger.

"You're one odd family, you know that?" he questioned with a grin.

Melanie returned the amused smile, putting the body brush away with the rest of the grooming kit.

"Dad's nearly normal, I promise."

"Somehow I doubt that," Johnny shook his head, following Melanie as she untied the horse and headed out to the paddock to put it away.

***

The Magic Millions yearling sales in Adelaide were almost immediately after the Melbourne Premier yearling sales. Wes had relatives in Adelaide and convinced a classmate – Kat – to come with her to attend these sales. They were on holidays from TAFE until mid-April and it was a great opportunity for the two young women to attend another sale, this time just as observers.

Most of the TAFE students had done their yearling placement in Victoria and consequently gone to the Melbourne Premier sales but one of their friend's had done her placement in South Australia and so was attending the Magic Millions sale. The complex was located near to the Morphetville Racecourse.

Wes and Kat had fun wandering around, looking at different horses and they were able to find where their friend was working as the catalog listed where each stud had their horses stabled, based on letters for each stable block and numbers for the individual stalls.

Finding their friend was able to take a short break, the three wandered around the complex, heading up to the sale ring which was set out quite differently to the Melbourne complex that Wes was slowly becoming familiar with.

Wes was surprised to see the small enclosure that you had to wait in with your horse before entering the sale ring. It rather reminded her of a cage and she questioned how much fun it would be to be stuck in there if a horse went off.

Up near the main reception there were a lot of advertising flyers and videos promoting stud services, stallions and their fees and even jobs in the industry. Wes picked up the four or so pages stapled together that advertised current positions available within the thoroughbred industry. She was amazed to see that there were a lot of positions going within Australia and quite a few overseas too.

One particularly caught her eye – a stud up in the Hunter Valley was looking for workers for the Easter Yearling Sales. The TAFE students had been informed that in Australia this was the most expensive of yearling sales – it wasn't uncommon for the young animals to reach the price of one million dollars – especially if it was by the stallion Danehill.

The sales themselves were just before they were due back at TAFE and Wes suddenly questioned if she couldn't get further experience while on holidays – and of course earn some more money.

Wes and Kat had turned up for the last day of the sale and went back with their friend who was working on this stud in South Australia until they were due back at TAFE.

The three talked late into the night, not having to worry about work the next day. Over dinner that evening they'd discussed with the owner and manager of the property the desire of two of them to attend the Easter yearling sales. He said he'd look into a couple of places for the girls which Wes was grateful for.

She and Kat stayed another couple of days on the property before making the twelve or so hour drive back to Victoria. Although on holidays, they soon came into contact with one of their TAFE teachers who stopped them in town.

"I hear you've been looking for somewhere to do the Easter sales," he directed at Wes.

She nodded her head.

"You could have asked me. I've had a chat with Bob and he's lined up work for your mate who's been working for him in Adelaide but I reckon I know a stud that would take you on for the week or so before and during the sales. Give me a couple of days and I'll get back to you."

Wes grinned, thanking the teacher before the pair headed on again.

Two days later it was confirmed and she was packing for a two week stint in New South Wales. The farm was located in the Hunter Valley and Wes was to take a train to Sydney which would be about a seven hour trip and then another up to the small town where she would be picked up by one of the workers.

The train trip up was overnight but Wes found it difficult to sleep on the trip. This didn't stop her from having a wander around the farm she was to be working on when she arrived the next day though.

Set up on a couple of thousand acres, the property was located between hills, seeming hidden in a valley. It took her breath away.

The breeding side of things was located on one side of the road and the yearlings on the other. Wes got shown the breeding side but had nothing to do with it in the week that she was on the farm.

The size of the draft of yearlings was large in comparison to the half a dozen she had just finished up with. Consequently the number of staff was a lot larger, too.

Wes quickly realised that to the numerous males she was considered fresh meat. She was amused by the sudden attention and had a lot of fun retaliating in response to their comments, trying to discourage the interest.

She'd been warned by a couple of staff members that one particular male would probably have asked her out by the end of her first day. She couldn't fathom that but was thankful for the warning for when it did happen, she was able to say no thanks without being put on the spot.

The accommodation was shared and she spent a lot of time in her room, being anti social but not sure about hanging out with so many men in their late twenties and older.

One woman named Colleen whom she guessed to be in her sixties took Wes under her wing for which she was thankful.

On the second day she was introduced to the manager of the property.

"This is the head boss. See him if you have any troubles," Colleen had informed her.

"She can see me if she has any troubles. I'll sort her out," Jaye grinned, winking at Wes.

"And if you're the trouble?" she smirked.

"We'll work something out... we can resolve it over dinner."

Wes had no reply to that comment. Instead she could only smile, which she feared would encourage him further.

The manager invited her, Colleen and one of the older male staff members to dinner that evening. Wes enjoyed spending the time in the company of older people who seemed genuinely interested in why she was working with horses.

The conversation didn't take too long however to get back to the three young men who were having fun stirring and flirting with her.

"They're alright boys, just a bit rough around the edges," Colleen offered by way of explanation.

"And just how many edges do they have?" Wes asked with a grin.

The other two men started laughing, her coworker nearly choking on his food. Wes clamped her mouth shut, working hard to not laugh also.

"Enough to be too rough in your opinion, it seems," Colleen replied with a grin and a shake of her head.

"You didn't hear me say that," Wes replied, smiling as she turned her attention back to the meal before her.

"No, but it did seem implied. Just remember, two of those boys will be accompanying you to that sale and I won't be around to keep an eye on you," Colleen said, a fact that Wes was already aware of.

The other worker, Steve, who was at the table said that he'd look out for her – a fact for which Wes was grateful.

April

Wes spent the next two days that were leading up to the actual sales working hard, finding herself at times in trouble with the young woman who was their yearling manager. That day she'd come in to help with the grooming and seeing a couple of staff scattered about the stables doing the same, picked a box and started brushing the nearly coal black Octagonal filly.

She'd been told once she was halfway done that it was illogical to start in the middle of the barn and that next time she needed to start at one end and work her way down. That way when people came in to help, they knew which horses had already been brushed.

Wes saw the logic and mentally kicked herself, making a note to do so next time. She didn't mind the manager – in fact quite possibly admired the 26 year old who oversaw the stables here, went home at lunch time to deal with her own yearlings that she was prepping for an upcoming sale and then came back to work to finish up with her boss' horses before going home to finish hers.

It was an example to her of how someone could earn enough money from prepping a few horses for clients that would cover the costs of putting their own through the sale. Anything made at the sale from her horses would then be solely profit.

Jaye had been having fun making his interest known over the past few days and Wes was a little relieved to hear he wouldn't be accompanying them to the sales. She didn't mind the interest but didn't like the fact that it was there despite his dating one of the women who worked over on the breeding side.

Jaye wasn't much of a fan of the yearling manager and Wes questioned if he resented having a woman of similar age in charge of him. She caught him complaining about her harsh tones one morning while doing boxes and had to stop and smile.

"Seems to me like you're taking her comments to heart," she cut in as she wandered past the two young men who rarely did work when in each other's company.

"I do – and yours – so don't hurt me too much," he replied all too quickly.

Glancing back she couldn't help but break into a smile at the sight of his gorgeously contagious grin. Shaking her head Wes continued around the other side of the barn to get started on another box.

Shortly after, Jaye and his mate were sent off to another small set of boxes, the yearling manager having asked them to muck them out. Wes questioned why she sent the pair when they both refused to work.

"If I send two people that don't like to work, the only choice is for them to put in and get the work done. They have no one to blame but themselves if the task isn't carried out. If I'd sent a conscientious worker with either of them, that person would do all the work while the other chose to do nothing. This way they have to work."

Wes smiled at the logic, concluding this young woman had a good head on her shoulders. The two young men returned not an hour later, having done the boxes requested of them.

By this time Wes was just coming in from one of the large paddocks that they used to walk the yearlings.

They were to be put on a truck the next morning and taken to the Newmarket complex in Sydney. Wes was looking forward to the sales, looking forward to seeing horses that would be sold for as much as a million dollars.

She exited the box and hung the head collar on the door, keeping a hold of the rearing bit that was to be packed away. Jaye paused at the door with another worker, the pair putting a large trunk down that was to go to the sales. He held out his hand to Wes and she gave him the rearing bit.

"That's to be packed away in the trunk for the sales... I'll pack you away in my trunk later," he stated smoothly, winking at her.

Wes grinned, unable to help it. She was entertained by the attention she was receiving.

At the sales Wes quickly became friends with Josie, one of the girls who generally did the feed run back at the farm but was helping out with the sales. The two were sharing accommodation with the young yearling manager while the other two men were sharing accommodation.

Wes was happy Steve was one of the two men but not so impressed the other was the male who had asked her out on her first day at work. He still seemed to be pressing to spend time with her. She was thankful they were kept so busy during the day with full parades to many clients.

Sometimes it was too much though and Wes found herself frustrated when she paraded a horse to one set of clients and put it back in its box to grab another, which was apparently the wrong thing to do. It wasn't until she'd taken out the third horse that the yearling manager told her she was supposed to be parading to a second set of clients as soon as she'd finished with the first.

Unsure where exactly, she followed after her boss, still leading the young horse. Quickly the young woman in charge disappeared into a spare box where they kept feeds.

"Where are the other gentlemen I'm supposed to be parading for?" Wes asked her.

"Out there," was the unhelpful terse reply accompanied by a general wave in one direction of the complex.

Wes headed to the end of the stable block with the filly and paused, seeing no sign of anyone standing around, waiting for a parade. Unsure she headed back to the box, fighting tears. The yearling manager watched her as she started to take off the gear.

"There was no one there," Wes said by explanation.

"They must have gotten sick of waiting," she replied, causing Wes to bite her lip to stop from crying.

The day didn't really improve with regards to her communication with the yearling manager and Wes questioned what she'd done wrong to be receiving such a cold shoulder.

The one time the manager did speak to her, she wished for the cold shoulder again.

One of the yearlings was refusing to go forward for a parade and needed to be hunted up to go into its box. The young manager informed Wes it was the way she was walking the horse that was the problem. She stared after her boss as that woman stalked off down the breezeway.

"That's it? It's my fault but no explanation why and how to correct?" she said to herself.

Frustrated, she exited the box, making sure it was properly closed after her before wandering after her boss.

"What was I doing wrong? I can't fix it if I don't know why the horse was behaving that way."

"You kept on going backwards with the horse."

"I couldn't keep going forward if she was going backward."

"No but you need to not look directly at the horse when you turn to face them. To look them in the eye is seen as a threat and they'll only continue to go backwards."

Satisfied that she had a reply that she could work on next time if the problem arose again, Wes nodded her head and walked off. She was happy to have a moment's rest before they would no doubt need to parade again.

Wes found other friends in the form of a young man and woman who were looking after four horses that were stabled next door. The male named Tom she guessed to be in his late twenties. He had a mentality for life that left her laughing any time she conversed with him.

It was common for the staff to head out to a nearby pub once the twelve or so hour working day came to an end. Wes was more inclined to hang out with Tom and Al, finding the young woman a bit more grounded and laidback than her boss and workmate. The pair spent most of the evening being amused by Tom's antics.

Wes was amazed to find one of Al's statements about her coworker to be spot on.

"The further back his cap recedes along his forehead, the more he's had to drink. It's amazing to see how far it can go without falling off."

Tom did indeed love to drink and Wes noted that as he became more inebriated, he'd knock at his cap and it'd move back a little further along the top of his head. She found the whole thing rather amusing. The three were having a good chat sitting on stools around a large wooden drum when suddenly Tom stood up.

"Well! I'm off to find my future ex-wife. Enjoy your evening, ladies."

Wes stared after the young man, concluding she'd never met anyone like him.

"One of a kind," Al agreed, seemingly reading her thoughts.

"You know what he said to me the other day?"

Wes shook her head, no.

"I was complaining I was bored – it was a quiet point in the day for us. Well the cheeky bugger says, 'I know what we can do to pass the time', in such a suggestive tone, I thought I knew exactly what he was implying and was ready to give him what for. Then he comes out with, 'Croquet. Wonderful game.' Would you believe it?"

Wes cracked up laughing; nearly overbalancing the stool she was on.

"Oh! That's a classic. Beats a cheesy come on any day, too!"

"He is one of a kind, definitely. Do you think we should get out of here and get some shut eye before it's morning and we're expected to work?"

Wes checked her watch and sighed when she saw it was just after eleven. She was due to be up at five. Nodding in agreement, she rose from her seat, Al doing the same.

It was only twenty minutes later that Wes was clambering into bed but she knew all too quickly her alarm would be going off to start another twelve hour day.

May

"We're going to need to bring in Mal Maree's foal for John to take a look at," Lise commented to Kaye, referring to the resident vet.

Her gaze lingered on the December born foal that had a half closed over eye that was quite weepy.

A grass seed was no doubt causing the irritation. Lise knew they'd need to have the foal in the crush to be able to get their hands on the baby and remove the offending grass seed and treat the eye. Kaye just nodded in response, seemingly bored as she did a circle around the half a dozen mares and foals that were enjoying their morning feed.

"You didn't answer my question, Lise."

"Oh?" Lise responded, working hard not to smile.

She really wasn't interested in answering Kaye's question, but didn't see how she could continue to put it off.

"About you and Declan..." Kaye continued, pausing at the gate so Lise could hop off the bike and open it for them to pass through.

"What about Declan and I?" Lise asked, seeming genuine in her innocently asked question.

She closed the gate after Kaye and stepped back onto the back of the four wheeler bike, legs dangling off the side as they continued on up the laneway to the next paddock.

"We all know he's a flirt, but he seems particularly focused on you, so what's going on?"

Lise smiled at the description, not convinced that Declan spent the rest of his time flirting with everyone else. She nearly started laughing when she considered the Irishman batting his lashes at Tony. Kaye frowned at the amused look on Lise's face, thinking she was being made fun of.

"Sorry, I was just picturing Declan flirting with Tony. You think he flirts with the whole staff?"

Kaye looked taken aback.

"He is rather friendly to most of the female staff..." she stated uncertainly.

"Perhaps that's all it is. I don't know many Irish men, but perhaps they're just particularly friendly people," Lise suggested with a grin, knowing Kaye wasn't feeling so sure of her line of questioning all of a sudden.

"Would you welcome his interest if it became more focused on you?" Kaye asked, trying a different approach.

This time Lise did laugh. It was hardly possible for Declan's interest to be any *more* focused on her, but she wasn't about to tell Kaye this.

"I don't think that's likely to happen," she replied truthfully.

The pair finished feeding the last paddock, Kaye seeming to have given up on her interrogation for the time being. Lise was quietly thankful, thinking that if the prying eyes were more observant, they'd note that Declan had backed off a little with regards to his behaviour toward Lise while they were in front of other's observing gazes.

It seemed obvious to her that this was because he was spending so much time with her one on one that he didn't feel the need to be such a flirt during working hours.

Lise was amused that those who seemed so curious about the idea of her and Declan as a couple kept on putting two and two together and getting five. Not that she minded.

Once they'd finished with the feed run, she suggested Kaye seek out their vet. Lise went back to the paddock to bring in the mare that had the foal with the weepy eye.

She had them waiting patiently at the crush by the time Kaye returned with John. The three worked to get the mare and foal secured in the crush before John hopped in beside the young foal, Lise restraining the small filly while he looked at her eye, removing the large grass seed before putting in some Opticlox, an eye ointment to help with the irritation that the grass seed had caused.

"The grass seed's been in four days," John commented as he stepped out of the foal crush.

Lise looked at him, frowning. *Fancy none of them having picked it up earlier!*

"How do you know it's been four days?" she questioned as she followed him out of the crush.

"The whites of the eye are covered in blood vessels. When aggravated, these grow at about one millimetre a day, so based on the length; I'd say it's been in there four days, irritating this baby's eye. Thankfully there doesn't appear to be any ulceration. She could do with some more Opticlox this afternoon when you redo the feed run and tomorrow. I'll have another look at her tomorrow afternoon."

Lise nodded her thanks; following behind Kaye who led the pair out of the crush and back to their paddock. She was annoyed to think that she'd been on the feed run two days earlier and not picked up the problem then. It worked as a reminder that she really needed to be more vigilant in checking over the young horses' eyes and legs for anything out of the ordinary.

Kaye let the pair go in the paddock before walking with Lise back toward the stables to check what everyone else was up to. It was near to break time.

In the stables the rest of the staff were working with a group of eight recently weaned foals. Being early May, the yearling sales were over and the Nirvana Park crew was able to solely focus on the thirty or so babies that were left to wean.

The August born foals had been weaned in February and with the staff working through them in lots of eight to ten, they'd been brought in for a week with their mothers and lightly handled, being introduced to head collars and the idea of being led. After this week the mares were removed and the new weanlings spent the next week getting used to being on their own and handled by staff.

This continued in a fortnightly pattern with the oldest foals being weaned first. The December born foals were due to be weaned at the end of the month. Lise enjoyed working with the youngsters but still preferred the babies when they were at a younger age, still reliant on their mothers.

There were half a dozen weanlings that were also in the stables, taking part in an eight week preparation in anticipation of the June Weanling Sales at the Oaklands Junction complex.

Lise had had enough of sales for the time being but was pretty sure she'd be attending the weanling sales due to her stature. She wasn't sure Declan would be coming along, thinking Kingsley would be making use of his petite female staff for the small draft of horses.

Once they had been sold, the farm would be quiet for a month or so with staff taking annual leave before the impending breeding season.

Trevor and one of the girls were currently on holidays, taking advantage of the quieter time of year. Kingsley tended to encourage staff to take their full four weeks between May and July but if they chose to only take a week or two off, he allowed this.

The manager refused to let staff work right through though, wanting everyone to take a break before the breeding season started each year. Lise was thankful that he did so, not interested in working with staff over such a busy time of year when they hadn't had a break beforehand.

She found she was missing Trevor though and hoped he was having a relaxing time and would come back refreshed for the breeding season. She questioned with a grin how many months they'd be into the season before he was complaining about stupid owners who couldn't make up their minds about which stallion they wanted to send their mare to.

The staff in the stables were just finishing up, leading the last two recently weaned foals up and down the breezeway while others picked up and straightened out their boxes.

Kaye positioned herself on an upturned feed bucket to wait for them to finish while Lise wandered over to those doing the boxes, checking to see if she could clean out waterers or top up hays.

She specifically offered help to Tony first, almost ignoring Declan due to Kaye's conversation being fresh in her mind.

She chanced a glance in his direction as she cleaned out a water trough and flashed him a smile when she realised he was watching her as he finished off the box he was in. He winked at her, moving aside as the weanling was put away, the stable door secured shortly after.

The staff of six deemed it time for a break and Lise questioned as she walked in one direction and Declan in another if it wouldn't just be easier to alert everyone to the fact that they were involved. Then at least she'd get away with joining him for lunch and breaks without brows being raised in question.

She wondered if Declan was feeling the same and decided it might just be worth asking him and having things out in the open. It was bound to come out anyway when the Irishman was so eager to wrap her up in his arms and kiss her when he deemed no one else was about.

***

Wes survived the Easter Yearling Sales, having enjoyed the two weeks work despite not getting to take any through the sale ring, and having a couple of unpleasant run ins with her boss.

In spite of the issues with the young boss, Wes concluded she had worked hard over the two weeks and hadn't gone out of her way to get on the young woman's wrong side. She did question if she could have done things differently so as not to have gotten herself into trouble on the odd occasion.

Putting the sale down to further experience, she was glad to be back in the classroom alongside her classmates and realised with an amused smile that she was the only one who had attended the Melbourne Premier Sales, visited the Adelaide Sales and then attended the Easter Yearling Sales in Sydney. It was a good feeling.

It was a Wednesday afternoon and the group of eighteen students were in the middle of a nutrition class with one of their teachers. They were discussing the requirements for a stallion over the breeding season.

The projector was on, a slide of typed notes lit up on the wall. Wes was working to write them down quickly while taking in what the teacher was saying. She'd just finished writing that B1 was good for settling stallions when the teacher threw a question at the class.

"Now why would you give a horse B1?"

"Because it settles them," one student responded, reading off the projector.

Wes smiled as the teacher looked at the student, frowning. He looked to the sheet on the projector and then back to the same student.

"Ok, aside from the reason I've already provided you with, why would you give a horse B1?" he questioned in a dry tone.

"Because it's better than B2," another interjected cheekily, looking up from her colouring in of 'Wisteria', a My Little Pony character.

"Are we talking bananas?" a third cut in, half-serious.

"No, you idiot, that's potassium," one of the boys informed her.

Wes laughed.

"Um, I think she's referring to bananas in pajamas," she commented, smirking as the teacher sighed and covered his face with his hands.

Taking a deep breath, he glanced up at the class full of students, Wes thinking he looked upset that they hadn't all magically disappeared.

"I want you all to think about why a stallion's nutritional requirements would be different over the breeding season in comparison to the off season. Next week you can hand in a one thousand word report on the differences required in energy levels, what might be included in a diet to improve libido and fertility and the feed you'd have a stallion on in the off season and what you'd have him on over the breeding months if he was covering a book of eighty mares."

A couple of students rolled their eyes, an assignment this early on in the term not appealing at all. Wes made a note of the rapidly assigned task, questioning if he'd given it just to spite them for being a bit cheeky in class.

"I'm changing slides in two minutes so I hope you've all got these notes down or are nearly done," he also informed them, smiling as a couple rushed to get out pieces of paper and a working pen.

Wes smiled, amused as she finished the last sentence before looking at the requirements of the assignment they'd just been assigned. She wasn't aware there was something that could be given to stallions to improve libido and fertility and made a note to check her *Veterinary Notes for Horse Owners* book that evening to get a head start on the assignment.

Her grin widened as she concluded it was good to be back in the classroom and learning more theory. She'd had enough testing practical work for the time being.

June

Maddie sat at the computer, reading in earnest. That night, watching the planes go over the property before going for a ride with Jack had planted a seed in her mind that seemed to be getting watered on a daily basis.

She was looking through a couple of websites relating to work in the equestrian world, the majority of jobs being advertised in the UK and US. Being nearly 24 she was within the required age bracket of 18-29 that most positions were advertised for. It seemed what once you hit the age of 30; it was more difficult to get a working visa.

Maddie still hadn't spoken to Jack, wanting to look into possibilities first and decide if she really did want to head overseas for awhile.

And of course there was the cost to consider but if she got a general idea now, surely it wouldn't take more than six to twelve months for her to save the majority of what she earned, giving her enough for a return airfare as well as some spending money. And of course she'd be earning something while over there... and would probably have no time to spend it.

The majority of positions offered one day off a week but there seemed no guarantee that she'd have access to a vehicle to get out and about.

One show jumping stable was offering a small house and positions to a couple that were keen to help out in the yard for three to six months, over the peak of the competing season. It seemed they needed two people to help bring on youngsters and keep others in work while the family were often on the road, competing.

Maddie grinned, questioning if it was out of her persuading powers to talk Jack into coming with her. Could he put up with living with her and working for six months though? She wasn't sure.

"What are you up to?" Melanie came into the study, peering over her sister's shoulder.

"Planning my great escape! Do you think you could look after Phoenix for me for a few months? Keep her up with her flat work and maybe over some low jumps?"

"Where are you going?" her sister asked in surprise, and then, "does Jack know?"

Madison looked up at her twin and smiled.

"Not yet and I promise I've no set plans but I'm thinking I'd like to spend some time in a show jumping yard over in England or Ireland. Who knows, maybe Jack will come with me."

"But you haven't even mentioned the idea to him..?"

"I think it'd be smarter to have a place, dates and costs in mind before chatting with Jack."

"He might feel like you're throwing it all at him at once and he has no choice in the matter, you've already decided," Melanie suggested, frowning at her sister.

"Or he might be appreciative of the fact that I've given him enough information that he can consider whether or not he wants to come too," Maddie retaliated, swatting at her twins hand when she grabbed the mouse, trying to scroll down and read one of the ads online.

"My idea, my time on the computer. If you think it's such a wonderful idea dear sister, you can have a look – once I've finished," she stated in no uncertain terms, poking her tongue out at Melanie for good effect.

Her twin just rolled her eyes in response, heading out of the room.

"I'm sure I could manage Phoenix while you're kind enough to leave us alone for a few months," she called back dryly.

"Perfect," Maddie stated to no one in particular, a large grin lighting up her face.

***

Wes said goodbye to the pair of girls, knowing she would see them again very shortly. She was on holidays from

TAFE and about to go out on a road ride. The two she was riding with from TAFE kept their horses a five minute drive away so had agreed to drop Wes off to get her horse ready and then head on to their own.

Wes knew she'd have Reign caught and tacked up before the pair and planned to head out along the path she knew they'd take to get to her. Chances are they'd actually meet up outside the TAFE facilities that were looking very quiet over the holiday period.

Despite not having classes, this hadn't stopped Wes from studying over the couple of weeks off.

The now second year students were due to finish early September and before then they had three major assignments due in. The three pieces tended to amalgamate into one major assignment but were marked as three separate assessments.

One required that the students find themselves a property within Victoria that they were to purchase and set up as a horse stud, catering to two stallions that covered a book of at least fifty mares each.

Wes had found a property that was close to 600 acres located on the other side of the Warby Ranges in Taminick that had a four bedroom house, basic fencing and was going for $1.15 million. She only hoped she could find such a place when she was in a position to be purchasing and setting up *her* own property.

Reign met her at the gate and she set to work brushing him as she thought about the set up of the property she wanted to have for her assignment.

The second assignment required that the students put together a twelve month calendar relating to the care of stud horses. They needed to consider farrier visits, vetting days, when the breeding season starts and finishes, sale dates for yearling sales and weanlings if they chose to do the weanling sales, when worming and injections were due such as tetanus and strangles and so much more.

They were also required to go into detail about the routine of their yearling and/or weanling preparations and different feeds based on different classes of horses - dry mares,

mares in foal, mares with foals at foot, stallions in the breeding season and when not in work as well as young weanlings and yearlings.

Wes was especially fond of this assignment as it seemed to her that once it was done, she'd have a calendar with dates and instruction on how to carry out the care of all classes of breeding horses, all year round.

The one assignment she wasn't so keen on required looking into how much water the stock would need over a twelve month period. Thankfully her property came with a bore with a large water source but she still needed to look into what sort of pump would be required, how many water troughs would be needed to cover paddocks and how the water system would be set up throughout the property.

This she planned to draw on a plastic overlay that sat above the design of her property. She realised what a large job the assignment would be and had been having fun working out the design of paddocks before being picked up by the pair of classmates that were to join her on a road ride.

Tightening her girth, she climbed into the saddle, putting Reign through a walk, trot and canter before heading out onto the road and toward the pair that were hopefully already on their way.

The three did meet on the road where the TAFE facility was located and it wasn't long before they were heading down a dirt track toward the Warby Ranges.

Wes was very quickly falling in love with the town of Wangaratta and looked around her in wonder at the slow incline of the properties backing up to the Warby Ranges. Many gum trees lined paddocks and roads, a couple of places covered with orchards.

The three chattered excitedly about the stud tour they were to partake in the following month.

The second years were due back at TAFE for July but were to spend the first week traveling around the Hunter Valley in New South Wales, going on about half a dozen stud tours. They were excited at the idea of seeing some of the larger studs and more expensive stallions that stood in the country.

Coming to the end of one dirt road, they turned left onto another, Wes' gaze resting on the small property at the end of the road. Being June the property was particularly green which Wes knew to not necessarily be the case in the dry summer months.

But for now it looked gorgeous with a number of thoroughbreds grazing, lovely fencing and trees scattered throughout the paddock to provide shelter and shade.

I think I'll be settling here, Lord. I haven't seen such a beautiful town before.

Her attention turned to her horse suddenly as the three came across a large puddle that they would have to ride through to be able to continue on in the direction they were going.

Reign stopped quickly, not convinced Wes would want him to walk through such dirty water. She smiled, gathering up her reins and squeezing with her legs to push him forward. The other two girls were doing the same, one finally being successful with her mount which convinced the other two that they could also go through.

"That's going to be fun to get back through," Wes stated with a grin, allowing her horse to trot a few strides before settling again into a steady walk.

The three actually made a trip around the large block, enjoying the scenery of the outer edge of town and doing a good job of tiring their horses out.

Wes was dropped off at her paddock before the pair continued on their way, vowing to come back and get her and her gear. She took her time removing her tack and washing Reign down with the hose attached to her paddock, before releasing him and watching him head straight for a patch of dirt and go for a luxurious roll.

Smiling to herself she gathered up her gear and started walking, not interested in sitting and waiting until her lift arrived; she knew she'd meet up with them eventually.

She smiled content with the way she'd spent the afternoon and hoped with all her heart that she would stumble across a property like the nearly 600 acre place she'd chosen for her TAFE assignment. Now all she had to do was work out how to make a million or two.

***

Lise sat down without ceremony, her feet nearly giving way beneath her.

"Tired?" Kingsley questioned with a grin from beside her.

"Silly question. We are nearly done for the day, right boss?" she asked, very thankful that they only had one day left of the June Weanling Sales and then they'd be headed back to the farm.

The last sale for the year. Indeed, Lise liked the sound of that.

"You know, I would have thought you'd have more energy at these sales," Dave Kingsley stated in sincerity, ignoring her question.

Lise looked at him in surprise.

"And why is that?"

"Well that Irish fellow isn't here chasing you around, flirting and carrying on like you were some couple," he replied with a knowing grin.

Lise felt her face flush, turning her gaze away from her boss when he chuckled in amusement.

"I worry at how dense my staff are when the rest don't seem to realise the pair of you are involved."

Lise couldn't help herself, a grin escaped, shortly followed by an amused laugh.

"I did question how they kept on putting together two and two and coming up with five," she responded, catching his gaze.

Kingsley looked at her, his eyes alight with amusement.

"Well for my enjoyment and perhaps for your peace, I hope their math skills don't improve any. You feel free to let Irish know that I'm on to him, however."

Lise grinned, standing up from her position beside her boss.

"I'll be sure to do that. I'm afraid by the time we get back to the farm he would have told Trevor and Jeremy anyway and suddenly Tony will know and the maintenance men and it'll only leave the women I'm currently working with to find out."

"I'm sure your secret will be safe with Trevor, though he may question your sanity, Miss Hemmingway. And I believe Jeremy will be over the moon," Kingsley replied, also mentioning she may as well get the feeds out and tell the others they can start rugging.

Lise smiled in relief, leaving her amused boss to his thoughts while she went to tell the girls that they could finish up for the day.

July

Wes groaned, stretching her legs as she questioned why the CD player couldn't just magically stop working. *Honestly, Lord... you could just make it go kaput. No one would be any the wiser.*

She was amazed to think that of the twelve or so students plus teachers, they only had two CDs between them. How wrong for such a long drive.

The students had met up at the TAFE facility at seven that morning and had now been on the road for about five hours; their lunch break having been an hour ago. Wes was excited about seeing all of the studs they were set to visit over the next four or so days but couldn't wait to get off the small cramped vehicle that had so many chattering bodies.

There had been some amusing moments already with one of the teachers taking too much enjoyment in changing gears with a sudden jerk each time another tried to take a sip of their drink. Wes concluded it was a good thing the cup hadn't contained something hot like tea or coffee when it was constantly being thrown in the teacher's face. *Who said you had to act like an adult when you were older?*

There had been a pause from the repetitive playing of the two CDs for awhile when one of Wes' mates suddenly remembered she'd brought along her guitar. Wary of letting others play it, Wes eventually caved, very quickly questioning why she had when what followed was off key versions of Hello World, American Pie, We Are One, Advance Australia Fair, Wheels on the Bus and countless others that were very repetitive. This was only stopped when the two males partaking in the course declared they needed to stop for a toilet break.

It seemed unanimous with the young women that they continue on their merry way while the boys relieved themselves behind a tree. Wes deemed the pair very lucky that a male teacher was sitting at the wheel and content to wait for them.

On the road again they bypassed a sign for Wagga Wagga, one of the boys proudly proclaiming this as his home town.

"I swear that town has grown in leaps and bounds over the last few years," their teacher driving interjected.

"The town used to be known as Wagga, actually," the young man stated with a grin, "mysteriously the population doubled as it was renamed."

Wes laughed, questioning how many from the town used that joke. The vehicle slowed as the terrain turned hilly and they climbed up through many rundown properties, the only sign of life the lush grass and cattle scattered in large paddocks.

"To your left you will see one of the largest thoroughbred properties in Australia. As you'll see, they take their cross grazing very seriously," the voice of one of their teachers rang out over their chatter.

A few sniggered as they took in the sight of the dilapidated property, cattle grazing in earnest.

"And to your right you will see the dry... heifers for the season."

"How many hours of sunlight do they get?" a student asked, playing the game.

Dry mares – that is mares that weren't in foal – that were to be bred for the season were left outside during the day and brought into stables at night where lights were left on to mimic daylight, tricking the horses' bodies into thinking the daylight hours were longer. This caused them to start cycling earlier in the year so they could be bred earlier.

"Eighteen hours. We do this in the hope of bringing them into season earlier. You'll see the man of the hour in the paddock next door by himself – he's a bit shy."

"A first season sire?" another asked.

"Yeah – he hasn't had any practice serves yet," came the serious reply, gaining a chorus of giggles from the amused students.

It was another two hours before they stopped at the first and only stud for the day. Wes was once again awed by the thousands of acres, questioning if all thoroughbred properties in the Hunter Valley were this big.

As they were taken through the facilities and shown the headstones of well known stallions that had stood at the farm, she questioned if it was these big names that were the reason the stud was able to be on such a large acreage. Good stallions could make an owner millions over the years.

One of the girls took out her camera, focusing on the headstone of the late great Vain.

"Hang on, one second!" one of the boys interrupted her, "it'll be a nicer photo of the boy if we have his attention," he explained, clicking his fingers at the headstone and earning a round of laughter from those standing nearby.

They were shown through the stables, the foaling area, the stallion paddocks and separate stalls for each stallion before being led toward the back paddocks where some pregnant mares were housed, the stallions they were in foal to being listed. Wes' eyes widened as she looked at a group of ten mares about nine months in foal, her head doing some quick sums.

With the stallions they were in foal to, the paddock was easily worth a couple of million dollars. Wes couldn't decide if this was awesome or just plain scary. She wasn't sure she'd like to be on foal watch the night any of these mares foaled down – what if something went wrong? Goodbye hundreds of thousands of dollars.

They bypassed some weanling paddocks, the babies soon to be yearlings as of August 1. The staff member giving them the tour explained the weaning process of the farm.

"We get them used to being handled, washed and walked over a two week period before they're weaned. They're also introduced to creep feeds out in the paddock so they have access to the grain they'll be on once weaned. This way when they are weaned, it's just basically that the milk bar is taken away."

Wes smiled at the description, questioning if this was the way the young foals saw it – surely their dams were more than just a food source to them?

A couple of hours later the students were headed back onto the bus, thanking their guide for the knowledgeable tour. One of the males on the course chatted excitedly about helping out with pedigree analysis on that particular stud once he finished the course.

Wes realised with a start that a lot of them could be working on these studs they were touring and it was only a few months before they would have finished their course and be out working full time. She made a note to keep her eyes and ears open for employment opportunities on the other tours they were to make in the days to follow.

The third day of the tour really opened Wes' eyes to how much money thoroughbred studs could be earning and putting back into the look and layout of the property.

She deemed the highlight on the third day to be when the students were taken down the stallion run of a particular stud and they got to pat Redoute's Choice over the fence. Wes marveled at the size of the stallion's jowl concluding she'd never seen one so big.

With Danehill no longer living, she questioned if this son of his was the most expensive stallion standing at the time, with a fee of around a quarter of a million dollars. *Imagine him getting one hundred mares in foal for a season... $25 million in the space of five months!*

After being taken down the stallion run of black painted post and rail paddocks of about an acre in size, trees lining them with shade and adding to the aesthetics of the place, the students were taken to an area enclosed by rich green hedges.

It took Wes a few minutes to realise this was a private viewing area for stallion parades.

She questioned how wealthy the client had to be to be treated to a private viewing. One in which clients could sit on glossy wooden benches, enclosed by twelve foot high hedges while million dollar stallions paraded up and down before them.

Maybe I could work here...

The properties that followed were just as impressive. Wes took many photos, making note of costs and measurements that would come in handy for the setup of her property for their final assignments.

She was rapt to hear that a couple of the larger places allowed staff to keep one horse on the property although she questioned when they'd have the time to ride or compete. However, she made a mental note to provide the same in her assignment, perhaps housing for her staff with a nearby paddock if they had a horse.

A couple of the studs also provided staff with a service to one of their lower fee stallions at the end of a twelve month working period. Even if the staff didn't have their own mare, they could sell this service on and with the lower end stallions standing for around $8,800 for a serve, Wes thought this a brilliant way to further encourage staff to stay put and reward them for a hard year's work.

By the end of the day she struggled to drag herself onto the bus, sitting down with a thump as she flicked back through her notes tiredly.

I hope these all make sense when I'm going back over them after the stud tour.

Groaning as the CD player was put on for the trip back to the hotel; Wes closed her eyes and willed sleep to come. She was exhausted and was happy for anything to stop her from hearing the same two albums again.

August

Wes pushed the wheelbarrow with a groan, struggling to get the overly full item to the shed where it was to be emptied into plastic drums and filled with water.

Not quite managing, she pulled frantically as the wheelbarrow teetered, threatening to spill the numerous small grains of triticale. Stamping her foot in frustration, she righted the barrow before using a bucket to scoop it back in. One of the young men in the course strolled over, offering a hand.

"Here, let me help."

Wes laughed as he picked up one grain at a time.

"Thanks, but I think that might be a little time consuming; perhaps more time than we have left this afternoon."

"Don't say I didn't offer," he shrugged, walking back into the stable block where the dry mares were being given their afternoon feeds.

Smiling to herself, Wes cleaned up the mess before unraveling the hose and filling up the tub, covering the triticale with about an inch of water before turning off the tap and putting the hose and barrow back where they belonged.

By the time she'd done this, the handful of students in the barn had finished feeding, topping up hays and watering the dozen mares that were stabled under lights to bring them into season quicker as breeding would be starting in a month's time.

Wes was on foal watch again that night and was thankful that they looked to be finishing the afternoon feed run by four o'clock, meaning she could rush home to shower, change and get back out to the TAFE facility for five o'clock.

Due to the mare's gestation, breeding started September 1 each year and foals generally should be born from August 1. However, early or premature foalings weren't uncommon.

Wes was glad it was back round to the breeding season as she'd quickly deducted that mares and foals were much more appealing than yearlings or weanlings.

There had definitely been appealing parts to the yearling sales, however. She'd been pleasantly surprised toward the end of the Easter Yearling Sales when their manager had handed each staff member a card.

It had contained a thank you note and $100 cash for the ten or so members and was from a couple that owned a horse that had gone through the sale.

Wes and her group of then workmates hadn't prepared the horse for the sale – this had been done on another farm. But the colt had been put in their sale draft and they had paraded him for potential buyers.

Wes concluded she'd probably only touched the horse a few times over the duration of the sale and was amazed that the owners had gone to the trouble to give each staff member a generous tip. Amazed and pleased.

It was another facet of the industry which she was happy to have her eyes opened to – generous and thankful owners.

She thought on this with a smile as she helped to sweep up the breezeway in the stable before catching a lift home with one mate, knowing she'd be picked up by another in a short half hour to take her back out to TAFE.

***

Lise finished another round of checking the mares out in the nearby foaling paddocks and pulled the utility vehicle up beside the foaling yards. She left the engine idling as she stepped out of the ute, pulling her jacket tighter around her body.

She did enjoy the start of the foaling season, always eagerly awaiting the first foaling, but was happy when November came around and she wasn't shivering in the evenings as she made frequent checks of the mares throughout the hour.

Taking a high powered torch with her she strolled past the four front yards, counting bodies, some that were dozing, others restlessly strolling from one pile of hay to another, pausing to munch at times.

So far things were quiet and she was struggling to keep herself warm and awake on this first evening, despite the number of horses to check.

Because there was so many in the yards that were close to foaling and a large number due within the month out in the nearby paddocks, by the time she'd made her rounds it was almost time to go out and start checking them all over again. This at least helped to keep things moving.

Lise ducked between the rails of the last yard where a mare was pacing up and down the fence line, heat radiating from her body.

She managed to still the mare for a moment, running the torch over her udder. Following this she checked under and around the mare's tail to see if the vulva was elongated and the muscles relaxed in anticipation for foaling.

Lise concluded the mare was showing the first signs of stage one of labour but didn't think she'd actually go that night.

"Sorry darling. I think it's going to be a long night and day for you," she commented, patting the mare on the shoulder before heading back to the idling ute.

The mare wasn't fully relaxed behind which led Lise to this conclusion. She was so caught up in her thoughts that she nearly jumped out of her skin when she stepped into the car and found another body sitting in the passenger seat. Reacting, she slapped Declan before making to get out of the car.

He reached across quickly and wrapped his arms around her waist, pulling her back in before moving himself over so that he was sitting beside her.

"Way to scare the life out of someone," she muttered, pulling the door closed and her jacket tighter around her body again.

"I just wanted to surprise ye. I thought ye might be cold and bored out 'ere."

"And you figured you were the perfect cure to both of those ailments?" Lise asked sarcastically.

"Indeed. What, ye don't?" Declan asked with a chuckle, wrapping his arms tighter around her body, resting his face in the crook of her neck.

"I promise I'm not bored; I don't think that's possible with horses, sorry to disappoint you, Irish."

"Why are ye mad at me?" Declan murmured, his lips resting at her ear as his hands made their way inside her jacket, pulling her closer.

"Who says I'm mad? If I wasn't before, I should be with you acting like you'll soon be running your cold hands over my stomach!" she ground out, swatting at his hands.

Declan laughed, placing a kiss to her cheek.

"The fact that ye called me Irish says yer mad at me. I wanted to see ye, is that such a bad thing?"

"When it could distract me from carrying out my duties of night watch, yes it is. And when you don't announce your presence and instead choose to scare the wits out of me, yes it is," Lise responded, putting the ute into gear with difficulty, Declan not volunteering to move out of the way as she put the car into motion and started the rounds of the paddocks once again.

The check proved unfruitful and so Lise pulled the vehicle up beside the foaling yards once again, turning it off. She leant into Declan's embrace, her gaze on the lit up yards before them.

"I'm glad Rocket didn't go back overseas," Lise murmured, leaning back to peck Declan on the cheek.

"Why is that and where did that thought come from?" he asked, looking down at her as she played with the cuff of his shirt.

"I was just thinking about the fact that you would both be in quarantine, close to being back on the farm if he had done so. Perhaps it's not good for the horse to have only done one season in the Northern Hemisphere, but I'm rather happy about you not being over there."

Declan smiled in the darkness.

"So I guess I'm forgiven for scaring the life out of ye, then?"

Lise leant up to kiss him soundly before turning the Ute back on, ready to make another check of the mares. Declan translated her actions to mean a resounding yes. He smiled again, thinking he was just as happy with that fact as she was – perhaps even more so.

***

Wes stepped up into the recreation room at TAFE, removing her gloves and jacket as she did so. She placed the torch on the charger.

"No change?" her friend and partner in crime for the evening queried.

"Nope. All quiet except for one maiden mare who is rather peeved that I keep waking her up with a bright light every half hour!"

Wes smiled as she sat back down at the computer, wanting to get back into her assignment before it was time to check the 'girls' again.

The TAFE students were required to go out every half hour to check over the mares as well as any time the foaling alarm went off. They were still taking it in turns in two hour shifts, doing four checks each before the other took over. Being about half past ten at night, both were wide awake, not yet taking advantage of the two hour breaks to get in a snooze.

Wes was currently working on her Care of Stud Horses assignment, having to detail the services offered on the property that would make her business money. These could include a mixture of breeding services, foaling down, weaning, yearling and/or weanling sales preparation, walk outs to farms as well as vetting services to line up mares for breeds.

Wes then had to detail the routine of each of these services. That is, the daily routine for the sales preparation, vet days and what time of the year this was likely to occur, whether the farm provided walk out services or just put the mare on a truck to visit particular stallions.

She also had to include farrier days, when the horses were to be wormed throughout the year and shots like tetanus and strangles to protect the horses and an outbreak on the farm.

The assignment was proving to be a lot of work but she was sure she had everything covered on her assignment sheet, having jotted down ideas as they came to her. Now it was just a question of elaborating.

All too quickly the alarm shrilled on her phone and Wes was up again, putting on her jacket and gloves, removing the torch from the charger and heading down the steps out into the cool evening.

Her check showed one mare pacing restlessly, steam rising from her body in the light of the moon as she made her way up and down the fence line. Not wanting to take any chances, Wes used the walkie talkie to contact the other student, asking her to phone the teacher on duty for the night.

Twenty minutes later the three were assembled outside, watching the mare from a distance after having moved her to a separate yard to foal down alone.

"You wouldn't believe the trouble I had getting here," their teacher commented, plucking at a piece of grass before twirling it around her fingers.

"Oh?" Wes inquired, thinking she'd arrived promptly.

"I ducked down Cribbes road as that's the best way at this time of night and was rushing to get here, not paying attention to my speed. As luck would have it, a coppa was heading in the other direction and the next thing I know there are lights in my rearview mirror flashing red and blue and I'm being pulled over."

Wes pulled a face, thinking what poor timing.

"So the officer comes up to my window and I'm gesturing frantically, nearly screaming 'No, no, no! You can't stop me now. I know I was speeding, but I'm having a foal!' Well you can guess how well that went," she stated with a chuckle, grinning sheepishly as the young students burst into laughter.

"What was the response of the cop who pulled you over?" Wes asked once she could get her breath back.

"To carry out a breathalyzer test," the teacher replied, causing the pair to again erupt into giggles.

They settled down shortly after as the mare's waters broke and she lay down to foal. As the young horse was brought into the world, Wes realised this was potentially the last foaling she would see at TAFE.

From mid September she would be on her last placement, being employed in the industry by November 1. The thought made her smile but she also realised how much she had to hurry to finish her last two assignments before that time came. Consequently, the rest of the evening went by very quickly for her.

September

"School holidays again, already!" Maddie groaned as she tugged her boots on at the back door before standing to head out toward the tie up area.

"At least you get the same group for a set period of flat, games, jumping and theory. I think that's easier than a day full of different classes and different levels of riders," Melanie countered.

"Maybe," Maddie replied to her sister, noncommittal.

"What are you going over with them with regards to theory today? I have three different lessons planned so can be a little flexible with my two theory days."

"I don't know... maybe I'll go over identifying a horse with them today."

"Maybe? Why on earth don't you plan these things rather than just wing it?" her twin asked, incredulous.

"Requires too much work that I don't need to put in," Maddie called back as she walked off to the tie up area, knowing her twin wouldn't follow her for fear of being seen by the half dozen students who were probably waiting eagerly to start their day of riding and learning about horses.

There were six students in total - a full class for a holiday program - and before too long Maddie had them all with head collars and leads, ready to catch their ponies and horses.

They went to the small ponies paddock first, picking up two mounts for the smaller of the children before returning to the tie up area to drop them off and head for the next paddock.

Maddie was glad to see that she had two small ponies, two larger ponies and two galloways assigned to the six kids she was teaching. This would make things very easy - and fair

– when it came to splitting them into two teams for the games session of the day.

It did however mean that the jumping in the arena would be difficult when trying to space things out for the different sized striding horses. Deeming herself a genius, Maddie concluded she could just set up a couple of single jumps, one on either side of the arena before taking the kids out to the cross country course that was already set up with three different sized jumps at each jumping point.

The six she had were regulars during the week and she was certain they could all handle the cross country course although a couple hadn't been out jumping in an open area in awhile.

Aware that the interest of her students tended to wane once they'd had lunch and were dealing with full stomachs, Maddie decided to put the theory lesson in before lunch but after their snack, hoping they wouldn't be too restless.

Before this session however she wanted to get the kids well warmed up by starting out with games.

Once all six children had their mounts for the day, she stood back and observed as each child got their equine ready, first undoing leg straps and then the front buckle of a rug before removing this and starting the grooming process.

Maddie stepped in to help with the removal of the heavy canvas rugs that were still on some of the horses but otherwise stayed out of the way and let them work along at a steady pace.

At the end of their games lesson, after having cooled the horses out at a walk around the outside of the arena, Maddie instructed the students to quickly brush down their mounts and put rugs back on due to the chill and the fact that the horses were still a bit warm from their exercise.

While the six kids enjoyed a short snack and play time under her mother's supervision, Maddie made sure the horses each had a chance to have something to drink if they so desired and offered them each some hay to munch on.

Five minutes before her students were due back she removed rugs from two of the horses, planning to use these as the two horses the students were to identify.

Upon their return she split them into two groups of three, giving them each a horse to focus on for ten minutes and told them to write down on the pieces of paper provided as much as they could about what the horse looked like. She gave them a few examples in the form of sex, colour and height and left them to their own devices.

When the ten minutes were up, she switched the groups over and had them do the same thing with a different horse. A small grin made its way onto her face when they noticed something on the second horse that made them question if the first horse was the same or different.

"Alright, tell me about Dundee," Maddie suggested, getting the group of six girls to sit down and read out from their lists.

They listed off her markings, the lack of brands, her dorsal stripe, different coloured hooves dependant on whether or not she had white leg markings, the fact that she was a mare and a general idea of her short height.

"Great! You guys found out a lot just from looking at her and if she got stolen, you would be able to give the police a good idea of what she looked like so that they could identify her… what about whorls?"

"Whirls?" one of the students asked, trying out the word with a frown.

"Similar. Whorls with an 'o' rather than an 'i'. Does anyone know what a whorl is?"

One of the older girls put her hand up, tentative.

"Go ahead," Maddie encouraged, grinning as the young girl rose and walked over to the horse, pointing out a particular spot on Dundee's neck.

Very soon the other five had stood and were looking at the odd spiral of hair that seemed to go in a different direction to the rest of Dundee's coat.

"Spot on! This is a whorl, girls and it's important because if we note exactly where they are on the horse's neck, it can further help to identify the horse. Horses generally have whorls but in different spots. Take a look at Sheila and see if you can find any on her neck."

The girls needed no further encouragement, hurrying to the other horse, exclaiming in delight and surprise as they found a whorl on either side of her neck, higher up than on Dundee.

Grinning, Maddie gained their attention again with a question.

"What about ermine markings?"

This question brought silence and Maddie strolled back toward Dundee, the group following her.

"Do you see the white stocking on Dundee's left front leg?"

"The near fore?" one of the older students asked, causing her to smile.

"Exactly! If you look close to the hoof you'll see a little black marking on the white. This is known as an ermine marking and is another way to identify your horse."

This new discovery had the girls rushing back toward Sheila, noting with disappointment that she didn't have any ermine markings.

"That's good to note too though. If your horse has a particular marking could be just as important in identifying them as recognising something that they don't have," Maddie told the girls.

"Now! Enough of this theory business, let's get the horses tacked up quickly and have a longer jumping session before lunch!" she exclaimed, gaining excited cheers from the group as they each went to their mount, again getting them ready to be ridden.

Maddie smiled to herself, enjoying the day. *Too easy indeed.*

***

The middle of September found WES on her last bout of work placement. She was working on a small stud in a small country town in North East Victoria. Small that is, in that around two hundred mares were on the farm during the season.

The town in itself was populated with around two and a half thousand people and when getting directions to the farm, Wes had been surprised by her boss' instructions.

"Turn left at the traffic lights when you get into town and travel out fourteen kilometres before you come to our road on the right. We're the third property on the right."

Having asked him which set of traffic lights, he'd simply responded, "Oh, you'll see them."

It was only later that she realised the town only had one set of traffic lights. The far from big town seemed a fitting place to have the small stud.

Wes was amused to think that two hundred mares was considered a small operation. However, taking into account the size of Nirvana Park, the home of her first placement, she guessed that this place was indeed small in comparison.

Consequently there were fewer workers, and therefore the opportunity to get to know the staff better.

Wes' mother had suggested - demanded more like - that Wes keep her mouth shut for the first week. As the young woman had grown over the duration of the two year course and became bolder due to being out of home, she was becoming known as some what of a smart alec and struggled to keep thoughts to herself. This was especially so if she considered them to be witty or amusing.

Today seemed to be such a case and she was only five days into her placement. She knew she wouldn't be employed at this farm after placement due to its size and the fact that a first year student was to be doing their breeding placement directly after her. That didn't mean however that she wanted to finish up her course on a bad note.

Having only been in the company of her boss and the stallion handler for such a short time, she hadn't yet worked out the tolerance levels of the two men she worked with, although both seemed to err on the side of being rather laid back.

Her boss, a man in his late forties had just recently been driving his large John Deere tractor and had managed to have a run in with the post and rail fence that provided a perimeter for the area where one of their four stallions was kept.

The two men were now working to fix the fence, her employer muttering about the 'damn tractor.'

"Never mind the tractor, what about the person driving it?" she questioned with a grin.

The older man looked over at her, seemingly taken aback.

"Are you implying that I caused this problem?" he asked with mock surprise.

"Do you need to imply fact?" Wes replied, seeing the stallion handler's large grin behind her boss and working hard to contain her own.

"Aren't you supposed to be catching some horses for the vet?" came the gruff reply, causing Wes to grin as she headed off to where the other worker on the farm, a woman in her forties was bringing in one of the dry mares for vetting.

Vet days on this smaller farm tended to happen on a Monday, Wednesday and Friday and as the season picked up, it wasn't uncommon for vetting to happen six days a week.

The protocol for bringing in horses seemed to be the same as what Wes had experienced at Nirvana Park, but on a smaller scale. Rarely was a mare and foal in the stable complex - of which there was one rather than the two at her first placement - and the property was small enough to bring in horses from each paddock on foot to the vetting area.

For efficiency however, the two all terrain vehicles were used to get to paddocks quickly and bring back mares or mares and foals at a brisk trot.

Wes found that if she puttered along in second gear, at about 12 kilometres an hour, any thoroughbred was generally able to keep up a steady trot. This worked if Wes had one hand keeping the four wheeler bike moving along and the other holding the lead rope attached to the horse.

Due to the small number of yards, it was possible that mares from different paddocks were kept in the same yard but they were still sorted based on different classes of horses – that is, dry and wet mares were kept separate.

Wes and her coworker efficiently managed to get in the twenty or so horses that were needed for vetting, one mare that was particularly hard to catch being left till last.

"She's a transitional mare so if we don't catch her it won't be the end of the world if she doesn't come in until next Monday," the worker informed Wes.

Determined to catch the horse, Wes followed her out into the paddock and twenty minutes later when the men came over to see if help was needed, the pair were still trying to get close enough to the mare to put a head collar and lead on her.

The stallion handler grinned, standing at the gate to the paddock, watching in amusement. Wes noted with a glance that her boss too seemed to find the whole thing funny.

"You need to learn from the master!" the stallion handler Brian called out across the paddock.

"That's fine – just show me where the master is!" Wes called back just as quickly, earning a hearty laugh from him in return.

Wes' first week turned out to be a very enjoyable one and she found she learnt a lot with the two men that were so laid back and willing to let her try out her skills at intravenous needles as well as subcutaneous for the Ovuplant that was administered to the transitional mares after a cover.

By the end of the first week Wes found that she was quite comfortable with holding the mares for the service as well as administering different kinds of drugs. She realised with a wry smile that this place was probably just the sort of place that she'd like to work on, making it a pity that her extra pair of hands wouldn't be needed after the last week of October.

Having met up with a few of her classmates on Thursday night due to others being placed on one of the other twelve horse properties on the outskirts of the same town, Wes was aware that they were expecting to stay on and be employed at each of their placements. It made her start to question if she should consider contacting Nirvana Park to potentially end up back there full time or try out yet another property and gain further experience.

Wes decided she'd chat with Brian, the stallion handler to see if he had any suggestions when he arrived for work on Monday morning.

October

Maddie sighed, rolling up her stirrups after dismounting. She loosened the girth on Phoenix before walking the mare around the outside of the arena to cool her down.

She was frustrated with the young mare's progress and decided she'd rather be on her feet to cool her out than to continue to convey her frustration to the horse while in the saddle. After a couple of laps around the perimeter of the arena she headed back toward the tie up area, noting that Jack was headed out to feed the galloways - a sign the working day was nearing an end.

The last lesson had cancelled and so Maddie had taken the opportunity to ride her mare earlier rather than later.

It hadn't helped her mood any, however with the day having been frustrating. She'd found it hard to get her students to focus or understand what she was trying to convey in her lessons. Usually such a thing wouldn't have bothered her but the fact that she'd ridden Phoenix twice in the past two days and had had two bad sessions with the mare on top of the average lesson, was getting to her.

This just topped off the day and the young redhead wasn't sure how to get through to her stubborn mare.

Phoenix had been jumping really well and settling due to all the flat work Maddie had been working on. Now however as the jumps were getting a bit higher she found the mare to be easily distracted and likely to shy at things that Maddie couldn't even see.

Currently she was so disheartened she wasn't sure the mare would be able to compete at the level Maddie was hoping to get to.

She quickly untacked her mare and brushed her down before heading out to the paddock, holding the end of the lead rope as the young mare strolled along easily beside her.

Maddie gave her a pat as she released the buckle on the head collar, not able to hold back a smile as Phoenix turned quickly and broke into a gallop, bucking as she raced to the end of the paddock where the rest of the horses were grazing quietly.

"At least you're smiling now," Jack's quiet voice came from behind the redheaded woman.

Maddie turned to face Jack, her brows raised in question as she closed the gate behind her.

"Your lesson didn't look all that fun. Phoenix not concentrating that well?"

"I can't seem to get through to her at the moment. I'm not sure what I can do to get her focused again on the jumps. Maybe we just need a break."

"Maybe. I can give her a workout if you'd like and see if she responds to the change in riders."

Maddie smiled her thanks, grasping the hand that was offered to her. The pair walked back quietly across the middle paddock toward the tie up area.

"I know you have tomorrow off. Rather than getting frustrated with your horse, how about you give her the day off and come out with me to watch some others ride?"

"Sounds great. What time are you leaving to reach the competition grounds?"

"About seven, I think. Will I swing by and pick you up on my way through? I should get here about seven thirty."

Maddie agreed and saw Jack off shortly after, thinking that perhaps a break was what the both of them needed.

***

Lise grinned as Declan groaned in frustration, turning back toward the day old foal that didn't seem certain it should be following its mother.

"No wonder you work with stallions," she teased him, laughing as he wandered lazily back toward the 50 kilogram or so baby horse, wrapped his arms around it, lifted it off the ground and promptly continued on his way, the mother following obediently.

Lise's laughter quickly stopped when her newborn foal did exactly the same thing, pausing indecisively near to a gate someone had left open.

"Typical. Only when a horse won't follow is there a gate open to entice them elsewhere," she muttered to herself, retracing her steps to get behind the foal.

Using the lead on the mare as a bum rope she wrapped it around the baby's rump, pulling on one end to encourage her forward, the mare helping to push as she strode forward.

Both mares were to get flushed. Due to a high occurrence of uterine infections the season before, their vet John had suggested flushing out the mares with a saline and penicillin solution the day after they'd foaled to help clear up any problems.

Lise thought this an interesting idea and couldn't wait to see if this extra precaution would result in cleaner mares for breeding and therefore a higher conception rate from first breeds.

Uterine infections could make it extremely difficult to get a mare in foal and put her out of action for a whole season, losing the owner money. Of course there was the loss of the stallion fee to the stud also if the mare didn't take after she was bred.

Declan put his mare in the crush first and went to the back to hold the mare's tail to one side while the vet John inserted a long tube through the mare's vulva and open cervix into her uterus.

Shortly after foaling was a good time to flush out any build up as the mare's cervix was still open, allowing access to her uterus.

After putting in the saline and penicillin solution the vet drew up a shot of oxytocin, handing the injection over to Declan to administer before releasing the mare from the crush.

The young stallion handler did so, giving the clear fluid into the vein and effectively straight into her bloodstream. This would bring on uterine contractions, expelling the fluid as well as any other build up from the recent foaling.

The same protocol was carried out with the mare that Lise had brought and shortly after the two headed toward one of the nearby nine day paddocks where mares stayed until they had gone through their foal heat which generally occurred around the nine day mark.

From this stage the mare could be lined up to breed starting the whole process over again.

Lise's thoughts wandered to the time of year and she marveled that it was already a month into the breeding season, three months from the end of the year.

She realised with a start as the pair let the mares and foals go that she and Declan had been an item for ten months.

The young Irishman stared at the tiny brunette as she continued to stand at the gate to the paddock after having locked it. Her gaze was on the equines in the paddock trotting about before settling to graze. He would have happily bet that her thoughts were elsewhere, however.

Glancing about he realised none of the other stuff were in sight and so came to stand behind her, his arms wrapping around her waist.

"What're ye thinking?"

"That the staff here at Kingsley's are incredibly dense," she replied, shocking him.

"How so?"

Lise turned around in his embrace and smiled up at him before kissing him softly.

"We've been involved for ten months and apart from Trevor whom you took great joy in telling, and Kingsley, no one else seems to be aware of it although I seem to be consistently harassed by Kaye about whether or not we are an item."

Declan smiled, grabbing Lise's hand as they headed back down the dirt path lined by tall trees and knee high green grass.

"Are ye starting to think it's time to stop creeping around and just get things out in the open?" he asked, the idea having crossed his mind often.

Declan hadn't wanted to pressure Lise but he was quite happy for their relationship to be public knowledge as long as she had no problems with the comments they would initially receive.

"Would you mind?" she paused, her eyes seeking his.

Declan smiled, his hand coming up to brush across her cheek before leaning forward to capture her lips in a firm kiss. Lise responded, leaning into his broad frame as he deepened the kiss, his strong arms embracing her smaller figure.

"If it means I get to do that in front of them all, of course I don't!" he joked.

Lise laughed, walking back toward the crush with Declan, questioning just what the Irishman would choose to do to let everyone know that they were involved.

***

Maddie's eyes lit up as she watched the familiar gorgeous liver chestnut mare with flaxen mane and tail enter the show jumping ring.

She and Jack had been enjoying the day watching other riders and their mounts carry out a dressage test followed by the cross country. Now the pair was watching the show jumping with Maddie's interest being further piqued by the mare that had taken her eye during the dressage earlier in the day.

It was initially the mare's stunning colouring that had taken her interest but then watching her impressive dressage test and catching a few of the jumps in the cross country had made her take note.

The pair settled into an easy forward canter before heading toward the first jump, clearing this successfully and moving onto the next, a double. They made it cleanly through the first four before the mare stumbled on landing after the fifth, throwing her off balance.

Maddie leant forward on the edge of her seat, not sure the pair would recover, the rider ending up on the neck of her mount.

Somehow she managed to get her balance back but the pair was off stride for the sixth jump which happened to be a spread. Maddie grinned in triumph when the mare took a massive leap, managing to clear the jump.

This success was short lived when they lost concentration and took down the top rail of the following vertical.

At the end of the round they only had four faults, having just taken down the one rail but Maddie realised their time wasn't as fast as a couple of previous riders – one having had a clear round while the other had taken down two rails.

"That was a pretty impressive effort," Jack commented from beside Maddie.

"You're telling me!" she grinned at him, her eyes lighting up with an idea.

Quickly her gaze went back to the pair that had recently exited the show jumping arena. Telling Jack she'd be back shortly she got up from her seat and headed toward the pair.

Maddie trailed them to a single horse float where the rider quickly attached her horse by a head collar, removing the bridle before loosening the girth on the saddle.

"That's some mare you've got there," Maddie commented, smiling as she caught the older woman's eye.

"Thanks. Blondie here loves her jumping. Thankfully she's a bit of a natural when it comes to dressage and has lovely movement too."

"Not to mention her striking colouring," Maddie replied, causing her owner to flash Maddie a brilliant grin.

"That's thanks to her sire. I fell in love with him nearly ten years back when he was doing the rounds at competitions and vowed when I had the money I'd be buying one of his progeny – preferably one with his colouring."

"What's the name of her sire?" Maddie asked.

"Golden Moment. I actually first saw him in New Zealand while on holiday but he has retired to stud in Werribee after being so successful in Victoria and around the Australian circuit."

Her interest piqued, Maddie made a note of the stallion's name and found out from the same woman where he stood at stud. This achieved, she thanked her for her help before making her way back to where Jack was watching the last rider put in a round that resulted in too many faults to be considered in the running for a place.

"You missed half of the show jumping," he said to her, surprise evident in his tone.

Maddie leaned over and pecked him on the cheek, her excitement reaching her eyes.

"Maybe, but it was worth it."

"I want to hear what you're up to – *after* we find out the results."

Blondie as she'd been affectionately named by her rider ended up coming in second despite the difficulty in the round.

"I think we need to go on a road trip on your next weekend off," Maddie stated cryptically as minor placings were announced and prizes given.

Jack looked at his girlfriend, trying to work out what she was up to but knowing he'd only get the full story when she felt like sharing – perhaps on their drive back home.

November

Wes smiled, once again surveying a new home, telling herself she was a nomad. Having finished her last day of placement - the end to her diploma - not four hours earlier, she now found herself in a new room, twenty minutes down the road from her last temporary home.

Brian the stallion handler at her last placement had secured her the job about a week ago at this larger stud that was also in North East Victoria.

Wes had been rather amused that her 'interview' had consisted of her and Brian stopping in for a cuppa and a chat. She'd been offered a position on the spot. Only as they were driving back had it occurred to her that she should have asked how much she would be getting paid, how often and how many days off she'd be getting. She made a note to find out that afternoon.

She had time to sort out her stuff, making her room in the three bedroom house that was staff quarters into some sort of order before heading over to the stables where her new boss was checking on a foal that was feared to have rattles.

"Ready already? Alright then, let me show you around the farm," he stated in a gruff tone, leading the way to the dilapidated work Ute.

He drove her around the farm, listing the names of paddocks as they went through each, Wes knowing she'd struggle to remember them all. After all, she'd been more focused on her struggles with each gate and the trick to opening it rather than the names of the paddocks.

Perhaps I'll just know them by how easy they are to open. This can be lean on gate while pushing in to open, paddock. Hmm, bit of a long name.

Smiling to herself she closed the gate with a small amount of difficulty before jumping back into the dual cab vehicle, habit causing her to reach for the seatbelt.

"Don't trust my driving, ey?" the older man queried with a grin, the vehicle jolting under his guidance.

"Habit," Wes replied with a smile, leaving the belt on the hook beside her.

"We're now heading into the long paddock. There's a half dozen colts in here that we'll be prepping shortly enough for the yearling sales. Do you like yearlings?"

"I prefer broodmares. They're usually more educated."

"It can be intimidating with younger horses," he nodded.

"I prefer broodmares - getting them in foal and raising the foals. I loved working with breaking in and weanlings though. They almost talked to you," he commented, causing her to smile.

"But, I started running out of patience so knew it was time to pack it in," he stated, immediately earning her respect.

Although Wes hadn't yet had a lot of experience in the equine industry, she had witnessed people that had a knack for working with younger horses and others that were insistent they did but seemed to cause more harm than good. It was a rarity to find someone who admitted to themselves that it was time for a change.

They entered the paddock of colts, Wes suddenly aware that one of her workmates was now also with them in the paddock.

"I mentioned before that ninety percent of horses is about observation," her boss commented, regaining her attention.

"Now there're two horses in here with problems. Take a look and see what you think," he offered, the challenge not lost on her.

Wes walked through the group of towering colts, reaching up to pat a nose that was sniffing at her. She frowned, questioning if her boss was referring to conformation of the horse or something else, her gaze immediately drawn to their legs.

Unsure, Wes looked to the older male, not quite managing to hold back a shrug. He smiled at her doubtful expression.

"That one there, take a look at his hock."

Wes did so, noting the near side joint was massive. She sighed internally, questioning how she could have missed such an obvious problem.

"The other is that brown fella standing behind you. He's stationary so it'd be hard for you to see. When he walks, his head is tilted to the side. We've the vet coming out tomorrow to look at the pair of them."

Wes nodded, digesting the information. Her gaze drifted to the slightly older woman she would be working with on a regular basis and she found herself surprised at the smug look that was on her face.

She's laughing at me. She's amused that I didn't notice either of the problems... guess I'm not going to be a threat to her in this workplace.

The three shortly after left the paddock, Wes once again struggling with the gate before they were all headed back to the stables. Here Wes and her workmate were dropped off, both heading for the staff quarters, the walk back a quiet one.

Wes quickly retreated to her room, not feeling particularly social. She left the door slightly ajar as she went about sorting her guitar music, looking for something relaxing that she could play.

Pausing at a difficult chord, her ears picked up the sound of muffled conversation and telling herself she shouldn't, she shuffled closer to the door, hearing a disdainful tone and realising with a start it was her coworker talking on the phone.

"This one's supposed to be a second year out of that TAFE College and she couldn't even notice a massive hock out in the paddock. I don't know what they're teaching those students."

Shrinking back against the bed, Wes felt her stomach drop at the critical yet true comment. Her immediate thought was to question if she could just return to her work placement farm not far down the road where she'd been led to believe she could achieve much with horses. *Maybe if I got more experience...*

She sighed, realising that another year wasn't going to make her any surer of herself or her skills. She did realise however, that things like this would encourage her to be a more observant worker and help to build her character.

And hopefully I'll have plenty of opportunities to do so while here. She smiled, promising herself she would stick this place out as she had planned rather than running like the child inside her was quietly pleading for her to do.

***

Trevor checked his watch for the third time in as many minutes before giving a sigh of frustration. It was six in the evening and the staff of Nirvana Park was waiting on a walk in.

"Why does Kingsley agree to walk-ins as the last cover of the day? We're forever waiting on people to turn up just so our day can finish!" he stated in frustration.

"Better that than they be booked in for six in the morning and turn up late and throw our whole day off. At least we're all done once they do get here and we cover the mare," Lise reasoned.

The older male wasn't in the mood to be consoled.

"He should make it a rule they have to drop the mare off the day before so we can tease her up properly and vet if there's any question of her being in season."

"Then it'd hardly be able to be a walk-in now, wouldn't it? It'd be a stop over or something of the like," Declan replied with a grin, pulling a small catalogue out of his back pocket and flicking through it, pausing now and again to inspect the pages.

This action caught Kaye's eye and she moved from leaning against a parked float to peer over his shoulder, her eyes widening in amazement.

"What do ye think of this one, Kaye?" Declan asked, working hard to hold back an amused smile.

"It's gorgeous. What're you doing looking at jewelry?" she asked in suspicion, her mind working overtime.

Her gaze moved to Lise who looked over at the pair in surprise, questioning what on earth the Irishman was up to. Declan looked at her briefly and winked, causing her heart to quicken.

"Or what about this one? It's real classy, like. Do ye think it's pricey enough for an engagement ring? I heard somewhere a fella should spend close to a third of his annual salary on such a commitment as a ring signifies."

This statement pulled like a magnet, three pairs of eyes to his frame, causing the young man to erupt into a fit of laughter.

"Ye should see the looks on yer faces! I was tempted to get down on one knee and propose but I don't think I could have kept a straight face. Just so ye all know, Lise and I are an item but I don't see that it's as big a deal as ye have been making out with yer questions, gossiping and assumptions. After all, tis not like we're getting married," he finished with a flourish, standing up.

A well timed vehicle with a float attached pulled up outside the covering shed.

Trevor stood quickly, rushing to get the teaser stallion they would use on the mare before introducing Rocket.

Lise stood slowly, her legs weak beneath her frame. She held Kaye's gaze, sure that her surprised look mirrored the fiery redhead's. Shaking her head in wonder she made her way slowly to the float to take the mare from the owner as she was unloaded.

Unsure what to think of the whole situation, Kaye watched dumbly as Lise took over the mare and headed toward the covering shed. Quickly she followed the horse and handler, the routine of the situation helping her to get the breeding boots and put these on as well as a rearing bit and a tail bandage.

Efficiently the group had the mare teased with the small farm stallion, confirming that she was indeed in season and shortly after she was placed in the middle of the covering shed with a twitch put on just before Declan entered the shed with Rocket.

The cover was quick and uneventful and not ten minutes later Lise was helping to load up the mare back onto the float and the owners were seen off the farm, the mare's identification papers having been sighted and signed with details of the cover listed in the small booklet.

Declan was amused by the stunned attitudes of his workmates and considered himself somewhat of a genius as he came back from returning Rocket to his stall. He noted with satisfaction that Kaye and Trevor had already dispersed but frowned when it occurred to him that neither was Lise around.

The young woman had headed over to the foaling paddocks, her mind a mass of questions. She was amazed by Declan's behaviour; stunned that he had chosen such a way to announce that they were involved. *Why would he bring marriage into the equation just to let others know we're an item, even if it was just in jest?*

Not quite sure why, she was suddenly uncertain of their relationship, not having questioned whether she expected things to be furthered by such a commitment as marriage and if this was something Declan would expect in the future. After all, they'd only been involved ten months.

She didn't have time to digest these thoughts as a pair of strong arms suddenly enveloped her frame, causing her to jump.

"I think I should be asking if I've scared ye - and I don't mean just now by sneaking up on ye," he murmured, his lips resting against her ear, his stubble brushing her cheek.

Lise stood stiffly, unsure as her gaze stayed ahead of her on the small paddock occupied by two mares and their less than week old foals.

Declan stepped in closer to the young woman's frame, his chest resting against her back as his lips sought out her neck. He smiled against her skin as he felt her relax in his embrace.

"Well at least yer not shying away from me touch," he stated softly, watching Lise closely as she turned in his embrace to look up at him.

"I'm not sure how I should be taking your comments this afternoon," she stated honestly, leaning her head against his chest.

Declan placed a kiss to her head, his arms gripping her tightly.

"Well, twas meant as a joke, just a bit of craic, really. I didn't mean to scare ye or make ye question me sanity! I love being with ye Lise but I'm not about to pull out a ring and pop the question. I was just so sick of them all that I thought I'd make a point."

"Well you sure did that," she stated, looking up at him with a grin.

"And yer not about to go running for the hills or demand I follow through with a ring?" he questioned with a cheeky grin.

"Agreeing to tie myself to you for the rest of my life may make others question my sanity," she replied with a smile, amused at his mock hurt.

"Ye pain me," he stated, putting a hand to his chest.

"I declare me intentions with regards to getting a ring and what do I get in return?"

"Nothing," Lise replied simply, reaching up to peck him on the lips.

"Why do I bother?" he questioned, his gaze going to the sky.

"Because you can't help yourself," Lise responded with a grin, reaching up and pulling his head down toward hers to kiss him, her hand playing with the hair at the base of his neck.

"Damn straight," Declan replied when Lise went to leave his embrace.

"And I don't plan on helping myself, either! C'mere," he grinned, pulling her back into his embrace.

***

Maddie closed down the internet page that had provided her with the pleasant information that she had just over four thousand dollars saved. She'd started putting away funds toward the start of the year - ever since the idea had formed to do some traveling.

Now she took great joy in logging into her internet banking on a frequent basis to see how the funds were accumulating and how much interest was being paid each month.

"Jack's here," Melanie called from the doorway as Maddie shut down the computer before rising from her seat and heading out of the room.

"Thanks, Mel. Are you sure you and mum will manage today without us?"

Her twin rolled her eyes, waving her away.

"Don't develop a conscience now, Maddie. It's not like you're going to cancel your plans because we would handle things a little better with you around - not when you know we'll manage. We'll just be a bit busy."

"True! Enjoy your day," Maddie stated cheerfully, ignoring her sister's glare as she strolled out the front door with Jack.

The pair made the hour and a half or so trip out to Werribee easily chatting about work and horses in general.

Jack was excited at the idea of seeing Golden Moment as he knew more of the stallion's competing feats than Maddie. Maddie was just interested in seeing the horse that threw such a gorgeous colour to his progeny. And just maybe she'd consider purchasing one that she could use to compete on and breed with later.

The property they arrived at was small in size - perhaps fifty acres but very well kept. White painted post and rail fencing lined the front of the property and continued down the drive which was matched either side with tall pine trees, obviously quite aged to reach the heights that they had.

Maddie grinned as she spied a few foals frolicking in the paddocks closer to the stables and what appeared to be the main house.

Jack pulled up outside the house and instantly a pair of kelpies was at the vehicle, resting their front paws on the door as they peered in the window at the pair.

"Gorgeous!" Maddie stated, climbing out of the car and calling them over.

"And so are the paw prints they left on my car," Jack muttered, wiping at the muddy prints.

"Sook," Maddie reciprocated, looking around and taking in a deep breath.

"Wouldn't it be nice living this close to the equestrian centre? Just a short trip to compete rather than the trouble we go to, to get here with our horses."

"I can't argue with that," Jack agreed, taking Maddie's hand and heading over to the stables where he had spied a couple of figures carrying out familiar chores.

A short and stocky woman appearing in her fifties watched the pair as they headed her way and shortly after stopped from filling up a wheelbarrow with shavings, wandering over to introduce herself.

"Maddie and Jack? Karen Fleming – pleased to meet you."

She offered her hand, asking the pair about their drive as she led them straight into the stables.

"The old man's just been tacked up, I thought with you coming this far that you'd like to see him put through his paces and over a few jumps. Then maybe I can show you some of his upcoming progeny."

"Sounds great!" Maddie enthused, squeezing Jack's hand in excitement.

He smiled at her before his gaze went to Karen.

"I think it's a good thing we don't have a float attached," he joked, causing Karen to smile.

The three made their way to an end stall where a dark chestnut stallion with flaxen mane and tail stood quietly while his handler finished picking out his feet.

Maddie took in his frame of 16.2 hands, his well angled shoulder, short cannons and back and smiled. *Perfect.*

Karen introduced the pair to Pedro, a young Irishman who looked after the stallion in all regards – feeding, exercising and the breeding side of things. Jack recognised the rapport that Pedro had with the stallion and felt that Karen had lucked out on her handler. It seemed Karen agreed. She talked easily with the young man, thanking him for having the horse ready and then instructed him to warm up the stallion.

Maddie watched the pair make their way out of the stables, ready to step after them.

"How about I take you where you can get a better view?" Karen asked with an amused smile, gesturing to a set of stairs behind her.

Maddie and Jack followed obediently, the pair pausing in awe when they reached the top of the stairs and entered what appeared to be a large room for entertaining.

The bit that most caught their eye however was one side of the room which was covered with glass and looked down on a large 70 x 30 metre arena where Pedro was already astride his mount and moving at a free and easy walk.

"Nice," Jack stated appreciatively, causing Karen to smile.

"I want!" Maddie exclaimed, eyes wide as she moved closer to look down on the pair that were carrying out square halts at every second letter.

"It is rather nice, isn't it?" Karen queried, inviting the pair to sit while she picked up something resembling a head piece with a microphone and placed it on her head, switching it to on.

"Now for the fun part," she stated cryptically.

It took Maddie a few moments to realise that as Karen spoke, depicting instructions for Pedro and Golden Moment and they carried them out that he was receiving the instructions through the head piece he wore attached to his helmet.

"How great would that be for a private lesson at ERS?" Jack questioned, watching the stallion extend at the trot down the long side of the arena and collect down the short side under Karen's instruction.

"It'd sure beat having to yell out across the arena, especially on a windy day," Maddie agreed, her eyes glued to the horse and rider as they carried out some lateral work before returning to a working trot and then moving up to a canter.

"Boy can he move," Maddie murmured, moving to the edge of her seat to get a better look at the pair below.

"And apparently he's even better at jumping than he is at dressage," Jack replied, in agreement.

The young couple watched as two other staff members shortly entered the arena and erected some jumps while Pedro walked Golden Moment on a loose rein.

"Now comes my favourite bit," Karen stated, looking at the pair with a grin.

"How old is he, Karen?" Maddie inquired, her gaze flitting from the arena to the older woman.

"He turned seventeen this year, getting on a bit is our Goldie. We don't tend to compete him much these days but like to keep him moving – it's good for his fitness and I get a kick out of watching others see him work," she responded, causing the pair to smile.

"So mainly he's used for breeding, then?"

"That and bringing on some of our young riders. He's a great confidence booster as he's so easy to manage and ride."

Maddie nodded, thinking how wonderful it would be to ride such a responsive and accomplished horse. She frowned as she thought of how Phoenix had been doing of late and suddenly knew that rather than buy one of Golden Moment's progeny, she'd put Phoenix in foal to him.

She sat quietly, thinking that it may be more cost effective to breed Phoenix than purchase one of the progeny of this stallion but then she'd have some waiting to do before she'd be able to compete with this horse.

The three watched the stallion as he was put through a course of six jumps a couple of times, the height being increased on the second round.

After the first two jumps Maddie had already made up her mind and by the end she knew that that was exactly what she wanted to do. The money she had saved to travel could perhaps be used to breed Phoenix then she could save again and gain some experience overseas while the youngster was growing up.

"Are you ready to see some of his progeny?" Karen asked at the end of the display, already knowing the answer.

The three headed back down the flight of stairs and the older woman led the way to some paddocks behind the stables where the colouring of dark chestnut with light mane and tail seemed to be a common occurrence.

"What's the likelihood of his progeny ending up with his colouring?" Maddie asked thinking of Phoenix's dark points and her brown body.

"We try to send our mares to him that are chestnut to ensure the colouring but it's possible from a different coloured mare to get a foal that is his colouring. The chestnut colour is a recessive gene which means to get a chestnut; both parents must pass on a chestnut gene. It's possible for a mare of another solid colour to also be carrying a chestnut gene and we've had many brown, black and grey mares produce foals to Goldie that have been his colour."

"And is it more cost effective to buy one of his progeny or breed to him?" Maddie asked casually, ignoring Jack's surprised look.

"It depends on whether you want to wait and how desperate you are to get his colouring," Karen replied, pausing to point out a two year old colt that was trotting up to the gate to say hello.

He was gorgeous but Maddie was sold on the idea of breeding.

"Generally his progeny start at ten thousand and with the demand there is for the liver chestnuts with flaxen mane and tail, it's not difficult for us to get a minimum of twenty thousand if they prove to be nice movers. This guy here has just been sold for thirty and he's to be picked up in a couple of days."

"And how much does Golden Moment stand for?" Jack asked; his gaze on his redheaded girlfriend.

"Five thousand, live foal guarantee."

"Live foal guarantee?" Maddie queried.

"That means the person who has bred their mare to him is able to send their mare back to our stallion the following year at no extra cost should the result not be a live foal despite getting pregnant. It's uncommon, but problems do arise with foaling."

Maddie nodded slowly, pondering this information as she absently patted the young colt. A nip to her hand caused her to retract it quickly, looking up at Karen who was obviously amused.

"Are you after a colt or a filly?" she queried, leading the pair on further down a tree lined laneway.

"Filly," Maddie replied, looking over the next chestnut, this one with four white socks and a star.

"She's gorgeous," she murmured, holding her hand out to the delicate nose that snuffed at it before putting her muzzle down to graze.

"But I feel she may be out of my price range," she stated with a rueful smile, her gaze catching Karen's.

"I think breeding to Golden Moment may be the way to go. Do you require the mare here?"

"No. We collect from him and breed using artificial insemination. If you have a vet who's happy to inseminate the mare, all we need is a warning when the mare is coming into season and then about forty eight hours before the best time to breed her, you contact us and we courier the semen to a specified address so the vet can inseminate her at the best possible time for her to conceive."

"So I need to find myself a vet, find out the likelihood of breeding my mare in the near future and do some sums," Maddie murmured, more to herself than to Karen.

"When you've got that sorted, just give me a call Maddie and I'd be only too happy to do business."

Ten minutes later the pair was headed back toward their car, Jack looking at his girlfriend in surprise.

"Where's the money coming from, Maddie?"

"I've been saving... I've got nearly four and a half and I want a chestnut filly with a flaxen mane and tail by Golden Moment," she replied, climbing into the car.

"Don't ask for much, do you?" Jack replied with a grin.

"Of course I do! And I tend to get it," she responded cheekily, leaning over to kiss him before putting on her seatbelt.

"Just you wait Jack. I'm going to breed Phoenix and end up with a gorgeous filly to work with in the near future."

"Somehow Miss Madison, I believe you."

December

Wes led yet another mare into the crush, expecting the vet to identify the mare as having ovulated recently. She'd been bred two days earlier and it was common practice for each mare to be brought in for an ovulation check after she'd been bred. If she had ovulated, then there was a higher probability of her getting in foal; if not, chances are she would need to be rebred.

It was improbable that a mare would get in foal if she ovulated three or more days after being bred due to the short lifespan of a stallion's sperm. The vet scanned her ovaries for activity, stating that she had ovulated and would need a caslick.

Wes adjusted her stance for the timely activity, aware she wasn't moving the mare soon.

At the farm she'd been at previously, it had been expected that she hold the tail out of the way for the vet after having washed down the mare's vulva with some diluted iodine water. This was to help him see and keep hairs out of the way while he did the suture work.

Here the vet did so himself, wrapping the tail with glad wrap to keep any hairs out of the way.

Wes deemed this a very clever way for the vet to be self efficient but felt she learnt more if she was actually able to watch the vet work and ask questions. She stood quietly however, making sure she was alert to the mare's state of being; ready to calm her down if need be.

Five minutes later the mare had been stitched, the vet stating she should be seen for her 15 day pregnancy check in a couple of weeks time.

The result of the vetting determined where each mare was put after being checked. Because she didn't need to be seen for two weeks and had been successfully bred and 'ovulated off', this dry mare was to be moved to a paddock further back on the farm.

Those kept close by were the ones that were due to foal or hadn't yet been bred for the season. At this time of year, the numbers were few although mares were still being bred and would be up until Christmas day.

Releasing her mare into a yard as directed by her boss, Wes then relocated.

She picked out a chestnut and put a head collar on her before leading her out of the steel enclosure to wait in the laneway with one of the other workers. On a reasonably large farm with a decent number of horses, Wes had been surprised to find that she was only working with three other staff, two of home she lived with.

The third was the gentleman in front of her, waiting patiently with his bay mare. Trent handled the stallions with the other female worker on the farm – something not overly common.

Stallions tended to be deemed a man's job and Wes was glad to see that this wasn't the case on this farm.

"Did you know we have thirty mares to vet tomorrow?" Trent asked Wes, gaining her attention from where she'd been looking over the horses left for vetting.

Her eyes widened in surprise.

"I know. At this time of year and on a Saturday, no less. How ridiculous."

"I think I'm glad it's my weekend off," Wes grinned, referring to the twelve day fortnight that each staff member worked.

"You're not going to stick around and help us out? Where's your dedication?" he joked.

"So not appealing," Wes replied with a grin, "And I can't, I'm going home to Melbourne and to Church on Sunday."

"God fan, ey? If there's a God, why is there so much suffering in the world, so much wrong?" he threw out of left field.

"So much suffering... and what are you doing about it?" Wes challenged.

"Excuse me?"

"All the suffering, what are you doing about it?"

That's what I thought, she concluded during the stunned silence.

"What's that got to do with things?" Trent finally asked.

"Not much… unless of course you liken blaming God for the entire world's problems to me blaming you," she stated dryly.

"Perhaps if you were helping, your eyes would be opened to all the hands He has helping those in need. Then again, you could just continue to blame Him. The vet's waiting on your mare," she gestured with an amused grin, causing him to disappear into the vetting shed.

***

"So how do you know that it's the correct time to inseminate Phoenix?" Melanie asked the vet, ignoring her sister's bored roll of the eyes.

"A number of things. A mare's cycle is twenty one days in length and on average five of these days are spent with the mare being in season and receptive to a stallion. Not having a stallion on the property however, it takes a more practiced eye to note a change in behaviour."

"Like Phoenix becoming more sensitive and irritable around her back end and with regards to me wanting to do things with her in general?" Maddie asked, frowning as she thought of the mare's bucks and uncooperativeness during their recent rides.

"That can be a sign, yes. Some mares actually become more affectionate and may even show their interest to another mare or gelding. When I scan her however, I can see uterine activity. Mares have follicles that tend to grow and one eventually erupts when big enough, releasing an egg. This is the point of ovulation."

"How big can the follicle grow?" Melanie asked, looking closer at the screen of the scanner as the vet scanned Phoenix.

"Up to around forty millimetres or four centimetres in a thoroughbred. It's common for live breeds to consider lining up a mare for a breed once the follicle has reached thirty five millimetres. However, we also need to take into account the tone of the uterus and the fold status."

"Tone I can understand, but what is the fold status?"

"Folds tell us the level of inflammation inside the mare. When a mare is in season there is a reasonable amount of inflammation. We tend to rate this from zero to four. The optimum is around three, if more than this the mare is too inflamed and this may be due to an infection. So at the moment Phoenix has a fold status of two to three which is good and she has a follicle just over thirty five millimetres."

"So she's ready to be bred, then?" Maddie asked.

"If you were sending her to a stallion, we'd be able to line her up to be bred shortly."

"But because she's getting inseminated, it's different?" Melanie guessed.

"Yes. When you inseminate a mare, you're actually inseminating through the cervix and effectively locating the semen closer to the egg, giving them less distance to travel. Because of this we try and inseminate as close to ovulation as possible to give the best chance of her conceiving."

"So how do you tell then when the best time is?" Maddie asked, interested in immediate results.

"When a follicle is close to ovulating, it gets a ring around it which can be seen on the scanner as a white ring around a dark sphere. After this it becomes irregular in shape and the fold status actually drops. We'll check Phoenix again tomorrow morning and I would guess that we'll inseminate her sometime tomorrow afternoon or the following morning."

Melanie helped the vet with wiping down the probe on the scanner and packing it away in her car while Maddie took her mare back out to the paddock.

"Are there courses you can do specifically on the reproductive side of horses?" Melanie asked the older woman as they stood at her car.

"There are but the more in depth courses will cover other aspects of horse care and some specifically focus on live covers due to the students completing their course and working in the thoroughbred industry. You can specifically partake of Artificial Insemination courses also, though. I take it this has gained your interest, Melanie?" she asked with a knowing smile.

"Just a bit," came the reply, the redhead grinning as the vet got into her car.

"I can bring you some leaflets on courses I'd recommend tomorrow when I scan Phoenix again, if you'd like," she said through the open car window.

"That'd be great, thanks Doc."

The young woman watched the vet drive off, thinking that such a course would be interesting indeed.

Year 5

January

Wes sat on the tractor, making note as one of her new coworkers pointed out the clutch, the gears, high and low drive which were on the same gear stick as reverse and the handle for lifting and dropping the carryall.

The day before she'd seen this same staff member reverse aptly up to the trailer, lower the carryall enough to line it up right below the trailer and raise the carryall so that the tow ball fit snugly into place, locking into position with the trailer.

The carryall was then raised and off she went to do the manure run.

Wes had made a mental note then that she wanted to have managed to do exactly that, rather than get off the tractor to pull the heavy trailer onto the tow ball. She hoped this was feasible, especially when she wasn't that familiar with tractors having only been on one a couple of times.

That afternoon she was happy with just having backed up the tractor successfully to the trailer so that it wasn't too hard to lift the trailer onto the tow ball and hear it lock in place. She grinned as she continued the routine, setting the gear to second and the other into high before putting the vehicle into motion.

A grinding sound caused her to apply the clutch quickly and slam on the breaks and she called out an embarrassed sorry to those in the nearby stables who were working with some yearlings. Shaking her head she quickly lifted the lever that activated the carryall, lifting it from the ground before continuing on her way - this time without the grinding sound.

The soiled shavings collected out of each box was dumped into this trailer which was then taken out into the middle of a back paddock and left in a pile to decompose.

By the time Wes had volunteered herself for her fourth day of doing the manure run, she was grinning excitedly as she backed up the tractor and lowered the carryall to line it up properly. Expertly lifting it, she caught the tow ball under the correct part of the trailer, hearing it click into place.

Rapt that she'd managed to achieve this in such a short space of time she told herself that if she managed to repeat this the following day, she'd consider it not a fluke and be excited that she'd mastered another skill.

A small laugh escaped her lips as she put the large vehicle into second and headed toward the back paddock. She shook her head, grinning as it occurred to her that she was so excited over being able to competently carry out the manure run. *Perhaps she needed help...*

***

"Is there any breeding season or Melbourne Premier Sales yearling preparation that we're going to have where Nirvana Park doesn't have a tafie?" Declan muttered, an exasperated tone evident in his voice.

Lise grinned, putting a reassuring hand briefly to his arm.

"Had enough for the day, then?" she questioned knowingly.

The most recent TAFE student who had been with them since the start of December had very quickly grated on everyone's nerves due to his incessant chatting. Lise had just as quickly worked out that if he was given something difficult to do, the talking ceased. It was hard for him to focus on conversation when all his energy was going into completing a task competently.

"Did I mention that Hunter's due today?" Lise asked innocently, her smile leading Declan to think this wasn't a pointless piece of information.

"And?" he questioned, leaning against the doorframe of the box she was leveling out.

"And he has a lot of younger yearlings that aren't for the upcoming sale that need their feet seen to. A lot of less handled horses that will be a bit of a handful but not too much for our overly zealous tafie."

Declan grinned at her triumphant smile.

"Lise?" he questioned, stepping into the box suddenly.

"A genius, ye are. Hunter is going to hate ye, but have I mentioned I love ye?" he asked simply.

Lise paused, aware that Declan was joking around but her heart rate increased at the unfamiliar phrase coming from his lips.

"No... you haven't," she replied, ignoring the fact that it was a rhetorical question.

Declan smiled softly, leaning in to caress her lips with his own.

"One of these days I may get around to it," he murmured, brushing the back of his hand across her cheek.

"But for now I'd better make sure our tafie knows which paddocks need to be seen to by the farrier. Great craic!"

Lise watched him go in a daze. She realised with a start that the eight yearlings on the walker needed to be turned around. Noting that Tony, Trevor and Kaye were all still to finish their first boxes she headed over to the walker, slowing the machine down before changing it's direction.

The young horses in the rounded enclosure changed directions in their separate bays and continued walking at a steady pace as Lise increased the speed slightly.

This done she headed back to the boxes, getting started on her second one but pacing herself. The yearlings were up to half an hour of walking in either direction, giving the staff plenty of time to get the boxes done, especially when four pairs of hands were seeing to eight boxes in the hour timeframe.

***

Melanie frowned in confusion, questioning how her sister could be so in love with the idea of having Phoenix give birth to a foal that she could later train and ride but not be interested in seeing the pregnancy in its early stages. The vet was due shortly to scan Phoenix - her mid scan which would hopefully confirm her to be about thirty days pregnant.

Both girls had been around for the first scan. This was fifteen days after Phoenix was inseminated. Melanie had been surprised that even though Phoenix had been inseminated at a point close to ovulation and it was expected that she would go on and ovulate within a short timeframe, she'd still been administered a drug to help her do so.

At fifteen days she had then been amazed to see the little sphere that represented what would in about eleven months time be a forty five kilogram foal. It just didn't seem possible.

Maddie was spending the afternoon at Jack's and had called to plead with her sister to bring in Phoenix and hold her for the vet. After all it was Melanie who was interested in that sort of thing, she'd felt the need to remind her twin. Melanie smiled as she thought over the conversation, ruefully thinking that Maddie knew from the start that she would do it.

I'm to juggle between the afternoon lessons and bringing in her *horse for the vet!*

Jade or 'Doc', as she was more affectionately known, turned up a few minutes later, Melanie meeting her at the gate to open and close it so that she could drive straight through to the tie up area.

Generally a mare was restrained in a crush to be scanned but the East Riding School didn't have a crush. They got around this however by holding up a front leg to keep the mare still.

Doc had a couple of restraining methods that she kept in her car for when needed but so far Phoenix had handled the unusual process without too much fuss.

"Tell me about this pregnancy check," Melanie said eagerly as the older woman got out her scanner and plugged it into a nearby power chord.

"It's the second of three, generally. We'll check her again in about fifteen days and if she's in foal at 45 days, then a pregnancy certificate gets filled in. You should see a marked difference in the size of the foetus from the last scan. Also, we should be able to see the heartbeat at this stage."

"Really?" Melanie asked, amazed.

"It can be difficult to see but I'll try and get a really clear shot on the scanner so you can have a good look."

***

Declan sighed, realising that Lise's idea to keep the tiresome TAFE student busy away from staff members was *almost* perfect.

The fact that Hunter had brought along Dave to get the horses done in half the time, meant however that Declan had somehow been nominated to be the extra pair of hands and now he had to listen to the sporadic pieces of conversation that were coming from Hunter and the young TAFE student.

Hunter it seemed had picked up on Declan's irritation and was milking it for all it was worth. The young Irishman was not impressed.

"Can't ye two pick another topic of conversation, or just quit with ye talking altogether?" he questioned, silently hoping for the latter of the two.

Hunter looked over at Declan, grinned and continued his conversation while rasping back a hoof.

"Not bloody likely. When you get Hunter started on the conformation of horses and corrective work, it feels like he'll never stop," Dave muttered from his position underneath a young bay colt.

"I'm not sure I could pick a topic I'd prefer him to discuss. At least the topic shows the young tafie is keen," Declan conceded, patting the fidgety thoroughbred he was holding.

"How's your woman going, Declan? Is she keeping you in line?" Hunter called out as he moved away from finishing the offside hind foot, stretching his back as he did so.

Declan's gaze flitted to Dave who looked at him with a large grin.

"A topic more to your liking?" he smirked, checking over the hoof he had been working on before letting it drop to the ground.

"Hardly," Declan muttered, and then to the older farrier, "I think ye chat with her more than me, Hunter. Why don't ye tell me if she thinks she's keeping me in line?"

"Well the fact that there've been no more proposals leaves me thinking her future is a bit safer. At least she doesn't have to work out some poor excuse to say no and therefore not tie herself to you for the rest of her life," he joked, leaning against the rail while Dave lit up a cigarette.

"Two months ago that was and ye still won't leave things alone. It's going to be great craic if I do propose and she says yes."

"Indeed it'd be an interesting day. Would I get credit for the relationship seeing as I talked Lise into working here in the first place?" Stuart called over his shoulder, grinning as he held out his hand for the next horse to sniff before getting to work.

"Maybe he can throw you a buck's party, too," Dave commented quietly, taking a last drag of his cigarette before dropping it to the ground and stepping on it.

"All this wedding talk is giving me the creeps," Declan concluded with a rueful grin, "what do ye think of that one's pins, Hunter?" he questioned, causing Dave to chuckle at the change back to the endless topic of horse conformation.

February

Wes led a colt toward the wash bay, pulling him forward as he resisted, but to no avail. Trent approached her with the britching rope, placing it over the colt's hindquarters and taking the lead from her hands, insisting on the colt coming into the closed off area that was the wash bay.

The colt resisted, backing up and then stepping forward a few steps before kicking out as another worker made sounds to encourage the young animal inside. Concluding all the fussing was only distressing the young horse, he turned the animal, leading him down the breezeway to return to his box.

After the third attempt, the colt entered the box and promptly Trent led him out again, up a few steps and into the next box, repeating this process again before heading back to the wash bay for a second try.

Wes watched the whole event earnestly, encouraged by her coworker's patience and persistence, telling herself this was what it was all about.

The colt paused at the doorway again, unsure. He took a few hesitant steps forward and again paused and found himself rewarded with a pat before the young man insistently pulled on the lead followed by the britching rope. Resisting, the colt was shocked by a sudden rap across his rump as another handler hit him with a stick, snapping the weak end.

Wes frowned, her gaze flicking up the breezeway of the stable to where their boss was watching the whole episode.

"Bring him up here!" the older man called out, brandishing a piece of poly pipe.

After being asked to do so a few times, Trent finally stopped trying to get the colt into the wash bay and brought him up to the manager, turning him as instructed.

He waited for the horse to react to the insistent encouragement of the poly pipe, his focus firmly on the young animal. He didn't have to wait long and on the third whack, the colt unhappily found himself in the wash bay. Closing the door behind himself and his equine partner, Trent patted the young animal slowly, rubbing his hand over the equine's forehead before removing the britching rope, dispersing it out the doorway and insisting on Wes joining him in the bay.

He smiled as she took a hold of the horse, closing the door and shutting out the other workers.

"I do prefer the more gentle approach and believe it works better," he informed her, helping to direct the wary animal around the bay so he could reach the hose.

"However, this is a farm with a large amount of animals where time is of the essence... oh, and I'm not the boss," he concluded with a grin, gaining one from Wes in response.

This was the third horse the pair was to wash for the day. They were methodically working through the barn, having introduced most yearlings to the wash bay and hose already, but not necessarily having shampooed them.

Fifteen minutes later Trent was scraping down the sleek body of the young thoroughbred to get rid of any excess water. Then he opened the door, allowing Wes to take him back to his box.

As she rugged the colt, Trent took the britching rope and another lead to a filly opposite, leading her out and again having issues when the pair reached the doorway to the wash bay.

Wes watched the pair in silence, having glanced around to see if their boss was nearby. He wasn't.

"Have you noticed how the first horse walked in fine but since we've washed him, the other three haven't wanted to come in?" Trent asked, his face looking thoughtful.

Wes pondered this for a second, realising the statement to be true.

"Thoughts?" she queried.

Trent handed her the lead rope, directing her to take the filly back to her box for a moment. She did so, watching with some confusion as Trent turned on the hose and started to wet down the breezeway from the wash bay to the said horse's box.

"There's a difference in the look of the surfaces now that the wash bay is wet. She may not like to step out of her box onto it, but I think once she does, she'll go willingly into the wash bay," he explained as he returned the hose to the bay.

It took some encouraging getting the unsure filly to step out of the comfort zone of her stall but Wes was delighted to find that once she did so, she happily walked into the wash bay and stood quietly in the corner while Wes removed the britching rope.

She smiled up at Trent, ready to deem him somewhat of a genius.

"Sometimes it really is just about assessing the situation and changing something, rather than pushing a horse to do something they don't want," he said by way of explanation, returning her smile.

He turned his attention back to the chestnut filly, patting her on the shoulder before turning the hose back on.

"Woah there, sweetie," he crooned as he started at the horse's leg and worked his way up, dousing the animal in water.

Wes kept a good hold of the filly while watching him rub shampoo into her coat before massaging it in with a curry comb. As he rubbed it deep into her backbone, he spoke up.

"If you're ever washing horses here, the back is the first place the old boy checks for dirt," he spoke of the manager before grinning, "and the belly is the second place," he commented, glancing under the horse and gesturing.

"See how I haven't got it all wet? Just when you think you've thoroughly doused a horse."

He let the hose run over her underside before continuing to massage in the shampoo and finished up with hosing the anxious filly off.

"Just hold her there for a sec," he stated, stepping out of the bay to grab a rag.

She smiled, holding the fidgety youngster.

"Woah there darlin'... if I were in your position, I wouldn't be complaining," she whispered with a small smile, thinking Trent to be very appealing with his looks and laid back attitude.

Shortly after, Trent returned with a rag to wipe over the yearling's face and body. Wes inhaled, a strong scent reaching her nose.

"Kero?" she inquired.

He nodded.

"It's good for finishing off and helps with irritations. Helps bring out their coat, too. I only mixed a little with water."

"Correct me if I'm wrong, but her back leg seems a bit swollen."

"On the joint there?"

"No, above her coronet band," she clarified.

"Oh, on the pastern," he gestured, taking in her nod.

"She's had that since she was a weanling. Have you heard of ringbone?"

Wes nodded, knowing a little bit about the calcification.

"If you run your hand down there, you'll feel it's actually hard. She's not sore on it though."

The pair finished with the filly a few minutes later, Trent deeming it must be near lunchtime. Wes checked her watch, affirming the fact and the pair rugged the filly before heading toward the feed room to find the rest of the staff and knock off for an hour.

***

Late February found the Nirvana Park team once again at the Oaklands Junction complex for the Melbourne Premier Yearling Sales.

Declan hadn't been surprised that he was working at the sales rather than staying back at the farm to tend to the stallions in their off season. Trevor tended to prefer that over yearling sales. The Irishman was pleased with the fact that Lise also happened to be along at the sales.

The major point he was struggling with however, was one of his roommates for the 10 day duration that they were at the sales.

The overly zealous tafie, Bob, was still working with the farm. Having finished his five week placement, Kingsley agreed to employ him for the remainder of the eight week yearling preparation, finishing with the young man attending the sales.

The previous night after arriving and unloading all the horses, all he'd talked of was his desire to lead at least one of the yearlings through the sale ring.

Declan questioned if maybe they could put the lot number on the young man instead and put *him* through the ring. *And I wouldn't even set a reserve price. First bid gets him.*

Kinglsey had packed it in early and wanting to get some time alone with Lise, Declan had opted to stay back at the pub where they'd had dinner. All he'd achieved however was encouraging Bob to stay out later. In the end Lise had left, giving Declan a sympathetic smile before making her way back to the motel.

Declan wondered if it was wrong of him to not so subtly tell the young man to leave him alone so he could spend some time with his woman.

Of course Kingsley had been dead to the world and Declan's weak excuse to stop Bob chatting hadn't worked seeing as the pair had been ridiculously noisy when entering the room, this not disturbing their boss' sleep.

The following morning's five am start left the Irishman with a small amount of hope, as Bob struggled to get up at such an hour. He had to focus hard to function and stay safe. This was especially so while handling the energetic and spooky thoroughbreds as their boxes were skipped over.

Declan smiled to himself as he realised that they'd be starting earlier on the first sale day due to the number of horses going through the ring. *Maybe that'll keep you a little less active.*

The day progressed quickly due to the large number of buyers coming around, a lot asking for a full parade.

Declan's stomach alerted him to the later hour as it grumbled at a quiet point in the day. He glanced at his watch, brows raised in surprise when he saw that it was getting on to two in the afternoon.

"Would ye like me to do the lunch honours?" he asked of Kingsley, squatting at his backpack to find his wallet.

"Great idea, Irish. Here, lunch is on me."

He handed Declan a fifty.

"Get a heap of rolls and cold drinks… unless anyone wants something hot?" he queried, his gaze going over the staff as they one by one wandered into the spare stall.

They shook their heads, saying no and he smiled knowingly, the near forty degree heat having already given him the answer.

"I'll give you a hand," Lise stated, joining Declan as he strolled up to the café area.

"Imagine that, the first time I've gotten ye alone in a long while and I can't actually take advantage of it!" Declan muttered, walking closely beside Lise.

"Oh?" she questioned, feigning ignorance.

"Don't ye play innocent with me, Miss Hemmingway. It'd hardly be considered good manners if I wrapped ye in me arms and kissed ye for all I was worth in such a public place."

"And since when do you follow good manners?" she asked in a teasing tone, bumping him with her arm.

"Don't ye tempt me either, Lise. If we go out tonight and that tafie insists on talking me ear off, I'm going to pick ye up in me arms and bail!"

"He'd be able to jog beside you and talk considering you'd be carrying me. I'll only slow you down," she stated with laughter, pushing open the door to the food venue.

"Hi Lise, Irish," Wes stated with a grin, entering the venue behind the pair.

"Hi! Who are you here with?" Lise questioned with a smile, taking in the uniform of the young woman.

"There's just something about North East Victoria, isn't there?" she smiled, recognising the name of the stud.

Wes nodded, thinking that indeed there was.

"Maybe I'll just keep moving around the studs in this area. I'm onto my fourth if you count the three lots of work placement through TAFE."

Declan cringed at the reminder of work placement students.

"Do ye need another student where yer working?" Declan asked, half serious as his gaze floated down toward the barn where Nirvana Park's horses were stabled.

"I can't say that he's good at holding onto horses, though..." he stated, his tone causing Lise and Wes to look also.

"Oh boy," Wes said, noting a figure on the ground, a horse running loose, the lead dangling between it's legs.

"Would that be your student?" she asked as he slowly got to his feet.

"Indeed it is," Declan replied, noting with relief that both handler and horse looked to be ok, a worker from another farm having caught the loose horse.

"You know, if that had have been a TAFE horse running loose, he'd owe the crew a slab," Wes stated, remembering the rule for weanling preparation.

"Hmmm... we may have to invoke that rule," Declan stated, a grin making its way onto his face.

Lise slapped him on the arm.

"Would you help me with these rolls?" she queried, having put in their lunch order.

"I'm sure you can just encourage him to take it easy and have an early night instead," she suggested, the idea ten times more appealing to Declan.

"Perhaps yer right," he conceded, grabbing some cans before nodding to Wes.

"Catch ye later, tafie," he teased.

Wes waved, returning the grin before her focus moved to the waiter who would take the lunch order for the stud she worked for.

March

"Why does it have to be so hot here?" one of Wes' workmates muttered, wiping the sweat from his brow before returning to mucking out one of the thirty boxes occupied by yearlings.

"Tell me about it! Someone forgot to remind the seasons that we've moved on to autumn! Perhaps next year I won't have to worry about this ridiculous heat," Wes replied, having recently stripped down to a singlet top.

"I have no issues with it being so warm," Trent replied with a wink, obviously happy with the lesser attire she was wearing.

Wes rolled her eyes.

"Does your girlfriend know you're such a flirt?"

"How do you think we started going out in the first place?" he replied, grinning like a Cheshire cat.

"Why wouldn't you have to worry about the heat of Australian weather next year?" the other worker asked, gazing at Wes from the box beside her.

"I'm hoping I'll be in the Northern Hemisphere. I've applied for the course at the Irish National Stud which runs from about February to June each year."

"Those Irish are mad!"

"And they sound wonderful," Wes replied, seeming to think that both facts were assets.

"So what makes you so sure you're going to get into the course?" Trent asked, sweeping in the door of the box he'd just finished.

"I'm not certain, but reasonably confident. I applied last year and didn't get in but they told me if I got another year's worth of experience in this industry, then they'd take me in. If they're true to their word, then I'll be doing the course next year," she explained, scooping out the small oat filled water trough with an old margarine container.

"While you're over there, you should head over to Chantilly in France."

Wes looked up in surprise at the other male worker, grinning.

"For the Living Horse Museum? We watched a segment on Bred to Win at TAFE on the Easter Yearling Sales and it also had a bit on the museum. I'll definitely have to try and get there."

"What's so great about this museum?" Trent queried, leaning against his fork.

"The story goes, that there was a prince who was obsessed with horses and thought he was going to come back reincarnated as a horse, I think. Because of his obsession he turned his whole domain into a tribute to the horse. Now there are over thirty rooms dedicated to the horse. Apparently they have different breeds there as well as things relating to the horse throughout history."

"Sounds a little bit nuts to me," Trent shrugged, losing interest and starting another box.

"Just a little," Wes replied with a grin, turning back to the other worker as he again spoke.

"What about the Spanish Riding School?"

"Don't get me started! I definitely don't have enough funds, but question if I have enough time to see all the places I want to see."

"Getting the travel bug before you've even traveled, that's a new one."

"Well perhaps after I've done the Irish National Stud course I'll have an excuse to have the travel bug," Wes concluded with a grin, turning her focus back to finishing the box she was mucking out.

***

Melanie paused at the tie up area, smiling as she took in the sight of Phoenix contentedly munching on some Lucerne hay. The girls had been instructed that throughout the first two trimesters of a horse's pregnancy – about 230 days all up – mares generally didn't need to be fed more than they usually were to be at a maintenance weight.

They'd also been told that it's in the last few months of the gestation that the foal doubles in weight and at this stage the mare needs to be fed more. Especially once the foal is born and the mare is feeding herself and her young. At this stage the nutritional requirements increase greatly.

Because not all of the riding school horses were given hard feeds however, it was a habit to bring in those that did get fed individually. Hence the young mare being fed in the tie up area.

Maddie had already given her a feed before tacking up a young horse that was being brought on in jumping. Melanie assumed her sister would put the pregnant mare away after she'd worked the young mare she was currently on.

"It's funny to think you're about four months pregnant and yet you look exactly the same to me," Melanie murmured, scratching the bay mare on her withers.

Her gaze turned to the arena where Maddie was putting the other young mare through the process of collecting and lengthening her strides at the trot down one side of the arena and through a grid of four jumps fairly close together down the other side.

Melanie smiled at the sight, getting enjoyment from the successful, fluid looking ride.

"I think Bellamy's going to be a great little jumper for the intermediate riders with the way Maddie's got her going," she said quietly to Phoenix.

"I hope she has just as much fun with your young one, girl. Perhaps I can breed future horses for the school and Maddie can bring them on, what do you think?"

Phoenix threw her head up and down, trying to dislodge a stalk of Lucerne that was stuck in her forelock. Melanie laughed.

"You know what? I'm taking that as an affirmative."

***

Wes smiled at the sound of the downpour of rain on the tin roof covering the stable complex. It was only a couple of days ago that she was complaining about the heat and humidity and now it was cold and raining. She didn't mind this but found it frustrating while carrying out a yearling preparation as the farm wasn't equipped for poor weather.

The walker didn't have a cover over it and the only way for the young horses full of energy to get a chance to stretch their legs was to be turned out one at a time into the covered round yard.

One positive with the time of year was that the stallions were out during the day - rain, hail or shine - and so the stallion boxes could be used to move a yearling to while their box got done.

Wes seemed to have acquired the fillies, putting them one at a time in the round yard while the colts were being walked over in pairs to the stallion barn by other workers who then came back to do their boxes.

Grabbing her third filly, Wes led the feisty young bay animal out of her box and toward the large round yard. The noise of the rain seemed louder here and the young animal rolled her eyes, snorting at the unfamiliar sound.

"You'll be fine darling. In fact, I think the unfamiliar noise will help you to react and burn some excess energy," she stated as she turned the young horse around to face the door in anticipation for releasing her.

The large door that closed the round yard was particularly heavy and the general protocol of the staff was to release their horse and then step back to quickly grab the door and close it. Generally this worked, as the yearling in question was focused on kicking up its heels. Not so for Wes this time.

As she stepped back to grab the door to close, the young filly stepped with her, pushing at the young woman and managing to get past her out into the stable breezeway.

Wide eyed, Wes rushed after the horse, questioning how she was to catch the young animal that was a bit spooked and suddenly free. The pair moved quickly down the breezeway, Wes praying that the filly wouldn't continue on outside of the stables and into the open.

The young horse paused indecisively at an open stable door that happened to lead to the walker. Seeing her chance, Wes quickly moved past the filly and then moved from behind her, encouraging the young animal into the open doorway.

The filly walked easily into the box and Wes closed the door, rushing to grab her lead rope before returning to catch the young horse and take her back to the round yard.

"Let's try this again," she muttered, her heart still racing at the idea of the young animal being loose and hurting herself.

This time she kept the lead on the filly and closed the door firmly behind her before unclipping the lead rope.

"And you'd better not knock me over when I open the door to come catch you once I've done your box," Wes warned half heartedly, silently relieved that things had worked out ok.

Wes was just heading back to her box when the men returned from having taken some colts across to the stallion barn.

"So I was thinking maybe you'd like to help me bring in the stallions this afternoon," Trent suggested to Wes as he started the box beside her.

Wes looked at him in surprise.

"Really?" she asked, unsure of her capabilities when she considered she'd just let a yearling filly loose, not that anyone had witnessed that incident.

"Sure! I'll be there with you and they have to come in anyway. I'll even let you lead in Redoute's Choice's full brother. How's that sound?"

Wes' responding grin was enough to cause Trent to laugh.

"I'll interpret that as 'Sounds great, Trent!'."

Although the stallion he was referring to didn't have a particularly high fee, Wes thought it rather cool that she was getting to lead him in. He was after all, the full brother to a stallion that commanded a $220,000 fee per mare that was sent to him.

"Sounds great, Trent, indeed," she smiled to herself, continuing on with the box, eagerly anticipating later that afternoon.

At about three that afternoon the pair strolled out toward the stallion paddocks, Wes having watched Trent already bring in two of the four stallions. She'd helped to put their feeds in and was amazed to find half a dozen decent sized stones in the feeder of one of the stallions.

Trent had informed her that that particular stallion had a habit of eating his feed so quickly it caused problems to his digestive tract. To try and manage this, they put the stones on top of the feed and the horse had to eat around them. It worked rather effectively.

Wes was amazed and amused at the idea, questioning if her parents had ever considered the same thing for her while she was eating meals with them.

Trent caught the stallion but very shortly after this he handed the lead over to Wes, directing her to lead him as she would normally lead a horse. The main difference was just to be aware of the nipping teeth and to keep moving forward at a steady pace.

In no time the large red bay animal was in his stall, Wes turning him to face the door before removing the bit and unclipping the lead. She handed both to Trent with a large grin.

"Thanks!"

"You're welcome. Might as well be able to tell people you've done something with stallions," he joked, strolling out to get the last horse in.

Wes raced back over to the main stable block, ready to help with feeding the yearlings their afternoon feed.

April

"So how long are you in Australia for, Randy?" Melanie asked of the young American man sitting astride one of their riding school horses.

"Why about a month, Ma'am," the late teen replied in a strong southern accent.

"I'm visiting with some relatives and thought I'd get in a few riding lessons while I was here."

"Works for me," Melanie replied with a grin.

"So what have you been working on at home?"

"I've recently started with some lateral work on my youngster and would love to keep practicing that so that I'm still familiar with the aids I should be giving for when I get back. He's having a six week break at the moment so I'm hoping by the time I get back we'll be able to pick right back up where we left off."

"That sounds fair. Well the fella you've got today is well established at responding to your leg and moving away from it, *if* we have his attention first. Sometimes it takes awhile to get him to tune into our frequency," she explained with a smile, directing Randy to push the gelding into a nice forward walk, stopping where he pleased around the arena.

"Got to make sure the birdie is home, ey?" Randy questioned with a grin.

"You'll have to explain that one to me," Melanie responded with a laugh.

"At home we ask, is the birdie home or not? If it's home, then our horse is with us but if the birdie is out and about, then our horse's attention is on that birdie, wherever it may be," he explained, causing Melanie to nod in agreement, smiling.

"Exactly! Now I'm certain that the birdie is home, so let's get that message through to this old man in our warm up. Randy, when you're ready you can ask him to take up the trot and focus on a nice steady rhythm once he's responding nicely to your aids. If he's a bit sluggish on the take off we're going to come back to a walk and try again with stronger aids."

The riding pair worked nicely through a warm up before Melanie directed them back to a walk on a loose rein while she set up a zig zag of poles.

"Now the idea here is that the poles are set up to nearly meet in a corner. The corner is the point where we're going to practice our turn on the forehand. Are you familiar with a turn on the forehand?"

At the young man's affirming nod she continued.

"Great. You're going to come up the centre line and continue walking with the pole on your right hand side, once you reach the end of that pole you're going to do a turn on the forehand, getting your mount to move off your right leg and continue with the next pole to the left of you. Once you reach the end of this one you'll be doing a turn on the forehand off your left leg and continuing on until the end of the zig zag, effectively changing which leg your horse has to move off each time. Does that make sense?"

"Perfectly clear," Randy responded with a grin.

"I guess that answers my next question then of whether or not you have any questions," Melanie replied, returning the grin.

"Alright, let's see it then. We want a nice rhythm established throughout our walk, not letting him lag behind or speed up."

They practiced this in both directions, Randy either starting from the centre line or if from the other direction, at the letter B in the arena. Having gotten his mount's attention in the warm up, the pair moved smoothly throughout the exercise, the young man's grin getting larger each time they executed the lateral movement correctly.

"Wonderful! I think you've got that one down pat. What I'm going to do Randy is place a cone in each of the corners and have you move around this while the poles are still in place. Then we're going to remove the poles and have you do so without their guidance."

"Easy!" came the confident reply.

"Good to hear. Now because that's so easy, you're going to execute it just as well for me and then I'm going to take away the cones and see the proof that the pair of you can work together effectively without the guidance of cones or poles. Sound fair?"

"You betcha. Let's see what we can do."

The three worked together, Melanie adjusting items in the arena as her client continued to work well with his mount, carrying out each task that she set.

"Is this too easy? Should I be setting you another task?" Melanie asked with a grin after having removed the poles, Randy working around the cones that were left.

"No! It's good for me to feel so good about this and things were going well back home but not this smoothly. It's nice to get a feel for the horse under me so I can better tell if my horse is stepping correctly under me."

"Ok. Well I'm going to remove the cones and I'll get you to try out the turn on the forehand without any guides and then let's see if you can do some around the arena, perhaps on the three quarter line at a corner."

"Sounds great."

Randy found his mount just as responsive without the aids of the poles and cones and managed to ask for the same moves as Melanie directed him around the arena. Once the pair had carried this out a few times Melanie set them to work on a circle, working on transitions between walk and trot, and trot and canter and back down to trot and then walk.

"You guys look great! Just before we finish Randy, I want you to do a lap at a relaxed walk on a loose rein and then try another turn on the forehand. The proof is in being able to do so anywhere you choose to ask and without aids such as the poles and cones."

Ending the lesson on this note, Melanie strolled toward the gate at the end of the arena, letting the young rider out and directing him to lap the arena once at a relaxed walk before heading on over to the tie up area to untack.

Maddie passed her sister as she exited the arena. It was quite a cool afternoon and she was rugged up, her jacket collar upright around her neck and flaming red hair hidden under the jacket. To a new client the fact that the pair were identical twins wouldn't have easily been spotted.

"Can I steal the arena now?" she asked, not really waiting for a reply as her young mount strode eagerly into the enclosed area.

"Could I stop you?" Melanie asked with a roll of her eyes, closing the gate after the pair.

Maddie kept her mount moving, aware that the young gelding was more inclined to act up when he was stationary. They got halfway around the sixty by twenty metre arena before he reared up on his hind legs, striking out with the forelegs.

Caught by surprise Maddie leant forward quickly, so as not to fall off. The young horse went up again and prepared this time she pulled hard on the inside rein, pulling him off balance. Quickly he returned to the ground, straining against the reins.

"Now, are you a quick learner young man or do you need me to unbalance you again while you're standing high up in the air?" she muttered, pushing her mount forward.

Another four strides and he went up again, Maddie responding quicker this time and again unbalancing him. Not liking this, the young horse continued around the arena at a forward walk, keeping all four feet on the ground.

"That's some riding!" Randy exclaimed, pulling up beside Melanie as he finished cooling out his mount.

"For some reason she enjoys the ones that are a handful," Melanie replied with a grin, rolling her eyes.

"Tell me, why is it that she sat quietly the first time, and then pull hard on the reins the next two?" he questioned, taking both feet out of the stirrups to dismount.

"I think he caught her unawares the first time. The idea with turning the horse while it's rearing is that it puts it off balance. She does so in the hope that this discourages the horse from going up in the first place. They seem to catch on pretty quick."

"You're telling me," Randy muttered, glancing back to the pair working calmly in the arena.

"Impressive, indeed."

"Just don't tell her to her face. Her ego's big enough already," Melanie joked, grinning.

Randy returned the smile, tying his horse up before starting to untack.

***

It was late April and Wes found herself once again at the Oaklands Junction complex for the Autumn Yearling Sales.

They'd been at the complex a couple of days and the third day had ended up quiet. Wes had been told that the morning rush was to be expected before people went off to the Saturday races and chances were that things would pick up again later in the afternoon.

"I guess it's nice to know we'll have a quiet day, but I think it'll drag. And then to top things off it'll pick up just as soon as we think we're done for the day!" Wes commented, kicking her feet out like a little kid as she sat on the bench placed at the end of the breezeway.

"Them's the breaks!" Trent stated with a grin.

"See what the horse industry does for your English? It's time to move on, Trent," Wes replied with a grin.

"But all I know how to do is pick up manure!" Trent replied, winking at her.

"Speaking of moving on... the boss man was asking if I knew what your plans were for the breeding season, so don't be surprised if he asks you."

"I was hoping to leave that chat for a bit, I'm not sure he'll look too favourably on me planning on staying on over the quiet season and then bailing in August to go back to where I did my last placement," Wes commented.

"I think you're spot on there and so I have a proposition for you," Trent stated with a grin.

"I'm not sure I like the word proposition coming out of your mouth," Wes joked, causing him to laugh.

"Well how about this? I know a lot of different studs in the area and I reckon I could get you work on one of them to tide you over to the breeding season if it ends up that you can't stay on with us over the quiet season."

"Sounds like a plan! I'd love to stay here until starting at the next place but if that doesn't work out, I'll be reminding you of that suggestion," Wes agreed.

"Now that that's sorted, do you think we should pick up some of the boxes and look busy?"

"Definitely, the job is about picking up manure after all," Wes replied with a smile, rising to her feet.

May

"All right you lot, I cave. I'll set up a small show jumping course for you," Melanie said, sick of the three young women nagging.

She'd managed to get them to at least focus on some flat work for twenty minutes and concluded the rest of the lesson could be based around jumping. Never one to miss an opportunity, Melanie decided to test their knowledge.

"Ok. I think it's about time you directed me with regards to setting up a course. I want at least one bounce, combination and related distance in it. Who knows what the difference between the three is?"

Jade raised her hand hesitantly.

"Go for it," Melanie smiled her encouragement.

"Well I know that a bounce involves a jump, landing and taking off again right away to go over another jump."

"That's correct. How about a combination?"

"A few strides in between?"

"A combination is made up of two jumps with one to two strides in between," Melanie corrected, informing the three.

"And a related distance is more than two strides?" another student guessed, pushing her mount out into a walk around the arena to keep him moving.

"It is. Any idea of how many strides a related distance can be at a maximum?"

"Six?" the third student asked.

"A related distance can be from two to eight strides in between jumps. Now that you know that piece of information, I think you should be able to direct me on where to put the jumps. Oh, and one last thing... I think there should be a rollback from the related distance to the combination."

Melanie took in the three different smiles, one excited, one smug and the other rather timid. She wasn't going to make this course easy for them but was certain they'd have fun, be challenged and learn a lot.

"Now, where shall we start?"

***

Wes sighed, knowing she shouldn't have expected any outcome other than the one that had come to pass. It made sense to her that her current boss wasn't interested in keeping her on over the off season when he didn't need to. And why should he do so when she wasn't going to stay for the following breeding season?

She realised that she'd have the job security if she gave her boss the word that she'd stay for the breeding season.

This wasn't part of the current plan however, as she was eager to return to working on the small thoroughbred farm fifteen kilometres up the road that she'd completed her last work placement on. She loved working with Trent and the others at this current farm but was aware she was given more opportunities and responsibilities at the other farm.

Plus, if Trent was true to his word, this way she'd get a chance to work at another farm, gaining further experience with different people and horses.

Wes' boss had given her two weeks to sort herself out, meaning she'd finish work in two Fridays' time. She smiled to herself, realising she'd definitely better chase up Trent with regards to the job he'd said he could get her.

She made a mental note to do so in the morning when the young man arrived at half past seven for work. Until then, there was no use worrying. Smiling to herself, she concluded now would be the perfect time to get stuck into some study. Having officially received her Diploma the month before, she'd quickly started up another form of study. This course she was doing via distance education.

The Certificate III in Recreational Coaching could be done at one's own pace and Wes had worked out based on what she was earning that to do the theory of one topic a month was feasible. It would also mean that she would have finished the theoretical side of the course in just thirteen months. Then it would be time to focus on some possible work in riding schools to get the correlating practical work marked off. And then, she'd be set to teach basic level horse riding and be insured due to the qualification she'd received. *One thing at a time.*

***

Having put the eight mares and foals through the crush in order to get head collars on the foals, Kingsley's staff then put each pair in separate boxes in the stables. These eight were the last to be weaned on the farm, having been born over the month of December. Now in May, the youngest were five months of age which was considered a time when the mare's milk provided the lowest nutritional value, prompting people to wean.

Each staff member assigned to a horse, they worked in pairs to get the mares back out of the box, leaving the young horse by itself.

Two of the mares were very light in condition, having given everything to their foals nutritionally. Consequently they were being paddocked separately so that they could be fed extra. The other six were being led to another paddock that was far enough away so the cries of the new weanlings couldn't be heard by their dams.

Lise and Declan took the lighter two mares while Trevor, Tony, Kaye, Kingsley and the other two girls took the other six. Jeremy was on holidays over the month of May.

The two mares to be separated left the stables calmly enough, having been through the same process many a time. Lise was glad that Kingsley had decided to separate them and even happier to find that they were going into a paddock that had been spelled for awhile.

She thought as she looked over the five or so visible ribs on her mare that the move was definitely for the benefit of the horse she was leading.

The pair walked their horses briskly up a steep incline, stopping close to the top to release the older mares into the lush paddock.

"We'll have to watch that these two don't colic on us," Declan commented as his gaze swept the fence line, double checking that things were in order and safe for the horses.

"True, at least it's not a change in feed; they'll just have more access to grass and hay after a couple of days. I'll make a note to check them thoroughly over the next day or two. Hopefully they won't gorge on this grass."

Turning the mares to face the gateway, the couple undid either head collar, releasing the pair at the same time. Lise laughed as they turned quickly and took off at a gallop across the paddock, tails high in the air.

"Silly old women," Declan stated with a grin.

"Silly old women that had better put some nick on in this paddock," Lise replied, closing the gate after the Irishman.

Declan nodded in agreement, heading back down the hill with Lise. They got halfway down when Lise stumbled, falling to her knees.

"Talk about an issue with proprioception," she muttered, pushing herself up off the ground.

Declan bent down to assist her, brushing some debris from her hands. Brows furrowed he stood with her.

"Proprio-what?" he asked, not familiar with the word.

"An awareness of one's own body," Lise responded, smiling up at him.

"Aah, I definitely have that," he replied with a grin.

"Proprioception?"

"Nope - an awareness of *yer* body," he responded softly, smirking.

"Where ye are in relation to me, where yer gaze wanders to... where yer lips are," he murmured, amused by the flush that crept its way along her face.

Smiling, Declan leant forward, resting his hand at the base of her jaw and rubbed his thumb across her sensitive lips before caressing them with his own. Lise responded, leaning into his embrace.

"I can't believe that I can still do that," he stated in wonder when they pulled apart.

"Do what?" she asked, a frown marring her features.

"Cause ye to blush. Great craic, I must say."

"And I think you'll forever be able to do so, McAlister," Lise muttered in mock annoyance, reaching up to kiss him again, fingers delving into the hair at the nape of his neck.

Needing breath, the Irishman reluctantly pulled away, resting his forehead against hers.

"We should get going with the afternoon feed run."

"Ok," Lise responded simply, turning from his embrace to head back down toward the feed shed.

After a few steps she realised she wasn't being followed and paused in confusion. She turned back to Declan, brows raised in question.

"What?"

"I was sort of expecting ye to fight me on that one," he stated, surprise evident in his tone.

Laughing Lise walked back to where he was standing.

"Expecting or hoping? There's a major difference, Irish," she stated with a grin.

"Indeed, a shame but too true. I guess I was hoping I'd have to be the one with the self control, ye see."

Smirking, Lise leant forward to kiss him again, pulling away all too soon for the young man's liking.

"Hope all you like. I fill those shoes," she stated with glee, turning quickly to run toward the feed shed.

"Forever chasing ye, I am," Declan muttered to himself, grinning as he raced after her.

June

Wes took in a deep breath, loving that the smell of horses calmed her nerves. Today was her first day of yet another job. Still in North East Victoria, she'd managed to land a nine week stint at an even larger farm than the last. This was thanks to Trent who had pulled a few strings for her. After the nine weeks here, she'd be heading back down the road to where she had completed her last breeding placement.

Being June it was still weaning time on some of the farms, which was the case for this one. In fact, the last lot of babies were being handled and would be removed from their mothers in a couple of days. This farm weaned rather differently to what Wes had seen at TAFE and on work experience.

She took note of the different process keenly, recognising some validation in the way things were done on this farm.

The mares and foals were brought into the large set of stables and head collars were introduced to the young horses. On the first day they were pulled around in the box with their mother being held quietly in the corner. Progressing from this - as time and the young horse permitted – the stable doors were closed over and the mare and foal lead out, and up and down the stable aisle.

One staff member lead the foal while the other led the mare, encouraging the young horse forward by leading the mare forward a few steps. The process was short, just enough to see the young horse respond.

At the end of the second day, the mare and foal were separated, being boxed next door to each other. The system was such that in the first box was a mare and beside her, her foal. In the box following this was the next foal and then its mother.

This was done to encourage the foals to seek comfort in each other and establish friendships for when the mares would be permanently removed.

The next morning the mares were introduced to the foals in their boxes and the babies were allowed to nurse. Then the process started all over again. This was continued for about a week before the mares were removed and the young ones stayed a further week in the boxes, being handled and getting used to life without mum.

***

Lise and Kaye headed out with the first pair of weanling fillies. The June Weanling Sales were on the following week with Nirvana Park taking along a dozen weanlings. Throughout this last week of their preparation the young horses were put out into day yards, beside each other. This way they had company but couldn't accidently hurt each other if playing rough.

Working in unison, both women walked with their horse into a yard before turning to face the gate. At the same time they undid the keeper on the head collar and released each horse before stepping out of the yard and checking the gate was secure.

One filly ambled over to her pile of hay, picking at it and munching thoughtfully. The other, once she realised she was free kicked up her heels, cavorting around the yard. The result was flicking up a large chunk of mud which landed on her rump. Both Kaye and Lise laughed as the filly snorted, jumping forward in surprise. As she did so, she let out a rather large fart, further scaring herself into a fast canter around the yard.

"Classic!" Kaye said, doubling over in laughter.

Lise sank to the ground, wiping tears from her eyes. She'd nearly composed herself when the filly slipped in the yard, scrambled quickly to her feet and after looking around – perhaps to make sure no one had noticed – continued racing around, further flicking up dirt and scaring herself into a faster pace.

"Don't run too hard, darling. You'll slip and hurt yourself," Kaye warned in between barely contained giggles.

She wandered over to Lise, offering her hand. Grinning, Lise took the hand offered, being pulled to her feet.

"Fancing a horse farting and scaring itself!" she stated in wonder, dissolving into giggles again.

The two women were still laughing when they entered the stables. Declan looked at them with a raised brow.

"I'm not sure I like seeing the both of ye in such an agreeable state. What happened?"

"Oh, we were just laughing at a lot of hot air," Kaye responded with a smirk, causing Lise to erupt into another fit of giggles.

Declan watched the redhead stroll down the stable breezeway before turning his attention to his girlfriend. He smiled as she worked to compose herself, stepping behind her and wrapping his arms around her body.

"I'm not sure I've managed to elicit that response from you," he murmured, resting his chin on her shoulder.

Lise shivered at the feeling of warm breath on her neck in the cool of the morning.

"What, laughing hysterically?" she queried, resting her hands on his.

"Mmmhmm... it's rather becoming," he whispered, kissing her neck.

"I'm not sure you would ever consider the possibility of making me laugh so much," Lise replied with a grin, turning in his embrace to face him.

"Not when you so often seem to be going for another response."

"And what response would that be?" Declan queried, brows raised as he smiled down at her.

"Oh, they each start out differently, but tend to end the same," she replied with a small grin, reaching up to kiss him.

"Why change a good ending?" Declan responded between kisses.

"I think Kingsley should be paying the pair of you one collective wage," Trevor called out as he strolled down the breezeway toward them.

"Heaven knows you're always together – and half of the time working," he concluded with a roll of the eyes, his amused smile telling the pair he was joking.

"Time for a cuppa?" Lise queried, following Trevor to the smoko room, Declan in tow.

"How are the farm horses?" Declan asked as he sat down, pulling Lise into his lap.

"All looking good," Trevor responded as he filled up the kettle and flicked the on switch.

"There are a couple of colts up in the back hill paddock. Each are rather sore, but on an opposite forefoot. With the rain we've had the past few days I think they've both developed an abscess and wouldn't be surprised if they bust out at the coronet in a couple of days. Hunter and Dave are due at the end of the week so if they're still sore, perhaps they can have a poke around."

Declan nodded, accepting the cup of coffee handed to him from the older male.

"Sounds fair enough. Does that mean Kingsley's booked in Hunter for while he's at the Weanling Sales with the girls?"

"Yup. Do you think we'll be able to cope – two stallion handlers with a bunch of young horses? You'll be separated at the hip for awhile of course; can you still handle horses without Lise?" Trevor queried with a strong bout of sarcasm.

Lise grinned, warming her hands around the mug of tea that Trevor handed to her. She leant back into Declan's embrace as his left arm tightened around her mid section.

"Very funny, old man. I'm sure we'll be just fine. In fact, a great chance to 'batch it' for the week! Perhaps we should have Dave and Hunter stop in for a few cold ones," he contemplated, taking a sip from his warm drink.

"How you can consider drinking alcoholic beverages on a morning like this is beyond me. Just thinking about it makes me feel cold," Lise replied, gulping down her tea.

"I'm Irish! It's me duty to consider drinking alcohol… on many an occasion!" Declan informed her with a grin.

The smile quickly disappeared when his girlfriend's response was to vacate from his lap.

"And scaring off the fillies, it seems," Trevor replied with a chuckle, seating himself beside the Irishman to discuss the rest of the horses he'd checked over on the feed run that morning.

***

Wes frowned, not liking the tone of her workmate's voice as it had passed over the radio system that they used to communicate. The farm was split up into three sections over 900 acres or so. This consisted of the dry mare area, mares and foals and young horses. The stallions were housed in the middle of the farm.

Being a Saturday, the plan was to feed and check over the whole farm and after this, having a long break before coming back for the afternoon feed up. The day was to be only as long as it took the staff members that were on for the weekend to feed everything and ascertain that all were well.

This appeared to not be the case, Wes reasoned as she jumped onto one of the four wheeler bikes and made her way to the 'young horses' side of the farm. As she drove along the graveled road marked between numerous paddocks, she was careful to stick to the 20 kilometre per hour speed limit. This was encouraged so as not to raise too much dust, lest it be carried across the paddock and inhaled by its occupants.

Five minutes later she spied the concerned workmate struggling to apply pressure to an area on a young mare's leg to stop the bleeding.

Oh boy. Sliding to a stop Wes hurried over, picking up some of the bandaging equipment that her coworker had managed to accumulate.

"Will I hold the pressure pad in place and you bandage?" Wes offered, not believing herself to yet be particularly proficient when it came to bandaging wounds.

In agreement, the other young woman took a hold of the bandaging materials, working quickly while Wes helped to hold things in place and limit the amount of blood lost.

"I've already called the equine hospital and let them know we'll be shortly on our way. One of the boys is bringing over the work ute and float."

Wes nodded, grabbing the Elastoplast to wrap a securing layer around the vet wrap that was holding in place the cotton wool. A few minutes later one of the other workers turned up with the ute and float and the three worked to support the lame mare as she painfully made her way onto the truck.

Wes took orders from the young woman who was in charge for the weekend, making a note to check over the paddock to determine where the young mare had managed to hurt herself. Thankfully no other horses were in the paddock, meaning that if any fencing required fixing, it could wait until Monday when the maintenance men would again be at work.

Resigned to be working the whole day, Wes returned to the all terrain vehicle and started it up before flicking into first gear and making her way through the gate, into the paddock to check out the perimeter.

Having stumbled across the mare halfway through her feed run, Wes' coworker hadn't finished feeding and checking over her side of the farm before she was required to head off to the equine hospital forty minutes away. Praying the mare would be ok, Wes set to checking over the rest of the farm, knowing she could prove her worth as a worker by getting that job done before her in charge coworker returned.

July

Maddie grinned as she looked over her twin's shoulder at the information laid before her.

"If I'd known your horse course was going to be so easy, I might have signed up for it!" she declared, sitting down beside Melanie.

"I doubt you'd last a week at being disciplined enough as to set your own study times so as to keep to the amount that they expect distance education students to cover," Melanie replied drily, marking the areas that she felt would require further reading on her behalf before being able to answer the questions.

"And, I'm not sure you'd take too kindly to all the science that is covered in an Equine Science Degree," she concluded with a smug smile as her twin screwed up her face in distaste at the chemistry work.

"I do believe you're right!" Maddie stated cheerfully, rising to her feet just as quickly as she had sat down.

"Have fun with that, Mel! I'm going to feed Phoenix and give Bellamy another ride."

Melanie nodded, her focus already returned to the paperwork before her. Having had a good chat with their vet with regards to study options, Melanie had opted to take up further study.

She'd been interested in Veterinary Nursing but had been informed that this was easier done if employed already at a Veterinary Hospital. Not looking to gain further employment at this stage, Melanie did some research and found that she could further her knowledge of a horse's physiology and anatomy by carrying out an Equine Science Degree.

After having discussed this with her parents and looking into costs, she'd applied to start mid-semester and been accepted based on her practical experience. She was now starting out part time with chemistry being the science subject and horse management the equine related subject for the semester.

Maddie had no such designs to tie herself to something for six years as would be the case with her twin. This was especially so due to her still considering the possibility of working abroad in the near future. She realised as she tacked up Bellamy that it was something she really should discuss with Jack.

Maddie had paid the service fee for getting Phoenix in foal to Golden Moment and just as promptly started saving again.

"What do you reckon, Phoenix? Do you think he'll want to come along too?" she asked of her mare that was now seven months in foal and contentedly munching on some Lucerne hay that had been given to her.

While Phoenix was eating, Maddie was determined to give Bellamy a ride over a low jumps course and then return the two to their separate paddocks. She warmed up the young horse over a fifteen minute period before giving her a decent half hour's work out.

This done, she cooled out Bellamy before returning to the tie up area. Her surprise at finding Jack there upon her return was evident.

"Hi! I thought you had some private lessons to get through today?"

"It's nice to see you too," Jack replied with a grin, "I did, but the second cancelled on me and I convinced the third to let me teach them earlier. And rather than sit at home twiddling my thumbs, I thought I'd come see a certain fiery redhead in case she was lacking in people to pick on."

"So kind of you," Maddie replied with a grin, removing Bellamy's tack and giving her a quick brush over.

"Phoenix is starting to look pregnant," Jack commented after a pause, his gaze resting on the mare's belly.

"Isn't she? It's just so frustrating to think it'll be a few years before I am on her young one's back! I can't wait till she foals down in November though."

"How are you going to practice patience until the foal is old enough to be started under saddle?" Jack queried with a smile, scratching Phoenix behind her wither.

The mare twitched her upper lip, showing her enjoyment.

"I was rather thinking I could keep myself particularly busy and distracted for some of that time," Maddie responded, thinking of her plans to travel.

"Oh?" Jack queried, pausing from giving Phoenix a scratch as he came over to take Bellamy's tack.

"I kept saving after paying the service fee for Phoenix..."

"You know, I didn't know that you were even saving in the first place. Then I found out you had the funds to send your mare to a certain stallion! Can I assume that you had something in mind then and you've got something in mind now?"

"I think it'd be a pretty safe assumption," Maddie replied with a grin, hanging up her bridle after having cleaned over the bit.

Jack leant against the stand where the saddle blankets were placed, his arms folded across his chest.

"So?" he queried, unsure if he should be worried, excited or indifferent.

"So there are a few sites online that advertise horse positions over many disciplines. The idea is to provide positions for those looking for experience in any field they desire."

"How does this relate to you?"

Maddie propped herself against one of the saddles hanging in the tack room.

"The positions are all around the world. I thought I might head over to the UK and work in an eventing yard over there. It'd be a great chance to travel, get some different experience and pass the time before I can start Phoenix's filly under saddle," Maddie explained, watching her boyfriend to try and determine his reaction.

Jack pushed himself away from the saddle rack's support and ambled over to his girlfriend. Reaching out, he took a hold of her arm, pulling her upright to stand directly before him. Maddie found herself quickly wrapped up in his arms as he kissed her soundly.

She stood for a moment, dazed and confused.

"Explanation?" she managed to get out in a quiet tone.

"For all I know Miss Jamison, you could have your bags packed and announce that your flight leaves early tomorrow morning. I wasn't sure I'd get a chance to do that for awhile."

"You'd accept it if I said I was heading off tomorrow?" Maddie replied, crossing her arms in front of her chest.

"Would I have a choice?" Jack queried, leaning forward to kiss her again.

Maddie leant back, evading his caress.

"That's it? No querying where exactly I'm planning on going, when, how long for?"

"What would you have me say Maddie?" Jack asked, frowning.

"How about, 'I'll come with you'?"

A smile escaped Jack's lips before he could stop it. His redheaded girlfriend took a step back, annoyed by his indifference. Jack stepped forward, refusing to let her out of the corner she'd backed into.

"Now you listen here, Maddie. I often don't seem to give the right response and never get away with it, unlike your charming self. But I will say this and you can choose to respond how you will.

You've already made up your mind to go and I doubt I could stop you. I'm not sure what your parents have said, but I'm sure they could hold the fort while you went overseas and gained more experience. If the two of us went however, how easy would it be for them to find two replacements? There aren't a lot of Level 1 accredited coaches around at the moment that could take over.

On top of that, I have a number of horses in work and clients outside of the ERS. I can't afford to drop things at the moment to try out something else. I think it'd be a great opportunity for you though and I'm not going to stop you from doing so. Just don't go charming some man over there, you hear? I don't think I'd cope too well hearing that the girl I love took my heart with her to the UK and promptly dumped it somewhere when she acquired someone else's."

Maddie stared up at her boyfriend as he leant down to kiss her tenderly before walking out of the room.

In a funk she tended to the two horses that were patiently waiting in the tie up area. This done she stomped into the house, thinking the whole time that that wasn't how she'd planned the talk to go.

"What's up with you?" Melanie queried from the lounge as she heard her sister throw her work boots to the floor.

"Jack told me he loves me," Maddie replied, storming through the room.

"Oh, well that explains it then!" Melanie replied sarcastically, staring in wonder at the quickly retreating form of her sister.

August

Wes grinned as she stood in the doorway of her boss' office. It was mid August and she'd returned to the last farm where she did work experience as part of her Diploma. She was to be here until the end of December when the breeding season finished.

"Why won't these machines do what they're supposed to?" her boss muttered, frowning at the computer.

"Well, it printed," Wes concluded, picking up a couple of sheets of paper from the out tray, "but I'm not sure it did so as you would like."

With a grin she handed him the two pieces of paper with the text jammed up on one half of the page, some lines reprinted over others to make an inky mess.

"Silly machine."

"Where would you like it?" Wes queried when the sheets were handed back to her.

"The round filing cabinet," came the put out reply.

Looking around the room, Wes found no such filing cabinet.

"Umm... where?"

"The bin, it can go in the bin," he responded, causing her to smile at the unfamiliar phrase.

"Never mind this silly thing. Let's get some horses fed. Come on out to the feed shed and I'll direct you on which part of the farm to feed."

Twenty minutes later, Wes' trailer was full of an oat and Lucerne chaff mix, ready to be bucketed out into feeders. She realised with a grin that her boss had directed her toward feeding the larger 'half' of the farm.

Riding across the creek she entered the first paddock on the left. This housed the dry mares that were soon to be lined up for breeding. Wes started a head count as she pushed the ATV and trailer through the gateway, swinging her arms and hollering to get the hungry mares to move.

All too quickly one made its way around the trailer and through the open gateway, the rest of the paddock just as quickly following suit. Wes sighed, sitting down dejectedly on the four wheeler bike as she watched a dozen thoroughbred bodies canter their way up the laneway.

Hearing a second bike, she looked across the creek and spied her boss making his way toward her. He stopped the bike just before the gateway.

"Well that was clever now, wasn't it bub? How'd you manage that?"

"Pure talent, obviously," Wes responded in a frustrated tone.

"Well nothing to it, let's go catch those horses. Might as well dump your trailer here and we'll go get them with just the bikes."

Five minutes later the mares were rounded up and secure in their paddock, Wes feeding the restless bodies as she mentally told herself off. *Oh well, maybe I can start a tradition. I let some mares out on my first day of placement here, too.*

Realising that her boss wasn't the slightest bit put out by the incident, she concluded she shouldn't be either and would best do to just get on with the day. After checking that all mares were settled at a feeder and that there weren't any lumps, bumps or cuts that needed tending to, Wes puttered out of the paddock. She made sure the gate was securely closed behind her.

She continued on around the farm, slowly working her way through the numbered paddocks down the left hand side of the farm. One of the furthest away was paddock thirteen, which currently housed some pregnant mares that would be brought closer to the foaling area in a month's time. This paddock of mares wasn't due until October.

After putting the break on, Wes hopped off the all terrain vehicle to swing open the paddock gate. This achieved, she hopped back on the bike and drove it through the gateway before hopping off again to close the gate.

"Well at least you lot aren't pushing your way out of this paddock!" she commented with a smile, watching one mare amble over to the trailer to get a mouthful of feed.

Hopping back on the bike Wes again puttered off, heading toward the far away and spaced out rubber feeders. She ducked in surprise as a magpie swooped her, diving awfully close to her head. Wes repeated this action as a second did the same shortly after, the two effectively creating a 'magpie pendulum'.

"Surely August is too early to be getting attacked by maggies!" Wes muttered to herself, working quickly to bucket out feeds so that she could escape the protective swooping of the pair of black and white birds.

Upon exiting paddock thirteen she glanced at the neighbouring fenced off area with nine equine bodies waiting impatiently at the gate. Concluding her feed trailer didn't have enough in it to continue, Wes headed back down the laneway to top up her feed, calling out to the waiting horses that she'd be back soon.

Later that night Wes sat in the quiet of her bungalow, reading her bible. Something that appealed to her about living on this farm a bit outside of Euroa was that she was the only staff member living in the bungalow. She'd shared at house with one other at the last farm, and two at the farm prior. Not that this bothered her, but it was lovely to have her own space and noise only when she wanted to have it.

Wes had concluded that based on its size, being alone was a very good thing! Her living quarters were made up of a joined bedroom, dining and kitchen area and an adjoining bathroom. She'd been very relieved to find out that the stallion handler Brian and her boss had found and secured a door between the two rooms.

As much as she was living by herself, she'd already found some spare blankets to hang over the windows as a sort of curtain. And she would have felt a little self conscious about showering near an open doorway.

The wind howled outside, causing Wes to pause from her reading and listen to the haunting noise. A grin crossed her features as she recognised a flash from outside to mean lightning. Wes loved storms. She continued to watch for further flashes of light and jumped a little when she heard a large bang that sounded very close to her.

Curious, the young woman headed outside with her phone and torch to determine what the loud bang had been. She looked in disbelief as she spied one of the previously proud standing poplar trees, now lying down on the ground beside her living quarters.

She glanced up in the darkened night, with her torch scanning the roof. This showed her an old television antenna bent to one side and a rather large dent in the corner of the roof.

"Well I'll be!"

Wes started as she noticed a flash of light moving sporadically nearby. Turning to face the oncoming light she realised that it was her boss checking out the noise also. She wandered toward the taller figure, avoiding branches grabbing at her in the wind.

"This is some storm! I think a branch just fell near my house!" her boss called out, causing Wes to smile again.

"It was a tree, and it fell on my roof!" she responded, grinning widely.

Her boss's torch flickered over her face.

"We'll be able to sort that out tomorrow but if you're panicking darlin', you can come inside my house," he offered.

"Why would I panic? I know I'm being looked after."

"Well! And what about me?" her boss asked, incredulous.

"I'm not sure I can answer that on someone else's behalf," Wes replied with a small laugh, turning back toward the bungalow.

***

Lise pushed passed Declan as soon as he opened the door to her.

"Hello to ye, too!" he joked, noting with a glance that it was windy and raining.

"Sorry," Lise responded, putting her wet jacket over a chair to dry before flicking the kettle on.

"I didn't want to be out in that weather any longer! Cuppa?"

Declan replied in the affirmative, heading to the fridge for the milk. He paused at the kitchen window, watching the branches being tossed about in the strong winds.

"I hope this doesn't continue until tomorrow!"

"Tell me about it, I hate working in this kind of weather and judging by the flighty animals we end up dealing with, so do the horses," Lise responded, putting coffee into a mug for Declan and a teabag into the other for herself.

"In a way, it makes me feel rather good about meself," Declan responded with an amused smile, taking the hot drink offered to him before making his way to the couch.

"And what would your Irish logic be behind that statement?" Lise questioned with a grin of her own.

"Well the weather is quite putrid, yes? And still, ye come by and visit! It's nice to know I'm worth visiting despite the disgusting weather outside."

"Always a silver lining. You're incredible, Irish."

"Thank ye," Declan replied with a grin, resting an arm around Lise.

"I hardly meant that as a compliment," she sighed, placing her cuppa on the coffee table before relaxing into his side.

"Like ye said, silver lining," he responded softly, pecking her on the cheek, his lips travelling quickly to her neck.

Lise shivered in his embrace, thinking her cup of tea would shortly be cold and far from finished, as a hand made its way into Declan's hair. The pair jumped as a loud crack and bang was heard from outside.

"I hope that tree didn't fall on any fence lines," Lise murmured, rising from the couch at the same time as Declan.

Making their way to the kitchen window, the pair looked out, rewarded with the sight of many trees still dancing dangerously in the wind.

"It's going to be a long day tomorrow," Declan predicted, wrapping his arms around Lise's figure as he finished surveying the parts of the property that were in view.

The tree had thankfully not landed on anything and was only partly blocking one of the laneways used to access the back paddocks for the feed run. There would be enough room to get past with the bike and trailer if need be, before the maintenance men managed to cut up and remove the tree.

"It's not getting any calmer out there, Lise... I think I've found another silver lining, though," Declan murmured, resting his lips close to her ear.

Lise turned in his embrace, looking up at him with a questioning gaze.

"Dare I ask?"

"I'm just thinking ye may have to crash here for the night," he responded almost smugly, causing her to laugh.

"Silver lining indeed," she muttered, returning Declan's embrace as he leant forward to kiss her.

September

Wes smiled as the vet indicated the small pregnancy on the screen. This was their first pregnant mare for the season. She was 14 days positive in foal, having been bred on the first of September.

"How early can you see a pregnancy on the screen?" she asked the vet.

"At around 10 days or so. It can be quite difficult. The embryo arrives in the uterus six days after conception but is too small for us to be able to identify at that stage."

Wes nodded, remembering day 6 as the first stage that her TAFE teacher had impressed upon the students during her study in Wangaratta. She grinned, remembering her friend Kat who had taken great joy in drawing cartoons of the main events.

"The embryo arrives in the uterus at day six. Prior to this it is making its way down the fallopian tube, where conception occurred," their TAFE teacher informed the class.

Kat nudged Wes, nodding toward a sketched cartoon she had hurriedly put together. Under the title 'Day 6' floated a little blob resembling an embryo. Wes chuckled at the evident arms and hands, each holding onto a suitcase.

"Between days six and fifteen the embryo moves freely about the uterus. This is thought to be an important part of maternal recognition, discouraging the mare from cycling again and coming into heat," their teacher continued.

For this stage Kat drew the embryo carrying out a little dance, partying and socialising in heels and a mini skirt.

"I guess it's a filly then?" Wes whispered with a giggle.

"They all start out as fillies, apparently… it may grow a goatee as it gets older," Kat replied with a grin, still sketching earnestly.

"At day sixteen of pregnancy, the embryo finally fixates, generally at the base of either uterine horn."

Wes chuckled as Kat drew the embryo pitching a tent and the family flag, showing she was settled for the rest of the gestation.

"That's gold. I don't think I'll be forgetting these points of the gestation anytime soon," she stated with a grin.

Later that afternoon Wes discussed with her boss what they had in store for the following day's work. It was still early in the breeding season, meaning that they were only vetting horses every other week day. This left opportunity to deal with any maintenance that may be required around the farm.

Wes was informed that she would be working with the other female staff member, straightening out droppers along the fence line of the yearling paddocks and the top paddocks, time permitting. She smiled and nodded, making a note to have her iPod with her if she was allowed to do the perimeter of a paddock by herself. Music often made her happy to do any task, even if others may find it a little mundane.

Before heading off to her bungalow, Wes was introduced to a couple of clients who had come up to check on their broodmares and a couple of foals that had been born in August. The pair of brothers were affectionately known as D1 and D2 on account of their last name being Davies. Wes had soon come to learn that it was a treat when they visited as they often brought food and loved to cook for whoever would eat it.

"Are you joining us for dinner?" Wes was asked by D2.

"Ummm..." she responded, looking to her boss to see if she should be deciding on an answer.

He just shrugged and smiled. *Up to me, I guess.*

"I think the more important question here is: do you like chicken?" D1 interrupted his brother's question.

Wes nodded.

"Well you shouldn't, it's fowl," he stated gravely, looking at her keenly.

"Much like that pun!" Wes responded, smiling at the pair.

"It's decided, she's staying for dinner," D1 commented, his brother nodding his agreement.

***

Melanie pulled the 2 in 1 tetanus and strangles vaccination out of the fridge in the East Riding School office, being sure to lock it after her. There weren't many treatments that they were able to use on the farm without veterinary permission. Vaccinations were a common one however. Because they were often made up of a small glass syringe and an attached needle, her parents were insistent on protecting their clients by having such items under lock and key.

The girls had been advised the last time their local vet had come to check up on Phoenix, that it was a good idea to give her annual vaccination about a month before she was due to give birth. This helped the mare's body to build up the appropriate antibodies in her colostrum before the foal was born.

Melanie strolled out to the tie up area, pondering this. Maddie had just brought in the heavily pregnant mare, and was tying her lead rope in a quick release knot.

"What time is the sand man due to arrive?" Maddie queried, leaning against one of the rails.

She was referring to the fact that the East Riding School was further establishing their second arena that was used for private lessons. It was smaller than their main arena that often housed a group of up to six riders.

Over winter, the smaller of the two had often been not useable, due to water logging. The girls' parents had finally decided to invest some funds in adding surfacing to the arena in the hope that this may help ease the problem should they receive a lot of spring rains.

"I know it was sometime this afternoon. I think we'd better get Phoenix's injection out of the way before a big truck comes looming down the driveway."

Maddie nodded her agreement. She untied the lead rope so that she had a hold of her mare, should she not react too kindly to receiving the vaccination.

Melanie pulled an alcohol swab out of her pocket and rubbed it over the area in the mare's neck where she planned to inject the vaccine intramuscularly. Making sure her sister had a capable hold of the mare, she took a pinch of skin with her left hand before applying the needle into a neck muscle with her right, pulling back slightly and then inserting the small amount of fluid.

"All done, girl!" she stated, patting the mare on her shoulder.

Maddie waited until her sister was out of the way before turning her broodmare around and taking her back to her paddock. Melanie headed back to the office to dispose of the used needle and syringe in their bright yellow sharps box. She grinned as she heard a large rumble nearby, guessing that their 'sand man' had arrived.

Good timing.

She headed out toward where the driveway broke into a fork, directing the truck to the right hand path that lead toward the tie up area. Having already put Phoenix away, Maddie was at the gate to this area, already holding it open and ready to direct the driver to where he could empty his full trailer.

The driver managed to turn his vehicle around and reverse up to the area where the sand was wanted.

The twins watched as the load was quickly dropped into a large pile on the ground, dust not surprisingly rising from it. Maddie laughed as the nearby ponies took fright, stepping high, some with tails bent almost horizontally over their backs.

"Would you look at them!"

"I guess if I was a horse, I'd find a large noisy truck and a lot of dust scary, too," Melanie replied with a smile.

The truck driver exited his cab to hand the girls an invoice for the East Riding School. Melanie accepted it, saying she'd place it in the office for her mother to organise payment.

The driver smiled his thanks and headed back the way he'd come, Maddie closing the gate again after him.

October

Wes grinned as she sat by her boss' pool out the back of his house. She took a small sip from her glass before placing the cup of coke back on the table.

"So do you think you'll stay in this game, bub?" her employer asked, his gaze on the nearby paddock of dry mares that were splashing in the creek that ran through their paddock.

"I think so! Well, horses anyway. I love thoroughbreds, but more so the breeding side of things than weanlings or yearlings. If I could have the breeding season all year round, I'd be set!"

"Guess you'll need to work both hemispheres, then," Brian, the stallion handler interjected.

"Well, I should find out next month about the Irish National Stud course... 18 months of mares and foals would be my idea of heaven."

"There's no hope for you then - you're hooked!" her boss commented with a small smile.

"Some things are predetermined," Wes replied with a smile of her own.

"Meaning?" Brian asked.

"Well I don't think I got a choice about being hooked on horses. I think it was a desire given to me at the start of my life."

"You mean... ordained?" the stallion handler asked, his eyebrows raised in surprise.

"I guess so. I just don't think I *decided* that I would like horses. I think it was something put in me..." she commented, questioning if she was about to be picked on by the two older men for her beliefs.

"So do you plan on running your own property?" Wes' boss questioned, looking at her intently.

"Absolutely. I'll buy some land and set up something horse related."

"And is God going to provide the funds for that, too?" came the next question, causing Wes to smile.

Brian finished the last of his drink and strolled away from the table, muttering something about hearing a horse float coming down the road. Wes realised that their walk in must have arrived.

"I didn't say that," she replied to her boss, pulling her work boots back on and finishing her drink also.

Her boss smiled, seemingly happy with that reply.

"But who's to say He won't?" she called back over her shoulder, running after the stallion handler.

The older man who was her boss stared after the young figure in surprise. Shrugging to himself, he headed to a nearby ATV to do a last check of the horses for the afternoon.

Nearby, Wes unloaded the mare that was being walked onto the property, finding her heavy and unresponsive to handle.

"A walk on mare that we don't know. I just love how there's not an extra pair of hands around incase we run into trouble," Wes commented with a wry smile.

Recently she and Brian had been deemed capable enough to deal with covers by themselves. Wes was rapt that her boss and other coworker felt she was doing such a good job with holding the mares for covers. She did however question if it would be a bit safer to have an extra pair of hands - just in case.

"Agreed. Especially with a drugged horse," Brian stated quietly, smiling at her surprised look.

"Drugged?"

"Look at her eyes. Maybe she's a bad traveler or hard to load on a float - trouble is, with her senses numbed she's less likely to show to the stallion. I hate doing covers like this. The boy should be keen enough but it's hardly natural to have an unresponsive mare," he stated as he opened the back door to the crush, standing back to let her take the mare through.

Wes closed the front door and waited for Brian to close the back before putting the rearing bit in the mare's mouth. The horse barely moved as Brian wiped her down behind. Generally with a mare that was in season, they were sensitive to touch behind but she just stood quietly.

"All set. Bring her out."

Wes did so, again closing the front crush door after the mare was out. She then stood the mare up away from the crush for Brian to put the breeding boots on. He muttered under his breath as he struggled to lift up the rear hind to put the left boot on. Eventually he achieved both and winked at Wes as he gathered the head collar, lead and bit for the stallion.

"The A Team will manage just fine. Just be aware she mightn't stand well when the boy mounts her."

Wes nodded, watching him make his way down to the third yard on the right where one of the stallions was housed. As the pair started up the laneway Wes tugged on the lead rope, encouraging the mare toward the teasing rail. She smiled at the couple that had brought the mare as they came over to watch.

"Bit of a bad traveler is she?" she asked curiously.

The pair nodded.

"We had to give her a bit of ace to be able to get her on the float."

Handy piece of information to have. Wes turned her attention back to the stallion and handler who were quickly approaching the teasing rail.

***

Lise smiled as she watched the three day old sniff curiously at Hunter's head. The seasoned farrier kept an eye on the young foal, but continued rasping back its mother's hind foot. He sighed as his four year old heeler, Please grabbed at some cut off toe, slinking away in the hope that his owner wouldn't see him.

Hunter bit back a smile as he watched the dog move only a few metres away before lying down and starting to chew.

"Please... the horse would feel a whole lot safer if you ate pieces of her out of her sight!"

Lise laughed, moving to the off side of the mare as Hunter put down the finished near hind. He moved to the mare's right side.

"I can't believe he still finds horse's hooves edible! Surely you can have too much of a good thing?" Hunter questioned, stretching his back.

"You would think a farrier's dog would tire of a diet made mostly of horses' feet. But maybe Please is just living up to his polite name and choosing to not complain?"

"Very funny," Hunter replied, running his hand down the mare's off fore before asking her to lift the leg.

"So how did your vetting go today?" he inquired, knowing that October and November were two very busy months on big thoroughbred breeding properties.

"Good! We had a couple of negatives, but they were early scans. Somehow it feels better if the mare isn't in foal on her first scan, rather than showing up as positive and then negative two weeks later."

"That's understandable. It'd be even more frustrating to find out your mare was pregnant for a month but on the final scan there was no sign of the pregnancy."

"Absolutely! On top of that, it can be hard to get them to cycle again, even if the foetus has been absorbed. There goes a year's investment in a broodmare. John was chattering to me about follicle aspirations, today," Lise continued, talking of their resident vet.

"I wasn't sure if he'd had much to do with artificial insemination or embryo transfers, but it sparked an interesting debate about aspiring follicles from mares. That is, until Declan cut in with a pun about every mares' follicles aspiring to be a size 40, surely!"

Hunter chuckled.

"Well I'm sure every owner of a thoroughbred mare would be hoping for a ripe follicle that's going to release an egg for breeding! I somehow doubt follicles aspire to be anything..."

"That's what I told him! Well actually, I think I just slapped him on the arm for being stupid," Lise conceded with a small smile.

Hunter laughed again.

"I'm sure the Irishman would have understood what you meant! That's this girl done. Do we have any other wet mares to trim today?" Hunter queried, tapping the inquisitive foal on the nose as it leant in close to the older man.

The young filly jumped backward in surprise, her mother nickering softly to her.

"I think that's us all done for the day," Lise called over her shoulder as she led the mare and foal back into the yard with the other 5 mares that had had their feet trimmed that afternoon.

"I guess we'll see you next week then, Hunter?"

"You betcha! Thanks for the update on how things are going at Nirvana Park, Lise. See you next Tuesday."

Lise waved goodbye as the farrier got in his car and headed off down the drive. She laughed as his heeler Please raced after the car, afraid of being left behind. Suddenly the ute paused in the driveway and the driver's door was opened for the dog to jump in.

***

Wes routinely threw on some track pants, a warm jumper, slid into her work boots and stepped outside. The foaling alarm Wes had momentarily switched off, her torch guiding the way to the paddock of heavily pregnant mares where she expected to find one dead to the world.

Running the high power light over the paddock, she spied the culprit for setting off the alarm - a chestnut mare named Coral Keys, lying on her side. Glancing at her back end, she spied a white bag protruding from the mare's vulva and grinned.

"Foalie time," she stated to herself, exiting the paddock to grab a lead rope.

Returning, she attached the rope to the mare's head collar and encouraged her to stand. She led her out of the paddock of other pregnant mares and into a small yard to foal down.

The labour lasted a short time, perhaps thirty minutes and on account of running smoothly, Wes saw no need to wake her boss. Spraying the foal's navel with iodine where the umbilical chord had broken away, she watched the mare licking the newborn filly for a minute.

Satisfied that all was as it should be at this stage in the birthing process, she headed back to her bungalow. It had become a habit - thanks to her laid back boss - to have a cup of tea before checking on the pair in a half hour or so to see how they were going.

Returning outside in the cool hours of the morning, Wes retraced her steps to the small yard that housed the chestnut mare and foal. Flicking the torch over the yard, she noted the filly in the corner, slowly trying to make sense of her long, uncooperative legs.

Moving her focus to the mare, she noted with satisfaction that she had expelled the afterbirth and was quietly grazing on the small picking available in the yard. Concluding the mare would happily accept something extra to eat, she left the pair, collecting a biscuit of lucerne hay from the nearby stable.

Returning quickly, Wes placed the roughage in front of the mare, watching her munch contentedly. Both mare and young woman turned their attention suddenly to the opposite corner of the yard as a loud splash sounded.

Only drawing one conclusion from the sound, Wes slid between the rails and rushed over to the water trough in the corner. A half moon provided her with enough light to establish that as the filly first found her footing, she had lost balance and fallen into the water trough. Responding immediately, Wes clambered into the trough, her small form struggling to get a grip on the struggling foal and then, to lift the forty or so kilograms of weight out of the round concrete container.

Successfully doing so, she then climbed out of the trough, breathing heavily but smiling to herself.

"What are the odds..." she muttered, realising with a wry smile that she could have at least first removed her shoes, and rolled up her pants before jumping in.

Her gaze roamed over the shivering filly as she picked up the torch to get a better look, her view blocked as the worried mother sniffed the newborn all over, checking to see that she was alright.

"Well, Shivers," she concluded dryly, naming the filly, "I wouldn't be surprised if you had a few scrapes and maybe some swelling tomorrow morning when I'm able to see you in sunlight."

Watching the young foal take her first gulps of the mare's colostrum, she smiled to herself, praying the young animal would quickly pass meconium so that she could shortly return to her bungalow to change, and then to bed.

November

Maddie groaned as the loud rapping at her bedroom door insisted. It wasn't until the door opened and she was being shaken that she sat up, slapping at the arms grabbing at her.

"What?"

"Phoenix looks like she's in the first stages of labour! Surely you don't want to miss your foal being born? Oh, and Jack's on his way over. I called him fifteen minutes ago as she seemed to be walking a lot and was working up a sweat."

Maddie looked at her sister in the now too bright room, not quite comprehending. Her gaze drifted to the digital clock beside her bed. *3.50 am. What kind of a nut job is up at 3.50 am watching a horse walk around?*

"Maddie!"

"I guess you won't leave me alone until I get out of bed and come watch my mare exercise?" the young redhead muttered, annoyed at her sleep being broken.

"You're incredible, and not in a good way," Melanie sighed, throwing her sister's jacket at her before rushing out of the room.

Maddie grabbed the jacket, putting it over her bed shirt before changing her shorts to a pair of jeans, just in case her sister was right and Phoenix's foal was coming. Slowly she headed outside, shielding her eyes from the floodlight that was on near to the stables and tie up area.

She frowned as she heard a car pull up in the driveway. *Who would arrive at this hour?* She nodded her head slowly in comprehension as Jack raced over to the pair. Melanie was standing, watching the mare as she paced up and down in a small yard.

Phoenix stopped and turned to look at the three, her ears pricked toward them. She started pawing at the ground and then rolled. Maddie frowned as water trickled from the mare's vulva when she stood.

"Thank you so much Melanie dear for waking me up to watch my mare pee."

"She's not peeing! Her water just broke, you idiot!" her twin replied, watching in awe.

"So… where's the foaling kit?" Jack queried, smiling as the two girls looked at each other, brows raised in question.

"So I guess it's still in the stables where you guys put it after you created one?" he questioned, laughing as Melanie raced toward the stables, around the pile of sand that was still to be put over the second arena at the riding school.

Melanie sighed in relief as she spied the kit. She opened it up and took in all the contents, wondering if they'd forgotten anything. It was while focusing on the individual items that she raced outside the stable block, forgetting about the pile of sand until it registered with her legs that she was running up a deep hill. Reaching the top she tried to slow, but momentum helped her to fall down, roll at the base and then land to her feet again.

She kept running with the kit toward Jack and Maddie. Maddie found herself suddenly very awake, erupting into a fit of laughter at the sight of her twin's mishap.

"Are you ok, Mel?" Jack asked, reaching out for the foaling kit.

He sighed as the most sensible of the pair quickly sank to her knees, also giggling. As this continued, Jack decided to take the kit from Melanie. He pried it from her grasp as she continued to sit on the ground, laughing a little harder as her twin started hiccupping between giggles.

Jack's attention turned to Phoenix as he heard her grunt. The mare was back on the ground, her legs taut as her body contracted, pushing the foal out.

Jack slowly made his way between the fence wires to get into the yard with the mare. He approached from an angle where she could see him, before making his way towards her rump.

"Hey girlie. Your owner and her sister are having a mad moment, so you're stuck with me helping if there are any troubles."

The delivery happened within twenty minutes, by which stage the twin sisters had composed themselves and were standing quietly behind Jack. Melanie started giggling again, causing Maddie and Jack to look at her in question.

"Do you see the nose and front legs clearly?"

Maddie nodded but frowned. What was her sister giggling at?

"Will we quickly guess what Phoenix is having? So far it looks like you're getting a chestnut like you wanted."

Maddie grinned as she realised her sister was right.

"Phoenix is going to have a chestnut filly with a flaxen mane and tail. I told Jack that when we first looked at Golden Moment."

Half an hour later the three were better able to see the filly's colouring as her coat had dried and she was first finding her legs.

"Maddie Jamison you are one lucky woman. Your mare has given birth to a chestnut filly with flaxen mane and tail on the morning of the Melbourne Cup. How cool is that?"

***

"She doesn't seem to be happy about her baby nursing. Is the squealing and kicking normal?" Tanja, the latest work experience student asked Lise, concern evident on her face.

"It's not unusual, but do you remember that this mare is a maiden?" Lise asked, gesturing for Tanja to follow her to the vetting room.

"That's right... so is she just not coping with being a mum?"

"I think it's more a reaction to pain. Her bag will be very full with milk at the moment and a newborn nudging between her hind legs might be causing her discomfort. We need to relieve some of the pressure of all that colostrum."

"How? I thought the foal needed the colostrum to get the antibodies so that it stays healthy?"

Lise smiled as she pulled a plastic bucket out of a cupboard and put it in the sink, filling it with warm water.

"You're right, Tanja. Can you grab me some cotton wool from that cupboard?" she asked, pointing in the direction where it could be found.

"What we can do is massage the mare's udder with cotton wool soaked in warm water. This may help to relieve some of the pain. Once the foal is nursing, this will release the pressure and mum will be more likely to let baby continue to nurse. If the massage isn't enough, we can milk out some colostrum into a bottle and feed it to baby to make sure he gets all the colostrum he can."

"That makes sense. But won't we get kicked milking out the mare?" Tanja queried, heading back with Lise to the yard where the mare had foaled down.

"There's always the danger of that with horses. So because there are two of us, one is going to hold onto her lead rope whilst lifting a foreleg. The other can do the massage and maybe milk out the mare a bit. Does that sound ok?"

"That sounds smart. Can I try the massage?"

"If you're happy to be in the firing line, sure. I'll make sure I have a good hold of her leg so that she shouldn't be able to kick out with a hind leg. Do you need any guidance about how to massage her udder?"

"Ummm... do I just put the cotton wool in the warm water and then apply firm pressure over her udder?"

"Give that a try, sure. Try not to get your cotton wool soaking wet – I think any drips may cause further irritation. She might try to kick at any drops running down her hind legs," Lise commented with a small smile.

Tanja nodded, putting the wool into the bucket of warm water with her right hand. She squeezed it out a little before advancing toward the mare. With her left hand she ran this down the mare's shoulder and side, working her way toward the hind quarters. Lise smiled, glad that Tanja was letting the mare know where she was.

The young student worked slowly, gently but firmly massaging the mare's teats and around them. Lise kept an eye on the mare's ears and eyes, watching for signs of nervousness, pain or annoyance.

"I think I should try milking out some of the pressure," Tanja commented quietly, smiling as Lise handed her a baby bottle with the top removed.

"Collect it into there if you can. We can test the colostrum level before we give it to baby."

Tanja nodded, applying pressure at the top of the bag with a thumb and forefinger, working the pair of fingers down the teat. This resulted in two thin streams of milk being pushed out. Once the bottle was half full, Lise suggested Tanja try the same for the other side of the mare's udder.

"Does this cause your fingers to cramp?" Tanja asked shortly after, causing Lise to smile again.

"At times! How about we test that colostrum and I'll show you a trick I've been taught that gives your fingers a bit of a rest?"

Curious, Tanja patted the mare on the side before moving away. Lise unclipped the lead rope, leaving the head collar on. The pair walked away, leaving the new mum to sniff curiously at her newborn. Lise entered the stud vet room, pausing inside the doorway as she waited for the lights to come on.

Heading to the far corner she opened a draw and pulled out the tool she used to test the colostrum level for each mare.

"Are you familiar with this, Tanja?"

The young girl shook her head.

"Is it a colostrometer of sorts?"

"Yup! It's otherwise known as a refractometer. All it needs is a drop of the mare's first milk onto this glass area here. Then we cover it with the attached piece of glass and look through the eye piece. Can you see a number in there?"

"I think so... does thirty one sound logical?" Tanja asked, unsure.

"It sounds great, Tanja. That tells us that the density of the mare's colostrum is good, which also tells us that antibodies should be present in her milk in a large quantity. The next bit is up to baby to drink a decent amount in the next six or so hours."

The pair jotted down this reading in the mare's file as well as what they'd witnessed of the foaling, timeframes and the issue with the foal's initial nursing causing pain to the dam. This done, they headed back out to observe the pair, Tanja eager to practice her bottle feeding skills.

After they'd fed this to the foal, Tanja queried whether they should be cleaning the bottle and putting it away. Lise shook her head.

"Remember I was going to show you a way to milk out a mare without causing your fingers to cramp so much?"

The work experience student nodded, watching as Lise pulled a 60 millilitre syringe from her pocket, removing it from the plastic casing. Removing a pair of scissors from the same pocket, she proceeded to cut off the nozzle of the syringe.

"A previous coworker at another stud taught me about using a syringe to collect milk. You place it up over the mare's teat and pull back with the plunger, and surprisingly the syringe fills with milk. One thing that makes this a little friendlier to the mare is putting a rubber casing over the top edge of the syringe that will be surrounding the mare's teat. The rubber of a bottle teat works great for it. Want a go?" Lise queried, demonstrating the task that wasn't perfect, but sure beat having hands that cramped up quickly.

"Sure!" Tanja replied, smiling at the invention.

***

Wes smiled as she headed down the laneway on the ATV, having just returned a mare to her paddock after a cover. She slowed on the bike as she realised her mobile was vibrating in her pocket.

Switching the ATV off she then heard the ring tone. The screen that was lit up showed the name 'Mum' on it. Wes smiled.

"Hi mum! What's up?" she queried, sitting on the bike casually.

"I'm sorry to call during work darling, but I had to call you! You got a letter from the Irish National Stud today – is it ok if I open it?"

"Of course! We won't know if I've been accepted any other way. So...?"

"*We would like to inform you that...* you've been accepted! I guess that means, you, your father and I are heading off to Ireland in January!"

Wes let out a whoop, thanking her mum before hanging up the phone and tearing off on the ATV towards her workmates to tell them the good news.

December

Wes smiled as she took Reign out for another road ride. Her boss had agreed to let her agist her palomino gelding on the stud over the months that she was working the breeding season.

She loved her work and adored horses. However, there were times when 10 or so hour days over a 12 day fortnight of working with horses, caused her to reconsider the desire to ride at the end of the day. The work in itself was physically demanding. At times Wes felt that this encouraged her to be more physically active, sometimes surprising her boss by going for a jog around the farm at the end of the day.

She realised that she hadn't fully taken advantage of having her horse on the property where she worked and should have taken him out riding a lot more. Whenever she did, they had a ball.

Wes had been nervous the first couple of times, remembering road rides back in Bangholme where she'd first acquired Reign. One particular ride she'd attempted to go alone, and been bucked off in the neighbour's driveway. This was still etched into her memory. She'd found out however, that in this quiet area of North East Victoria, 15 kilometres from town, that Reign seemed to settle more with a lack of traffic. Wes felt it also had something to do with the fact that she sang at the top of her lungs, focusing on keeping her notes true.

She found that singing helped to calm her, and consequently her palomino gelding calmed.

"I'm really not sure what I'm going to do with you for six months whilst I'm overseas, mister. Boss man made it clear that he's happy for you to be here while I am, but then you have to be re-homed. Maybe I can ask Brian if he'll agist you at his property."

Wes shortened up her reins as her gelding tensed below her, snorting air quickly through his dilated nostrils. She scanned the area ahead, trying to find what it was that had spooked her horse. Applying firm pressure to his sides with her calves, she started laughing as she spied the scary culprit.

"I guess you've never seen an echidna before, ey boy? They're the cutest little things! I'm sure this one won't hurt you."

She urged Reign forward; still chuckling as he tip toed past the creature that was trying to make itself invisible, burying deeper into the hole it had dug on the side of the dirt road they were travelling. Eager to get past the scary object, Reign picked up a high stepping trot, trying to break into a canter as they came alongside the native animal.

Wes sat tall and deep, keeping pressure on her reins. She made sure to loosen her legs, not wanting to accidently tell Reign that he was welcome to run away from this small creature that was scaring him.

The pair relaxed as more distance was put between horse and echidna. Coming to the end of one dirt road, Wes looked left and right. Wanting to continue around the perimeter of the farm on which she worked and also up for a run, she pointed her gelding to the right, pushing him into a canter up the dirt hill.

Wes knew Reign liked a buck every now and again, and so figured whilst out riding alone; pushing him into a faster pace up a hill was the safest way to avoid trouble if he did buck. By her reckoning, a buck would throw her forward and seeing as Reign was moving forward quickly, he should keep himself underneath her body even if he did choose to display some high spirits.

Luckily for Wes, he kept up a steady collected canter, coming back obediently to a trot as they reached the top of the hill. Wes smiled, thinking that riding her quarter horse cross arab gelding around the perimeter of a thoroughbred stud on which she worked was something she would surely miss whilst in Ireland.

***

"Do we have enough rugs? I think we'll need a few more that are five foot six," Lise commented, looking at the pile of horse rugs sorted into varying sizes.

"There's more in the store room if we need them," Kaye responded, grabbing a couple of five foot nine rugs and heading to the far boxes in the stables.

"Do ye want a hand laying out the rest?" Declan queried, picking up a pile of six foot length rugs.

"Sure... then maybe you can show Jodie how we rug the yearlings for the first time?" Lise queried, unsure if her boyfriend would entertain the idea of such an uncertain task with a TAFE student.

"I get to help put the rugs on?" Jodie asked timidly, having been at Nirvana Park for the past couple of days.

"Of course, Tafie! I'll hold, ye'll put the rug on! That is, after I've shown ye how to fold them up so as to make the rug less scary to these young horses."

Lise smiled at Jodie, hoping the young woman would become a bit surer of herself by the end of her placement. It seemed to Lise that those who arrived timid often left with a bit of self assurance and a long list of skills they had acquired. Lise tended to prefer these students over those who arrived full of themselves and left having learnt very little due to an attitude problem.

"Oh, leave that one at Bob's door, Declan. He's built like Mal Maree's yearling from last year. I think that rug will fit him well."

"You haven't yet put a rug on a colt but you think you know what size rug he'll fit into? How can you remember all of the previous year's horses? Is it worth retaining that information?" Jodie asked in surprise, putting a five foot nine rug down as Lise directed her.

"Absolutely! Often I've foaled them down so I tend to remember the foals individually well before we wean them. Working with them as weanlings helps us to further remember which horse is which and as they come in as yearlings, having fed them out in the paddocks, it's easy to remember which horse is which body type. Comparing their type with a previous year really helps with working out what size rug will fit them. Can you see a name on the near side at the shoulder of the rug you're holding now?"

"I think it says... Jackson?"

"That it does. He was a fairly short little colt, but with a really stocky build. His wide chest meant we had to put him in a larger rug even though he was short in the body. We have a filly similarly built this year. Perhaps you can put that rug outside her door, it's box number 10."

Jodie smiled, following the directions before heading off with Declan. Lise watched her go in to catch the yearling in box number one after Declan had shown her how to first fold up the rug into thirds so that it wasn't as imposing when introduced to the young horse.

***

Wes and her Canadian coworker puttered along on the ATV, having just checked over some mares that were close to foaling. The pair had pondered one mare who wasn't alarmed and decided that she would foal down soon, but not that night, deeming her not worthy of having a foaling alarm on.

Wes grinned as she heard another bike revving behind them. With the horn tooting, encouraging her to quicken her pace, Wes knew it was her boss with another coworker on the back of his bike. Smiling, Wes stopped her ATV as she was halfway across the creek bridge.

"I'm sorry, was I going the wrong way?" she asked, proceeding to reverse into her boss' bike.

Whilst he was in a state of shock, Wes managed to push her boss' bike backwards with the pressure of hers. Waking up from his surprise, he applied pressure to his accelerator with a laugh. Deciding it not worth getting into a battle of two bikes pushing against each other, Wes changed gears into drive, speeding up over the hill, laughing.

"I'd never do that to my boss!" her workmate commented, shock evident in her tone.

"Guess you'll just have to enjoy me doing it then!" Wes replied cheekily, grinning at the older woman.

"Did you want to reverse the bike and trailer while I put some lucerne and oats into the mixer?" she queried, receiving an affirmative nod.

Wes leapt off the bike, leaving it to *Canada*, as the young woman was affectionately known by the other staff. She strode into the farm's feed room, working to quickly untie two large bags of lucerne chaff before lifting them up onto the stand near to the feeder.

Her boss came in to join her, lifting buckets of oats up to Wes so that she could tip them into the feed mixer before turning it on.

"Not many sleeps now, bub," he commented, referring to her impending trip to Ireland.

"Not at all! And I'm already planning another trip," she replied, grinning.

"Ey?" he questioned, a brow raised.

"I found a horse stud in South Africa that focuses on trail rides and endurance. The only cost to me would be an airfare, insurance and play money. They provide accommodation, food and of course, the horses. Sounds great!"

"Well, darlin'... as long as you come back here each year from August 1 to December, you can do as you please," he decided, turning the mixer on.

"Oh, and how long for?" Wes asked with a smile.

"Bah, ten years, if you want!"

She turned to the silo, a grin spreading across her face as she filled buckets with oats, her mind quickly doing sums. *Save two hundred a week... that's around four grand from August to December... do yearlings somewhere, save some more. Take off May-July and spend two of those months travelling... South Africa next year, New Zealand the year after and America after that!*

"Yup... could definitely manage that for the next few years," she muttered to herself, still smiling.

Year 6

January

Wes smiled, waiting with her parents for the tour bus. Her mother and father had decided before Wes received her acceptance letter into the Irish National Stud, that they would go on a holiday to Ireland and accompany her for the long flight over to Dublin. The 21 year old was relieved to have her parents come with her halfway across the world.

The flight in itself had been 24 hours from Melbourne, to Singapore for a 1 hour stop and then onto London. Wes had been amazed that it was necessary for herself and her parents to catch a bus at Heathrow, to get to the other side of the airport. The flight to Dublin from London was short, but once boarded on the plane the passengers had had to wait over an hour for ice to melt from some part of the plane's wings before they could safely take off.

The travel in all had taken over 30 hours and was made up of a lot of turbulence, awkward sleeping, a mass of movies and finally a cab ride to the hotel. With the time difference between Ireland and Australia, Wes was glad she hadn't slept so well on the plane.

Half the trick she'd been told by her parents was to stay awake longer than you normally would, so that you could fall asleep by the new country's normal timeframe.

Another thing that had surprised Wes on their first day in Ireland was the hour at which it grew dark. Having just come from daylight savings in Victoria's summer, she'd been surprised by the early hour at which the sun set. This surprise further turned to alarm when it wasn't yet five in the afternoon, and Wes found herself disoriented, in the dark and unsure which way led back to the hotel where her parents were safely housed.

Now on their second day in Ireland, Wes was thankful that she'd managed to navigate her way between old stone buildings, passed the green rugby field and amongst the strong smell of cars to find their hotel. The three had achieved staying up until the appropriate hour to sleep in Ireland, helping their bodies adjust to the new time zone.

Their first day of visiting Dublin, they went on a bus tour, where they would 'hop on' and 'hop off', the bus driver explaining history and punning while he drove them to their destinations. The visits had included Trinity College, the Irish Museum of Modern Art, Phoenix Park and the National Museum of Ireland.

Wes had taken delight in the driver's tale as they bypassed the Guinness storehouse. This was housed next door to a psychiatric hospital that now treated mainly people with alcohol problems. *Only in Ireland would you find a mass of alcohol available next door to a place where they treat alcoholics.*

Later in the day Wes and her parents visited the National Gallery. She found herself smiling in surprise at familiar artist names. She didn't know the artists in themselves, but was familiar with the names as she knew stallions by these names. *Bianconi and Perugino... cool.*

Yeats seemed to have a fascination with horses, this suiting Wes just fine as she took in paintings and statues. She paused as her ears picked up the sound of some screaming, giggling girls.

The giggles belonged to a group of three. One was obviously leading the other pair, the second in line seemingly amazed with the gallery.

"See? I told you... a horse!" the first stated smugly.

Wes smiled as she watched the three display obvious excitement over a marbled piece shaped in an equine form. She thought suddenly that she'd like to teach children in the future who were that excited to see anything that portrayed an equine. *After all, I still feel that way.*

As the group of three wandered into another room, Wes started to retrace her steps, knowing her parents should be nearby. Her stomach was telling her it was time for some dinner.

***

Maddie paused at the end of the driveway, noting that the front gate was unlocked. She questioned with a smile if this meant that Jack had come to work some of the horses. Melanie was out with Johnny and her parents had embarked on a two hour drive to check out a gooseneck that had been advertised for sale online.

Their old double horse float was getting on and proving to not provide enough room when both girls were competing and taking along all their competition gear. The three horse float that was on sale seemed well priced and worth a look.

Maddie did think it amusing that her parents were considering such an investment when she'd talked with them about heading overseas shortly. If she was overseas, suddenly they wouldn't need so much room as there was one less daughter competing, surely?

Maddie put the car into park as she pondered this, strolling to the two bins now empty on the side of the road. Dragging them back, she hooked them onto the back of her old Holden Ute before getting back into the vehicle and driving slowly toward the house, the two bins in tow. She realised that if Jack was about, she'd probably better broach the subject of heading overseas with him again. The first discussion hadn't ended as she'd expected, but Maddie realised that she did seem to have her boyfriend's blessing, something for which she was thankful.

She slowed down more than the expected 15 kilometres per hour along the riding school's driveway as the paddock housing Phoenix and her filly came into sight.

Maddie paused the car, smiling as she watched the now two month old filly nursing vigorously from her mother. Not impressed with the insistent head butting between her legs, Phoenix pinned her ears and turned to give her filly a small nip.

"That's the way, girl. Best to keep your child in line from an early age," Maddie murmured, taking her foot off the brake and ambling down the rest of the drive.

Jack was at the car park, leaning against his vehicle as he changed a pair of sneakers over to some riding boots.

"Hey! Just got here?" Maddie asked, getting out of her car.

"Yup. A few minutes before you, it seems. I thought this place was going to be empty whilst I worked Bellamy. Jacinta rode her for the first time last week and I think the pair went fairly well together. I told Jacinta I'd give Bellamy a little schooling before her lesson next week."

"Do you think Jacinta enjoyed riding Bellamy?" Maddie asked, an idea forming in her mind.

She knew that the young woman's mare Geira was on stall rest due to having sprained a tendon. Maddie had also recognised that Jacinta's riding was improving to the point that she may need to take on another horse - one that had the potential to compete at a higher level than Geira.

"What are you planning, Miss Jamison?"

"You mean apart from a trip to the United Kingdom next month?" Maddie asked, knowing Jack would forget his current train of thought.

Besides, I need to check with mum to see if she's willing to sell Bellamy before I have Jack accidently telling Jacinta that she's for sale. Maddie looked at her boyfriend, his gaze one of surprise.

"That soon? You're really going, Maddie?"

"I did tell you back in July about my plans," Maddie replied, grabbing Jack's hand as she headed over to the tack room to grab a couple of head collars and lead ropes.

If Jack's planning on working Bellamy, maybe I can ride with him.

"You did... and we haven't talked about it since. I can't believe you're planning on leaving me next month."

"Jack... we tend to be quieter at the riding school over the hottest month of summer, so I figured that would be a good time to be overseas working on my skills… and Phoenix's baby is a couple of months old, so it's a long while before I can consider putting her under saddle."

"So how long are you going for?" Jack questioned, stopping outside the tack room with the redhead.

"I'll be back in time for Christmas," Maddie responded with a smile, heading past Jack to grab a couple of head collars from where they were hanging in a row.

"A year! You're going overseas without me for a year?"

"No! More like… ten months," Maddie replied, smiling as her boyfriend grabbed a head collar from her and stormed out of the shed.

"Come on, Jack! I'll be back before you know it!" she called after him, concluding she'd better jog to catch up with the quickly retreating form.

***

Wes had enjoyed a couple of days travelling the Republic of Ireland with her parents, but was glad once she'd gotten past the nervousness of first driving into the Irish National Stud, located in County Kildare. Her parents had gone in with her, met some of the teachers and checked out the facilities.

A lot of students had already arrived, whilst still others were yet to come. The breeding course at the Irish National Stud attracted students from European and non European backgrounds. Wes later found out that 25 or so students were taken into the course, with half each being from within and outside of Europe. Half each also happened to be male and female. This made for quite a mix of individuals.

Classes weren't due to start for a week and Wes was relieved to find that she had a short time to get used to the routine of working on this 900 acre or so property before she was expected to study. She'd already recognised – and was thankful for – some small mercies.

Wes had desperately wanted to take her guitar with her, knowing she would miss playing it for six months. She'd concluded logically that unfortunately, it wouldn't be so easy to take on the plane and back again. She'd been rapt consequently to find that her German room mate – a young woman a little older than her – happened to have a guitar and Wes was informed she was welcome to play it as she pleased.

The other things, for which the young brunette was thankful, were that on her floor where most of the females' rooms were, she was next door to the communal bathroom. The laundry was directly after this, too.

The idea of sharing a bathroom with potentially 9 other females daunted her a little. The fact that she only had to duck out of her room to use it made this idea a little less scary.

Another small mercy arrived in the first week, with Wes sitting in her room with the door ajar, reading her bible on her bed. A French girl had wandered passed, noticed the bible and invited Wes to attend church with her if they happened to have weekends off together. Wes gratefully accepted.

On the first day of staying at the stud, Wes met her German room mate, an Irish, French, Canadian and New Zealand woman. She was pleasantly surprised by the number of different nationalities that she'd met within the first 24 hours. She decided very quickly that the talkative French woman, aptly known as 'Frenchie' was going to be a good friend.

It also amused Wes to find that a couple of the students, who didn't have English as their first language, had learnt their English whilst living in Ireland. Consequently, the German and French women both sounded a little Irish when they conversed with Wes.

She thought over this with a smile as she lay in bed that night, excited and nervous at the idea of her first day of 'work' starting in the morning.

February

Lise smiled as she met Jodie at the stable door. The work experience student had just put a cantankerous colt away after a parade to a potential buyer. Jodie looked very relieved to have unclipped the lead rope from the head collar and close the door on the excited horse.

"Are you ok? You did a great job with him, Jodie."

"Thanks, Lise. I feel a little bit shaken up - I don't think I've had a horse rear up beside me before! I'm glad he didn't strike out with his foot."

"I think he's a little bit over being asked to do the same thing so often. It's a pity for him that he's so popular with viewers! If you do find that he does that again and you're leading him, try to hold the lead rope up as high as you can. This way if he does strike out with a leg, he won't get it caught over the lead."

Jodie nodded as she processed the information.

"I'll take him out the next time that he's needed," Lise commented quietly, earning a relieved smile from the young woman in return.

"Lise... do you think that Kingsley would let me come back for the breeding season this year? I only have one more work placement to do for my course and have really enjoyed working with the staff at Nirvana Park."

"I think you'd have to ask him about that one! Or you could wait until you get your feedback from your work placement if you like, Jodie. Do your TAFE encourage you to work at a place you like?"

"I'm not sure... I think they like us to do our three lots of work placement at different studs. Then we have three places that potentially we can chase up for work at the end of our course."

"That's a very wise move for your career in general. Perhaps when you feel the timing is right, you could ask

Dave if he would be willing to employ you once you've finished your course... that's in November, yes?"

Jodie nodded.

"Well we'll still be busy - in the peak of the breeding season. Perhaps your problem may be that the last place you did work experience at offers you a job and you've already secured one with Nirvana Park. It's nice to have choices!"

The young woman nodded, smiling. Lise watched her head over to their boss before telling a questioning client that'd she'd be only too happy to show them Lot 51.

The young colt pinned his ears as Lise came in towards him. She spoke softly to him, aware that he was tired and over the constant parading.

"It'll all be worth it boy, I promise. Someone will buy you and then you'll get left alone for six months or so before you start a racing career. Now let's show them what you're made of," she whispered to him, brushing his forelock from his eyes and checking that no shavings were stuck to his coat, mane or tail.

Jodie sat watching as the older worker led the colt out of the stable block and stood him up for a client. She noted Lise's reassuring hand on his neck as the colt fidgeted. Aware of how he had been behaving, Lise was ready for his rear and stayed well to the side of the young animal, her lead rope high in the air.

She smiled as the client directed her to walk him, glad for the excuse to keep the colt moving.

"Steady boy. It's almost the end of the day, and then you can rest a bit."

Not ready to slow down, the fiery colt resisted Lise's right hand that was directing him to turn away from her. She placed her left hand up near his eye and he shied, shaking his head before rearing up and striking out.

Not quick enough, Lise didn't manage to get the lead out of the way and the colt came down, the lead rope now under one of his forelegs.

She talked quietly to him, moving quickly as he backed up against the pressure. Able to move a little faster than the colt was, Lise grabbed at the bit of lead above the horse's forearm and managed to get the whole lead out from under his leg.

This done, she continued walking him back toward the watching client. Aware that the young horse was still too forward, she asked him to stop well before they reached the onlooker, grinning as the colt obediently halted. After a quick second glance over the colt standing still, the client thanked Lise and left. Jodie met her at the stable door.

"That was close! What would have happened if he'd gotten away?"

"I promise you, that has happened to me before! And, it's not the end of the world," Lise commented with a smile, unclipping the colt's lead and closing the stall door behind her.

"A great thing about horse sales is that most of the people around are horsey. So if ever a horse ends up loose, someone will catch it. Of course, it's easier if they don't end up loose in the first place," Lise concluded with a wink.

Jodie smiled, following Lise into the tack room to pull out the rugs as Kingsley had directed her to do. It was time to pack up for the day. Lise made a note to chase up Jeremy who she'd spied passing when she was parading earlier in the day. She knew he was working on another stud in the Seymour area and had managed to catch up with him a couple of times since he'd moved on from Nirvana Park.

***

Wes soon found out that the Irish National Stud was made up of varying yards. These were on different parts of the large property and housed mares in foal, mares that were to be bred that season, mares with foals at foot, the stud's 10 stallions or the yearlings for that year.

Between the twenty something students that were there to do the course, they were divided up and put to work on a weekly basis in a different yard. One week Wes may have two workmates and a 'boss' – the yard foreman. The next week she may have seven other workmates and two yard foreman. This depended on the yard and the number of horses housed within it.

It was a great way to quickly be introduced to all of the staff at the stud, the different classes of horses and different routines depending on what stock was in the yard. Wes loved knowing that she would definitely be working with stud horses, but if she didn't like a particular yard or working with someone, the following week it was bound to change.

Generally the students' days were made up of working from around 8 in the morning until 4 in the afternoon. Wes found this a breeze, having previously worked on 3 stud farms with hours ranging from 6 or 7 in the morning till sometimes 5 or 6 in the evening.

Another thing Wes was really enjoying and finding easy, was the weeknight classroom sessions. They only ran for an hour but focused on teaching the students about the thoroughbred breeding industry.

Not strong on pedigrees, Wes was excited about the prospect of an assignment where they had to source a number of thoroughbred broodmares. Once they'd detailed the mare's breeding and racing history and each purchase price, the students then needed to find appropriate stallions to send them to. Wes already knew of a couple of male students who were pedigree savvy and made a note to check with them for her assignment.

Not surprisingly, Wes found the classes on the reproduction side of broodmares to be the most fascinating. She was disappointed to find however that it was often in this class that she found herself struggling to stay awake.

The hours weren't difficult at the stud. However, working eight or so hours, then being fed an early cooked meal by the kitchen staff and having to stay awake for an hour of a lecturer giving them lots of information proved to be difficult when it came to staying alert.

Wes was very glad that she'd already done a diploma focused on horse breeding and gained confidence when she realised that this course had given her a knowledge already far beyond most of the students that were attending the breeding course with her. She found also that as she helped to explain it to some students, that it further imprinted the same knowledge in her own mind.

She wondered if the three other Australians who were studying alongside her also found this. One had won the scholarship the year after Wes had applied for and not gained hers, causing the two to be studying side by side.

In spite of studying 5 days a week and working 20 days straight before getting a day and a half off, Wes was loving her time in Ireland.

March

Madison grinned as she mucked out her fifth box for the morning. *And it's only 6am!*

Things hadn't turned out exactly as the vivacious redhead had thought they would. Her flight had been incredibly long and uncomfortable, but she'd managed to spend a lot of the time watching movies, sleeping and chattering away with the gentleman seated beside her.

The flight survived, she'd managed to gather her luggage and find a taxi to take her to the address of the farm in which she'd landed a position to gain some experience for six months. Maddie at this point was optimistically thinking that she could convince the family she'd be working for that it was worth their while to employ her for a further few months. This way she wouldn't have to look for a second job before returning home.

The job she'd flown over to the United Kingdom for had sounded great online:

'Eventing couple with two horse riding children looking for an equestrian nanny. Board and weekly wage provided for capable horse rider to look after children, instruct them in horse riding and attend events on the weekend with parents as their groom.'

Upon reading this she'd envisaged riding with well turned out kids, all three of them on prestigious warmbloods and strapping for a competitive and talented couple of parents on weekends.

The wage offered hadn't been brilliant, but when Maddie converted it from pounds to Australian dollars and took into account the fact that she wouldn't have to pay rent for a place, she considered it worthwhile. That and the fact that she could teach during the week and attend competitions on weekends had sounded very appealing.

Unfortunately, a week of working at this place proved to be less than appealing. Maddie had found out through conversation with her employers that the pair hadn't competed in over two months and that of their three mounts, the most promising was 'mysteriously' lame.

Maddie's suggestion of a vet check had been shot down quickly. Shrugging this off, the redhead decided that she could at least focus her energy on teaching the young boy and girl who were the children of the couple.

She was disappointed to find that although the parents were said to be eventers, the two kids aged 9 and 11 were keen to run fast on their ponies and jump high. This wasn't surprising. Maddie dealt with this often at the East Riding School. What was surprising was the lack of riding style that both kids had, considering she'd been told that they had been riding for at least 5 years.

Maddie had very quickly concluded that although she had a reasonable place to stay and was paid promptly for her first week, that the environment didn't appear to be one in which she could improve her riding and see the competition scene in England. What had surprised her even more was the nonchalant way in which the couple had accepted her resignation.

Looking back on her interesting introduction to horse work in England, Maddie was glad she'd spied a nearby racetrack. Thinking that maybe she could get some work here whilst she hunted for another eventing position, she'd walked the half hour trek to the track and gone from stable to stable, seeking out work.

It was the third stable block that she entered where she was given a job as soon as she asked. Maddie questioned if she should be concerned about how easily she'd acquired a job when she was from another country and this new employer didn't know her.

After she'd explained where she'd come from, the man in his forties had smiled slowly and said he'd be more than happy to hire her. Maddie questioned if there was a story behind this, but accepted the job gratefully, smiling as she was told the hourly wage that was paid out each week. She'd been thankful to find that in spite of the early hours and split shifts, the rate of pay was more than her last position. By the end of the first day, she'd also managed to find someone at work that lived not too far away and was willing to put her up whilst she found a place to stay.

Now on her third day of work, Maddie felt that although she wasn't a morning person, the staff members were nice and knowledgeable, and it was great to be learning about a different discipline.

The young man who'd agreed to let her board with him over the short term was very helpful in explaining to Maddie the routine and how certain tasks were done at a racing stable. In the first couple of mornings she'd learnt from Tom how to swim the racehorses and tack up with a racing pad.

Most of the other work wasn't foreign to her. Although the boxes were straw instead of shavings, mucking out was easy enough, as was putting horses on and off an automatic walker and lunging some stock. Maddie was pleasantly surprised, too, that the young thoroughbreds were well educated, colts included. Those that were a bit of a handful were assigned particular staff to handle them, so that they were educated appropriately when they misbehaved.

Maddie was keen to find another eventing stable where she could work, but in the mean time, she was willing to make the most of this unexpected opportunity. She made a note that she should Skype Jack and let him know all that had been happening since they last talked. *Boy would he get a shock!*

***

Wes found herself working in early March in the foaling down yard at the Irish National Stud. This was her second time in this particular yard and she loved it. One unique thing about this yard was that a few falabella ponies were kept in a fenced off part of the hay shed. They were an attraction to children visiting the stud.

There were about five students in total assigned to work with one yard foreman for the week. Wes had come to realise that although the students she worked with and the yard she worked in changed on a weekly basis, the foreman for each yard stayed the same. This made sense to her, as there needed to be some form of continuity between the weeks at each different area of the stud.

Wes found the stable arrangement and foal handling to be very different to Australia. She had fun telling the Irish staff of the 200 horses that she and two other full time staff managed during the breeding season in Australia.

Here, because the horses weren't able to be out all day in a paddock - or field, as they called it in Ireland - a lot more man power was needed to bring horses in at night, put them out the next day and muck out their boxes on a daily basis.

All of the boxes were straw instead of the shavings Wes was used to. She was glad to remember that at TAFE they'd been made to do both kinds, but having worked in the industry for a year, she'd become very used to mucking out shavings boxes in Australia. Getting used to using a pitch fork and not have the manure and straw slide between the wide gaps was an art form she was still learning!

Luckily she had plenty of opportunity to practice. Although it may be seen as double handling, each student was directed to muck out their boxes into the open yard. Later one of the maintenance men came along with a tractor and large trailer and the soiled bedding was then thrown by all students onto the back of the trailer.

Wes loved that on this stud, each stall opened out into a large yard area. This particular yard was designed in such a way that the stalls lined the perimeter of a square, with them all looking in on each other. This way it seemed that the horses could see each other across the yard, look outside and enjoy some fresh air entering their stall.

Each morning it was the students' duty to remove the mares from their boxes, pick out their feet with the hoof pick they'd each been given and told to have in their pocket at all times and after checking over their bags and bodies, take them across the road to a large field where they were turned out.

Wes had been surprised to find that although the way of leading horses was the same, the lead ropes were very different. Rather than clipping up to the horse's head collar, they were a wide, fairly thin piece of material that was about one metre in length. This fed through the ring in a head collar where a lead rope is normally clipped up. With the material folded over, students lead the horses.

When they needed to release a horse, it was just a question of letting go of one side of the rope and allowing it to slide through the head collar – if the horse didn't take off at a quick speed as soon as it was released! It took Wes a little while to adjust to the fact that if she accidently let go of one end of this lead, her horse could pull away and walk off if it so desired. Thankfully this only happened to her on a couple of occasions when she was letting horses go.

Because this yard was full of heavily pregnant mares, the yard foreman assigned one student to go out to the field where they'd been released and check them over for signs of foaling. This was to occur every twenty minutes because of the mare's short labour period. It wouldn't be good to find a mare had foaled unassisted in a paddock!

Once the boxes were stripped of any soiled bedding and manure, the task of refilling them with fresh straw started. Whilst some carried this out, others cleaned out waterers and topped up hay.

Large rolled bales of hay and straw were brought into the yards for these tasks. Wes had a lot of fun learning to master how to take a large chunk of hay off the round bale and pile it into a wheelbarrow for distributing. She and 'Canada' carried out this task together.

Piling up the hay as high as they could, Wes and the blonde bombshell looked at the full wheelbarrow with pride.

"Brilliant!" Canada stated with glee.

"Indeed," Wes agreed, staring at it thoughtfully.

"Do you reckon… that'd be comfortable?" she asked slowly, smiling.

Her blonde partner nodded, grinning also. She helped Wes to climb onto the large pile before positioning herself at the back of the barrow. The pair erupted into giggles as Canada steered the large barrow at as fast a pace as she could manage, dodging tourists that looked at them in surprise.

"Totally forgot about tourists!" Wes hissed, still laughing as Canada came to a sudden halt, Wes toppling from the wheelbarrow.

The pair meekly looked around, concluded it was safe and started piling hay into the far corner of the closest box.

The Irish National Stud was open to the public at certain times of the year. This allowed people to see how a stud worked and learn about the greatness of the thoroughbred breed. Of course, the fact that the stud also boasted an Irish and Japanese Garden and a gift shop didn't hurt either.

Wes made a note to be careful of what shenanigans she got up to when there were paying clients around. She didn't want to get in trouble whilst studying in Ireland!

April

Melanie smiled as Jack joined her at the fence line, watching the young filly cavort around the paddock with a couple of pony mares. She questioned how long it would be before the filly would realise she was going to be a lot bigger than her paddock companions... and then act on this feeling of superiority.

Phoenix's filly – currently named Phoebe by Melanie – had been weaned a couple of weeks earlier after things had been worked out logistically.

Melanie had read up on the weaning process and been learning a bit about it through her university course. Because the East Riding School wasn't a large property, Jack and Melanie had spent a little while working out where to put the mare and foal once they were separated. Melanie had read that it was advisable to put the pair out of hearing and sight of each other, to try and minimise the stress of separation.

Having had a nanny suggested to her by a study mate, Melanie had suggested to Jack that they place Phoebe in with another horse or two so that she was able to learn about behaving like a horse. Jack had suggested the pony mares might be a good substitute. He'd also recommended taking Phoenix for a month or so to the place where he agisted his horses so that the mare and foal were completely separated.

Jack hadn't admitted to anyone that having Phoenix under his care made him feel a little closer to his girlfriend. He and Maddie talked a couple of times each week via Skype but Jack was glad at the end of each month when he could turn the calendar page over and know that the fiery redhead was a little closer to coming home.

"She's going to be as opinionated as her owner, isn't she?"

"I'm not sure it's possible for a horse to be that full of itself," Jack replied with a smile.

"Guess I'd better get ready for this lesson. It looks like Jacinta's just pulled up."

Melanie nodded, watching the young man stroll toward the tie up area. Jacinta was currently leasing Bellamy and the pair were doing great together. Melanie had been surprised to find out that Maddie had put forward the idea of Jacinta buying the mare before she headed overseas.

The suggestion so far was working out really well, with the pair achieving a lot together. Melanie made an extra effort for her twin to keep an eye on the determined young woman, who still made her interest in Jack clear. She wondered if Jacinta would be bold enough to push past her consistent flirting with Jack. For Jack's sake, she sure hoped not.

***

Wes sighed, sitting down in the chair of the classroom, relieved.

"I thought today wasn't going to end!"

"Not enjoying the stallion yard, then?" Frenchie asked with a grin, grabbing at the camera Wes had made a habit of carrying with her almost everywhere.

The young Australian woman found that she never knew what her classmates were going to get up to or what she could discover with regards to a horse that was worth getting on film. Thinking back, she realised she was glad she'd had the camera on the stud today, as one of the boys had agreed to take photos of her leading in the stallions from their paddocks.

Wes had paused for a photo, increasing the pressure on the lead of the stallion Alamshar, causing him to come to a halt.

"Ok! Go for it!" she had instructed her partner in crime.

Nodding, he lined up the camera, snapping a few shots. Wes wanted this as her "proof" that while on the other side of the world, she'd been deemed capable of handling a majority of the stallions standing at the stud that season. As the photos were taken the bay stallion leant forward, sniffing her hand, finding a scent he was unfamiliar with. In perfect 'flehmen's' style, his top lip curled up; trapping the scent in his nostrils as he breathed in, further assessing the scent. Wes grinned as she heard the click of the camera.

"That'll be a keeper," she had commented, smiling.

Wes recognised that she was being given a great opportunity to work in the stallion yards. There were 10 stallions standing at the stud, two stallion handlers or yard foremen, and herself and a young Irish woman.

Wes loved getting to see the covers that were happening daily, and helping out with regards to preparing the farm mares or mares that were walked in to one of the 10 stallions. She'd been amazed to find on her first day in the yard that there was no foal crush like she'd grown accustomed to in Australia. It had surprised her even further to find out that the foals were restrained during a cover by one of the staff.

Having not had a lot of hands on with foals in Australia, Wes recognised that she was a little behind most of the other European students. She was frustrated with her lack of control of a foal that day that had managed to escape her embrace just when the stallion was mounting the mare. The foal had raced behind its mother and distracted the stallion, much to the two yard foremen's dislike.

To make matters worse, each breed at the Irish National Stud was recorded to have proof of stallions being bred to mares. One of Wes classmates was on camera duty and took great joy in showing her the point where she lost control of the foal and then fumbled to try and catch it again.

"I don't think stallions are my thing… I find them intimidating and have been in tears a couple of times already this week," Wes whispered, earning an understanding pat on the back.

"At least it's nearly the weekend and we get to go to church. You can talk with that Irish guy you like," Frenchie commented with a conspiratorial wink.

Wes laughed, thinking that much was true.

"Lads, the barn is on fire!" a student burst into the classroom.

Twenty three students stopped their bickering, doodling on paper, checking of emails and looked up at the figure that had just burst into their classroom.

"You're joking, right?" was the general response, but not certain, many stood to their feet and headed for the door, the rest soon following suit.

The view nearby tourists had of the next few minutes was twenty five bodies bursting forth from a building, all running a sprint across the well manicured lawns, dodging trees and flowers as they rounded the lake and burst forth into the main yard and through it to a set of gates that were being hesitantly held open for them.

Rounding the corner together, the students stopped in their mad dash and took in the almost incomprehensible sight of the hay barn, its whole contents ablaze with reds and oranges.

Hands made their way to cover mouths as it sunk in that the jeep that had been carting them to and from yards and the horse box that all had sat in, holding on tightly as their driver took corners a little too fast – it was all ruined.

"Is it likely to blow? Should we get back?"

"Too late – already has," they were informed quickly.

"The falabellas – we need to get them out!"

Minds turned to thoughts of the three gorgeous ponies, favourites of the many children that tourists brought with them; two heavily in foal.

"Too late," came the sombre reply.

The rest hardly seemed worth saving, but jumping into action, fire hoses were suddenly remembered and bodies scattered everywhere, pairs of hands working together to join up the long pieces of hose while other bodies unraveled and dragged the heavy mass around the corner to where it could be connected to a water supply.

Still more bodies moved the few mares and foals that were housed nearby and others checked on all the heavily pregnant mares, closing skylights in boxes, aware that if the wind picked up, a flame could all too easily head in their direction, and make an entrance through the open window, onto the inviting straw below.

The hose although a good idea, was near to a waste of time as the water pressure proved to be not enough. Once all horses were seen to, the student bodies found themselves returning to the hungry flame, watching with dark fascination as it continued to burn, seemingly eager to take all it could before the fire brigade arrived to put it under control.

Upon arrival and seeing the flame being attacked, the student's minds turned once again to the horses and under staff instruction, they separated the two groups of mares. A dozen or so students and horses headed across the property in one direction, the other dozen heading in the opposite direction, all minds eager on getting their steeds to safety.

It was an interesting sight as leads for the horses were not enough and students utilised shirts, jumpers and belts to drag the expecting mothers away from the danger.

Still more students rushed around, putting together the bare essentials to make up a foaling kit while others volunteered to go on mare watch for the time being, resting their frames on the top rails of the dark wooden fences, overlooking the lush green fields in a so green and damp environment that a fire could not be imagined.

The wind picked up and smoke blew across the property, winding itself around the uneasy mares in the fields, causing bodies to again be put into action as it was decided they should be moved to another part of the farm.

But first, boxes had to be bedded down. Another crew of workers was decided and they hastily raided the pitchfork supply before making their way out of the main gate and across paddocks, each with a fork over their shoulder as they wove between pregnant mares down to the two empty barns waiting to be filled with thick beddings of straw, fresh water and hay.

May

Lise ran her hand patiently down the young colt's leg. The June Weanling Sales at the Oaklands Junction complex near Melbourne weren't far away and yet this colt that had been stabled for the past month hadn't seemed to have settled at all.

Lise made a note to check with Kingsley about putting him on Ulcerguard, a product that helped to protect the lining of the horse's stomach. Lise was aware that stress could upset a horse in many ways, including putting them off their feed. Ulcers were an internal sign of stress, sometimes hard to diagnose. Lise did know that this colt wasn't eating as he should, in spite of keeping weight on his body.

If a horse didn't consistently have something moving through its gut, it was possible for acid levels in the stomach to increase to such a point that ulcers were created. To exacerbate things, the ulcers could then cause it to be painful for the horse to eat, continuing the cycle of not eating properly and increasing ulcers.

This particular colt hadn't seemed impressed at the start of the sale preparation, but neither had any of the others as they'd just been separated from their mothers. The others seemed to have grown used to their separation and gotten into the routine of stable life. All except this one.

"I think we should take him into the wash bay, Lise," Declan commented quietly, as the woman ran her hand halfway down the cannon of the hind leg to have the colt kick out again.

"Ok. Remind me to talk with Kingsley about putting this fella on Ulcerguard, too."

"You think he's got ulcers?"

"I think he's stressed, definitely. If he improves, maybe then we can know that it's ulcers causing the problem."

"Fair play to ye. We'll mention it to the big fella when he stops by before lunch."

Lise nodded, opening the stall door for Declan to lead the young male out of his box. The pair made their way down the breezeway of the stable, Declan applying pressure to the breeching rope if the colt hesitated in his stride.

The Irishman had suggested they go to the wash bay in the hope of using water to get the young horse used to having pressure against his leg. Once he came to accept this without kicking out, then it might be safe to move back to running a hand down his leg. The pair worked with him for about ten minutes before heading back down the breezeway.

"Lise, will ye grab Mal Maree's baby out of box 9?"

Not sure what he had in mind, Lise followed Declan's instructions anyway. She smiled as she stood in the breezeway with her colt, watching Declan place his in the box she was previously in.

"Do you think the box swap will help him to settle?"

"I'm not sure. But maybe now that he's got a friend on either side of him, he'll be a bit happier. Two friends to talk to is better craic that one."

"I guess we'll see tomorrow, McAlister. So did you want to speak to Kingsley or will I? I think I just heard his car pull up outside."

"Ye have a way with words, ye can talk to him," Declan replied with a wink, whistling merrily as he strolled after Trevor who was up the other end of the stable block.

***

Wes grinned, thinking that she was indeed living and studying with a mad bunch. This week she was working in the yard Maddenstown, one of the largest at the stud. Consequently she was working with six other classmates.

A couple of students were discussing the reproductive cycle of the mare in the box next door where they were piling hay into one corner.

"Ye should have been in this box when I was mucking it out earlier! Boy is this girl hot on! It seems she's peed all over the box!" an Irish student commented.

"The bit that I don't understand is that you give this shot of PG to the mare that is looking at any stallion like she'd like to rip his head off, a few days pass and suddenly she's a smitten, giggling school girl that goes weak at the knees at the sight of a boy," Canada commented to the Irish woman.

"You give me a PG shot and in three days I'll be all yours," one of the boys commented with a smirk, causing Wes to laugh.

The blonde Canadian slapped the English boy on the arm and picked up the wheelbarrow, declaring that she was going to get some more hay.

Wes didn't feel it was timely to mention that the reason prostaglandin worked so well on a mare was that it broke down a structure on the mare's ovary that then resulted in her coming into season and being receptive to a stallion. Consequently, there was no guarantee that the same drug would have anywhere near a similar effect on males who didn't produce eggs or ovulate.

Nevermind that 1 milligram affects a 500 kilogram horse... how would it affect an 80 kilogram person?

Wes watched in surprise as the Englishman raced after the Canadian woman, not eager to let her out of his sight.

"You really like that wheelbarrow, don't you? Why don't you ever look at me like that?"

Laughing at the odd statement, Wes headed towards the crush where she knew the last few mares were being vetted. She paused at the doorway as she heard one of the yard foremen talking quietly with the resident vet, a woman in her mid to late fifties.

"So I glanced out of the last stable block to make sure the students were ok putting the last mares out and what do I see? That blonde one is astride one of the mares, cantering her out to the field! I was too shocked to tell her off."

Wes grinned as she realised that her Canadian friend had indeed been seen by the teachers in charge of this yard.

Thankfully it sounded like she wouldn't get in trouble, but Wes made a note to mention it in case Canada was planning on repeating the exercise.

***

Maddie found herself questioning how things had fallen into place so neatly. She was still working at the racetrack and was glad. A couple of weeks into working at the track she'd discovered that her boss had a history with show jumping. Curious, she'd brought it up one morning, only to excitedly discover that he and his two sons had a side business of turning ex-racehorses into show jumpers and selling them on when they found the right buyer.

Upon hearing that currently things were too busy on the racing scene for her boss, Maddie suggested that she could help out keeping the jumpers fit and in constant practice on her days off. Noting her keenness, the older gentleman named Jim had agreed.

A month later Maddie was rapt to find that her working days related to racing hours were cut down to four and she was given a day and a half to focus on riding show jumpers, giving her a day and a half to herself. The tenacious redhead dedicated these days off to riding anyway and found this keenness rewarded with being put in nearby shows at the expense of her boss.

Jim had watched Maddie ride and commented on her skill, throwing in a couple of pointers of his own. Having researched his riding career online, Maddie listened keenly, a newfound respect evident for this man who had made a decent living from show jumping fifteen years earlier.

***

Wes looked at the shaking newborn, frowning.

"That doesn't look normal," her foal watch partner stated, peering over the door.

"No," she agreed, thinking the young equine looked like it was gasping for breath.

"How long has she been like that?"

"I'm not sure... since I came to check on her at least. So, ten minutes."

The foaling attendant nodded, digesting the information. She mentioned to Wes that she felt a vet was needed and was going to call the stud groom to get his permission to contact the vet. Wes nodded, leaving the foal for a moment to do another check of the pregnant mares in the yard.

Upon her return five minutes later the foal seemed to have deteriorated and Wes thought that maybe it was unable to stand. Wes looked away from the foal as her workmate stopped at the box next door, a mare being led beside her.

"The vet is on his way and the stud groom's coming to help us, too. And I think... we may have another foal before the vet arrives," she commented.

Wes watched the mare pace her new location, sweat evident on her neck and flanks. Her tail was elevated as was typical of mares in their first stage of labour. Wes concluded that it was going to be a busy night. She started as she heard a rough barking sound and frowned when she realised it was coming from the foal they'd called the vet out for.

That can't be good. Under the foaling attendant's instruction, Wes got into the box with the mare and foal and helped the foal to stand up. The idea was that maybe this would help the foal to breathe better. Often dummy foals – as both women were guessing this one to be – had issues because of a lack of oxygen around the time of their birth.

The vet arrived shortly after and put a tube through the foal's nasal passage to provide it with oxygen. The stud groom helped the vet with this.

Wes stood with the attendant who was watching the mare next door pacing around, pawing at the ground intermittently. She looked to Wes like she was quite uncomfortable.

"Might be a red bag."

Wes nodded, having not seen one of these foaling mal presentations before. She questioned how the attendant knew it was a placenta that had failed to break open.

"I've only seen one, but this mare is behaving like the one I saw when I studied at the Irish National Stud. If we're lucky, once the placenta is broken, the delivery will proceed as normal. I think we should take a look."

Putting on a glove, the foaling attendant had Wes hold the mare whilst she felt inside the birth canal.

"Yeah, it's a red bag. Come have a feel."

Wes switched positions with the young woman, feeling something inside the mare that felt thicker than the birth sac she had grown accustomed to.

"What now?"

"Put a hole in it... with your hands, try to break it. Oh, and stand off to the side so you don't get drenched when the mare's waters break," she ended with a grin.

"Ok... done," Wes commented, surprised to find it was easier to pop than a balloon.

"Really? It must have been a thin placenta. They can be quite thick and hard to break," the attendant said, again switching to see.

Some allantoic waters were suddenly released from the mare, proving the afterbirth had indeed been broken.

"As long as the presentation is correct, she should foal fine unassisted now," the older woman commented as she determined that the foetus' forelegs and muzzle could be felt.

"Ok, we'll leave her alone."

The two quietly exited the box and closed over the door, peering through the top of the door to judge her progress. They assisted once where the foal got stuck at the shoulders – a very common point for problems to occur – and then left the pair to bond once the foal was expelled completely.

Whilst the foaling attendant got together the necessary items for the mare and foal from the foaling kit, Wes went to check the mares again. The other mares were quiet; most snoozing, some munching on hay or bedding.

Wes paused in surprise upon peering into the box of her favourite mare, frowning when she saw the creature cast in the box - upside down and stuck. She only fully comprehended the situation when she spied the placenta behind the mare and a dark brown newborn in another corner making its first attempts to stand.

Questioning if she'd be able to flip the mare without a rope and without getting herself kicked she slid open the door, closed it behind her and went to the mare, opting for the back leg closest to her. After the third attempt she was able - with the mare's help by writhing about - to pull the legs away from the wall and therefore turn the body. Once the mare was up she ran to get the foaling attendant. It was indeed proving to be a busy night!

June

Wes grinned at the older male heading across the road toward her. Things had quietened down a little on the stud. Consequently the students found themselves participating in random maintenance jobs to keep the horse property in working order and looking neat and tidy. Some had complained, but Wes figured it came with the territory of running a property. She did realise that if she was doing this in Australia, her iPod would be a welcome addition.

"Need a haircut?" she called out to the Iranian man who had just crossed the road, snapping the secateurs shut with a grin.

He shook his head, returning the smile.

"Nope. C'mere."

She frowned in confusion, standing while he dropped the bucket, sponge and brush that he had been carrying, onto the ground before bending down and gesturing to her to hop on his shoulders.

"Wha? No... no!" she squealed as he rose up into the air, balancing her on his knees before realising he'd forgotten the washing implements and had to lower both their weight in order to pick them up and pass them to her.

Giggling as she rocked unevenly on his shoulders, Wes took the heavily dripping sponge and ran it across the sign that pointed to their yard. Her laughter increased when the water and suds made a dive from the sign into their unsuspecting victim's hair below her.

"Hey!"

"Bet you're not considering this such a smart idea now!" she retaliated, continuing to clean the sign and thinking that this was more fun than trimming back the hedge she'd previously been working on.

Very soon a few other students joined the pair and then one of the maintenance men. The group of five was informed that they were needed in one of the larger paddocks across the road for some weed removal.

Having finished with the sign, Wes was grateful to be lifted back down to the ground and followed their leader up the road. The equine students paused at the fence line in surprise.

"We got out of painting fences to do this?" one young man questioned dubiously, staring at the field full of long grass and many, many weeds.

Wes shrugged mentally as she heard the young men complaining around her. *Not much we can do about it!*

"Well? C'mon lads!" the maintenance guy instructed as he climbed over the fence into the field, gloves on and ready to pull out any dock within site.

Grinning, Wes followed suit concluding both jobs weren't high on the entertainment list, but the company she was keeping was amusing, so it would do suffice. This resulted in an afternoon of lying down in the surprisingly damp summer grass for periods of time, listening to others moving around; chasing each other with dock that had been pulled up and making large piles of the unwanted weed.

Wes wasn't too sure about stealing dock from another's pile, but she spied two boys doing just this, perhaps in an attempt to make it look like they'd worked harder than they actually had. She kept a close eye on her pile, however, not eager to let them have any of her hard earned proof.

***

"Look, Emmy! That horse is burping – how rude!" 12 year old Geordie exclaimed in surprise, pausing from doing up the rug on her mount.

Hannah looked up from her pony to see what the fuss was about. Melanie smiled, holding back laughter.

"And the other one is, too! Matty taught Nikki how to burp!"

"How do you know Nikki didn't teach Matty how to burp?" Melanie queried, her grin remaining.

Geordie frowned, not finding an answer.

"Actually, neither of them is burping. It's a bad habit that some horses pick up and it's called crib biting. Have you heard of it?"

Geordie shook her head, pondering the word. Hannah peered at the bay gelding as he repeated this odd behaviour.

"Did one of them teach the other to crib bite?"

"Some people think that's a possibility but horses tend to crib bite because they aren't able to find something better to do with their time. Because we just bought these two ponies, it is possible that where they came from they started to crib because they couldn't do other things, like spend a lot of time eating out in a paddock. They might have both started to do it without having seen the other one do so. It just happens that we now own both of them and we see them doing it at the same time."

"Will they stop now that they spend a lot of time out eating in the paddock?"

"I'm not sure. Because they have done it quite a bit, it may be hard for them to stop doing so. It's sort of like if I learn to rise to the trot and then I find it really difficult to sit to the trot because I'm so used to rising. Does that make sense?"

Both girls nodded, glancing at the pair of ponies each time they made a deep burping sound. They finished putting their rugs on their mounts to protect them from the winter chill and then strolled out with Melanie to the pony paddock to put them away.

Melanie accepted a promise of a date later from Johnny when he came to pick the pair up. She smiled as she watched the car disappear down the drive, concluding that both Hannah and Geordie had improved drastically since Melanie had started teaching them. She realised with a start that that was five years ago. *How had the time gone so quickly?*

***

The blonde bombshell, sarcastic dark haired woman and effervescent brunette burst into giggles, each setting the other off in a contagious run of laughter as they hung precariously off either side of a bridge in the Irish 'St Fiachra's' garden, attempting to direct each other on how to catch the midges darting around in the water below.

"Quick, quick!" Canada urged them on.

"Left, on your left! No, other left!" Wes directed the French woman, "You got some, lift! Don't fall in - you'll drop the fish!"

"And that's how it's done ladies," the blonde Canadian commented proudly.

"Agreed! With quiet, calm and patience," Wes cut in causing them to all burst into laughter again as they watched the larger of the small fish circle the bucket at a rapid pace.

It was nearing the end of their six month course at the Irish National Stud and Wes had suggested they carry out a couple of tasks to commemorate their time in Ireland. More giggles ensued as the three managed to transport most of the fish from the large bucket to a small drinking bottle.

Other fish escaped back into the water of the flowing creek as they were poured out of the bucket, the three young women suddenly quiet with concentration. The plan was to let these fish go in the fountain of the main foaling down yard. The girls had originally considered the idea of putting bubbles in the fountain but concluded that fish might be a little less obvious.

Bypassing some tourists visiting the open garden on the stud, the girls snuck around corners of buildings, Frenchie humming the James Bond theme song much to their amusement. Peering around the passageway into the yard, Wes commented that the coast was clear, causing the three to make their way toward the main fountain whilst no one was in sight. Double checking their surrounds, two kept guard whilst the third emptied the contents into the base of the fountain.

The girls managed to keep their composure as they made their way out of the yard. That is, until the yard foreman passed the girls and the French woman called out to him,

"Top of the morning to ye!" causing the other two to cough and splutter as they worked hard to hold back laughter.

Wes was glad to know that soon she would be able to be on home ground and see her family. She was excited to know too that she would get her certificate for doing the breeding course, find out how she ranked amongst her classmates with regards to yard work and assignments and then be off with a few of the girls to check out Northern Ireland.

Most exciting of all was the fact that as she left this place, she was leaving with contacts that spanned 11 different countries. Life indeed was promising.

July

Lise paused from making up the afternoon feeds as she heard the rumble of a bike and then jogging footsteps. Declan's frame soon appeared in the doorway. Lise watched him head toward a nearby cupboard, removing a ready made foaling kit for emergencies. She put down her feed scoop and grabbed a handful of gloves, trying to think who was due to foal first.

"The earliest girls are due in the first week of August. Who is it?"

"Kaiya. She's foaled out in the paddock - two weeks early; tore a bit, according to Trevor. Better go see the damage."

Jumping on the back of the bike Lise held on tightly as he took off for one of the nearby paddocks where the first due mares were housed. Trevor was waiting at the gate, holding it open for the pair.

"Will you two be ok? I need to finish the feed run with Kaye."

Lise nodded, her gaze sweeping the paddock. The other twelve mares were eating; leaving the new mother and foal in peace for the time being. Stopping the bike a few metres from the pair, Declan hopped off, directing Lise to hold the mare while he checked her behind, holding her tail off to the side.

"Ouch. I'm not sure this one will be a contender for a foal heat breed, Lise. Then again, seeing as it's not yet August, maybe she'll be right before she needs to be bred," he stated.

"How far up is the tear?" she questioned, rubbing the mare on her forehead.

She made a note to give the new mum some bute to ease any pain from the unexpected foaling. The mare nickered as the bundle near her feet flicked its front legs out before its body, making an attempt to move.

"High. She's got a rectovaginal fistula. Maybe Kaiya's owners will be ok with sitting to see if she heals or give her the season off."

Lise nodded, hoping for the mare's sake that this would be possible if necessary.

"It doesn't look like baby's been out long. I guess Trevor and Kaye just missed it, pity mum couldn't hold on a little longer so they could have helped. Maybe the tear could have been avoided."

"Hmmm… so shall we go for a stroll?

"Perhaps we should get the ute so we can move this baby. He's not on his feet yet."

Declan caught Lise's gaze, grinning. Moving away from the mare's back end, he squatted down to check out the little brown colt, spraying the umbilicus area with iodine to discourage infection. This done he put the bottle in his back pocket.

Lise grinned as she spied her boyfriend wrapping his arms around the chest and rump of the foal, picking him up.

"Ye can drive Lise. I'll sit on the back and I'm sure mum will be more than happy to follow."

Lise walked quickly with the mare, leading her with the head collar and lead that Trevor had put on her. She noted with thanks that the other mares were more interested in their afternoon feed than what the humans were getting up to. Sometimes trying to get an unexpected foal out of a paddock with its mum could prove to be difficult with other curious equine bodies.

Lise led Kaiya around to the left side of the all terrain vehicle and sat on the seat of the bike. Declan sat himself on the back, the foal resting across his lap.

Lise put the vehicle into first gear and puttered along at a pace where the mare could keep up a stately walk. Every now and again Kaiya turned to sniff at her foal, pulling at Lise's left arm that was holding the lead.

"'ere, give it to me. She just wants to know baby's ok."

"Ok."

Once the group of four made it down to the foaling yards, Lise left Declan to carry the colt into a yard, mum obediently following her newborn. Rummaging through the foaling kit she found a small tub of phenylbutazone and drew up 10 millilitres into a small syringe.

Lise administered the bute and then stood back to watch the pair while Declan cleaned himself up in the vet room. The young colt was again focused on his legs, awkwardly placing them around his recumbent body.

"They'll make sense soon enough, young man. Then you'll be tearing about the paddock with mum in hot pursuit," Lise said to him with a smile.

She squealed suddenly as Declan wrapped his hands around her, creeping them under her jumper and shirt.

"Declan! You're hands are freezing from the water, and not to mention wet!"

The Irishman burst into laughter, causing Lise to turn and face him with a frown.

"I don't love you anymore."

"Do ye love me any less?" he queried innocently, earning a smile from Lise in return.

"I guess I lied," she laughed, "you seem to have a knack for making me love you more each day."

"Tis all in the accent," Declan replied with a wink, stepping forward and wrapping his arms around her.

"If that's the case, McAlister, then you'd better not take me to Ireland."

Declan smiled, leaning forward to kiss her, his lips trailing to her neck.

"Did ye just give me permission to not introduce ye to me folks?" he murmured in between kisses.

Lise frowned as she felt the vibration of his laughter against her neck.

"I think I just did... that's it - I definitely don't love you anymore!"

Declan smiled against her lips, his fingers making their way into her hair. Lise returned the kiss, leaning into his frame.

"Yer actions seem to disagree with yer words," he stated as he leant back to catch her eye.

"I don't hear you complaining, funnily enough," Lise responded with a grin.

"Damn straight, woman."

***

Wes drove her laden car over the last rise of the Warby Ranges, her eyes suddenly opened to the numerous lights illuminating the town of Wangaratta. Images from memory of the green acres below her that were currently covered by a blanket of darkness sprang to mind and she smiled. *Home.*

There was no doubt in the young woman's mind that north east Victoria was where her future home lay. She had no idea when exactly she would settle in the town of Wangaratta but was content to know that for now she had work lined up an hour down the road in Euroa.

Upon finishing the course at the Irish National Stud, she'd headed to Northern Ireland with a few of her classmates, visiting many places and hostels along the way. A highlight had been getting to see Giant's Causeway and walk across it.

Wes had naively known of the stallion by the same name, but it wasn't until one of the other girls suggested they visit this phenomenon that she came to realise that the stallion had been named after an incredible place worth visiting in Ireland.

Wes had been blessed whilst studying at the national stud to visit some large properties, such as Kildangan - Darley's set up in Ireland, Coolmore and Ballylinch Studs. Seeing these gorgeous properties, with just as beautiful equine occupants, Wes was determined that she would one day have her own property in North East Victoria on which she could teach others about horses and the wonderful careers they can offer.

Her next step involved heading back to the farm where she'd last worked and completing a third breeding season in a row. She decided with a wry smile that skipping the yearling season again was more than appealing but didn't know if that would be a possibility the following year.

Having found a website that advertised working and riding holidays in South Africa, she decided that this was her next aim. *After all, who wouldn't want to spend a holiday riding horses on the beach?*

August

Madison grinned as she rose over the jump with her mount, the pair landing correctly on their left lead before cantering three strides and jumping a spread to finish a course set up by her boss. It was nearing the end of summer in the UK and the redheaded woman was having a ball competing on this current mount, a 16.3 hand high thoroughbred gelding.

Jim had allowed the tall thoroughbred time to grow and mature, knowing full well that he wasn't going to be a two year old performer. By the time the gelding had reached 5 years of age and not managed to achieve better than a 5th in a local race, the trainer had conceded that he might as well see if the young horse could perform over jumps.

When Maddie had first arrived at the track 'Tiny' had been tested at two foot jumps by Jim's sons. Maddie had fallen in love with the big boned horse as soon as she'd gotten in the saddle. Jim would often find her riding him after work, taking advantage of the current increase in daylight hours.

Consequently the pair had worked their way up to jumping a neat course of four foot fences, Tiny looking like he had plenty of potential to improve on this height. Jim had at first encouraged Maddie to pursue show jumping with the large gelding. Maddie had happily obliged and upon finding the gelding to be showing a lot of promise, entertained the idea of eventing.

She'd tried to keep their dressage work away from prying eyes but Jim's sons had one afternoon stumbled across the pair working nicely on a frame in an outdoor arena on the property. Upon seeing the gelding collect down the short side of the arena and extend at a trot and later at a canter down the length of the 60 metre long enclosed area, they'd decided to speak to their father about the horse's potential.

As Maddie cooled out the gelding on a loose reined walk, she chattered with Jim as he walked the perimeter of the arena alongside the pair.

"I was thinking of giving Tiny a day to rest tomorrow and then trying him once more over some cross country jumps before the event this weekend. What do you think?"

"I think you're going to hate me," Jim responded with a wry smile, having watched the Australian woman grow more attached to the thoroughbred gelding daily.

"Because you disagree with my idea and that never happens?" Maddie asked in a mocking tone.

Jim laughed.

"I'm sure a lot of people have disagreed with you at different times Miss Jamison. I doubt they'd be brave enough to do it in front of you, however! I had the boys send those videos of you completing dressage and a show jumping round last weekend on to someone who is looking for an eventer for their teenage daughter. They're very interested in the prospect of purchasing Tiny."

Maddie imagined herself wrapping her arms around the big gelding's neck, hugging him protectively. *Perhaps if they did badly at the event this coming weekend, these people wouldn't want to buy him.* She smiled, realising that was an appealing idea, but completely unethical. *And besides, Tiny isn't mine. If he was, I wouldn't sell him!*

She looked down at Jim standing stationary beside her, realising with a start that she'd lost her focus on the gelding below her and he'd stopped.

"This boy is a real gem. Any eventing enthusiast would be lucky to have him," she commented with a grin, earning one from Jim in return.

"That's my girl. Do you think we could keep you here instead of you returning to Australia at the end of the year?"

Maddie laughed, shaking her head in the negative.

***

Wes thought back over her first few days at work as she drove toward the town of Euroa. Being a Thursday night and the breeding season, she was looking forward to this first of a weekly catch up with locally working ex TAFE friends and coworkers for dinner at one of the pubs.

Having made use of her contacts in Australia, Wes had managed to find a job for Frenchie at one of the larger studs in the local area. She'd been rapt to find that a number of other students had also decided to continue on with the breeding season, coming to Australia or New Zealand to gain some experience in the Southern Hemisphere.

Her German roommate from Ireland and another German gentleman who had undertaken the course at the National Stud had landed jobs on the same stud near to Tullamarine Airport. This was a couple of hours away from the French and Australian woman, but Wes had agreed to take Frenchie to pick up the other two and head to the Royal Melbourne Zoo if they could find a weekend when all were off work.

Tonight Wes was keen to find out how her friend's first week on an Australian stud had gone. She was also dying to know how all her friends - whom she hadn't seen for six months - had fared over the yearling and weaning seasons.

There ended up being a group of eight stud hands together, two of whom Wes had studied with at TAFE in Wangaratta, one who was currently on work experience from the same TAFE and a few who she'd worked with in June the previous year. These last few now had a new workmate in the form of Frenchie.

Wes loved that she'd been able to 'bring over to Australia' some of her classmates from Ireland. She felt that in some weird way, it delayed the end of her time in Ireland.

"So has anyone had any foals yet?" Wes asked the table after they'd all said hello and ordered their various meals.

"Two for us!" Frenchie replied with a grin and a wink, holding up three fingers.

Wes laughed.

"You dag. I don't think our first mares are due for another week, but hopefully we'll have some babies on the ground soon! I love the breeding season but things get more interesting once there are foals on the ground and we're allowed to start covering mares."

"Don't wish September on us already! Then things will start to get busy," one of her TAFE friends cried in mock alarm, "two of our stallions have over 100 mares booked to them."

"I'm happy for October to come around!" another declared, "at least then we won't have to worry about dry mares under lights and all the boxes that need to be mucked out," she concluded, screwing up her nose.

"How many boxes do ye have?" Frenchie asked with a slight Irish lilt, having learnt most of her English in Ireland, "it seems to me that every horse in Australia is paddocked throughout the year!"

Wes smiled, thinking that she thought the exact opposite of horses in Ireland when she'd first started at the stud. *I think that's something that makes the horse breeding world more affordable in Australia. We can have more horses and less staff because there aren't so many boxes to clean out on a daily basis!*

Wes managed to catch up on what all of her friends had been up to, including any mishaps at the yearling, or following weanling sales at Oaklands Junction. She and the others around her ended up in a fit of giggles when one of her TAFE mates sheepishly told of getting some sedazine on their hand after giving it to a yearling before loading the horse onto the truck for the trip down to the sales.

The sedative that was able to have an affect on a large horse caused the young woman to feel a little bit off and not with it. Feeling further sheepish, she commented that she didn't even realise why she felt that way – it was the yearling manager who picked up on it, had a chuckle and made sure she was aware of wearing gloves in future instances of handling medications.

Wes was delighted to find that Frenchie was enjoying her time down the road on another stud. She seemed to have hit it off with the farm's farrier, who also happened to frequent where Wes worked to trim the mare's feet.

"I haven't had to hold many horses for the farrier in Ireland, but it sure was entertaining today! We have one filly that is spelling and needed her feet done. She has the biggest head I've ever seen on a thoroughbred, is a bit narrow and has one bad club foot. Do ye know what the farrier says when he looks her over? 'This filly wasn't beaten with the ugly stick at birth... she was beaten with the whole forest!' Great craic!" she finished, causing the others to burst into laughter again.

Wes laughed, thinking that sounded just like the man who had a couple of years earlier nicknamed her 'grumpy' because of the foul mood she was in the first day she met him. To this day he still didn't call her by her real name. It was great to be home.

***

Maddie sighed as she dropped the reins, letting Tiny stretch out at the walk. They'd just finished their cross country phase of eventing and were well positioned for the show jumping that would be carried out the following day. It was a bittersweet moment for the Australian. She was so proud of how far the ex racehorse had come, but knew that his talent and genuine nature were going to result in him being sold and Maddie having to cease riding and competing on him.

She'd at least met the potential owners of the thoroughbred and was glad to find that they seemed a lovely family. To further put her mind at ease, the young girl Jessica who was planning to compete on Tiny was also entered in the event that weekend.

Although at a riding level below Madison, it was easy for the young woman to see that the 16 year old had talent and her current mount wasn't promising enough for where the teenager could go with her riding. Tiny was to go to a promising future home.

September

Melanie sighed in contentment, letting the reins slip through her fingers until she was just holding onto the buckle. She'd just had one of her best horse rides ever.

This gelding worked easily in a frame, was forward moving and responsive. And best yet, she'd achieved a couple of flying changes after being encouraged by her onlookers.

The young woman had been toying with the idea of investing in a new riding horse for a few months. Not understanding horses, but realising that they made his girlfriend happy, Johnny had suggested that they check out any within a couple of hour's drive that were for sale and appealed to the young woman.

Melanie hadn't been sure at first, but when she ran the idea by Jack and then her parents and all three agreed with the idea, she accepted Johnny's offer. The Sunday prior she'd tried out three horses and found one that she quite liked but after sitting on the idea for a few days, she realised she could sleep at night without having to own the horse.

Melanie made herself a promise that if she didn't find a horse that she felt could help her to compete at higher levels in dressage and perhaps eventing, then she wouldn't feel pressured to use the money she'd saved so far. It could sit and acquire interest until something came along that convinced her it was worth buying.

The seven year old she'd just tried - a gelding named Tuppeny - was out of a thoroughbred mare and by a warmblood stallion. Melanie had researched the performance history of the two.

The mare had only had a racing career, which wasn't largely appealing, but the sellers of this horse had been able to show Melanie the mare that was now aged, but still beautiful. They'd also been able to provide her with a DVD containing videos of previous progeny and after seeing this and riding the horse in question, she was excited about the idea of purchasing this willing gelding.

She discussed with the older couple payment terms and the option of a trial. It was decided that Melanie would pay a deposit, could trial the gelding at the East Riding School for a week and then pay the balance if she still wanted the horse. The young woman wrapped her boyfriend up in a hug once they got into the car. *She was getting a new horse!*

***

Wes nodded to Brian, indicating that she was willing to let the foal go. Generally in Australia mares were lead with their foal at their side. Wes had been telling Brian that whilst studying in Ireland, she'd been amazed to find that head collars were put on the first time the foal needed to be led somewhere.

What had surprised her further was that staff members were accustomed to leading the mare on the left and having two fingers looped through the foal's head collar, the foal positioned on their right. This seemed so foreign to Wes, as she'd always been taught to not get between a mare and foal. On top of this, because the foal wasn't used to pressure on its head, the natural reaction would be to pull back, rather than move forward.

She'd been amused to find that a solution to this was the handler kicking up a leg to tap the foal on the rump. More often than not this would encourage the foal forward. Consequently, the equines learnt from a young age how to walk alongside their mothers with a head collar on.

The seemed to have a lot of merit to Wes. She'd not had a lot of experience so far in weaning foals, but could easily remember the effort that went into first getting a head collar on a young untouched horse.

Following the success of this, teaching the young animal to lead required an experienced hand. The larger the young equine was when first introduced to a head collar and lead, the more damage it seemed they could do when they resisted.

Brian had jumped on Wes' eagerness to handle foals early. Hearing her explain the method overseas, he encouraged her to get into a habit of touching the foals as often as possible. It was easier to handle any horse when they weren't afraid of human touch. Having finished with the filly by the stallion More than Ready, Wes knew that the plan was to take the pair out of the stall in which they'd been housed overnight and put them into a day yard.

This filly had been born two nights earlier and the strong winter weather had convinced her boss to lock the pair up from the safety of the elements the past two nights.

"I think this girl's more than ready to go outside," Brian commented with a grin.

Wes groaned.

"I'm more than ready to stop with the puns for the day."

"That's fine, I can continue without you!" Brian laughed, "Ready?"

"More than," Wes bit back, smirking.

Brian led the mare out of the stable block, with Wes following behind and to the left, ready to encourage the filly after her mother if necessary. The young horse followed on her long legs, keeping close to mum.

Wes closed the gate after Brian had led the mare and foal inside, turning the mare back to face the gate before taking off her head collar. The pair watched from the fence as the mare broke into a trot, her tail sticking up in the air as she snorted. The little filly whinnied and cantered after her mother.

"Look at that! Phar lap!" Wes commented enthusiastically.

"Phar from it!" Brian responded with a wink, causing Wes to grin at the bad pun.

"I'm sure we have other work to do. And I think that requires me going with Canada on the feed run and leaving you to your puns!" Wes stated with a grin, laughing as Brian pulled a mock sad face.

"See you in time for the cover before vetting!" Wes called over her shoulder, jogging toward the feed room as she heard the ATV being started up by her coworker.

***

"Here."

Maddie took the envelope with her name on it, curious. It looked just like the pay envelopes that each worker was given at the end of a week. Why would her boss be giving her an envelope mid week?

She looked up with an enquiring gaze to find that Jim had already walked down the breezeway and into the feed room.

"Guess I'll only find out if I open it," she muttered to herself, peeling back the sticky top of the envelope to pull out a folded piece of paper.

"What's that?" Tom asked, peering over her shoulder.

He let out as wolf whistle as Maddie stared at the 1,000 pound figure, not comprehending.

"What did you do to get that? Who's it from?"

"I'm not sure..." Maddie responded, confused.

In a daze she headed toward the feed room, leaving Tom curious. Jim ignored Maddie as he dished out different feed stuffs into a row of buckets. Maddie failed to notice the small smile on his face.

"Jim?" she asked, unsure.

"Yep?" he questioned, continuing to put feed into buckets.

"I don't understand. Why the cheque?"

"To put in your bank, silly. It won't be much use to you otherwise," he replied with his back to her, grinning widely.

"I understand where they go... but why do I have a thousand pound cheque?"

"Oh, that! Well the money just cleared for Tiny, and the wife and I have been talking and came to the conclusion that this was one practical way to thank you for helping us with all of the horses that we've been able to find good homes for and sell on because of your help."

Maddie nodded to herself, a grin making its way across her face as she realised that she'd inadvertently earnt one thousand pounds through doing something she loved. She knocked over a couple of buckets in her haste to hug the older man. Jim laughed, telling her to get out of his feed room before she made more of a mess.

Maddie obliged, skipping back down the breezeway to tell Tom the cool news. *Celebratory drinks were on her tonight!*

October

Wes groaned, reaching across her small bed to grab the foaling alarm. It had just projected a piercing short sound, three times. This indicated that a mare in one of the foaling paddocks was either lying down and snoozing, or giving birth.

Switching the small pager to 'off', she climbed out of bed and pulled on a pair of track pants and a jumper before heading out to check the horses, a torch in hand.

She walked quickly to the nearby first foaling paddock, shining the strong torch beam over the paddock, counting the number of equine bodies within the confines of the fence. There were the expected three, one mare lying on her side and groaning.

Wes jogged to the nearby stable block, turned off the still beeping foaling alarm unit inside and then switched on the outside floodlights. Grabbing a lead rope off a hook in the stables, she headed back out to the mare, no longer needing the torch.

Slipping between the rails of the fence, Wes made her way to the foaling mare and clipped the lead rope up to her head collar, encouraging her to stand. She wanted to move the mare away from the other two in the paddock and know that she could foal down without the other mares curiously inspecting her progress.

Putting her into one of the small holding yards nearby, Wes removed the alarmed head collar and closed the gate behind her. Now that the mare was foaling, there was no need to keep the head collar with the attached foaling alarm on it. This could be used for the next mare that was deemed close to foaling.

The mare's waters had broken by the time Wes was woken by the foaling alarm. The foal was born within forty minutes of Wes moving the mare into a separate yard. Wes noted these details down in the foaling book, including the fact that this mare had given birth to a chestnut filly.

Not two hours later, Wes was foaling down another mare that had set off the alarm. She'd managed to grab an hour's sleep in between assessing the other mare and foal's progress with regards to the foal nursing and the mare passing her placenta.

She'd placed the second chestnut mare into a yard beside the first and watched things progress into the second stage of labour. The mare managed fine without any intervention until the coming foal seemed to stop progressing at the shoulders. Wes stepped into the yard to help, tugging on one leg when the mare pushed with a contraction.

Not making any progress, Wes rang her boss to ask for help. He and their Canadian coworker were outside in a few minutes, offering assistance.

It took the three of them pulling when the mare pushed, to assist with getting the shoulders through the birth canal. After this difficult point, the foal was expelled in a sudden rush. The three workers laughed in delight.

"That was a tight one!" Canada remarked.

Wes nodded, watching her boss size up the chestnut colt that had been born.

"I'd reckon he weighs around 70 kilograms. What a monster of a foal."

Wes agreed, thinking that his mum was big but the large size of the foal was probably what led to it being so difficult for him to be pushed out.

"He is a big boy! I'm glad he's out safely. Thank you both for the help! I can keep an eye on them now."

"Sounds good, bub. I think I'm up for a coffee and then back to bed."

Wes grinned, concluding her boss was the only person she knew who wasn't affected by caffeine when it came to sleep. If she had a coffee at three in the morning, she would stay awake until work was due to start!

***

Declan grinned as he headed back toward the covering barn. They'd just finished their last cover for the day and it felt good! As the season was picking up, they'd recently had covers three times a day for one or two of their stallions.

Today had been incredibly busy, with in excess of 100 mares to vet and 3 covers for 3 of their stallions. It was a relief to know it was the end of the day.

"So, how did ye like today, kid?" he asked their most recent work experience student with a grin.

"Great! Do you think Kingsley would let me hold another mare when we have covers tomorrow?" 18 year old Danni asked in a hopeful tone.

Lise smiled, slapping Declan on the arm when he started laughing.

"Ye won't be that keen after a year or so in the industry! Days like today are great when they're over!"

Danni smiled, shrugging her shoulders.

"I think stud work is wonderful. Is it always this much fun?"

"That depends on if you're referring to work with mares and foals or not," Lise replied as she sat on Declan's knee.

"It's seasonal and some people find the young horses and sale preparation to be more enjoyable. Others prefer the breeding season. I'm glad you're enjoying your work experience, Danni. Are you on foal watch tonight?"

Danni nodded, telling the pair that she was covering the dog watch and would ask their night watch staff member to call her if any mare foaled. She wanted to see as much as she could over the next few weeks.

Declan chuckled as he watched the young woman make her way out of the covering barn, heading off to check the pregnant mares.

"She's super keen. I like it."

"I hope she stays that way – she'll be a great asset to any stud and the industry in a few years. She listens, follows directions and is very thoughtful about any task. I think she'll make a great teacher to other TAFE students that turn up for work experience."

"So she's another like ye?" Declan questioned with a smile, wrapping his arms around Lise.

"Passionate about the horse breeding industry? I think so," Lise replied with a smile, resting in the Irishman's embrace with a content sigh.

***

Wes yawned, thinking the working day wouldn't end. She hadn't gotten a lot of sleep the night before due to the two foalings and was feeling a little irritable. Consequently, Brian had been picking on her a lot.

"Argh, I can't wait till this day ends and you can leave," Wes muttered, earning a laugh from the stallion handler in return.

"Your day will get worse when I leave!"

"Quite the opposite... that's weird..." Wes frowned in confusion as they pulled up out the front of a yard.

This was where the two mares that she'd foaled down the night before had been housed together. Wes and Brian were carrying out the afternoon feed run and then would be finished for the day.

"What's weird?" Brian questioned, hopping off the bike to fill two buckets with oats and chaff for the hungry mares.

"Those foals have switched mums!"

"Are you sure? They're both nursing fine and the mares aren't discouraging them. I know you had a tiring night last night with the foalings."

"I'm sure. I foaled down the filly first, out of the other mare. It took three of us to pull the big colt out of this first mare. However it happened, they've switched mothers!"

"Ok. Then we need to do something about that."

Wes watched uncomprehending as Brian grabbed a head collar and lead off the ATV and headed into the yard, putting it on the closest mare. He directed Wes to open the gate for him as the two mares and foals walked together.

"Just don't let the incorrect foal out with me. Let's see if we can pair them back up correctly."

Wes manned the gate, thinking it a stroke of luck that after she managed to stop the wrong foal from following the mare it thought was its mum, that the other foal followed after Brian and its correct mother. She was surprised further to find that the big colt stayed with its genetic mother, in spite of having seconds ago nursed from the other mare.

Wes threw a feed in with the left over mare and foal before taking the other bucket to Brian. He had placed the other pair in one of the yards that had been used for foaling the night before.

"That seemed too easy!" Wes stated, handing the bucket through the fence.

"It did seem to be done without fuss. I think these foals haven't yet learnt to distinguish who mum is. It may be best for us to keep them separate for a few days so they can truly bond. Then it should be ok to put them all out into one of the paddocks across the creek."

Wes nodded, feeling tired again as she walked back to the bike and sat down, yawning. She perked up at the thought that tonight was another chance to catch up with her previous workmates. *I'll have to make it an early night, though.*

November

The flight back to Australia for Madison Jamison seemed a long one. Her head full of ideas, the 25 year old woman wasn't able to settle and sleep the hours away. She was too busy thinking on an idea that had been forming in her mind since Tiny had been sold in August.

Maddie loved to ride and loved the challenge of taking on a willful horse and turning it into an efficient performer. She'd loved the willingness of Tiny but also found joy in taking on some of Jim's less cooperative thoroughbreds and getting them to perform to the best of their capabilities.

Suddenly the idea of acquiring off the track thoroughbreds and reeducating them for an eventing career was extremely appealing. Living in the South Eastern suburbs, Maddie recognised that there were a decent number of racetracks not too far away. Consequently, she felt it wouldn't be difficult to source horses that were deemed no longer suitable for a life of racing.

The young woman also spent a lot of her flight thinking of her boyfriend back home. She knew Jack was a talented horse riding instructor and that his students loved his lessons. She also knew that she had a consistent income via teaching at the East Riding School, but wondered if she couldn't build up extra income in bringing on and reselling racehorses after their racing career had finished.

Maddie recognised that the facilities at her parents' property were sufficient for taking on such a project and trying it out to see if it was a feasible income earner. However, an idea of getting some land with Jack was forming in her mind. This way, they could run a property, teach outside of their lessons at the East Riding School and build a future together.

The young woman decided that 25 years of age was the perfect time to start her own business. She also concluded that if Jack liked this idea, she should throw another one at him. Perhaps 25 was perfect age to get engaged, too.

***

Melanie scanned the university website, eagerly looking at the subjects that would be available for study in the first semester of the following year. She'd completed 6 units of her equine science degree over the past year and a half and was eager to take on a little more.

Because she was studying via distance education, the learner guides and subject information were sent out by post. It was a requirement that she attend the university twice a year to complete practical tasks and get assessed, but otherwise she could study when she had time at home. So far she was sitting on a credit average and seriously contemplating the idea of transferring into veterinary science once she finished her equine science degree.

Aware that this would take up a lot of time, she had decided to take on an extra subject to see if the increased work load would be doable. Full time students did four subjects per semester, but Melanie was happy to increase from two to three and see how the following semester went.

Deciding that statistics wouldn't be appealing at any point, she chose this subject to get it over and done with. *Besides, dad is knowledgeable in this area. I can ask him if I'm unsure.*

Choosing this unit, she clicked on the enrol button before logging off and shutting down the computer. It was time to work her new horse!

Tuppeny had impressed Melanie, her parents and Jack, whilst at the East Riding School for his one week trial. This was enough to convince the young woman that she would keep him. They'd been rewarded the following weekend by placing second in a dressage event that Melanie had decided to test the waters with.

She'd been rapt at the result, knowing that the test wasn't a difficult one but also concluding that she and Tuppeny were just getting to know each other. There was a lot of room to improve. Something the redhead twin hadn't envisaged was that Jacinta and her acquisition of Bellamy had led to the pair also progressing up to a level at which Melanie would be starting out with Tuppeny.

Upon discovery of this, the two women had decided to work together as time permitted. The 22 year old had done a lot of growing up over the past six months.

Melanie wasn't sure if Jack had had a word with her, but she had noted that Jacinta had stopped flirting with him. Her focus seemed to be solely on her promising new horse and gaining as much competition experience as she could manage between her shifts at a local feed company.

Melanie was relieved to know that Maddie would return soon, too. It wasn't fair on Jack that her sister was halfway across the world.

***

"You're home!"

Jack embraced his girlfriend on his front doorstep, thinking that it seemed so long since he'd been able to touch her.

"I thought your flight was coming in tomorrow? I've taken the afternoon off to pick you up at the airport! Your parents agreed."

"Well in that case, I guess we can spend an afternoon together," Maddie stated cheekily, causing Jack to blush.

"I managed to organise an earlier flight a week or so back and told mum and dad, but I asked them to keep it a secret so I could surprise you," the redhead explained as Jack ushered her inside his two bedroom rental property, not fifteen minutes from the riding school at which he worked.

"I was coping with the fact that I would get to see you tomorrow but this is so much better," Jack said with a smile, sitting down on the couch to digest the fact that Maddie was back home.

"If you're going overseas again, I'm coming with you."

Maddie grinned, climbing onto his lap.

"I love that idea. But I've got a lot of things in mind that require being in Australia for a long while yet."

"Such as?" Jack asked, not sure whether his girlfriend was about to throw him a curveball.

Maddie pressed a kiss to Jack's cheek before telling him about what she'd been considering on her flight home. He was already aware of Tiny and the other horses she'd been bringing on as the pair had been constantly in touch via Skype. Jack listened with growing enthusiasm, thinking Maddie's plans sounded like the logical next step for the pair of them to take on.

Maddie finished her large spiel, watching Jack who was sitting quietly.

"You do know I'm expecting you'll help me with all this, right?" she questioned, suddenly not so sure that she was on the same wavelength as the man she'd been away from for the past ten months.

She caught Jack's large grin just before his lips came crashing down on hers, taking her breath away. Maddie laughed once she was able to catch her breath.

"Thank God for that! I wasn't sure for a second there."

Jack started to tell Maddie about an acreage he'd been driving past and eyeing off for the past month on his way to and from work. Maddie thought it sounded worth checking out and told him so before occupying his lips again. There would be plenty of time to talk later.

December

Wes smiled as Frenchie continued the story of her day, detailing how some of her coworkers had been in town at lunch time and managed to distract the local loudmouth that worked down the road. The pair were sitting cross legged on the floor of the bungalow that Wes had for the breeding season.

"I don't know what possessed them to take off with his trailer! But it was mighty difficult keeping my mouth shut while I watched two of them back up their work ute to his car and unhook the trailer full of wood. Thank goodness the other two were able to keep him occupied! I had to mask my laughter with a coughing fit when they puttered off down the main street, towing someone else's trailer!"

"My goodness! Did he catch on to it?"

"Apparently shortly after I'd left to get back to work. The farrier fella claims ye could hear him screaming down the street about killing the pair that'd taken his trailer of wood!"

Wes laughed, finding further amusement as Frenchie remembered to tell her about the stud's exciting morning of staff members chasing sheep off their property.

"I'll be sad to leave Australia next week!" she concluded with a sigh.

Wes nodded, thinking that at least the French woman got to go back to the northern hemisphere in time for the breeding season. *Then again, that's exactly what I did by returning home after the season in Ireland.*

"So where will ye be doing yearlings? I know ye mentioned that ye only do the breeding season here. Will ye be back working where I am, or the other place in Euroa where ye got to do yearlings?"

"Neither," Wes replied with a grin, "I really love the breeding season, not so much the yearlings. And before going to Ireland I was completing a course in coaching horse riding. I've done most of the theory, but not a lot of practical. There's a riding school Melbourne way that has agreed to take me on part time as a stablehand and give me riding lessons! And another is willing to take me on a trial for teaching and potentially pay to put me through my Level 1 in instructing with Equestrian Australia. I think I'll try this for six months and see how it goes!"

"Well! Have ye had a break from study since school?"

Wes smiled, nodding.

"The year I had working in Euroa before Ireland counts, right?"

"But that was to get you into the National Stud! Ok... it counts, just!"

Wes grinned, thinking that increasing her knowledge and skills on a consistent basis was a particularly appealing idea. *Besides, all of it will help with my future property. And it'll be great to be back home with my parents for a little while. Bring on next year and whatever it's got in store for me!*

***

Maddie raced out the door as she heard Jack's car pull up in the drive.

"Jack's here, mum!" she called back over her shoulder, thinking her boyfriend had taken a long time at his parents place.

It was Christmas day and the Jamison's were having a family lunch, plus a few extras. Johnny and Jack had been invited, the twins' parents eager to include the men in their lives.

"What took you so long?" Maddie demanded as Jack opened the car door.

"And it's nice to see you, too," Jack replied with a grin, nearly falling over as the redhead threw herself at him.

"If I'd known I was going to get this warm a welcome, I'd have come sooner!" he joked, accepting a few fervent kisses from Maddie.

"Johnny's here chattering away with mum and dad, and Mel of course. We… ok, *I've* just been waiting on you!"

"Well you could have come with me to mum and dad's, you know Maddie? They were commenting this morning that they were surprised I didn't bring you with me. You've not seen them since you got back from England!"

"It's only been a month! How about we go and visit them next week?" she asked, dragging Jack toward the house.

"Deal."

The six adults enjoyed a companionable meal together, the four younger ones talking of their plans for the new year that would follow. Johnny seemed eager to accompany Melanie to every competition she had mapped out on her calendar. Maddie was amused to find that he'd turned into quite the handy groom.

Maddie and Jack had been working out sums and excitedly concluded that by the end of the next year they'd be in the market to purchase a small acreage and start their dream together. Prior to that Maddie planned to take on a couple of off-the-track thoroughbreds and try her hand at reeducation in Australia. She'd run the idea by her parents and they agreed that as long as it didn't interfere with her teaching, she could make use of the facilities at the riding school.

Jack suggested a short ride after lunch, inviting Melanie and Johnny along. The pair declined, happy to let their meal go down. Maddie grinned, not interested in sharing any more of Jack's time. She dragged him outside to get a couple of head collars.

"I'm rather glad the other two didn't come with us," Jack confided sitting on a bale of hay.

Maddie grinned, hanging the head collars over her shoulder.

"I think that makes two of us! I was silly enough to have a play overseas without you and now I don't want to share you at all!"

Jack grinned, pulling Maddie onto his lap.

"The feeling's mutual," he commented, cupping her face with a hand before leaning in to kiss her.

"In that case... will you marry me, Jack?" she questioned suddenly, catching him unawares.

Maddie peered up into his face, searching for a sign of what was going on in his head. Jack reached into his pocket, pulling out a small velvet box.

"On one condition, Maddie. When people ask about our engagement, you say I asked you," he responded with a grin, opening the box to reveal a simple silver ring, an emerald stone in the centre.

Maddie laughed.

"Deal!"

***

"Excuse me, Please," Hunter stated, making his way from the table of food, a full plate in his hand.

"Oh, sure," Tony replied, trying not to move too quickly due to the amount of alcohol in his system.

"Not you, him!" Hunter called back over his shoulder, referring to his dog.

"Is anyone keeping an eye on how much he drinks?" he questioned with a grin, sitting down beside Lise.

"I doubt it. As long as all the girl workers and any work experience kids know to steer clear of him, it's all good. In fact, great craic!" Declan replied with a chuckle, earning a slap on the arm from Lise.

The staff and associated workers of Nirvana Park were enjoying a Christmas dinner, as provided by Dave Kingsley. It was an annual event that Lise had come to really enjoy. Most chose to take advantage of the free alcohol, but Lise preferred to stay sober. Often there were young work experience women to keep away from Tony and besides, most of the staff members were working the following morning.

Just because it was Christmas didn't stop the fact that they were preparing in excess of thirty yearlings. She was more than happy with not having to nurse a hangover the following day.

Declan and Lise chattered away with Stuart and his wife, discussing the horses that were currently in the stables.

"So are there any fillies that I should be keeping my husband away from?" Stuart's wife Kerrie questioned with a smile.

Lise grinned. Each year Hunter seemed to acquire another horse. He had a particular interest in fillies that he could hold onto for residual value. Kerrie didn't see the point in investing in any broodmares at 18 months of age, unless her husband was willing to give them a chance at a decent racing career. Consequently, Stuart was only allowed to buy one horse, instead of the three he insisted he needed to buy each year.

"Mal Maree's brown filly," Trevor joined in the conversation, pulling a chair over to the group as he sat down with his second plate of food.

"But you can't, Hunter. Kingsley's already agreed to sell me a half share if she doesn't make the reserve."

"And who would own the other half?" Stuart queried, an idea forming in his mind.

"The boss man himself. He likes her, too. Said it makes more business sense to sell her but if she doesn't make what he thinks she's worth, he's happy to hold onto her."

Stuart turned to his wife with a grin.

"Hey Hon, if I buy half a horse... does that mean I get to buy two this year?" he questioned sincerely, causing Lise and Declan to burst into laughter.

"So, Trevor – is there another filly you'd like to talk my husband into buying?" Kerrie asked dryly, shaking her head.

Trevor grinned, excusing himself from the group, insisting it must be time for dessert.

"I don't know how you guys do this every year. I think my 9 to 5 office job and weekends to share with my kids – and my husband when he's home – are more appealing."

"That's horse fanatics for you, Kerrie. I think you'll find by next Christmas you'll be making a similar statement. Kingsley's great to work for, this farm is one of the biggest in Victoria and most of the time the staff get on great. I think you'll find the main staff here for many years to come," Lise replied with a smile, relaxing as Declan placed his arm around her.

"Yep. Nirvana Park's home. Wouldn't have it any other way," Declan agreed with a grin.

About the Author

Christine Meunier considers herself introduced to the wonderful world of horses at the late age of 13 when her parents agreed to lease a horse for her. She started experiencing horses via books from a young age and continues to do so, but recognises that horses cannot be learnt solely from books.

She has been studying horses from age 16, starting with the Certificate II in Horse Studies and is currently undertaking her Bachelor of Equine Science via distance education.

Christine has worked at numerous thoroughbred studs in Australia as well as overseas in Ireland for a breeding season.

She then gained experience in a couple of Melbourne based horse riding schools, instructing at a basic level before heading off overseas again, this time to South Africa to spend hours in the saddle of endurance and trail horses on the Wild Coast.

Particularly passionate about the world of breeding horses, she teaches equine studies focused on breeding, at a TAFE in Victoria, Australia.

She also writes a blog about equine education which you can view at http://equus-blog.com/

For details regarding Horse Country including reviews, author interviews and more, visit http://www.horsecountrybook.com/

www.ingramcontent.com/pod-product-compliance
Lightning Source LLC
Chambersburg PA
CBHW020918020726
47495CB00002B/240

* 9 7 8 0 9 8 7 5 3 3 2 0 3 *